PEPPER WINTERS

FOREVER

NEW YORK BOSTON

Copyright © 2016 by Pepper Winters
Excerpt from *Ruin & Rule* copyright © 2015 by Pepper Winters
All rights reserved. In accordance with the U.S. Copyright Act of 1976, the scanning, uploading, and electronic sharing of any part of this book without the permission of the publisher constitute unlawful piracy and theft of the author's intellectual property. If you would like to use material from the book (other than for review purposes), prior written permission must be obtained by contacting the publisher at permissions@hbgusa.com. Thank you for your support of the author's rights.

Forever
Hachette Book Group
1290 Avenue of the Americas
New York, NY 10104

www.HachetteBookGroup.com

Printed in the United States of America

RRD-C

First edition: January 2016
10 9 8 7 6 5 4 3 2 1

Forever is an imprint of Grand Central Publishing.
The Forever name and logo are trademarks of Hachette Book Group, Inc.

The Hachette Speakers Bureau provides a wide range of authors for speaking events. To find out more, go to www.hachettespeakersbureau.com or call (866) 376-6591.

The publisher is not responsible for websites (or their content) that are not owned by the publisher.

Library of Congress Cataloging-in-Publication Data has been applied for.

ISBN: 978-1-4555-8938-8
LCCN: 2015953517

Thank you to those who took a chance on my work, for enjoying my slightly twisted world, and for letting me into yours.

Prologue

Kill

I thought fate finally agreed that I'd paid enough.

That justice would set me free.

That the woman I'd loved since childhood would be mine again.

Once again, I was fucking naïve.

Cleo made me sin and she made me suffer.

With her resurrection came deceit and war.

But then they took her.

Stole her.

And my carefully laid plans for vengeance were now my reality.

They'd brought everything I was about to do on themselves.

They had no one else to blame, nowhere else to hide.

War had begun.

It's time to rewrite our destiny.

Chapter One

Cleo

*H*e was a bully.

Ever since his voice deepened he'd been mean and short-tempered. Mom told me that he was at a point in his life where he had to lose himself to find himself. I had no idea what she meant. I just... I just really missed my best friend. —Cleo, diary entry, age nine

Amnesia.

A curse or a blessing?

Memory.

A helping hand or a hindrance?

The things I'd forgotten and remembered had been both enemy and friend—solace and pain. They'd been constant companions, fighting over me for years. Amnesia traded my first life for a new one—with new parents, new sister, new home. But then the boy with the green eyes brought me back—showed me the path to my old world and a destiny I'd forgotten.

For eight years I'd struggled, always fearing I'd left loved ones behind. I'd hated myself for being so selfish—knowing my brain had deliberately cut them out in an act of self-preservation. I'd always wondered what I would do when I finally remembered everything... *if* I finally remembered.

I didn't have to wonder anymore.

Even after the consequences of following a mysterious letter, the snake pit of lies, the confusion of blended pasts, the rough way Killian had treated me—I wouldn't change a thing.

Those trials were a worthy payment for my broken memories. I was whole again...*almost*. I was on the right path to patching my life together and finally understanding it all.

However, as I stared around the freshly painted room, all alone and imprisoned, I wished that I was stronger, smarter. I didn't suffer from fear or terror of what would become of me, but I did suffer regret—regret for not anticipating retaliation, for not being prepared.

Enough! Focus. This isn't the place for stupid reminiscing.

I forced myself to shove aside worries. Now was the time to fight harder and stronger than ever before.

I'd endured one captivity: a caging of my mind with no walls or locks but with endless darkness and unknowing. Now my mind was intact for the first time in years, but I had a new prison.

I'm not bound by rope or chains, but I'm trapped all the same.

I sighed, smoothing Arthur's black T-shirt I wore. Before, the cotton softness was comfort and safety—the perfect wardrobe to wear beside my sleeping lover. Now, it was vulnerability and no protection.

Locked in a room, stolen from Arthur's arms, I was lost, lonely, and most of all bristling with fury. I would've traded everything I owned for the strength to destroy the men who'd taken me. I'd end their evil tyranny and pay them back for not one wrongdoing but two. *They'd* burned down my house. *They'd* murdered my parents. *They'd* tried to kill me. And most of all *they'd* destroyed the boy from my past.

So many tithes to pay.

And I had every intention of stripping what was owed and balancing the scales of justice once and for all.

The truth is despicable.

My eyes fell on the forged police report Rubix Killian had given me to read. He expected me to buy his lies?

Stupid, stupid man.

He'd done me a favor. His lies had set my memories free. I saw it all now. Nothing was hidden and everything revealed.

I'd never been a victim. Even as a little girl, I'd always fought and spat, inheriting the swift temper said to be the curse of having blazing red hair. Even when I was lost in the blank sea of amnesia, I put faith in my tenacity, trusted my instincts, and followed my heart.

Now my instincts were screaming a message I'd never heard before.

This will never stop.

Unless you *stop them.*

The past would forever suck me back if I didn't deal with the men who continued to puppeteer me at their whims.

They have to die.

They couldn't be allowed to live because they would never be satisfied. And men who could never be satisfied could never be trusted.

Arthur "Kill" Killian, my childhood lover and green-eyed Libran, wanted these men dead.

He'd plotted and schemed for eight long years to claim closure and payback for all that they'd taken.

He wants their blood.

And now...so do I.

My name was Cleo Price. *I've had so many names.* Sarah Jones died the moment I willingly embarked on this crazy odyssey—just like Cleo had died the night she crawled from a burning building. The FBI had tried to keep me safe until they found the true culprit of my attempted murder. But now Cleo had been reborn, and not only did I remember my upbringing...of burly men, cigarettes, and battles fought on the backs of Harleys and choppers...but I also remembered the glue forming our communes: *revenge.*

Revenge to those who threatened our loved ones. Swift punishment to any traitor. In our world, society's rules didn't matter. We followed our own black-and-white laws with no leniency and swift punishment.

And these men deserved *severe* punishment.

After what they've done to me ... to Arthur.

Vengeance wasn't just Arthur's cross to bear anymore—not alone at least.

I remember what they did to him.

I no longer saw blankness when I tried to recall. I saw everything that happened that fateful night, and it was up to me to save him from his own self-loathing.

Arthur Killian killed my parents.

He pulled the trigger and ended their lives.

But it's so much more complicated than that.

However, at the same time, it was exceedingly simple. He was innocent and I would make sure the guilty paid. I would ensure their wickedness was struck out for all eternity.

Sitting taller on the bed, I embraced my cold conviction and turned my thoughts to present matters.

How many hours had passed since I'd left Arthur bleeding and unconscious?

Was he still alive?

Could he come after me?

He'll come for me if he's able. I didn't doubt that for a second. But I also couldn't wait around for him ... just in case. *Don't think like that.*

Climbing off the single mattress, leaving behind the daisy-decorated sheeting, so similar to my old childhood room, I circled the small space searching for any weaknesses for escape.

I'd done this already when I first arrived.

How long ago was that?

And just like before the door was still locked.

The window still barred and sealed shut. Its pane painted black from the outside, obscuring all illumination and passage of time.

The only light was a bedside lamp just bright enough to read the police statement that'd sent Arthur to jail for a crime he didn't commit.

Well, he did commit it ...

Sighing, I spun in place. The room was a tomb with no way out.

I wished I hadn't been so *stupid*. My recklessness had brought me here. I'd come like a lamb to the slaughter the moment I was summoned.

Here I was—at their mercy, while Arthur was bleeding and alone...possibly dead.

Stop thinking that way.

Taking a deep breath, I prepared for whatever came next.

Any weapons?

My eyes skated over the unhelpful bedspread and empty dresser.

No weapons.

Engine noises purred outside the blacked-out window conjuring ancient memories of being lulled to sleep by the grumble of motorbikes and masculine voices.

My heart flurried, stretching within the thought.

I'm home.

Gritting my teeth, I shook my head. I wasn't home. I might be across the compound from the charred remains of my own house, but this wasn't home. Not anymore. Not after the massacre and betrayal.

These men weren't my friends. They weren't my childhood saviors who I'd trusted blindly.

They were the reason I'd lived the past eight years in a different country. Why I'd spent my teenage years in foster care, and why my brain was broken.

Scott "Rubix" Killian had taken great pleasure in welcoming me back into his lies and treachery.

A sharp tang existed in the back of my throat—the residual effect of being drugged. I didn't know what they'd shot into my veins, but its effects lingered far longer than I wanted. I struggled against the sluggishness in my blood, trying to keep my thoughts in order.

Don't give in.

I yanked on the door handle again. Still locked.

Making my way to the window, I pried at the sill. Still unmovable.

Dropping to my knees, I tried ripping up the carpet, desperate for a weapon or freedom, but the threadbare covering was glued firmly.

Frustration sat like a vise around my lungs.

"Dammit!" Climbing to my feet, I ran my hands through my hair. "There has to be a way out."

But there isn't.

I had to concede.

I was locked in there—for however long they wanted, and there was nothing I could do about it.

Chapter Two

Kill

I was a stalker.

Shit, I'd even researched the definition to see if it was true. It was. I willfully followed, watched, and coveted Cleo Price. There. I admitted it. I was in love with a child. I had dirty thoughts about a girl who didn't even have boobs yet. But that didn't stop me. It made me worse. Because not only was I a stalker, but I was an addict, too. An addict for any glimpse of her, any sound of her voice, any hope that I could ever possibly deserve her. —Arthur, age fourteen

"What the fuck?"

I tried to sit upright, glaring at Grasshopper and Mo. "Let me up, you assholes!"

The room refused to stay still. The edges of my vision were fuzzy and the god-awful pounding in my skull wouldn't give me a fucking break.

"What the hell do you think you're doing?" My breathing was broken and short; my eyes burning with light from the diabolical fluorescents above.

Where the hell am I?

Where's Cleo?

Rage battered away my pain, granting me temporary power.

I shoved aside arms holding me down and swung at the faces of my captors.

My knuckles met flesh.

A bellow sounded in the square, white room. "Christ, man!"

The incessant beeping sliced through my eardrums turning my headache into a brass fucking band of horror.

I'd never been one to panic but I couldn't control the overwhelming sensation that something awful had happened.

Something I needed to fix straightaway.

The door suddenly swung open.

I paused just long enough to take in the balding man with a stethoscope around his neck and baby-blue scrubs, before struggling with renewed determination. "Damn bastards. Let me up!"

The doctor inched warily into the room. "What on earth is going on in here?"

"He's just woken up, Doc," Hopper said, trying to grab my shoulders but unwilling to risk another fist to his jaw. "Ain't got his bearings yet."

"I've got my fucking bearings, asshole. Let me up!"

"You gotta do something, before he makes it worse," Mo growled. His lip was bleeding, his nostrils flared in pain.

Did I do that?

The headache turned feral, crumpling me in its agony as if I were nothing more than a sardine can. Clutching my skull—finding bandages instead of hair—I bellowed, "What the fuck is going on? Someone tell me before my brain explodes out of my goddamn ears!"

My heartbeat clanged to one name. A single name siphoning through my blood over and over again.

Cle…o.

Cle…o.

"You're in hospital, Mr. Killian. I need you to relax." The doctor used his calm-the-unhinged-patient-down voice as he crept closer. Grabbing the chart from the foot of the bed and scooting backward as if he would get bitten or infected by being too close to me, he flipped the pages and scanned the notes.

I couldn't breathe properly.

I couldn't see anything in my peripheral vision, and that damn fucking beeping was getting on my nerves.

"Someone shut that thing up!"

Grasshopper ignored me, coming to the side of the bed and bravely laying a hand on my chest. "Kill, you have a concussion. Doctors said if you move too much before the swelling goes down, you might do some serious damage."

My headache came back with ten-ton pressure.

"Concussion? How the fuck did I get a concussion?" My eyes flew around the room.

I wasn't in my bedroom, that was for fucking sure. White morbid walls looked like a bleached coffin, while an outdated television hung like a spider just waiting for death. The entire place reeked of antiseptic and corpses.

Hospital.

I'm in the fucking hospital.

Clutching my head, I tried to gather my temper and relax. Screaming only drove pins of agony through my eyeballs and terrified answers away. "Speak. Tell me."

Mo looked at Hopper, unsuccessfully hiding the nervousness in his eyes. They waited for me to explode again. When I didn't, Mo admitted, "Eh, you were struck in the head."

My headache tripled its efforts to turn me into a vegetable almost as if on cue.

Then…everything came back.

Finding Cleo after all this time.

Loving Cleo after all this time.

Holding Cleo after all this fucking time.

She's not dead.

She was never dead, just missing.

They took her!

I soared out of bed. The wires, the sheets—nothing had any power to hold me in my wrath. "Where is she?!" Shoving aside Grasshopper with superhuman strength, I swallowed hard as the room spun like a fun house. "They have her! Goddammit, they have her."

Grasshopper, Mo, and the doctor sprang on me, each grabbing an arm or a leg. I grunted, buckling beneath their weight. In ordinary circumstances, I would've let them win. I would've been rational and collected and listened to what they had to say.

But this wasn't ordinary circumstances.

This was motherfucking war!

My father and brother had broken into my house, got past security, and taken the only thing of value I had left.

They'd stolen her from me all over again.

"Shit!" I screamed. "Shit, shit, shit!"

"Kill, calm down!"

"Let us explain!"

"Get the fuck off me." No amount of arms could hold me down. Adrenaline tore through my blood, giving me a merciless edge. My vision might be faulty, my head might be broken, but I still knew how to fight.

They weren't listening to my voice. Perhaps they would listen to my fist.

With no effort at all, I punched the three men in a connecting roundhouse, and tore at the IV in the back of my hand.

Yanking it out, blood spurted over the white sheets and linoleum floor. The stark crimson spread macabre patterns, whispering of murder and revenge as I launched out of bed, battling sickness and vertigo. "Someone better start talking." I breathed hard. "Now. Right fucking now."

Mo and Hopper stared transfixed at my bleeding vein. "We should patch you up, dude."

Waving my hand, splattering the bed with more red droplets, I snarled, "Leave it. It's not important. I don't even feel it." Strangely, that was the truth. There was nothing that could overpower the pain of knowing they'd taken Cleo. That agony was enough to drown me. Over and fucking over again.

I groaned under my breath as scenarios and horror-filled daydreams tormented me.

Please, please, let her be okay!

My eyes flickered to the door. All I wanted to do was leave. To chase after my rotten enemies and give them what they deserved.

Suddenly, nausea raced up my gullet. I stumbled to the side. Crashing against the bed, I gritted my teeth against the swirling room.

The doctor sidestepped, avoiding me as best he could. "If you could sit down, Mr. Killian."

"Do what he says, Kill. Just behave for once in your damn life," Grasshopper growled. "Let us explain before you kill yourself, you bloody asshole!"

A wave of brutal heat tackled me to the bed. The nausea turned to sickness. My teeth chattered as the agony in my blood came back full force. Having no choice but to lean against the bed like a fucking invalid, I muttered, "Why the hell aren't you out there looking for her? She's your responsibility, too!" The light stabbed my eyeballs as I stared at my trusted friend and vice president.

Grasshopper's black mohawk hung limp, floppy without gel. His blue eyes ringed with stress lines and bruises. He swallowed hard, refusing to answer my question.

"Well?" I prompted, holding my pounding skull. "What the fuck have you been doing to get her back?"

"Kill, back up." Mo inched forward, wiping at the blood on his chin with the back of his hand.

Hopper never took his eyes off me. "We had to make sure you would survive. Been for a ride in an ambulance, helped dress your naked ass into a hospital gown, and stood by you while you were given scans and all that other medical bullshit to make sure you didn't croak."

Pointing at my bandaged head, he added, "You were out of it. Talking nonsense; wouldn't wake up. The doctors thought the swelling might affect your speech. What were we supposed to do? Strap you to your bike and drag you with us to kill your own flesh and blood?"

My fists clenched. Blood dripped from my torn vein, splashing faster to the floor.

I couldn't contemplate that the two brothers I trusted above anyone had let my woman get taken. And then not gone after her the *second* she was stolen.

It's not their fault.

She's yours and you failed her, asshole.

This is all on you.

"Fuck!" I groaned, tearing at the bandage around my head, trying to reach inside and turn off the incessant throbbing. Why was I so weak? I'd failed her *again*!

The room swam; my eyes worked like a faulty camera lens unable to focus. "You know what she means to me. You know how damn important she is." Glaring at Grasshopper, I couldn't bring myself to be grateful for his loyalty or attempts at keeping me alive. I didn't *want* to be alive if Cleo was hurt.

I deserved to rot in hell for letting her be taken again.

"We did what—"

I slashed my hand, cutting off his sentence. "No, you did what *you* wanted to do. Not what I would've done. You know damn well I would've gone after your woman—regardless if you lived or fucking died." Punching myself in the chest, I growled, "*That's* what I wanted."

"Kill, what were we supposed to do?" Hopper snapped. "We'd go to war for a girl who would hate us if she knew we did nothing while you bled to death. No point in that fight. No one wins."

I couldn't see his logic. It was flawed. Ridiculous. Cleo would understand if I died while my men rescued her. She would expect such a gallant act.

At least she would be safe.

I didn't want to listen to fucking reason.

I want blood!

I didn't care that my ass was hanging out the back of this paisley printed apron. I didn't care that blood dripped from my hand, staining my bare feet and floor. And I definitely didn't care about the viselike agony in my skull.

All I cared about was Cleo.

The nausea faded and I charged at Hopper. In a jumble of leather and hospital gown, I pinned him against the door, threading my fingers around his throat.

"Mr. Killian, unhand him!" the doctor shouted, swatting the back of my shoulders with the clipboard.

I ignored him like a lion would ignore a flea. He was nothing.

However, the rush of energy, coupled with moving reluctant legs made me squeeze Hopper's throat more out of support rather than rage. My vision blacked out. I blinked, trying to see. "How long? How long was I out?"

Mo slapped a warning hand on my arm, tugging me away from Hopper. "Let him go, then we'll tell you."

My brain didn't feel right. The sequences of numbers I relied on all my life, the ingrained knowledge and intelligence I'd taken for granted was muted…*faded*. Missing beneath a storm of pain and swelling. My temper was fucking insane.

Grasshopper didn't try to remove my hand. Instead, he stood taller, breathing shallow as I slowly suffocated him.

"Two days."

My world fell away.

I stood on the brink of suicidal mayhem.

Don't snap. Do. Not. Snap.

My headache consumed me until I felt sure I would explode into bloody particles and devour the entire world with my fury.

Letting him go, I staggered backward. "Two days?"

Two fucking days where my father could've done anything to her.

Hopper shrank before my eyes. "Rubix took her about fifty hours ago."

I shook. Fuck, I shook.

"Fifty hours?" I couldn't do anything but repeat him. It was all I could do to force English through my lips and not revert to primitive grunts and growls.

I wasn't human. I was an animal. An animal drooling at the thought of tearing my enemies limb from limb for what they'd done.

"Why was I out for so long?"

Mo answered, "They hit you a few times over the head with a baseball bat. The scans showed—"

"The PET, MRI, and CT scans all came back conclusive," the doctor jumped in.

I'd completely forgotten he was still there.

"You have a hairline fracture in your skull and heavy swelling on the prefrontal cortex."

I turned my attention to the man severely pissing me off. I didn't want to hear what happened to me. Didn't he get it? None of that fucking mattered!

"We kept you in an induced coma for thirty-six hours, hoping the swelling would recede to acceptable levels."

"You. Did. What?" My heartbeat exploded. "You kept me fucking drugged when my woman is out there with men who won't hesitate to rape and murder her?"

I couldn't fucking believe this shit.

"You need to get back into bed, Mr. Killian. The swelling hasn't decreased as much as I'd hoped. Your rage is a side effect of your injury. The prefrontal cortex is in charge of abstract thinking and thought analysis. It's also responsible for regulating behavior. I don't believe—"

I laughed. "The bump on my fucking head isn't the cause of my behavior; it's because my woman is *missing*."

Mo placed himself in front of the doctor. "Kill, this is serious. If you don't let yourself heal, you might suffer long-term effects."

"Yes, like…eh…" The doctor scrambled. "Your normal reactions and moral judgments might be impaired. Choices between right and wrong could be compromised. You won't be as quick to predict probable outcomes. The prefrontal cortex governs social, emotional, and sexual urges."

"I don't fucking care!" I roared. "All I care about is getting her safe. Healing can come later."

"But you might not heal correctly if you damage yourself further!" the doctor yelled, finally finding some balls. "I refuse to sign you out until you are well. You're my patient. Your recovery is on my conscience!"

Putting one bare foot in front of the other, I shoved aside Mo and towered over the doctor. "Listen to me, and listen good. I am no longer your patient. I can take care of my fucking self and if that means I damage myself in order to save her, then so be it." Bending so our eyes were level, I glowered into his mousy brown ones. "Get it?"

He swallowed. "Fine. I'll let you leave. But you'll sign a waiver saying you refused treatment in case you become a damn vegetable." In a flurry of blue scrubs, he dumped the clipboard on my abandoned bed and shot out of the room.

"Kill, you really should stay. Everything depends on you and that genius brain of yours. How will you run the Club, the trades—shit the whole fucking operation if you can't—"

I snarled, "Shut it, Hopper. This is the way it has to be. I won't waste another moment arguing when Dagger Rose has my woman."

Mo sighed. "Despite what you think of us, we did send a couple of men to the compound to spy and report back. They say they've seen her. She's alive and unharmed, Kill. You could afford to heal and let us take care of this."

That didn't make me calm down. If anything, it made me worse.

I couldn't speak. I only glared. It was enough for Mo to shut his hole and nod.

My father had Cleo.

The same fucking father who'd orchestrated an entire murder, sent me to life imprisonment, and left my lover to burn.

I'll fucking kill him.

Screw my plans. Screw my vengeance. I wanted his soul. And I wanted it *now*.

The heart monitor squealed as my pulse skyrocketed with another dose of adrenaline. Reaching down the front of my hospital gown, I ripped off the sticky sensors and threw them on the floor. "Call reinforcements. The entire crew. We're going after her."

Grasshopper grabbed my elbow as I swayed a little to the side. The room faded in and out, an irritating fog consuming my vision. As much as I hated to admit it, the doc was right. The ease and supercharged highway of my thoughts was blocked and faulty.

I wasn't myself.

But it didn't matter.

"Kill, seriously, man, you're not in a condition—"

I shoved Grasshopper away. "He's hurt me for the last time. This time there will be no elaborate schemes, no long-winded plans to destroy him piece by piece. This time...I want his head at my feet, his blood on my face, and his soul hurtling toward hell." Pointing a finger at Hopper's chest, I said coldly, "Don't try to stop me. You'll lose."

Hopper nodded. "What do you want to do?"

I know exactly what to do.

My lips stretched over my teeth. "We kill them, of course. Slowly, painfully. I want them to scream."

Chapter Three

Cleo

We climbed on the roof of the Clubhouse again tonight.

We ignored our parents and stargazed until the bugs drove us inside. Lying beside him, discussing Orion's Belt and the Milky Way, I'd never felt so close to him. When we're up there, we aren't boy and girl or neighbors or even friends. We're infinite…just like the stars shining upon us. —Cleo, diary entry, age twelve

More time passed.

How much, I had no idea. There was no way to tell.

Hunger twisted my stomach, my head ached from dehydration, and my bladder was uncomfortably full.

I'd investigated until I'd memorized the pattern in the brown carpet and become best friends with every streak in the terribly painted walls. There wasn't a rusty nail, paperclip, or even a pencil to turn into a weapon.

Nothing.

No tool to pick a lock or phone to call for help.

But I had a more pressing problem: I couldn't stand another moment without a bathroom.

As much as I didn't want to bring attention to myself, I had no choice.

Swinging my legs from the bed, I stomped over to the door and banged on it. "Hey!"

I paused, straining my ears for any movement outside.

Only silence returned.

I hammered again. "I need the bathroom!"

My mind left the confines of the room and traveled through the house that I'd been in so many times as a child. Would it still look the same? The Killian household wasn't big: three bedrooms all joined by a short narrow corridor with one bathroom in the middle. The lounge was open plan with a kitchen where Art and I would spend many hours watching his mom bake and complete our homework.

My heart punctured with daggers.

Please, let him be okay.

He's okay. He has to be.

And if he *was* okay, I had no doubt he would come for me.

He might already be on his way.

I just had to stay hopeful and strong and bide my time until Kill, the president of Pure Corruption, cutthroat killer, and hardass protector, came for me.

It would be a bloodbath.

Pressing my forehead on the door, I knocked as loud as my knuckles would let me. "Someone let me out of here!"

Silence.

"Are you awake, Buttercup?"

My eyes snapped open, staring directly into the soulless gaze of Rubix Killian. I winced at the pain in my bladder and the weakness of hunger.

He smirked, leaning against the door frame. "Did you still need the toilet or did the past hour push you to the breaking point?"

Sitting upright, I gritted my teeth. "If you're asking if I disgraced myself, then you'll be unhappy to know I haven't." Standing, I hissed, "Let me use the bathroom."

He chuckled. "Still so high and mighty. Always giving demands as if I have to obey." Pushing off the door frame, he came forward in creaking leather and smoke. "You're not the princess around here anymore, *Cleo*."

Cocking my chin, I didn't back down. This was a man I'd been raised with as an uncle. The vice president of Dagger Rose and best friend to my father. My temper banded around me until I throbbed with the urge to make him pay. "We trusted you. I loved you. How could you be so cruel?"

He grinned. "Who's to say I'm cruel? Your father didn't see the potential of what our brotherhood could be. He was weak ... and there ain't no room for weakness in our Club."

"There's no room for liars or murderers, either."

Rubix lost the gloating glint in his eye, replacing it with rage. "Tell that to my fucking son."

I shot forward and slapped him.

We both gasped at the same time.

My brain transmitted the message to cause bodily harm without being filtered by rationality. My palm stung from connecting with his scruffy five-o'clock shadow.

His green eyes narrowed as he grabbed my wrist, jerking me painfully close. "You shouldn't have done that, Buttercup."

My stomach turned inside out with revulsion.

My nickname. It was blasphemy on his tongue.

My hands curled. "Don't *ever* call me Buttercup. You lost that right years ago."

"I can call you whatever the fuck I like."

Asshole.

"Why did you frame your son? What did he possibly do to deserve his own father betraying him?"

Rubix turned from rage to savagery. "Don't talk about that motherfucker in my presence." Dragging me forward, he carted me from my prison and threw me into the bathroom two doors down—exactly as I remembered it.

"You have three minutes."

He slammed the door.

I had no doubt he meant I had *precisely* three minutes. He'd always been a Nazi when it came to time. Tardiness was as much an affront to him as disobeying a command or spilling brotherhood secrets.

Turning to stare at the bathroom, I pursed my lips. The grout between the tiles was blackened, the shower curtain covered in grime, and the toilet filthy. The air was rank with mildew and smelly drains.

Who lived here? Was it just Rubix and his second son, or had he patched in more members and shared his home? I remembered the layout of the compound from when Arthur and I would explore from fence to fence. The piece of land had approximately twenty homes all dotted in an ever-widening circle. But the Clubhouse and my parents' home had been the crown right in the center.

Quickly relieving my bladder, I splashed my face with cold water and drank as fast as possible straight from the tap.

The door wrenched open before I had time to dry my face. Not that I'd touch his towels—probably covered in *E. coli.*

Rubix narrowed his eyes, his gaze trailing down my nightshirt-encased body. He smirked as he took in my scars—the scars *he* put there. "Pity the burns make you ugly, isn't it?" He licked his lips, looking at my left side. The ink that ran from my collarbone to my little toe was an intricate mural of blues, reds, and greens. "If it were me, I would've covered up the scars with the tattoo. Hide your awful disfigurement." His forehead furrowed. "Why didn't you?"

Because I'm not ashamed of wearing my scars or from finding strength in them.

Yanking a few squares of toilet paper free from the holder, I dried my face and threw the wadded tissue in his direction. "Curious or just trying to figure out how I survived you?"

He ducked my missile, green eyes darkening. "Neither. Just making conversation."

I snorted. "Everything you say is loaded with ulterior motives, never *just* conversation. Always has been." My mind skipped back to snide comments over the years as I grew up in his shadow.

"You really shouldn't draw that way. It's not very good."

"Your father sure doesn't care about your welfare if he lets you walk around wearing that."

"Jesus, Cleo, could your voice be any higher and annoying?"

Most of them had been said in jest, with a cheek-pinch or a licorice allsorts being given, but the desired effect never failed.

His words were the only way he could hurt me back then.

Now he could hurt me any damn way he wanted.

My father was dead. The men loyal to him most likely dead, too, or joined with Rubix under fear of torture.

I was alone.

My heart panged for Arthur. I didn't care that I had no one to rely on—I'd spent most of my life that way—but now that I'd found Arthur again, those feelings of togetherness only amplified the echoing emptiness of loneliness.

"You're right. I never quite grasped the art of straight shooting." Rubix grinned. "Always preferred to deal my true thoughts in thinly veiled bullshit." His nostrils flared, his eyes taking yet more liberties of my scantily dressed figure. "How about I forgo the veils and just tell you point-blank, hey?"

My skin crawled. "Fine."

Tilting his head, he said, "I think you're a stuck-up fucking princess who was raised by a redneck and pampered by a whore. You warped my son's mind and used your pussy to divide my family."

In a flash, he pounced. Shoving me against the vanity, he wrapped fingers around my throat, the cold porcelain dug into my lower back. "How's that for the fucking truth?"

Tears sprang to my eyes as he squeezed my neck. My hands shot up to cover his, clawing at his hold. "Not...truth...," I gasped, hating the way my larynx squeaked from being crushed. "Insanity."

He choked me harder.

Our faces were so close, his nose brushed mine. It was as if he tried to wring me dry—waiting to see what lies and secrets spewed forth.

My eyes bugged, the pressure of not being able to breathe pounding in my head.

Then...he let me go.

I collapsed at his feet, sucking in air with loud inhales.

His large boots stayed glued to the floor as I panted and coughed and slowly dragged enough oxygen into my bloodstream to halt the screech of death.

Keeping my head down, I muttered brokenly, "What you believe...it's not the truth—just lies you fed yourself over and over." Rubbing at the blazing pain in my throat, I wheezed, "I loved you. You scared me and I always felt as if I disappointed you, but you were the father of the boy I loved. I wanted your blessing. I wanted to be a part of your family as much as mine." Every word bruised my larynx but if I could somehow get him to believe me...perhaps I stood a chance at getting free without more pain.

A few endless seconds ticked past.

With each one, I tried not to let my hope run out of control.

I stood on shaky legs, praying that he would see sense.

But just like every time, he believed lies over truth.

Rubix's face shaded with hate and disdain. Disdain that I'd somehow stripped him of his righteous anger by fighting him not with loathing but with love.

A love he didn't deserve.

A love that finally died completely inside me.

He was no longer my uncle. No longer a father figure from my childhood. He was a monster and deserved to die.

His arm came up.

I twisted to avoid him, but he was faster.

His fingers wrapped in my hair, yanking me close. "Enough of these games." His eyes flickered to my lips. "Are you ready?"

My heartbeat exploded. "Ready for what?"

Rubix smirked. "Ready for your penance, of course."

His hair was longer, tied up with twine at the base of his skull. His leather jacket had streaks of rusty red from blood of his countless victims. It was strange to think as a child I looked up to him. I believed he would be there to protect me always...now I knew better. I was no longer blinded by young naïveté.

Every inch of me wanted to spit in his face. "I have nothing to repent for."

Rubix chuckled. "Always were argumentative, even as a little girl."

"Stop it!" Having him talk about our shared past infuriated me. I didn't want to fight memories of happiness when I wanted to embrace the coldheartedness of murder. I was done with this production.

I snarled, "You've lost the right to talk to me. You're dead to me, and soon you'll be nothing more than a rotting corpse."

For the first time in my life, I surprised the ruthless biker.

His fingers loosened in my hair, a sharp inhale on his lips.

My eyes darted behind him, down the dingy corridor to the small slice of sunlight bouncing into the lounge. If I could get past him, I could sprint to the boundary and escape.

I'd done it before while burned and bleeding.

I could do it again.

Rubix lost his shock, fisting his hand deeper into my hair. My scalp burned but my anger overrode any pain. "You really didn't change, did you? You still have the same runaway fucking tongue as you did when you were ten."

"You don't scare me anymore." I dragged my nails down the back of his hand holding my hair. The lie came out brutal and fierce—sounding truthful rather than a fib.

Rubix smiled, not flinching in the slightest from my scratches. "You should be afraid, pretty Cleo. Because unfortunately for you, your life just became a goddamn nightmare." His breath reeked of stale coffee as he pressed a rancid kiss against my mouth. His fingers wrapped harder in my hair like an awful cage. "Don't panic, little

princess. Nothing will happen that you can't handle." He added under
his breath, "After all, I want you alive."

Chills darted down my spine.

My heart stopped.

Fear tangled with fury and I wanted to carve out his eyeballs and
flush them down his disgusting toilet.

"Let me go!" Struggling in his hold, I kicked his leg. Hard.
Extremely hard.

My toes screamed and I hoped to God I hadn't broken them, but
the pain was worth it because his fingers unlocked just enough for me
to throw myself into escape.

I shoved him backward.

He stumbled.

A gap opened up between him and the doorway.

I was free.

Run!

I leaped past him and pushed myself as fast as I could.

Run, run, *run*.

I skidded into the lounge, tasting the breathy relief of freedom.

But it all came crashing down.

I didn't get far.

A few steps, that was all.

Rubix launched himself at me; his heavy leathered bulk knocked
me off balance and sent me sprawling to the sickening carpet below.

I cried out as my arm bent painfully; air shot from my lungs.

Rubix breathed hard in my ear, his body crushing mine to the
floor. "You try that again and the outcome won't just be a few fucking bruises." He kissed my cheek, then climbed to his feet. With a
savage jerk, he yanked me upright. Capturing my chin, he snapped
my head back to glare into my eyes. "The result will be a lot worse.
Understand?"

His green gaze glinted, sending me whirling into a sudden flashback.

"We have to kill him, Thorn. There's no other way."

I peeked through the stair railings, eavesdropping on my father and his vice president when I should've been sound asleep.

My father bowed his head, looking tired and stressed. "He's one of us, man. Teach him a lesson but don't fucking murder the son of a bitch."

Rubix scowled. "He broke the code. He's got to pay the punishment."

I didn't know who they were talking about, but I didn't like the sound of it. Ever since I was old enough to understand, I knew the lifestyle we lived was high risk and often dealt in high penalties for disobedience, but I'd never witnessed or heard of people being killed before.

My tummy rolled as I tiptoed back to my room. I loved my parents, but I couldn't handle hearing my sweet father who'd bounced me on his knee, painted my room my favorite buttercup yellow, and shared his desserts with me could kill someone just for disobeying.

"You're not going to ruin my plans a second time, bitch." Rubix shook me, dispelling the memory. "I'm through with you fucking everything up."

He spun me around and twisted my arms behind my back. "Move," he ordered, kicking at the back of my knee with his boot.

I bit my lip at the pain, refusing to cry out. My leg buckled, stumbling forward before my balance saved me from face-planting again.

Without another word, Rubix marched me from the house.

I didn't struggle—what would be the point? I had to save my strength for another opportunity and this wasn't it.

I blinked at the brightness after being in a gloomy house. The sun hung low in the sky. I guessed it was late afternoon.

Late afternoon.

It'd been nighttime when I'd been drugged and stolen from Arthur's arms. I tried to work out if my abduction took place last night or the night before...or even before that.

It depends how strong the drugs were.

An icy chill coated my insides. If it was more than a day...why hadn't Arthur come for me yet?

Because he's...

I slammed up a mental wall, not able to think of him dead or gone.

Deciding to believe in miracles, I clutched blindly to hope. I visualized Arthur and his Club storming the perimeter and mowing down these men. I fantasized about him thundering in on his bike and rescuing me.

And if that doesn't happen . . . then what?

I had no answer to that. I would just have to save myself—through whatever means necessary.

"Where are you taking me?" I asked as Rubix pushed me forward, forcing me to lurch faster toward the large Clubhouse in the center of the complex. My bare feet landed on sharp stones and weeds. Cigarette butts littered the pebbles and black splodges of oil-stained concrete pads outside small community houses.

This was Dagger Rose.

This was my old home.

To a child, the compound had been a treasure trove of magical machinery, gruff teddy-bear men, and interesting finds of bullet casings and dirty bandanas. Now it was just destitute and unhygienic. The aura of poverty and violence sat heavily like a rain-clogged cloud, shadowing everything with black greed.

It was the exact opposite of Pure Corruption. There, men had families, love, wealth, and a president who *earned* their loyalty rather than demanded it. Arthur had turned a tarnished lifestyle into something safe—a true brotherhood rather than a bunch of criminals.

Men appeared from behind closed doors, all watching me with evil in their eyes. I shuddered as I remembered the rules I'd been forced to recite as a little girl.

No getting caught.

No using the merchandise.

And above all else, no going against family.

Rubix broke the third one. He went against family. He *murdered* my family.

Hatred effervesced in my stomach.

He'll pay. Somehow, I'll make him pay.

Rubix forgot one important thing: Once a member of Dagger Rose, you were no longer a single entity. You were absorbed by the clan—a cog in a machine that ran on unquestioning fealty. He broke that fealty and owed his life to pay it back.

He'll pay forever in hell.

The concept of individual ownership was nonexistent, as was the tolerance for secrets. Men ate, slept, fucked, and fought as a family—unfortunately that family was now governed by a traitor. With Rubix as top dog, everyone else, including children and wives, all came second. Nothing was more important than the Club.

It was an age-old tradition to obey such strict guidelines—people said it forged bonds that were unbreakable. However, I thought it encouraged resentment. No one had anything to be proud of. No family to love or belongings to cherish. Everything they had belonged to the prez.

Arthur ran Pure Corruption so differently. His men were their own. They had freedom and happiness. Their loyalty was unswerving because it came with no conditions, no threats.

"Happy to be home, Buttercup?" Rubix's fingers pinched my wrists.

I flinched as a sharp stone stabbed my toe, adding to a long list of discomforts. I should curb my tongue. Hold my rancid loathing and play along quiet and meek. If I did, I might have a better chance at lulling him into smug laxness and escape.

But I couldn't hold my tongue.

My parents couldn't stand up to him. Arthur couldn't. It was up to me to point out what a twisted and deluded bastard he was.

To remind him that he's a dead man walking.

Tilting my head, and with the airs and graces of a biker princess, I said, "This ceased to be home the day you murdered my parents."

Looking over my shoulder, ignoring the pressure around my elbows, I added, "You sold your soul, Scott Killian, and I'll make sure you die for it."

Rubix laughed. "Didn't you read the report I gave you? It wasn't *me* who slaughtered your family." His fingers squeezed hard. "It was my lowlife pussy of a son."

My heart stumbled as Arthur's face played bright and true in my mind. His winged eyebrows, chiseled jaw, and fathomless emerald eyes. He was a romance novel. A fairy tale. My past, present, and future.

My hands fisted. "He was always too good for you." I raised my voice. "You never deserved him. He's a hundred times the man you will ever be and I'll dance on your grave when he delivers the justice that you deserve."

Rubix slammed to a halt, jerking me close so I crashed against his body. The pungent whiff of cigarettes and staleness wrinkled my nose. "We'll see who will be dancing on graves, little princess."

"I guess we will." Our eyes locked and I had no doubt that if he meant to kill me, he would've dispatched me right there in an ocean of gravel. My blood would've poured through the dusty pebbles to the earth below and stained the sanctity of Dagger Rose.

But no matter how hot his temper, he didn't slaughter me.

Why? Does he have more self-control than I thought? Or is keeping me alive more valuable than killing me?

What did he want?

Men looked up from their menial tasks around the compound, summoned by our wordless rage and silent death stare.

You won't win. I won't let you.

Rubix tore his eyes from mine, taking note of our audience. Smiling thinly, he propelled me farther from the home I'd been imprisoned in and toward the communal Clubhouse.

My skin prickled as more eyes fell upon me. Brothers young and old emerged from homes, falling in behind us to form a biker parade.

Tendrils of fear gathered like ghosts inside my stomach.

What are they planning to do?

Staring straight ahead with blank eyes, I forced my terror not to show on my face. However this ended, I would not show my fear.

Rubix looked behind us, grinning at his entourage. "See, Cleo... everyone has come to welcome our runaway pet. I have half a mind to collar you and make you crawl."

"Do it, Prez!" a man shouted.

"I'd pay to see that kinky shit!" another yelled.

My body begged to whirl around and attack—to show them how rabid a pet I could be. Instead, I remained outwardly frigid, ignoring their manipulation and taunts.

I had no amnesia to hide me this time.

No protection from what would happen.

I knew these men too well and my mind filled with painful imaginings of what they would do.

Rubix laughed, shoving me the remaining distance to the Club-house. I tripped and winced, my feet becoming bruised and dust-painted from the gravel path. My attire of T-shirt and panties had been perfect for sleeping beside Arthur—the material enticing and sensual for my lover's tender fingers and soft embrace. But here, with Dagger Rose devils gnawing on the fringes of my courage, it was woefully too revealing.

Then again, no wardrobe would be equipped to defend against being biker-napped and held hostage. The only armor I had was my mettle and ability to be dauntless in the face of certain torment.

"I want some clothes," I snapped as Rubix pushed me up the stairs of the meetinghouse. "I'm still a Dagger, after all. What's yours is mine and I demand some clothing." The lessons Detective Davidson taught me when he prepared me for my foster family came back.

"If you ever find yourself in a situation where help fails, remember you did nothing wrong and to remain strong."

I glanced up. My new name, passport, and documentation had been completed. I'd been in the state's care for a few months while waiting for the final go-ahead to locate overseas. "What do you mean?"

"If you get taken, try to keep the kidnapper talking. Get them to see you, not as a victim, but as a fellow human being. Don't beg or grovel, just be yourself. Appeal to the soul."

I traced my pink burns. Bandages still covered the worst ones and pain was a constant daily war. "And if they have no soul?"

"Then it's their life or yours. And yours is paramount."

Rubix snorted. "You're demanding clothes?"

"Yes. I'm cold."

"And you're calling yourself one of us? When you just told me you'll try to destroy me?"

I held my chin high even though navigating the steps with my arms behind my back took concentration. "Yes. I know what I'm entitled to. I'm hungry as well. Add that to my order—clothes and food."

A man chuckled behind us as if I was highly entertaining.

Rubix gripped me harder. "No."

"If you won't feed me, then you should know I'll have no energy to play your little games—whatever you have planned. Oh, and by the way, my feet are bleeding from the damn gravel." Wriggling my toes, a fresh cut oozed with blood and grime. "Clothes, food, and shoes. That's the very least I'm owed after everything you've done."

You owe me more than that, you bastard. You owe me your life.

"Fuck no."

I kept pushing. Each argument undermined his power in front of his men. It was stupidly defiant, but I'd be lying if I didn't enjoy pissing him off with reminders that once upon a time I was his ruler. "I'm your prisoner. You said yourself you want me alive. It's your job to ensure I have the things I need in order to stay that way." My back straightened regally. "Give them to me. Now."

Rubix chuckled, rolling his eyes. "I said I'd keep you alive, not in a life of fucking luxury."

"Food, shelter, and medical attention are bare necessities, not luxuries."

His voice snaked down my ear. "And you would know, wouldn't you, princess? Always had everything you ever wanted. Keep talking, bitch, and I'll show you how much worse life can get. Then we'll argue about what counts as fucking luxury."

Slamming his palm on the large door of the meeting hall, the entry swung open, revealing the same high-lofted, bare-boned structure from my childhood.

Oh, God.

Such twisted memories. Such happy times now tainted with bad. My heart filled with Arthur and the past.

"Come on, Buttercup."

I shook my head, crossing my ten-year-old sticklike arms. "Nuh-uh, we'll get in trouble. Daddy says to never go in there. It's adults only."

Art rolled his eyes, stalking toward me with moonlight as his ally. "It's ours as much as theirs. I want to explore. I'm sick of the forest. I'm sure there's plenty of juicy things to read in those locked filing cabinets." Reaching out, he touched my hand.

Instantly, the same electricity that only strengthened year after year crackled between us.

He froze.

I froze.

The moon froze.

We were too young to have these feelings. Too young to have found our soul mates.

But that was exactly what'd happened.

Rubix let me go, shoving me away from him and into the cavernous room.

I skidded with inertia as the late afternoon sun became gloomy interior.

"See, Cleo?" Rubix stomped his boot. "Tiled floor. You don't need shoes. And the air is warm, so you don't need clothes." His eyes stole liberties, slithering over my body. "In fact, I rather like what you're wearing. You sure don't look like a fucking child anymore."

Ignoring him, I drank in the meeting hall where Art and I had explored, stolen kisses, and ultimately planned our leadership when we came of age. So many memories inscribed the walls. So many laughs faded with time.

Pain crippled me thinking of him hurt or dead. I couldn't stomach the thought of finding him only to lose him all over again.

Please be alive.

My agony morphed into blackened hate, reinforcing my desire to slaughter Rubix and ultimately cure the world of his evil insanity.

I expected darkness and quiet, the hazy world I remembered of swirling cigarette smoke and the anticipation of new conquests. Instead, I was interrogated by blinding overhead lights and thirsted after by a hall of vile men.

Every pair of eyes trained on me.

And every atom inside me sprang to a feverish fear.

"Well, fuck me. There she is."

"Our own little queen back from the fucking dead."

"Fuck, her hair looks like the fire she burned in."

"Show us your scars, pretty princess."

The voices all crashed around me, eddying in my ears, decomposing with their intentions.

Keeping my face haughty and void, I glanced at the men sitting around the huge wooden table. Empty booze bottles and odor-spewing bongs rested by filthy hands of at least thirty brothers. Unlike Pure Corruption, Dagger Rose's Club room was messy and untended. Empty beer cans littered the floor and condom wrappers stuck to the stained couches shoved in the corner to make space for the huge table. The walls were covered in graffiti and cracked out Club bunnies lay haphazardly in chairs and on the floor.

There was something to be said for cleanliness washing the

wickedness out of one's soul. Dagger Rose needed a compound-wide disinfection.

A man with a bald head and a tattoo in the shape of a striking cobra licked his lips, wolf-whistling in my direction.

Cobra.

I remember him.

He'd whacked Arthur across the back of the head whenever he caught us doing homework. He said we wasted our time on education when Arthur was destined to always be a bitch.

Another man with long, greasy black hair slurped a wad of tobacco and probed me with his gaze.

I remember him, too.

Sycamore.

Named after his love for making shanks and weapons from the sycamore tree.

He smiled, teeth stained sepia from his nasty habit. "Hello, little Cleo. Fancy seeing you alive, after all these years."

Snickers and chuckles echoed around the space.

"Fancy seeing you alive and still chewing cud like a cow."

Sycamore's fingers dug into the table. He spat the brown mess into an overflowing ashtray. "Your father should've used the strap to shut that fucking mouth of yours."

I cocked my chin. "My father should've done a great many things."

Like murder you all in your sleep before you murdered him.

Rubix sidled closer, his fists balled by his side. "You're right, Cleo. Thorn failed on so many accounts. Pity my hell-bound son put him out of his misery like a fucking dog."

My heart free-fell as Arthur consumed my soul.

Arthur never wanted violence. He'd been content with love and numbers, only to be smothered by a life he didn't choose.

Arthur … I'm stalling. I'm doing everything I can to drag this out. But I need you to get here now. Where are you?

The fear I'd been keeping in check crested again.

My time was swiftly running out.

Sighing, as if I'd grown bored of my tiresome subjects, I placed my hand on my hip, hoping no one noticed my tremble. My eyes fell on another biker at the end of the table.

Him.

The one who'd burned me in the Dancing Dolphin motel.

Alligator.

My skin crawled and the acrid scent of my own skin burning haunted my nostrils.

Traitor!

His beady eyes pinned me to the spot. He no longer wore a tan Pure Corruption cut but downgraded to a black Dagger Rose.

I struggled to stay in place. I wanted to launch myself across the room and see how he liked being held down and set alight.

Hiding the flush of rage and fear, I demanded, "What is this all about? You write me a fake letter. You burn me when I follow your breadcrumbs, then steal me from Arthur all over again. If you wanted to kill me—why not just kill me when I didn't remember? Why not shoot me when I was alone in England?"

Rubix came up behind me, poking my lower back with a gun to march me forward. I recoiled but had no choice. I moved closer and stopped at the head of the table.

"Because this isn't cut and dry, Buttercup. This isn't about murdering you to hurt him."

The wooden table barricaded my way as Rubix jammed me hard against the edge. His hand lashed up, encasing my nape.

"I don't understand." I winced as his fingers turned to pincers.

"No, you wouldn't. How can I put this?" Nudging my ear with his nose, he breathed, "This isn't about you. No matter what we do to you, remember that you aren't the target—he is. If I wanted you dead, you'd be two fucking feet under and the beetles would've already enjoyed your taste. After all, you are a fucking delicacy." His tongue slimed over my cheek. "But that isn't my plan. My plan is to show him that all this time he thought he was better than me. Better than his own flesh and fucking blood. Well, he isn't and it's time he learned that the hard way."

Shoving my head against the table with a vicious push, he glowered at the cracked out whores who'd traded their souls to pleasure devils on earth. "Get out, bitches. All of you."

Cobra, who sat in the vice president's seat, glared at the scantily dressed girls. "You heard the fucking prez. Move!"

Slowly, the rustling of cheap fabric and abused bodies shuffled from comatose into movement. The bikers smirked and occasionally swatted a woman on her behind as the girls traveled the gauntlet to the main exit.

My heart charged thickly, my body growing frigid from pressing hard against the table. Everything inside me wanted to follow them and leave this godforsaken place.

Take me with you!

The men stayed silent until the last girl disappeared in a flash of nakedness and cheap polyester. The anticipation hummed with an electrical charge—all eyes pinned on me.

With a curt nod, Rubix ordered a man I didn't recognize to shut and lock the door.

The nucleus of fear grew larger until it opened its jaws like a consuming black hole. It sucked and swirled, urging me to jump into its terror and give in.

With every attention zeroed in on me, my skin goose bumped and prickled. Their interest cramped my stomach. Their lack of empathy and blatant disregard for right and wrong ratcheted my heartbeat until my palms sweated and legs begged to bolt.

Arthur...hurry.

Pausing just long enough to make a dramatic beginning, Rubix shouted, "We have her boys. Sarah fucking Jones."

Some of the men frowned. "That ain't a bitch called Sarah...that's—"

"Hey, wait...what?"

"Thought this bitch was—"

Rubix rolled his eyes. "For fuck's sake, you're a bunch of twats." Pulling my face off the table, he choked me with his savage hold around my throat. His body singed mine, pressing hard like a living coffin behind me.

Even as terror suffocated me, I still scoffed at how stupid these men were. Before them stood a woman their president had waged a vendetta against for years. Yet they didn't know my state-given name.

They should all die just for being half-wits.

"I know her name isn't Sarah Jones, you dumb fuckers. That was the name witness protection gave her. Ain't that right, Cleo Price?"

My mind filled with memories of the tender FBI agent who swooped me away and gave me a new life. What would become of me now that I'd walked from protection and into bloodshed?

I know what will happen. Arthur will come for me and we'll end this nightmare together.

A collective grumble of excitement worked around the table. An elderly biker with white hair growing from his ears said, "Well, shit."

Rubix nodded. "It's time to fucking celebrate. The plan's in action, boys, and there ain't jack shit that my son can do about it."

Questions danced on my tongue. What plan? Why had Rubix penned that letter to get me back after all these years?

"Goddamn, I can't wait." Cobra drank from his beer bottle.

Sycamore leaned forward, his nasty eyes never looking past my breasts. "Payback's a bitch, little Price. And it's been a long time coming."

My palm itched to slap every self-righteous asshole before me. "You're right. And you'll get what's coming to you for what you've done."

The men frowned, hurling insults and profanities in a chaos of voices.

Rubix grinned, basking in the temper of his men. "This little bitch was stolen right from beneath that cocksucking son of mine. He thinks he's better than me. He thinks he can start up a Club and not fucking beg for my approval. Well...I have news for him."

The men nodded, their hatred for Arthur thickening the air until the large space became stiflingly claustrophobic.

Rubix grabbed my breasts, squeezing painfully.

I bit my lip, fighting against the urge to struggle. If I fought now, I wouldn't stand a chance. I had to come across as scared, docile. Arthur was too late.

I have to get myself out of this mess.

"Time for the fun part," Rubix muttered, pinching my nipples. "Time to send a warning." Grabbing my hair, he tugged hard. "Time to steal something that's fucking precious to him."

Oh, God.

Suddenly, he shoved me forward. I crashed against the table. My arms sprawled sideways only to be captured by the two men closest. Cobra and Sycamore pinned me down, their breath reeking of beer and tobacco, their eyes glowing unnaturally bright from substance abuse.

"Good plan, boss." Cobra laughed.

Sycamore asked, "So...she's ours?"

Rubix pressed against me, grabbing my hips. "She's all ours."

Chapter Four

Kill

She was trying to kill me.

That was the only reason I could come up with. One moment she was the sweet, funny, terribly bad at mathematics little girl I loved more than anyone; the next, she was a little vixen, looking at me with something foreign in her green eyes, watching my lips, gasping whenever I touched her. The real Cleo—the girl—I could handle. I could love in the way I was permitted. But this new Cleo—this woman—I couldn't. She terrified me because she made me want. I wanted her so fucking much. But I wasn't allowed. —Arthur, age sixteen

The wind in my face and salt on my tongue never failed to grant me freedom.

Riding alone or with others; day, night, summer, winter—it didn't make a difference as long as I had a stretch of road before me and no commitments. It was the only way I could find some resemblance of peace.

But not today.

Not this fucking ride.

My hand curled around the accelerator, feeding more and more gas to the snarling engine. I was already way over the speed limit but I didn't give a rat's ass.

If I could strap wings to my bike and fly to Dagger Rose, I would.

Come on. Faster.

I'd been raised on a motorbike, and tonight was the first time that I didn't find that freedom—that peace. The loss of Cleo ate at my soul. The pain of failing her all over again threatened to crumble me into destruction.

I rode fast.

I rode hard.

But I felt as if I treaded water. Fought against demons. Got fucking nowhere.

The hum of tires and growl of engines only worsened my emotional torture. Peace? What was that? I'd never find peace again if I failed her a second time.

Fuck!

The speedometer needle climbed higher, teasing the boundaries of red danger.

Hurry up, for Christ's sake!

The journey from Pure Corruption to Dagger Rose was an endless fucking marathon.

Every stop sign was a mortal enemy, every traffic light my ultimate nemesis.

An hour we'd been driving and we hadn't even passed the half-way point.

My teeth clenched harder as I hunched farther over the bike.

We were late.

We were late and I was fucking pissed.

I was livid at my weakness.

I was furious at my condition.

And I was incandescent with rage at Mo and Grasshopper for not finding some way to fix this clusterfuck.

The nurse at the hospital had filed charges against me and called the police. She'd done everything in her power to detain me, all because I couldn't leash my temper. She'd refused to give me the forms to sign out. She'd held my fucking clothes hostage. She'd deliberately antagonized me to the point where I would've probably killed her if Grasshopper hadn't taken me into a janitor's closet, stolen some fat man's clothes, and thrown them at me.

I growled under my breath, anxiety and anger circulating hot in my blood. I needed to fly. I needed this journey to fucking end.

I need her.

I shivered as hurtling wind sliced through the horrific Hawaiian print shirt encasing my broad torso. The sleeves were too short, the chest too tight, and I couldn't look at the god-awful track pants clinging to my legs.

I missed my leathers.

Shit, I missed my own damn bike.

Grasshopper's custom Triumph was all wrong. The acceleration sluggish compared to my beast. The Pure Corruption logo of skulls and all-important abacas was drawn freehand with glowing flames on the frame.

The flames seared my heart.

Cleo.

My mind whooshed with burning houses, smoking remains, and charred dreams of ever growing old with the girl I loved.

She'd witnessed her parents' double homicide.

She'd almost burned to death.

All because I wasn't strong enough to save her.

And I'm not strong enough to save her now.

The agony of the never-ceasing headache hollered in agreement.

I'm a liability. I don't deserve her.

Every mile we charged, my injuries and shortcomings became more apparent.

My head hurt like a motherfucker.

My vision was frighteningly narrowed.

My mind slothfully slow.

The joy of thinking in algorithms, the speed of dealing with figures and equations was...damaged.

I was fuzzy.

I was lost.

I hated to admit it, but the doctor was right.

There's something wrong with me.

Everything raged inside. I couldn't find that calm—that control. I was on the cusp of wreaking my revenge—on the precipice of having everything I'd been working toward coming true.

I couldn't afford to be broken now.

I can't bear to be ruined when she needs me.

The roar of another Triumph coasted beside me.

I looked to the side.

Mo matched my speed, still managing to look badass even with Grasshopper riding bitch on the back.

I felt empty, vulnerable at not having my usual weapons. But I'd refused to waste more time by returning home. Instead, I'd commandeered Grasshopper's knife and his unregistered pistol and straddled his machine without asking.

What was his was mine. He'd get over it.

He worked for *me*. Not the other way around.

I'd been dead for too long believing Cleo was lost. I wouldn't live in such hell again.

Yes, I had a shit-stirring headache. Yes, something was seriously fucking wrong with me.

But none of that mattered.

Cleo.

I have to get to Cleo.

Then, I could worry about myself.

Then, I could die happy knowing I'd finally avenged and saved her.

Fifty-four hours they've had her.

My mathematically tuned brain clunked and wheezed, no longer the streamlined super machine but a rusty fucking cog.

Fifty-four hours they'll have to pay back in blood.

Hunkering over the bike, I fed another twist of petrol to the roaring engine. I didn't need to look at the speedometer to know this speed would kill me three times over if I buckled beneath the pain in my head.

My patience snapped.

My hatred overflowed.

Nothing else fucking mattered.

Only her.

I'm coming, Cleo.

Don't you dare leave me . . . not again.

Chapter Five

Cleo

He was still being a dick.

*Last week, he'd wanted to hang out with me. Now he wanted noth-
ing to do with me. I'd tried everything. I'd baked him his favorite white-
chocolate-chip cookies. I'd worn my hair in pigtails like he loved. I'd even
stuffed my bra so he could see that a woman existed inside this stubborn
flat-chested thirteen-year-old body. But no matter how he treated me,
he couldn't hide the truth. He* did *care for me. I knew he would always
come for me. Always protect me. I knew because he was mine. He was my
guardian angel.* —Cleo, diary entry, age thirteen

There hadn't been a single moment in the past eight years when I'd
awoken and wished I could forget.

Every morning had been a struggle to remember.

Every night a battle between needing to know and needing to
forget.

I'd tried to trick my mind into remembering, but either I was too
stubborn or too afraid, because it never worked. And…as the days
turned from hell to heaven and Arthur fell back in love with me, I
didn't really mind that a chunk of my life was missing.

I had him back. Larger than life and even more perfect than any
recollection could do justice.

I was content with that.

But living in the silver haze of amnesia, with no past or present, came with its own burdens and trials. It meant I couldn't find my true self, but it also granted unusual freedom. Freedom *because* I couldn't find my true self. I had the latitude to be stronger, braver—all because I had no notion of who I'd been or what I was risking by choosing certain paths.

I'd be lying if I said I didn't like that indulgent laxity . . . that *power*.

It'd granted me silent strength to chase Arthur even when he seemed unchasable. And it'd helped me find the truth that I'd been missing all these years.

But now, pinned to a table with men gawking at my half-naked form, I wished I could disappear into the void where my mind had vacationed for so long.

I wished I could delete whatever was about to happen.

I struggled against the fingers around my wrists, unable to look up at the men holding me down. My cheek squashed against the table; my toes ached as I dug into the tiled floor, trying to stop myself from sliding and becoming completely helpless.

Rubix stood behind me. The heat of his thighs against my T-shirt and the roughness of his fingers sent my heart spiraling.

Please, don't let this happen.

Rubix was many things, but a rapist? Would he stoop that low?

The unequivocal answer reverberated through my head.

Yes.

Especially if such a thing would hurt the one person he hated above all. Arthur would never be able to forgive himself if I was violated so terribly.

It will kill him.

My heart shattered into kaleidoscopic pieces at the thought of destroying Arthur in such a way. Me? I could brave it. I could heal. But him? He'd never be able to look at me again without suffering such awful guilt.

"Why do you hate your son so much?" I whispered, fearing his answer.

Rubix chuckled. "You never guessed?"

Never guessed? "No." *How would I ever guess something so wrong?*

"He was supposed to be like me. Instead, he was like *her*."

"What?" My forehead furrowed. "Like her...your wife?"

"Yes," he snarled. "So fucking soft. She was always so meek—riddled with indecision and then later with disease. Arthur was supposed to make me proud—but all he did was make me a laughing stock."

"All because he preferred to use his brain over his fists? Because he chose to go to school instead of smoking crack with the rest of the lowlife prospects?"

Rubix tucked my hair behind my ears. "No, pretty Buttercup, because he chose your family over his own."

My stomach ruptured. "He didn't choose us over you. You gave him no choice. Arthur wanted to be good rather than follow morals he didn't believe in. That doesn't make him soft. That makes him strong."

Stronger than you'll ever be.

He bared his teeth. "He was mine. His blood was mine. His destiny was mine. But then you and your fucking kinder-than-thou family stole him from me."

"We didn't steal him. We loved him. Just like you should've—"

Rubix fisted my hair. "How could I ever love someone who could settle for second best? How could I tolerate my own flesh and blood thinking he was fucking better than me because he wanted diplomacy over violence?" His face turned puce with rage. "Our world is governed with fists not democracy. Arthur refused to follow my orders. He was a fucking pussy and no son of mine."

Had Rubix ever loved his son? Was that all it took for so-called love to turn into bitter resentment?

Perhaps there was hope. Perhaps Rubix hurt because he felt

Arthur abandoned his family. Perhaps they could reconcile and whatever awful misunderstanding could end. Even as I thought it, I knew it wasn't possible. Too much time had passed. Too much hate had gathered.

"Don't do this, Scott," I implored, keeping my voice low, controlled. *You're wishing for a miracle.*

Standing tall, he grabbed my hips. The stiffness of his erection dug into my ass. "Do what?"

The bikers snickered as Rubix rubbed disgustingly against me.

"Hurt me to hurt him."

He laughed, running his fingertips up my rib cage. "Now where would the fun be if I didn't?"

I squeezed my eyes as Cobra muttered, "You heard the prez, you're ours now. Ours to do whatever the fuck we want with."

My breasts ached from being pressed so hard against the table. The awful metallic taste from being drugged never left my tongue. I wanted nothing more than to slip away from this part of my life and pretend it never existed.

I hated myself for being weak. I hated that my strength to escape dwindled by the second. But helplessness didn't stop me from searching inside my compartmentalized brain, begging for the gift of amnesia to sweep me away and save me.

If I couldn't run physically, perhaps I could run mentally.

Like I did all those years ago.

Hadn't I endured enough at the hands of this man?

Hadn't I paid whatever debt I owed?

"Do you know what your father planned for me, little princess?" Rubix's fingers stroked my spine, digging into each vertebra. Each pinch left a resounding bruise on my flesh.

"He planned to teach me a lesson. To cut me from the Club, all because I had balls big enough to imagine a better way of life than he ever could."

His touch slid over my ass, tracing my thigh and disappearing up the hem of Arthur's T-shirt. "He was weak, your father. He believed in redemption instead of retribution. He believed in leniency instead of law. And look what happened to him."

The men chuckled.

My eyes stung with unshed tears. My father had been a good man. Despite his chosen lifestyle and rule-breaking, he'd been kind and generous and loving.

This man... he was just a coward, a snake, an *insect*.

"Can you see the irony, princess?" Sycamore said. "Can you see how soft that motherfucker was?"

Cobra jumped in, ensuring I wasn't stupid enough to miss their punch line. "Your father was a pussy and now he is dead."

Rubix's fingers skirted higher; repulsion tugged on my gag reflex. "Your father didn't deserve this Club. And my son didn't deserve me as his father."

"Just me, Prez."

That *voice*.

It sliced through the heavy stares and whipped around me with filth. I sucked in a breath as the owner ducked by my side and stared into my eyes. "Hello, baby Cleo."

My cheek ached from kissing the table but it faded as my blood washed with wrath. "You."

Arthur's older brother grinned. The family resemblance was strong, with matching aquiline noses, symmetrical features, and sculptured lips. However, Arthur had prominent cheekbones that stretched his tanned skin, turning him ageless, whereas Dax "Asus" Killian had full cheeks and a dimple on his chin.

I bared my teeth. "I hoped you were dead, Asus."

He grinned. "Didn't you figure it out already? Life doesn't care about your hopes."

He looked pudgier than last I'd seen him—sitting too long on his butt hacking innocent people's laptops with his own Asus computer. That was how he earned his nickname—by being a geek with bad intentions.

Turns out gifts with numbers runs in the family.

My nose crinkled at his horrendous aftershave. "I didn't understand at first, but now I do."

When I didn't elaborate, Rubix pulled my hips back, grinding himself on me. "Understand what?"

Asus threaded his fingers through my hair, slowly tightening his fist until agony bloomed. Two Killians tormenting me and all I craved was the third to make it go away.

"Continue, by all means."

My blood turned to dry ice, smoking through my veins. "I couldn't understand why Arthur didn't kill you the day he escaped prison, but now . . . I do."

The men in the room grumbled under their breath. The stench of violence and cruelty thickened.

Rubix growled, "I suggest you think about what you're going to say, otherwise—"

"I know what I want to say," I snapped, cutting him off. Turning my attention back to Asus, I smiled. "He doesn't just want to exterminate you; he wants to rip everything from you like you did from him."

Asus leaned forward, drawn by my quiet voice. "He'll be dead in a few days; then we'll see who won in the extermination."

Rubix's questing fingers pressed against my inner thigh. "Everything he's been working toward, everything he thought was secret will come to bite him in the fucking ass." Raising his voice, he demanded, "Cobra, if you will."

The bald-headed tattooed biker nodded and stood, leaving my left wrist unfettered.

Tucking my hand beneath my torso, I willed sensation to enter my shoulder and arm. If I spied an opportunity to fight, I needed my body to move swift and sure.

The men watched in silence as Cobra moved toward another door that led to a meeting room where Arthur and I used to eavesdrop on the men while they discussed world domination. He disappeared for a moment before returning with a prisoner.

A woman.

Her head was covered with a black cloth, her body naked and bleeding.

Oh, God.

The ground became quicksand as my hope sank into grainy despair.

"Let Cleo go, Sycamore," Rubix ordered.

Immediately, my other wrist was freed, relinquishing me into Rubix's control. Rubix yanked me upright, molding my body against his and holding my chin with biting fingers.

I squirmed. My flattened breasts smarted as blood rushed back.

"Recognize her?" His breath wafted hotly in my ear. "You should. She was there the night my son kidnapped you."

I blinked, wishing I could ignore his every word. I didn't know who stood before me but my heart hurt for her—for the obvious torture she'd endured.

One kneecap looked shattered. The right side of her chest was concave, and she couldn't stand upright without being supported.

She'd been demoted from healthy human to emaciated marionette.

Nobody—regardless of their crimes—deserved to be so thoroughly broken.

"Remove the hood," Rubix said, gathering me tighter against him. The hollow of my back burned as he ground his belt buckle against me.

Every part of me demanded to struggle and run. Everything about him repulsed and petrified me but I swallowed back the insane pressure to fight and stood stoic. On the outside, I looked queenly and unaffected but inside the pulsing of my blood and the panic whooshing in my ears drove me faster into madness.

Cobra grinned. "With pleasure." With one hand, he held the girl's bound wrists in front of her naked body, somehow propping her up, and with the other ripped off the hood.

Blonde hair once the color of sun-warmed wheat was now matted and stained pink with blood. Her eyes were like broken moons in a face butchered and swollen.

I didn't recognize her.

But wait...

The longer I stared, the more my memories tugged at some vague recollection. She'd been there. She'd been in the truck when we'd arrived at the scene of mutiny with Arthur and his men. She'd stood in line with me as we all stripped and delivered ourselves into Pure Corruption's control.

I sucked in a breath.

Rubix laughed softly. "So you *do* remember her."

I shook my head. "I don't know what you're doing or what you want me to say, but I won't do it." My heart was tied to an anchor, slowly sinking deeper and deeper into desperation.

"You do know and you're far too bright not to see the point I'm about to make."

No!

I would've sold every worldly possession to save her.

But I was bankrupt.

Cobra slapped the blonde girl, dragging her forward and kicking the back of her legs so she slammed to her knees before me.

She screamed, her shattered kneecap excruciating.

It ricocheted around the room like a voice boomerang, ringing in my ears.

My stomach convulsed.

Instant sobs escaped her mouth. She looked up and our gazes locked—hers full of begs and pleas while mine were no doubt bleak and desolate.

"Arthur Killian, my useless treasonous son, stole this whore from Chainsaw's bed. Do you know who Chainsaw is?"

I shook my head, unable to tear my eyes from the girl.

She trembled. Every rib stuck out from malnutrition. How long had Rubix held her as a captive? It couldn't have been more than a few weeks. How had he damaged her so swiftly?

"Chainsaw is an honest member of Dagger Rose—he earned this bitch when I gave her to him as a gift for pleasing me. However, she was stolen and given to the president of a Club past our borders." Rubix's voice grew angrier the longer he spoke. "Not only was she given as a token, but it also solidified an agreement between the Night Crusaders and Pure Corruption."

My brain tripped in its urgency to understand. There was so much Arthur had been planning—so many carefully laid parts to his overall vengeance. Why had he stolen women from his father's bed and given them to other presidents? What did he hope to gain?

Rubix shook me. "My son tried to buy the Night Crusader's loyalty. He made them pledge their allegiance to fight against me when the time came, all for the price of a girl and a few measly dollars."

Art had paid men?

My mouth fell open.

He's creating an army.

An army to destroy any enemy who'd supported his father and ruined his life.

No, not just his life.

My life.

Tears swelled behind my eyes. All of this: Art's thirst for revenge and his obsession with retribution was all for me—for what they'd broken the night I disappeared.

Rubix snapped, "He enlisted other Clubs to fight against us. He went against every code and took the coward's way out of hiring other people to do his fucking dirty work. But it didn't go the way he wanted."

Rubix forced me to stand over the girl, bending me as if I were her judgment and executioner.

Cobra smiled, fisting the blonde girl's hair and jerking her head back. Her throat strained, exposing translucent skin and blue veins.

She was so close. So terrified.

I wanted to say I was sorry. I wanted to save her so desperately.

"This is what happens to those who defy me." Rubix thrust his erection against my lower back as Cobra reached behind him and withdrew a hunting blade.

"No!" I fought. "Don't!"

Slamming my head back, I tried to make contact with Rubix's nose. But it was no use.

In a horrible heartbeat, Cobra dragged the sharp knife across the girl's neck, slicing sickeningly deep. Her blood fountained from the wound, red—the color of love and valentines spritzed the air with metallic mist.

She gurgled and twitched as her life force drenched my half-naked body, staining my hair, my eyelashes, my lips. I bathed in her blood. I wore her death like a mortal sin.

Every part of me rebelled. I wanted to throw up. I wanted to hide. I wanted to bite and tear and *kill*.

But all I could do was be there for her as she faded before my eyes. Every pulse of her heart spewed more hot crimson down her front, slowly pushing her into a deep, dark sleep.

The room remained silent. No one coughed or laughed or spoke.

And that final moment, when the last pitiful beat of her heart sent her from living to dead, a spark, a tingle, an all-knowing sixth sense radiated out like a chime.

Her soul escaped.

She was free.

Closing my eyes, I found I didn't have to fight tears or nausea. I was numb. Numb and cold and terribly, *terribly* angry.

You'll suffer for your sins. You'll watch as they're torn from you like you've torn them from others.

Rage twisted my insides until I housed a nest of poisonous snakes. "I'll kill you myself," I hissed. "I'll avenge that poor girl and rip out your blackened hearts."

Rubix laughed as Cobra let go of the girl's hair, tossing her to the side as if she were trash. Her body was graceful even in death, languishing on the tiles like a heartbroken ballerina after an ill-fated tryst.

"You're not strong enough to kill me, pretty princess. And neither is anyone else. You're a walking corpse, just like my son. And it's time to send him a message he will never forget."

His hand disappeared down my front, groping me brutally in front of his men.

I gasped.

I fought the urge to vomit.

My lips pursed with revulsion.

But I didn't give him the satisfaction of crying out. My body was just a tool. It was my soul…my mind…that was the true part of who I was. As long as I remained untouchable inside, he couldn't hurt me the way he wanted.

His fingers wrenched my nipples.

The pain was hot and consuming but I'd had worse.

Anyone could see I was a survivor of pain by the scars adorning my body.

I'm invincible to them.

Because I'd survived far worse than they ever had.

A laugh bubbled in my belly. I swallowed it down. I might be strong enough to endure whatever came next, but I wasn't stupid enough to antagonize them by proving I was impenetrable.

"What's the matter, Cleo? Is my son such a bad lover he's turned you frigid?"

I couldn't breathe without inhaling blood. I couldn't lick my lips without tasting murder.

I stayed silent.

Rubix grunted under his breath as his hand trailed possessively down my stomach. Kicking my ankle with his boot, he forced my legs to spread as his hand cupped my core.

I stiffened—I couldn't help it.

No matter how removed I was, it was still a direct violation of somewhere only my lover was permitted to touch.

"Ah, so you are alive, after all." Rubix's fingers probed further, indenting my nightshirt.

I breathed harder though my nose, doing my utmost to hide my rapidly building repugnance.

His tongue lashed around my earlobe, sucking it into his horribly wet mouth.

I'm not here.

I'm far away from this.

My mind—for once—obeyed me. It skipped backward through time, trading this monstrosity of a Club for the one where I'd grown up happy and carefree. Dagger Rose was once a joyous place—a sanctuary full of love and laughter.

I'd fallen in love here.

I'd been groomed for my destiny here.

My father knew he couldn't give the Club to me. I was a girl. But I was also his only child. Royalty within the ranks was governed by blood rather than dictated by votes. Therefore, the man I chose as mine would've been the next president.

Arthur would've been president.

My heart bled dry. Was I the reason why Rubix had done what he did? Was jealousy of his son's future ranking enough to push him to such dreadful things?

My limbs turned to stone. The reason was so superficial—so vain. How could anyone possibly be envious of their own family?

"You got what you wanted, didn't you, Rubix?" I said coldly.

The men around the table froze, straining to hear what I had to say.

Rubix's fingers stopped in their appalling exploration. "What are you bullshitting about now?"

"You couldn't stand to think your son was more man than you. More deserving to rule in my father's stead. You had to murder my family and pin it on him to remove him from the picture." My blood thickened until my brain swam with an overdose of oxygen, preparing to flee or fight. "What I don't understand is why did you try to kill me? What was the point in dispatching me when I would've only made your claim more concrete by taking me for your own?"

Rubix glanced at the men before bending to whisper in my ear. His hands flattened on my belly, curving my ass into his crotch. "You're very perceptive, little princess. A pity, really." He paused. "I did want you for myself. I left you in that burning house only long enough to scare you. I was going to save you, turn your gratefulness into love and your putrid hate for my murdering son into adoration for me. I had it all planned out. Yet you didn't wait for me to save you."

"No, I saved myself because I could see through your bullshit."

"Not true. You're as blind as you were when you were ten. You're still in love with him. Still letting him sink between your fucking legs. But no matter what you think you remember about that night, Cleo Price, he *did* murder your parents. It was *his* finger on the trigger. No matter how you twist the fucking facts."

No matter how much I wanted to believe Arthur didn't do it, I couldn't deny Rubix told the truth.

I was in love with the man who stole my family.

But I had my reasons why.

I could forgive him because of what *truly* happened that night.

"I know what you did, asshole," I murmured. "I know the truth."

Rubix chuckled. "Doesn't make a shit load of difference, though, does it? He'll still die." He licked my cheek. "Just like you will do, pretty little girl. Which is such a shame, as I would've so enjoyed your company."

All reminiscent and favored memories of Dagger Rose evaporated. The laughter, the connection—it all vanished as if it never existed.

I *hated* this place.

I loathed it.

I wanted to burn every damn house to the ground with every member inside.

I wanted them to die by fire like they'd almost done to me.

Wriggling in Rubix's arms, I managed to dislodge his touch and spin to face him. "What do you want?" I spat, gritting my teeth against his horrible touch. Everything about him—from his scruffy chin to his greasy black hair pissed me off. "I'm done with whatever you're doing. You want something from me? Spit it out so I no longer have to be subjected to your filth."

Men laughed.

Cobra guffawed. "Holy shit, Prez. You gonna let her talk to you like that?"

"Yeah, Prez. Give her to us and we'll set the bitch straight." Sycamore's sickening drawl webbed around the room.

Rubix laughed blackly. "Oh, believe me, boys, we'll make her fucking pay." Shooting his hand down the front of my body, he fingered me cruelly. "And what I want from you, princess, is a fuck load more than you think."

"Get your hands off me!" I tried to slap him but only succeeded in being slapped myself.

My cheek bloomed with fire.

He snarled, "Make me."

I flinched as his hand gathered my T-shirt, revealing my behind to the table of disgusting onlookers. They never moved, drinking in the scene with devil-soaked eyes.

"Do you want money? Shares? Let me go and I'm sure Arthur will give you both."

Arthur would never pay—I knew that. But I would've bequeathed anything if it meant I could escape. I could take his punishment. I would survive it. But I would be stupid not to fight. Hell, I would've pledged millions if it meant I could walk out of there and be done with this ignoramus vendetta between father and son. I would've promised the world, but the moment I was free, I would've reneged on every single one.

Murderers, liars, and thieves didn't deserve promises.

They didn't know the value of an oath. Why should I be any different?

I bit my lip, swallowing my disgust as Rubix marched me back to the table and held me prisoner against the wood. I flinched as his fingers entered me forcibly, but I didn't reward him with a cry.

He smirked. "I see you're not going to make me stop. Haven't you figured out that I don't want money or whatever else you think you can fucking bribe me with?" His finger drove deeper, making me wince. His head tilted as coy smugness entered his eyes. "You're not wet...so it isn't just the last name that turns you on."

He pushed my chest so my shoulders slammed against the surface. Bending over me, he thrust his jeans-clad cock against the mound of my pussy.

Oh, God.

I'm not here.

I'm not here.

I'd always been the type of person who guarded herself carefully. I supposed that was why my mind had tripped into amnesia when faced with something too hard to handle. I didn't let emotions overwhelm me—I had a natural defense that probably wasn't healthy but I couldn't circumnavigate.

I had the tendency to shut down.

A switch.

And if I shut down, it was over. Done. Whatever happened from that point on couldn't affect me because there was nothing inside to affect.

"Did you hear that the father is twice the man his son is?" Rubix's breathing was thick and fast. "Don't you want to sample the better version?"

I bucked, trying to get him off me. The bikers who'd held my wrists before captured them again, flattening me down, turning me helpless.

"You'll only embarrass yourself," I snarled. "Arthur isn't just twice the man you are—I told you, he's a hundred times."

Cobra and Sycamore licked their lips, watching me with over-bright eyes.

"Go on, do whatever you think proves you're a bastard. But just know the entire time I'll be laughing at you. Laughing at how worthless you are. How lacking you are compared to a real man."

Oh, God, Cleo. What are you doing?

I swallowed my terror. I hadn't meant to say that.

Too late now. I only had myself to blame.

Rubix laughed, bunching the T-shirt higher.

My teeth clamped on my bottom lip. I poured every inch of hate and repugnance into my gaze.

If he wanted me scared—he'd achieved it.

If he wanted me to scream or beg or cry—he'd be sorely disappointed.

I won't.

Cobra and Sycamore pulled my wrists, jerking me flatter against the table.

"Tell me again...what you said about Arthur," Rubix demanded.

"Yes, tell us the part where he's a hundred times more man than us," Cobra chuckled, blowing a kiss in my direction.

"Yeah, the part where you'll be laughing at us." Sycamore's eyes were luminescent with toxic lust.

Don't fall into their trap.

I knew they were taunting me, but at the same time, I couldn't let them talk ill of Arthur.

I looked at all three Dagger Rose bastards and said loudly, clearly, and with utmost conviction. "Arthur is a thousand times the man you will ever be. He'll find and kill you. And then you will see for yourself how pathetic you truly are."

Rubix laughed softly. "I guess we'll see, won't we, Cleo? We'll see who wins this coming war." He placed his chilled hands on the paper-thin skin of my throat.

I froze.

Our eyes locked.

With the barest of voices, Rubix ordered, "Prepare her. The sooner we do this—the better."

I wanted to ask what would happen.

I wanted to disappear and never open my eyes again.

But Cobra moved so fast.

A blur.

A shout.

What—

Then pain.

Impossible, profound pain.

Cobra struck me with something I didn't see.

Pain against my temple. Agony around my throat.

I moaned as the agony intensified, casting out waves of black fog. My mind sank deeper into the ink, faster and faster, succumbing to whatever they'd struck me with.

"Again," Rubix shouted, slicing through my thick haze.

I tried to speak but my tongue wouldn't work.

I tried to move but my body had disappeared.

There was nothing but thoughts and whispers and pain. Endless, measureless pain.

Cobra obeyed.

The agony struck again.

It smashed through my consciousness, sending me into drunken spirals.

Around and around.

I'm on a merry-go-round.
I'm slipping.
I'm falling.
It came again.
One last strike.
The world turned from solid to swimming; I was sucked down a drain into a whirlpool of sickness.

Chapter Six

Kill

*R*unning away had a certain appeal.

> *If I knew he wouldn't come after me, I'd steal a bike and put Dagger Rose in my dust. But to leave, I'd have to cut my heart out, because I'd never be whole unless I was with her.*
>
> *She'd saved me all while ruining me.*
>
> *And now I was trapped.*
>
> *Indefinitely.* —Kill, age fifteen

There were approximately five liters of blood in an average man.

Rubix owes me every last drop in his body.

Cleo had been in their clutches for fifty-five hours.

Ninety thousand seconds since she'd slept angelically beside me.

Fuck…

No, wait. That's wrong.

Three thousand six hundred seconds were in an hour. So that made it one hundred and ninety-eight thousand seconds since I'd last seen her.

A cold sweat dripped down my spine.

Another mistake. Another mathematical solvent I'd fucked up.

Shit.

Had this injury stripped me of whatever gift I'd been given? Were all my trading sequences, tricks, and secret formulas dashed upon the rocks of my useless fucking brain?

My mind was darkness and smog.

My neurons faulty and extinct.

Snippets of knowledge were there, but not in their entirety. The codes were broken—unconnected and fragmented.

Shit, I am defective.

Fear stalked me, closing its claws around my thoughts.

I forced my bike faster.

It doesn't matter.

I didn't have time for self-fucking-pity.

Cleo had been held hostage for one hundred and ninety-eight thousand seconds. In order to pay the grim reaper, I had to extract the perfect amount of vengeance before killing those who hurt my woman.

My headache intensified; sludge coated my synapses. I was swimming upstream and out of breath.

There's approximately five liters of blood in an average man.

Punishing the bike with another burst of speed, I beat my brain into submission. In a spark of intelligence, a figure came to me.

A figure of exact revenge.

My thoughts turned from chaos to calmness.

Five liters spread out over fifty-five hours.

Zero-point-zero-zero-five drops of blood for every second.

That's how much they'll pay when I get my hands on them.

Darkness was our ally as we purred through the sleepy township run by Dagger Rose.

With a growl of mechanical power, we slipped through suburbia.

My old family.

My old home.

It wasn't too late—about midnight—but the streets were abandoned. There were no teenagers playing on the seesaw and swings where I'd kissed Cleo for the first time. No couples stumbling out of the diner.

Vacant.

Soulless.

Just us.

My body ached as if we'd been traveling for days, and my head—shit, my head was a damn wasp nest of agony.

Every mile we traveled, it grew worse.

I could barely move my neck to check for traffic. I couldn't see without blinking through black spots and swallowing back nausea. Everything was a herculean effort.

The second Cleo was back in my arms, I was passing the fuck out.

And taking drugs.

Lots and lots of drugs.

We didn't stop until we navigated our way through town and onto the outskirts. Our engines cleaved through the stagnant silence like a chainsaw through bread. My skin prickled with anxiety and adrenaline. Now that we were close, I wanted to charge into the compound and pummel to death the bastards who'd done this.

I wanted to howl and turn berserk with no regard for anything but delivering justice.

Turning into the same dead-end where I'd parked the bike when I'd brought Cleo to jog her memory, we rolled onto the grassy uninhabited verge. The undergrowth had claimed any attempt at landscaping by municipality councils, offering natural protection to hide the bikes.

The second we killed the engines, warm air chased away the chill on my skin from riding for so long without a jacket. The man's clothing that Grasshopper had stolen didn't invoke fear or hint at my credentials as ruthless president. The sweatpants were too short and I would've preferred to go bare-chested than wear the god-awful Hawaiian shirt another fucking minute.

"You look like a homeless bum, Kill." Mo snickered, climbing off his bike once Grasshopper had jumped off the back.

I threw him an icy stare. Even that small action sent clammy sweat over my forehead, threatening to topple me into unconsciousness.

Hopper cracked half a smile. "He's right, though. Perhaps you can kill them by making them laugh to death?"

"Shut the fuck up, both of you." I locked the handlebars and swung my leg over the hot machine. The instant my feet touched terra firma, I wobbled like a drunk.

The night sky glittered with our intent; silver stars and waxing moon shone ready to turn bloodred in retaliation.

Grasshopper cleared his throat. "The rest of Pure are already in position. Got a text about five minutes ago."

Turning slowly, so as not to upset the unbalanced pandemonium in my head, I nodded. "Good."

Reinforcements had been sent ahead. I'd made the call while we stormed from the hospital.

In all the years I'd been president, I'd only summoned their help twice in battle: once when fighting off an invading cartel and again when I'd wanted to expand our reach and absorb more Clubs under our name.

Each time my men had fought bravely and loyally.

Each time they'd been rewarded handsomely.

This time would be no different.

But this time *everything* would be different. Different because this was the start of everything we'd worked toward. The beginning of change.

I want more than this. I deserve more than this lifestyle provides.

"Let's go." Mo cocked his head at the undergrowth. "The sooner this is over, the sooner we can blow some shit up and get home."

I tried to hide my slight sway and the way even the darkness hurt my eyes. But of course, he saw right through it.

Mo came closer. "You're the prez, Kill. You're the one pulling the strings on this party. But tonight, let us be the ones in front, yeah?"

Grasshopper froze. I was well known for being on the front line. I never asked others to do what I was afraid to do myself. I shook my head, then stopped immediately.

Motherfucker, that hurts.

Swallowing my groan, my shoulders slumped. "Normally, I'd take a swing at you for sprouting such bullshit. But…you might be right."

Honesty was a weakness, but it was also a strength. My men trusted me because I wasn't stupid. If they had a better idea, I listened. If they had reasons to avoid something, I paid attention.

And this was one of those times.

Grasshopper's boots crunched a twig as he shifted. "You're still the boss. We aren't protecting you or doing shit on your behalf; you're just doing us a favor by not getting in the way."

As if anyone believes that shit.

"We'll get her back, dude. And we'll destroy those motherfuckers." Grasshopper slapped a hand on my shoulder.

I winced as my headache flared, but I appreciated the gesture. Fuck, I appreciated everything he'd done—even if I was livid.

I owed him.

If it hadn't have been for Hopper, I might've bled out or turned into a damn zucchini before anyone noticed. He'd been the one to pop around when he couldn't get me on the phone. He was the one who found me passed out.

Mo pulled his gun free and clicked off the safety. "Let's go." Like an evil spirit, he dissolved into the tree line.

Grasshopper took off after him, leaving me to bring up the rear—like a rookie or some idiotic prospect.

The trees were watchdogs.

The shadows were death's pockets to hide in.

We remained silent as we merged with the darkness, slinking stealthily through leaves and cobwebs.

Every step throbbed my head.

Every duck to avoid branches sent queasiness splashing through my skull.

Cleo was nearby and we were about to rescue her.

That was all the incentive I needed to do my fucking job as a Pure Corruption president and lover to my woman.

I'm stronger than a damn concussion.

However, the closer we got to the large wooden fence barricading Dagger Rose, the more I feared I might not be a help but a hindrance. Mo was right to put me at the back. My muscles trembled and the cold sweat of illness never let up. I could barely stomach the pain of walking, let alone running into battle and firing a loud gun.

Shit.

Moving past the glade where I'd brought Cleo, my fists tightened as I recalled her peering through the hole in the fence and witnessing her old home.

It hurt like hell that she couldn't remember everything we'd shared, but at the same time, I was glad. Glad that she couldn't recall the night we both lost everything.

My stomach convulsed as a rancid thought crusted my mind.

She'll know.

She'll remember what I did.

My father would've had ample time to tell her what happened. To show her the false statement and guild lies into truths.

Everything he said would reek of dishonesty—but one fact remained.

One undisputed fact that would make her hate me for eternity.

What I did was unforgivable.

I was the one who pulled the trigger.

I was the one to slaughter the two people she cared for most in this world.

How can she ever forgive me once she knows?

More pain morphed into my heart. I could barely place one foot in front of the other at the thought of her turning her back on me.

I truly would end up in hell if she cast me away.

Hopper and Mo appeared from the undergrowth, forming a wall in front of me like good footmen in war. Their large boots tiptoed, cracking twigs and scuffing falling leaves. Their bulk and the added weight of leather and denim didn't exactly make a silent ambush.

Our jilted movements threaded with the buzz of night insects and occasional scurry of something in the bushes.

Time moved interminably slow as we made our way down and around, following the perimeter toward the main entrance where the rest of Pure Corruption had gathered.

The Pures were reliant.

I didn't have to chase or remind. I didn't have to second-guess or plan. The men knew what was expected and it got done.

"What the fuck?" Grasshopper muttered as we rounded the final corner.

I slammed to a halt, cursing my head as my bruised brains sloshed like chum. What the fuck was right.

"I don't get it," Mo grumbled, picking up the pace.

My heart thundered, panic dousing my blood as we closed the distance. Pure Corruption brothers stood congregated around the main entrance rather than hidden and preparing to attack. All but one had their backs to us, the emblem of our Club gleaming in silver thread in the darkness.

The man facing us, Matchsticks, rubbed a hand over his face before waving in acknowledgment. His huge feet flattened fallen bracken as he came forward. He was one of the tallest brothers in Pure Corruption—built like a mountain with a gut to match. Despite his size, his face was kind and unscarred, and his long hair made him seem as gentle as a puppy dog rather than vicious like a pit bull.

Something's not right.

Fear whipped around like a hurricane inside me.

Craning my neck, I tried to see what the men were crowded around. *Why do I smell smoke?* Anxiety heightened. I hated the smell of burning after what'd happened.

It hurt like a bitch to arrange my face into question marks and authority. "What's going on here?"

"Prez." Matchsticks nodded in respect before straightening his shoulders as if preparing for bad news. His long hair did nothing to hide the beaded sweat on his brow. "We, eh—there's been a development that we didn't see coming."

My eyes tightened, my vision ebbed. "You have precisely two seconds to spit it out."

Grasshopper and Mo flanked me, pistols cocked and fingers on the trigger by their sides.

My attention darted to the Dagger Rose compound. The gates were wide open like teeth in a giant wooden skull, beckoning us into the belly of our enemies.

Matchsticks looked back at the compound. "I was one of the first here. Came as soon as I got the call from Hopper saying you were out fucking cold and your old lady had been stolen. I brought Bas and Coin, and we staked out the compound."

My breathing climbed with every word.

"Nothing happened. We couldn't see the girl, and nothing seemed to be out of the ordinary. I swear on my life I didn't look away in the two days we've been here, but somehow..."

I roared, "Somehow what?!"

Ah, fuck, my head.

"There was an explosion—about thirty minutes ago—and the front gates blew wide open. Our backup wasn't here by that point, so we couldn't make a move, ya know? Didn't have the firepower to secure the scene and catch the fuckwit who did this. So the three of us waited. I got Bas to hide in one of the trees to act as sniper and Coin to wait in ambush if the entire Dagger brotherhood spilled out to dish us some cold justice. But then, well... nothing happened."

My legs wobbled. It was all I could do to stay upright. "What do you mean *nothing* happened?"

Matchsticks grabbed the back of his neck, rubbing away his discomfort. He looked guilty as sin. "We gave it ten minutes—to see if they'd come out bullets blazing. But when they didn't, we inched forward to survey the scene. And found it completely empty."

Mo shook his head, playing with the cocking action on his pistol. "Empty? Well how do you explain the vanishing act of over forty Daggers when you were right fucking there?"

My blood pressure rose. My skull threatened to crack at any moment.

Matchstick pointed to the clustered bikers. Their leather-jacketed torsos blocked whatever they were so fascinated with.

Was that smoke in the center?

They're gathered around a damn bonfire?

Matchsticks motioned us closer to his brothers. We followed. My hands clenched around my gun.

Matchsticks said, "We've done a full recon. The compound is deserted. All the vehicles are gone. Documents have been shredded; houses locked up tight. We followed the tire marks to a back exit they'd made in the north perimeter."

I pinched the bridge of my nose, stumbling a little over tree roots. "So, you're saying Rubix and the rest of his fucking Club have pulled a runner and you didn't catch them?"

This can't be happening.

My temper morphed into something fire-breathing and mortally dangerous.

Matchsticks looked away, unable to keep eye contact. "She's here, Prez."

Every muscle instantly locked. My mind filled with horrible images. Blood. Torture. Pain.

If they touched her, I'll do so much worse than kill them.

"They left her for you." Matchsticks waved at the gaping entrance. "Just in there. We didn't move her. Didn't want to touch her, just in case..."

Mo shot forward, but I was faster.

Even with a goddamn concussion, I still outran them and shoved men out of my way. I bowled through their ranks, growling like a damn beast.

Brothers stepped aside, letting me charge through the gates of Dagger Rose and slam to a halt at the scene.

The second my feet hit Dagger ground, I suffered a fleeting feeling of homecoming.

Then it was gone, replaced with heavy hatred soaking into my bones.

This place.

This madness.

This was where evil began.

This is hell.

True to form, the scene before me was worse than I could've ever imagined.

Cleo!

My lungs stuck together as I took in the message my father had left. I wanted to collapse to my knees. I wanted to tear out my fucking heart.

Goddammit, Cleo.

She lay naked like a human sacrifice. Curled up on her side, her legs tucked into her chest, she looked like a fallen angel—a vision of purity damaged by so much wrong.

Lying on her right, her scars and burns were hidden, displaying the mosaic colors of ink on her left. My eyes trailed from the tip of her toes to her shoulders, taking in the vibrant tattoo and intricate clues etched into her skin.

I knew the design by heart, but most of it was obscured by...

I swallowed bile.

Blood.

Her porcelain pale skin was smeared in rusty red. Splashes on her arms and legs; huge puddles patterned her face, throat, and chest.

"Cleo!" I bellowed, ignoring the screech in my skull.

Was it *her* blood? She didn't look alive. Her vibrant red hair fanned out in the churned dirt, matted and clumped with yet more awful rust.

I moved to go to her, rushing toward the excruciating heat. The rest of the scene came into view. I was so consumed with making sure she was alive, my broken mind had blocked out what surrounded her.

It was the past all over again.

The terror.

The helplessness.

Fire.

"Somebody get a fucking extinguisher!"

Mo darted past me. "On it!"

Why the fuck did no one get one before?

My father had wanted to send me a message.

He'd fucking succeeded.

My woman lay unconscious in a ring of blazing fire. Even though she was naked, she was dressed in the same orange flames that'd transformed her when she was barely fourteen. Flicking flames and licks of shadows danced over her like a spell or voodoo.

The circle of fire had been conjured by a seasoned pyrotechnic. The flames were high and black smoke filled my nose, caging her in and barricading us.

My knees locked against the sudden wave of ferocity and sickening horror.

"Why did no one move her, for fuck's sake?"

The fire wasn't hurting her. The flames danced more like friend than foe—protecting the girl already marked by their power. But I hated the orange glow on her skin. I hated the patterns they cast as if every second they sucked more of her soul into the underworld.

"Get me a mattress, a door—anything to make a pathway." I was done waiting. I'd walk through the fire if I had to. I had to get her *now*.

Matchsticks disappeared, grabbing two men to help him. The sound of a window smashing and a door being kicked overrode the crackling of the flames. Grasshopper returned first, proving once again why he was my most trusted friend and VP.

Between him and Matchsticks, they dragged a double mattress.

I moved to help, but my head held me hostage. There was no way I could lift something so awkward and cumbersome and remain standing with the pressure in my skull.

Instead, I waited for the men to drag the mattress into position. With a sharp push, they tipped it over so the large spring-covered bed smothered the fire and opened a gate.

Stepping onto the mattress, I braced myself.

Cleo moaned.

Fuck this.

I leapt.

In stolen Converse sneakers and too-tight sweatpants, I threw myself through the gap of hissing heat and slammed to a stop beside Cleo's bloody form. The mattress singed and charred, the flames doing their utmost to devour their new enemy.

I didn't have long before it ignited and locked us both in here.

Mo returned with a fire extinguisher.

Looking at the men from this side was surreal—as if I were already in hell and permitted one last glimpse of life.

"Shit, Prez. You could've waited another few seconds for us to kill the fire!"

A second was too long!

Didn't they understand a second was fucking purgatory when Cleo was hurt?

Slamming to my knees beside her, I touched her cheek. "Buttercup?"

She didn't move.

Her skin was slippery with blood and sweat, and hot—terribly hot.

The gushing sound of foam faded into the distance as Mo attacked the fire like a veteran. He barked commands at his brothers, rallying them into throwing buckets of dirt and any other debris they could find to kill the flames.

I blocked them out. I didn't care.

My whole world was in front of me. And she wouldn't wake up.

"Cleo...open your eyes for me. Please."

Brushing her hair back, I inspected her quickly. My hands shook as I searched for the wound causing so much blood. Nothing on her neck, chest, rib cage...her skin was covered but there wasn't a single puncture or slice. My hands trailed down her side, rolling her gently onto her back. I convinced myself it was to ensure once and for all that she wasn't bleeding out, but in reality...I had to check.

I had to know if my father had raped her.

Clenching my jaw, I traced the muscles in her stomach down and down. Following her hip bone, I glanced between her legs.

There were no bruises, no blood...but that didn't necessarily mean...

Fuck, please don't let them have hurt her that way.

I could fix her physical injuries. I would make it my life's work to ensure she was cured and untarnished in every way possible, but rape...that I couldn't cure. That might ruin her. That would ruin me.

And I would never be able to undo the pain inside.

Unable to withstand her silence any longer, I cupped her face. My headache increased, migrating to throb behind my eyes and in my ears.

I shook her gently. "Cleo, I need you to wake up."

Nothing.

My eyes fell to a tintype photograph peeking out from beneath her shoulder.

What the—

My heart stopped beating as I picked it up.

The picture was of all of us. Cleo's parents, my parents, and my brother. I remembered that evening. Hot and muggy—the entire Club had come together to celebrate a windfall. At the time, I'd had no idea how they'd earned. Thorn Price wasn't into skin trades or guns, but he wasn't averse to drugs. I guessed now cocaine had been the explanation in the sudden accumulated wealth.

It'd been a great evening of laughter, fun, and a secretive kiss on my cheek from a bold Buttercup.

I froze.

The image wasn't just a memory, but another fucking message.

Flipping the photograph over, I recognized my father's scratchy scrawl instantly.

Arthur,

This is just the beginning. You thought you were untouchable, that you could outplay me. You thought you could keep her hidden. I've been one step ahead of your useless fucking plans the entire time.

You can take her home, but she'll never be safe.

Not until you're dead.

Then I'll make her mine and give her the life she was always destined for.

Queen of my motherfucking Club, not yours.

Until the day of your death, son.

My throat closed over with anger so violent, I struggled to breathe. I hated to admit it, but I'd underestimated my father. I'd been too arrogant thinking I could wipe him out at my convenience without worrying if he had the same agenda.

I hadn't waged war.

We both had.

Like father like son.

Grasshopper suddenly crouched beside me. Foam stuck to his mohawk from the fire extinguisher, face blackened with soot. The flames were no match and existed no more.

Without a word, Hopper read the message. "Well, shit. Fucking bastard is more resourceful than we thought."

I nodded, scrunching the photograph in my fist. I didn't want to look at the image again. He'd just ruined any happy memories I had left.

"I want him dead, Hopper. I want it so fucking bad." Looking down at Cleo, I couldn't breathe at the thought of my father winning and taking her as his prize.

I will never let that happen.

"He's already a corpse, dude." Grasshopper rested his hand on my shoulder, his blue eyes landing on Cleo. "Ambulance is on its way. Thirty minutes."

Glancing up, I noticed Mo loitering. "Get me a damn blanket."

"Right." Mo touched his temple in a halfhearted salute and took off into the house that'd been ransacked for its mattress.

Pressing my thumbs into my eye sockets, I wished I could pop the pressure in my head. Just lance the shit and let the pain trickle out somehow.

Keep it together a little longer.

Dropping my shaky hand, I cupped Cleo's cheek. "Thirty minutes is too long."

Cleo moved minutely, sending my heart racing. Her lips parted as a breathy moan escaped. Her forehead furrowed either in pain or nightmares.

Fuck this.

I couldn't sit here and do nothing. "Where's that damn blanket?" I muttered.

Almost as if he'd heard me, Mo appeared and tossed me a bundled up black duvet.

Crouching over Cleo, I gathered her shoulders and did my best to wrap her and hide her nakedness. Once I'd covered her front, I draped the rest over her sides and tucked it tightly beneath her. I hated the finished effect—she looked as if she were dressed in a shroud ready for a funeral pyre.

Standing upright, I towered over her. The next part would kill me. I needed to pick her up.

Don't do this.

I ignored my inner voice. It was my job—my *right*—to be the one to carry her away from here. Screw my head, fuck my concussion. I would battle through the pain because sure as shit no other man was touching her.

Ducking, I scooped my arms beneath her neck and knees and inhaled hard.

"Kill, you sure about—"

"Mind your own goddamn business," I growled. With a grunt of agony, I stole Cleo from the ground and hoisted her into my arms.

She hardly weighed anything, but even the slightest pressure sent my head blaring with sirens and more pain than I thought I could endure.

Shit, I hated being so *weak*!

Blinking back dark spots, I turned to face Grasshopper and Mo. "I'm done with hospitals and doctors. Get me a car. I don't care how you do it. Beg, buy, or fucking steal it, but don't come back without one."

Grasshopper clenched his jaw, the urge to argue bright in his gaze. My fists tightened around Cleo, fully prepared to sock him in the jaw even with my woman sprawled in my hold. "I'm not asking, Hopper."

"Fine." Running a hand through his mohawk, he nodded at Mo and jogged toward the blown apart entrance. Once he'd bypassed the bikers, who all looked at a loss of what to do, he broke into a full-out run.

Good. One thing I could stop worrying about. Grasshopper was reliable and fast. I had no doubt I would have wheels and driven away from this town before the ambulance arrived.

Can you drive?

Once again, I ignored my brain. My flickering vision would make it dangerous to navigate at high speeds. It wasn't rational for me to drive. But that cool-headedness I always prided myself on was missing.

All I focused on was getting Cleo home by *me*.

Healing her by *myself*.

Proving to her I was worth all the shit that just happened. And all the crap to come in order for me to win. I needed to ensure she couldn't live without me, so when she found out the truth, she might somehow forgive me and not leave.

I have to do this.

I had to if I had any chance of deserving her.

Hoisting Cleo higher in my arms, I looked at her beautiful features. Her full lips were smeared with blood—whose blood? Her temple was bruised and a large bump decorated her hairline. It drove me to distraction thinking we both suffered the same injury—both incapacitated by a concussion at the hands of my asshole family.

Matchsticks came closer, peering into Cleo's heart-shaped face. "She gonna be okay?"

I narrowed my eyes. "She better be." Cocking my head at the compound behind me, I ordered, "Grab her some water. She has to wake up."

Matchsticks nodded. "Right." Sprinting to the nearest house, his gut wobbled and bounced. A few moments later, he returned with a plastic pink cup brimming with water.

I shuffled Cleo so her head tipped back a little over my arm. "Feed it to her gently. Don't make her choke."

Matchsticks tipped the overflowing water in the general direction of Cleo's mouth.

It went fucking everywhere.

"Goddammit, what are you trying to do? Drown her?"

He froze. "Sorry, Kill." Tipping some of the water out, he tried again, this time lucking out and managing to get some into her mouth.

Cleo mumbled incoherently, moving her chin away.

"Cleo, you need to open your eyes."

Another moan.

Anger sneaked over my concern.

"Buttercup," I snapped. "Open your fucking eyes."

Men moved past me, forming small groups to ransack the compound. I let them go. I was too wrapped up in Cleo to care.

The pounding in my head never ceased as I wrapped my arms tighter around her. I forgot about Matchsticks and Dagger Rose. I forgot about what I would have to do to make my father pay. All I focused on was the girl who owned my heart.

Pressing my forehead against hers, I begged, "You have to open your eyes, Buttercup. I'm a fucking mess without you. You can't do this to me. I won't let you. Do you hear?"

I groaned as my headache became endlessly heavy, compounding deeper and deeper until I felt like Atlas trying to hold up the world.

Tucking her against my body, I moved past Matchsticks and left behind the smoking ring where Cleo had lain. Marching to the gates, I found Mo, who was busy coordinating the gathering of oil, gasoline, and diesel. In his hands, he held an assortment of lighters, matches, and a long rope made of knotted sheets that'd been soaked in what I assumed was bourbon thanks to the empty bottles by his feet.

My lips twitched into my first smile since I'd woken in hospital. "Good idea."

Mo tilted his chin at the compound. "You up for it? They're not here; everything important has been taken or destroyed. We won't gain anything by keeping it standing." Glancing at Cleo, he lowered his voice. "The only person we came across was one of the bitches we stole and gave to the Crusaders. Her throat was cut from ear to ear..." He trailed off.

My eyes widened, looking at the war paint of someone else's blood covering Buttercup.

That's how she became so covered.

She'd been made to watch as another woman was viciously murdered in front of her.

My heart lurched.

Fuck. Fuck. *Fuck.*

"The men have explored the place. It's worthless, Kill. We should—"

"Dagger Rose isn't worthless."

In fact, it had great value. But that value would only increase if the compound was destroyed. "Torch it," I growled. It was time to purge the place where evil resided. Cleo would understand.

"You sure?" Mo moved to stand beside me as we faced the compound that'd been my home for so many years. Instead of happy memories, all I could think about was the day when I'd been so terribly betrayed.

Clutching Cleo harder, I nodded. "Yes, I'm sure." My voice was cold, merciless. "Burn it to the fucking ground."

Chapter Seven

Cleo

He hated me.

I didn't know what I was doing wrong, but he did.

My dad told me that Art was dealing with issues with his father. It hurt, because the moment Dad mentioned it, I knew. I just knew what those issues were. I was so selfish and stupid not to see. How did I miss the bruises on his arms? The puffy lip the other day? His father hurt him. And it was my job to protect him. That was what love was, right? Protecting those you cared for? Well...tomorrow, I was going to tell Rubix to leave Arthur the hell alone. —Cleo, diary entry, age thirteen

I'm cold.

Why am I so cold?

Before, I'd been too hot—far too hot. But now, all that heat had gone, leaving the sweat on my skin to chill and the warmth in my blood to freeze.

Curling into myself, I snuggled into the hardness surrounding me and tried to make sense of this strange new world.

It was dark.

It was painful.

Slowly, in the tiniest of increments, my body awoke and took stock of what'd happened. I couldn't open my eyes—I was so *tired*. My mind seemed disconnected from my limbs and organs, floating freely, but the throbbing pain growing deeper with every heartbeat shackled me to the mortal world.

I flinched as horrible dreams bombarded me. Images of throats erupting and blood waterfalling. Fire consuming and ash raining.

I didn't want to remember but this time there was no amnesia, no blankness to protect me.

I recalled everything. In vivid, perfect detail. The girl dying at my feet. Rubix touching me. Cobra and Sycamore holding me.

Then...pain.

I didn't know what'd struck me, but it'd sent me hurtling into darkness.

I squirmed, no longer finding comfort in sleepiness but a sinister syrup housing monsters and nightmares.

Wake up!

The more I forced myself, the more pain exhausted me. The thick throbbing haze was absolute. A sickening roll reminded me all too keenly of the *Seahorse* ship where Arthur almost sold me.

Something jiggled me, pressing me harder against firm muscles. "Open your eyes."

The demand sounded familiar—as if it'd been repeated over and over again.

I strained toward it—reaching with eager hands to latch on to the kindness in their tone.

"Buttercup, open your eyes. Please...for me."

Arthur!

The sinking sensation disappeared.

The anchor snipped free and I soared buoyantly to the surface.

I opened my eyes.

"Oh, thank God." The jostling sensation came again. "Can you see me?"

I hooked on to his deep baritone, willing my body to fall back under my control. Slowly, shadows and shapes came into play.

And then...there he was.

Tangled jaw-length black hair, strained green eyes, and kissable full lips. High cheekbones made him exquisite, while two- or three-day growth made him human. He was the perfect contraction of fantasy and fate.

The most heartbreaking love glowed in his gaze, undoing me with besotted pain.

"You came," I croaked.

"You can see me?" His question was an urgent demand.

"Yes." I swallowed, lubricating my throat. "I can see you."

He deflated before my very eyes. "Thank God."

He crushed me close, forging us together into one statue of bleeding souls.

I moaned a little as my body complained at being hugged.

Along with my vision, feeling in my limbs returned. The flurry of my heartbeat hammered against my ribs, joined by a steady drumbeat of grumbling hunger in my stomach. The abnormal strangeness of not feeling tethered to my body disappeared as I wriggled my toes and clenched my fists. The tips of my extremities tingled as if reacquainting themselves after being separated and free.

"What happened?" I swallowed again, trying to wash away the taste of soot and metal.

"It's over. That's all you need to know." Arthur's arms tightened around me.

The softness of relief and sparkle of love wiped away the past few horrors. Being in his embrace again, seeing him alive—I couldn't ask for a better gift.

I thought I'd lost you.

I burrowed closer to him, seeking confirmation that this wasn't a dream—that he was real and safe and here. "I knew you would. I never doubted."

His muscles bunched. "Knew I would what?" Fear burned in his eyes. Panic made him shake.

I frowned. What could he be so afraid of?

My stomach clenched with the need to absolve him, to assure both of us that we were all right. "That you'd come. I never stopped believing."

Never stopped hoping you were alive.

"The only way you wouldn't have come for me is..." I trailed off.

Arthur cleared his throat. "Is if I'd died." His exhale layered with grief and torment. His lips kissed my forehead. "Of course I came. How could I not? Even if I was dead, I would've found a way." He closed his eyes, cutting me off from his persecution. "I'm just so fucking sorry it took so long."

I moaned again as he tucked me protectively close. Nuzzling into his warmth, I did my best to eradicate the ice still living in my blood. "How long?"

Arthur shook his head, the tips of his hair tickling my forehead. "We'll talk about it when you're better and we're home."

Home.

I liked the sound of that.

"Can we do that, Buttercup? Can you forgive me for everything and stay with me? Can you give me the chance to explain when we've dealt with this mess and we're alone?"

You don't need to be afraid of me.

My heart perished. "Arthur, I need to tell you something."

"Don't," he growled. His eyes turned glassy. "Don't. *Please.* I can't do this here."

I hated to see him in pain—especially when I could grant him relief—but I nodded and respected his request. "Okay."

Arthur kissed my cheekbone, his muscles twitching to lift me higher. "I was so afraid. When you wouldn't open your eyes...fuck, it killed me."

I stroked his rough cheek. "I'm sorry I hurt you."

He pursed his lips, anger mixing violently with heartbreak. "Don't you dare apologize. This was all my fault. I'm the one who should beg for forgiveness." His face shadowed, filling with thoughts I couldn't chase. "Just...I hope you can forgive me—for so many things."

Once again the underlying message played on my soul-strings. I ran my thumb over his dry lips. "You're already forgiven." Narrowing my eyes, hoping he would understand, I added, "For everything."

He sighed, but his suffering didn't ease. Looking away from me, his body stiffened with duty. "I need to get you away from here."

"As long as I'm with you, I'm happy." I curled tighter in his arms, giving in to a bone-wracking shiver.

"You wouldn't say that if you knew," he barely whispered.

"You're wrong." I shook my head. "There's nothing you could do to make me stop loving you."

He flinched. The moonlight cast a silver glow on the side of his head where a small patch of hair had been shorn. *What*—

Reaching for it, I found a large bump—similar to the one gracing my own skull. Any remaining fogginess disappeared as nervousness slammed into me. "Are you okay?"

His brow fell as he snorted. "Forget me. What about you?"

Not letting him change the subject, I tried again. "When they took me...when you were left lying there, bleeding..." My blood flowed faster. "How badly did they—"

"They should never have been able to get inside and take you." His face twisted. "I swear on my life, I'll make it right."

"That wasn't what I meant. I need to know if *you're* okay."

Tell me!

My heart picked up its pace with a worried staccato.

Something happened. Something he's not telling me.

"Arthur, if you're not well, we need to—"

A hand landed on my head gently, breaking the moment and tearing me away from the lies Arthur was about to sprout.

Grasshopper came into focus, a soft smile on his lips. "Glad to see you're awake. You don't want to miss the best part." He glanced at Arthur. "By the way, got the car. It's ready to go."

Arthur grunted; the sound threaded from his chest to mine. "Good." He turned and Dagger Rose sprawled before me. The houses, the Clubhouse, the scuffed and blackened circle with a singed mattress and dirt.

What on earth happened here?

I tried to remember, but this time I had no memories being blocked by a stubborn wall. I'd been out cold and never witnessed a thing.

Arthur said, "We'll wait to see the first spark, then we'll go."

I didn't know if he was talking to me or Grasshopper.

Gingerly, I inspected the bruise on the side of my temple. It was more like an egg-shaped bump than a bruise. And it hurt—a lot. I flinched, sucking air between my teeth as I prodded it. "What exactly are we waiting for?"

As much as I appreciated Arthur holding me, I wanted to get down—to test my legs and hurry along my recovery.

"You'll see." Arthur cocked his chin at Dagger Rose. A few lights had been turned on in houses with broken doors and smashed windows, but that was the only illumination in the dark. Pure Corruption members dashed around, pouring rivers of gasoline from one house to another.

My heart panged to think of my childhood once again going up in flames.

Arthur hugged me harder. "Tonight, we take back what was stolen from us. Tonight, we begin our true vengeance."

I didn't say a word as men continued to tip any combustible liquid they could find into small trenches kicked into the mud, all leading to a center point where a small beehive of jerry cans, turpentine bottles, and half-empty spirits rested. The reek of chemicals and petrol swirled around us on the intermittent breeze.

Arthur didn't move or put me down as we watched the commotion before us. It didn't take long—the men worked efficiently, rigging the entire place to disintegrate.

A biker I didn't know with greying hair and a large belly came toward Arthur and presented a tequila bottle with a rag already drenched hanging from the mouth. With the pomp of ceremony, the biker lit the dripping rag and held it away as the flames gusted into being.

He made eye contact first with me, then Arthur. "All yours, Kill."

Arthur shifted me in his arms, somehow balancing me to take the bottle all while protecting me. He held the flaming Molotov cocktail reverently, almost as if he were about to give last rights to something sacred.

The glisten of rainbow oil on the dirt a couple of meters away beckoned for someone to start the catastrophe waiting to happen. The houses poised—as if they knew their existence was at an end.

"Ready to say goodbye?" Arthur murmured.

A twist of emotions filled me. This place had held so much love and family. So many happy memories. But all that happiness had vanished the night Rubix tried to destroy me.

Anger boiled in my stomach. "Fire already ended my world once. Let it burn this one, too."

Arthur smiled, then…he handed me the bottle. "Burn it, Cleo. Put an end to this place."

I gasped, accepting the volatile torch uncomfortably. "I don't think…" Stretching out my arm, I did my best to keep the fiery rag from getting too close. "This is your closure, your triumph."

With a soft but dangerous look, he said, "It's both of ours. I want you to be the one to do it."

I held eye contact for a long moment. This was *his* retribution—not mine. He needed this to find an ending.

Arthur held me firm. "Do it."

The fervor in his voice forced me to obey. My blood flowed faster.

With a pathetic swing and an arm that didn't completely remember how to throw, I tossed the tequila bottle toward the liquid fuse.

I jumped in Arthur's embrace as the bottle bounced. It didn't shatter against the soft dirt, but the fire didn't care.

We held our breath as it rolled the remaining distance, spitting out liquor and flames until it hopped straight from the rag to the path laid before it. It took a second... one second and that was it. Almost as if the universe held its breath with us, waiting to see what would happen.

In a blink, an electrifying yellow and blue whip tore up the center of the compound, devouring the road set before it and branching off seamlessly into each abode.

For a minute, there was no noise. Just the gentle hissing of fire devouring gasoline. It lulled me into a false sense of anticlimactic apprehension.

Then... the first explosion sounded.

It ricocheted around the world like a ring of Saturn.

Both Arthur and I cried out at the pain ringing in our ears. He stumbled backward as the windows of the Clubhouse suddenly detonated outward, raining in an almighty storm of glittering shards.

"Boom!" Grasshopper laughed, clapping his hands as Arthur staggered toward his brothers.

"Perfect night for fireworks, huh, Kill?" Mo winked, his face alight with erupting fire.

Another explosion followed, thumping through the night sky like a battle drum. The pressure of it sent shock waves pulsing around us.

Larger and larger.

Hungrier and hungrier.

Dagger Rose was completely engulfed.

The bigger the flames became, the more entranced I was.

Fire had hurt me. Fire had almost killed me.

But I couldn't hate or fear it.

That was the thing with flames. It was neither friend nor foe. It had no feelings or agendas. One moment it was a necessity of life: a giver of both heat and safety; then, without warning, it could become the greatest of enemies.

I'd crawled through its painful embrace.

I wore its mark upon my skin.

I was part flame, part human.

And in a way, I understood it. Appreciated its singular purpose with no favorites between wicked and right.

We stood silently, each wrapped up in the symphony of explosions rocking the night around us. And as I watched my old home become consumed by fiery teeth, I felt a purging.

A release.

I hoped Arthur felt it, too. I hoped he'd finally begun the journey to moving past the hatred and finding salvation.

My amnesia still toyed with my memories, but I knew enough of my birthright that our enemies should quake in terror at the formidable force Arthur and I would create.

This was just the beginning.

This was the start of our reign.

Holding out my arms, I hung in Arthur's embrace, giving myself once again to the fire.

Only this time, I didn't burn.

I glowed.

Chapter Eight

Kill

I could solve any equation.

I could find any sequence or pattern.

But I was completely idiotic when it came to understanding Cleo Price.

She said she wanted me as her friend. Yet when I did my utmost to remain in the parameters of friendship, she demanded more from me. And when I told her I wanted to give her more but she was too young, she no longer wanted to be my friend.

What did she want from me? And more importantly, what did I want from her? —Kill, age sixteen

Holding her in my arms was sheer fucking torture.

Watching our old home disappear into smoke was a triumphant honor.

I was both happy and sad. Relieved and terrified.

Cleo was safe. Dagger Rose was destroyed. But my father was still out there... plotting my demise as I plotted his.

These cat-and-mouse games had to stop.

I thought of all the times I could've dispatched him. I could've slaughtered him the moment I was released from jail. But where was the glory in that? Where was the joy in delivering an easy death to a man who deserved agony instead?

I wanted to make him pay.

So, I'd worked tirelessly on plans and elaborate conquests, concocting ideas to bring him to his knees.

I wanted him suffering.

I wanted him to beg me to chop off his head with my rightful vengeance.

That pleasure belonged to *me*. I was *owed* that.

So why did I feel as if I'd failed Cleo all over again?

Why had she paid another fucking price in my quest for perfect revenge?

Because something deeper than revenge now rules you.

Cleo eclipsed everything. She was my Sagittarius, my soul mate, my best friend. Not only had I failed her once and persecuted us to eight years apart, but she'd also been harmed twice at my father's hand. She'd suffered more than she ever should and it was all because of me and my need to settle the score.

I wanted to forget about my goal—to halt the guillotine hovering over both our futures—because if I didn't, if I continued chasing death, then I didn't deserve her.

And I want so fucking much to deserve her.

While I'd been busy preparing for Rubix's death, he'd been busy preparing mine.

Twin graves.

Twin murders.

And if he won, he would take Cleo.

That can't fucking happen.

This wasn't about my need for perfection anymore.

This was about ending it so Cleo was safe.

There was no time for pleasure or precision.

War was no longer coming.

It was here.

Chapter Nine

Cleo

*M*om had taught me how to apply lipstick and mascara.

She said makeup could be used in all forms of warfare. She said I could use it against Arthur. To make him fall, make him stumble. She said I had all the power. But I didn't agree. No matter what weapon I chose, I couldn't break through his walls. I couldn't get him to admit the truth. He hid behind secrets—trying to protect me with silence. He didn't understand that he hurt me more by ignoring what was between us, rather than facing it and giving me a chance. —Cleo, diary entry, age thirteen

"Where did you get this car from?" I asked as Arthur gently placed me on the beige leather backseat. The front consoles gleamed with newness and a Mercedes logo glittered on the steering wheel.

Arthur gave me half a smile, tucking the duvet around me and brushing hair away from my blood-sticky cheeks. "No idea. It's Grasshopper's new . . . acquisition."

My ears pricked at the half-truth. "He stole a car?"

His eyes narrowed. "Seriously, after everything that's just happened you're pissed over a boost?"

Trying to soften my shock, I smiled teasingly. "Just because you have money doesn't mean you can take anything you fancy."

He relaxed, light returning to his strained gaze. "I think you'll find that's exactly what having money means. Look it up—I'll bet you that's the definition in the dictionary."

Rolling my eyes, I winced as my head throbbed in response.

Note to self: don't roll eyes.

"What do you bet me?" I never looked away from him. The moment stretched like a kitten, aged like a fine wine. It was so nice to just *be* . . . to enjoy a tiny respite of normalcy.

How long had it been since Rubix took me?

Time felt both longer and shorter.

The past eight years had faded to inconsequential along with every other second that we were apart. Vibrancy only entered my life when he was in it.

"I bet you . . ." His voice trailed off, thoughts flickering like colors in his gaze. "I bet you an orgasm."

"A what?" I giggled, ignoring my hammering head.

"You heard me." He glanced at my lips. "I'll show you that wealth means you can have anything you want. If I'm wrong and you win, I'll give you the best orgasm you've ever had. I'll obey whatever you ask. I'll do whatever you need."

My heart faltered in favor of a quivering clench. "And if I lose?"

His lips turned up into a wicked smile. "If you forfeit and *I* win, you have to do what I want. Submit to whatever *I* desire." His arms bunched as he planted them on either side of me. "Let me rule you."

Rule me now.

I shivered as the air crackled with belonging.

I was mostly naked, Arthur was in pain, and Dagger Rose was in flames behind us, but our desire was a stronger force—knitting us together after our time apart.

I'd never get used to the intensity between us.

Untangling my hand from the bedding, I held it up to strike our bargain. "Deal."

Arthur shook his head, amused. Taking my hand, he shook firmly and rolled his shoulders to slide backward out of the door. "Deal."

He looked happier than before—less burdened and bruised, but his gaze still held acres of pain. "Oh, and, Buttercup? I already know what I'll make you do when I win."

My mind ran amok with sexual scenarios. Blindfold me again? Tie me up?

I know.

The one thing he never let other women do.

A blow job.

My mouth watered at the thought of kneeling before him. Of submitting to him, but ultimately controlling him.

"I like a man who is decisive."

He laughed quietly.

Leaving me lying on the backseat, he stumbled a little as he stood upright outside the car.

My heart deflated and I scrambled into a sitting position. The world swam for a second, before righting itself. "Wait, Art?"

He ducked again, his eyes connecting with mine. "What?"

Leaning forward, I grabbed his hand and looped our fingers together. "Are you okay? Truly?"

He squeezed my grip, all while trying to untie me from him. His eyes skittered from mine, doing what he did in the past—hiding things from me. *I hate that he's so good at that.*

A distance that hadn't been there before sprang up. It hovered like a warden, overseeing every spoken word and weighing them with meaning.

Managing to free himself, he said gruffly, "I'm fine."

I shook my head. "No, you're not." Shuffling higher, my voice grew demanding. "What happened to you?"

He ignored me, backing away from the vehicle.

My pulse rose. Terrible conclusions filled my head. "Arthur Killian, you tell me right now. I'm done with you keeping things from me." My voice softened, but my anger didn't fade. "You already keep so much. Secrets upon secrets. Concerns upon concerns. You're not alone anymore. How many times do I need to tell you that?"

When only silence replied, I slouched against the leather. "I want to help you but I can't unless you let me in."

You didn't let me in in the past. You didn't let me console you or brainstorm a solution to stop your abuse.

My hands curled at the thought of how different things could've been if he'd confided in me or my father—if he'd trusted others to help him.

"You can't keep hiding behind walls, Art. Not anymore."

He ducked, his knees creaking under his large bulk. "I'm not hiding. And you can't push me to discuss things I'm not ready to."

"Just like you won't talk about that night?"

He stiffened. His nostrils flared. "I told you why."

"You want to be behind closed doors. But why? I know what happened. Let me tell you so you can—"

He shot upright, staggering against the Mercedes and grabbing the roof for support. "It's so damn simple for you, isn't it?" He bared his teeth. "Can't you stop and think for just *one* second how this is for me? I'm the asshole. I'm the fucking murderer. Is it so wrong of me to pretend that you'll still want me if we talk about that night? Is it so fucking weak of me to ignore it so I can keep you for a tiny bit longer?"

I froze.

His green eyes locked on mine.

We stopped breathing.

He's completely clueless.

He was more screwed up than I feared. What had his father done to him all those years ago? How had he been so brainwashed and blinded?

"Arthur. It wasn't like that. You don't have to ignore or pretend—"

Holding up his hand, he snapped, "Stop it. Just once in your life, stop trying to fix me. I know what I did and I know I can't ask for forgiveness." Breathing hard, he winced through a wave of pain. "Just like I can't ask forgiveness for lying in a fucking bed with a damn concussion while you were being tormented."

I sat straighter, gathering my gown of bedding. "A concussion? So you aren't okay! You're lying to me about how bad—"

"That's not the fucking point, Cleo! Goddammit, don't you see? What happened that night was because of me. And what happened now is because of me. It's *all* because of me." He punched himself in the chest. "That's the shit-awful truth."

So much torment. So much incorrectly harbored guilt.

This poor man who I loved more than anything was festering in shame that wasn't his to bear. "You're so wrong," I whispered. "You're killing yourself by not seeing the truth."

He ran his hands through his disheveled hair. "Not seeing the truth?" He pointed at my blood-smeared cheeks and rust-daubed chest. "You're drenched in blood and there was a corpse in the Clubhouse. They made you watch while they killed someone. They scarred you physically as a kid and now emotionally as an adult. I can guess the rest, Cleo, and I don't fucking like it. You can't hide things from me—you've never been able to hide things from me."

Crap, he's good at guessing. Always had been.

My temper overflowed. "No—never like you, of course." I slapped the billowing blankets. "I've never been able to hide—not like you. I don't have your talent. I could never compete with the Great Secretive Art."

He shook his head. "Are we seriously having a fucking argument? Here?"

"You started it!"

"You won't let things go!"

"You won't let me tell you the truth!"

"You're just trying to push me away because of what I did!"

"Ah!" I grabbed my hair. "You're impossible!"

Pain slammed into me, reminding me my temper might want to fight but my body definitely didn't.

I slumped in the backseat. "I can't deal with you right now." I couldn't look at him. Had he always been this frustrating? This hard to convince?

Yes.

So many times we'd locked horns and screamed until we were torn apart by worried family members. We fought over everything. When we were younger, our battles were over stupid things like stationery thievery and bicycle tampering. When we were older, it was about lipstick smears on his cheek from two-bit hussies and innocent messages to me from boys in my class.

We were jealous.

We were possessive.

We were passionate and explosive and consumed.

And that fiery combustion never ceased because we never gave in to what existed between us.

But now we are *together. Shouldn't it be easier?*

Silence was heavy and breathless as our cease-fire lengthened.

Tears pricked my eyes. My head bellowed, my stomach was empty, and all I wanted to do was have a shower and get rid of the sticky blood and memories. But I also wanted to clear the air between us. To let him know that he didn't need to fear—

Of course!

Sitting higher, I said urgently, "All this time and I didn't see it."

He frowned. "See what?"

"The past few weeks I hurt you with not remembering us, our past—of leaving you behind. When you took me to the beach, I knew how much you needed me to remember, but at the same time, you were hoping I would never recall that night—"

He reared back; his face shut down. "We have to go. We're going around in damn circles."

Slamming the door, he didn't hear my whispered, "Everything you think you know about that night is a lie. You went to prison believing a lie. And you're pushing me away because of a lie."

How could I be so stupid? How could *he* be so stupid?

Arthur thought I would leave him. Did he honestly think after the trauma of the past few days that I wouldn't remember in explicit detail? If I had to thank Rubix for anything in my life, it would be that. For smashing through the panic, shame, and bitter grief and showing me I was strong enough to face the one recollection my mind had tried to delete.

Sirens sounded on the horizon, splicing through the thick smoke from burning Dagger Rose. I'd wanted to witness the houses turning to dust. I'd wanted to laugh at the symbolism of a new beginning. But that wasn't possible with the compound being so close to civilization and me covered in blood. Questions would be asked. Men arrested.

Arthur was right. Talking would have to wait. And then by God, I would make him listen, even if I had to hit him over the head with another baseball bat.

A tap on the window wrenched my head up. Grasshopper grinned, waved, then took off in a roar of thunder on his bike.

A torrent of leather-jacketed men followed him, their motorcycles kicking up dirt like angry stallions galloping through the darkness. Roar after roar of super-charged engines devoured the silence, turning night into nightmares.

A thrill went through me at the sound. The purr of motorbikes no longer scared me. It was my heritage. My home.

Sliding into the driver's seat, Arthur slammed the door and slipped the key Grasshopper had given him into the ignition. The engine was so quiet, it didn't sound like the car was on after the raucous of bikes.

Tension and awkwardness prevailed from our unresolved fight.

Rather than address it and bring our tempers back to boiling point, I said quietly, "I feel like you're my taxi driver."

The rigidity of his back softened a little as he looked at me in the rearview mirror. His eyebrow quirked. "Why?"

"Whenever we're in a car together, you're always in front and I'm in the back." My mind slipped back to the day he'd thrown me into the 4WD and shot across town to the harbor to sell me. We'd had a massive argument then, too. Seemed the only way to slap any sense into this man was to fight through his pigheadedness.

Art didn't say a word. Locking his fists around the steering wheel, he looked as if he prayed for patience . . . or pain relief.

My heart twisted at the void between us. "I love you, Arthur," I breathed. "No matter what, I hope you always remember that."

His head shot up, a low groan escaping his throat. He made eye contact in the mirror again, his face contorting with so many things. His gaze glowed in the car's gloomy interior before he leaned forward and rested his forehead on the steering wheel. "You kill me every time you say that, Buttercup."

The agony in his voice wrapped around me like sad, tearful mist.

"Oh, Art." I couldn't stand him hurting like this. Despite my bruised body and my killer headache, I shoved aside the blanket and wrapped my arms around the back of his seat, stroking his shoulders.

He reclined, folding himself into my embrace. His back rested against the beige leather, and he sighed heavily as my arms locked around his chest, holding him tight. "I'm going to say this once and only once, so pay attention." I kissed the shell of his ear. "That night won't change how I feel about you. I give you my ultimate promise. But I understand your need to wait to talk about it."

He went deathly still. "You . . . you remembered?"

I hugged him harder. "I told you. All of it."

He twisted out of my embrace, turning to face me with wide, incredulous eyes. "You're telling me you remember me shooting your mother and father point blank, yet you still love me?" He shook his head. "Are you insane as well as amnesic?"

God, give me patience with this man.

I wanted to scream at him but we were both too tender and sore for another battle. Instead, I took the calm road and kept my voice even and soothing. "You didn't kill them."

"I pulled the trigger."

"You weren't yourself."

Leaning forward so his nose almost touched mine, he seethed, "They're dead because of me."

I balled my hands. "They're dead because of Rubix!"

My outburst stopped him long enough for me to spill the horrific memories of that night. Screw waiting. Screw his ideals. "*Yes*, you pulled the trigger. *Yes*, you were the one my parents saw the moment they died, but they knew as well as I did that it wasn't you!"

"What do you mean it wasn't me?" Arthur roared. His temper blazed as vibrant as the fire behind us. His features were harsh and brutal from his awful concussion.

My mouth parted. "You honestly don't know, do you?"

He snorted. "I know just fine. I remember the weight of the gun in my hand. I remember the stink of gasoline. I remember the soundless bullet as it tore through your parents' hearts. Don't tell me I don't know, Cleo, because I know too fucking well!"

His chest pumped, sweat shone on his upper lip and brow, and the sounds of sirens were no longer on the horizon but just around the corner.

"We need to leave," I said softly. "There are two sides to every tale and you're remembering the wrong one."

For the longest moment, I worried he would ignore me and continue fighting. I doubted he had the strength to argue much longer or wish to be here when the fire brigade came screeching around the corner. But at the last second, he clenched his jaw and turned away from me.

Throwing the car into gear, he stomped on the accelerator; we tore away in a spray of gravel and soot.

I pursed my lips as I slid recklessly on the slippery leather, knocking already bruised elbows against the door. I didn't protest. In a way, we weren't just escaping the scene of an arson, but also running from a past that'd scarred both of us.

The sooner we were on neutral ground the better.

Keeping my eyes trained on the road, the only scenery illuminated was the golden strip from the headlights. The rest of the night was a blur of blackness.

Arthur didn't speak as he took a left at the bottom of the gravel road and sped away just as the red and blue lights of help appeared from the right.

The car purred, chewing up ground faster and faster until my heart wedged itself in my throat. A few minutes passed before I squeaked, "Arthur, they're far behind us. We're safe. Can you...eh... can you slow down, please?"

He kept his eyes locked in front, but obeyed. The speed went from bullet to racecar, still too fast for my liking but an improvement nevertheless.

"You okay?" I asked. For some reason, I couldn't shake the fear that no matter his assurances, he *wasn't* okay. Something was wrong. Yet again, he was hiding. And yet again, I was lost.

"I'm fine. Stop asking that."

I stiffened. Just because I couldn't voice them didn't mean my questions stopped. They kept me company as we drove in silence for a while. Finally, after miles were between us and the remains of Dagger Rose, I couldn't stand the noiselessness any longer.

I carefully chose a topic that wouldn't lead to an argument. "What exactly are you wearing by the way?"

The random question of his awful sweatpants and shirt made him laugh, cracking the tension. "It was this or a hospital gown with my ass hanging out. Be grateful it's this." He cast me a look in the mirror. He looked terrible. Feverish and white.

My heart tripped. "I want to know the full story of why you were in the hospital, but I'll wait. However, I do need to know if you should be driving with a concussion."

He looked away. "Probably not."

I shuffled forward, reaching for him again, but he twisted in his seat and slammed his palm against my thigh. "Stay there. If I'm concussed, so are you. We both have pretty lumps and until you've been checked out, I don't want you moving." His voice turned bossy. "In fact, lie down. I don't want you sitting up, especially without a seat belt." He added deathly quiet, *"Especially as I can barely see the road."*

"What was that?"

His skin stretched over his aristocratic cheekbones. "Nothing. Buckle up."

Ideally what I wanted to do was crawl into the front seat so I could watch him closely, but Arthur's fingers tightened around my leg. "Buttercup...do it."

Huffing, I slid sideways. Once I was settled, he took his hand off my leg and placed it back on the wheel.

"Happy?" I asked.

He shook his head. "I won't be happy until the shit inside my skull is sorted and I know you're okay. Seeing you covered in blood is driving me insane." His eyes flickered to mine, then back to the road. "You sure they didn't cut you. You're not bleeding anywhere?"

I smiled softly, loving his concern for me. His protectiveness. "Yes, I'm fine. Just the head bump." He didn't need to know what else his father did. I wasn't raped—thank God—but the violation of his touch between my legs was a distant echo that I doubted a shower could wash away.

I didn't know if it was shock keeping the past events from consuming me or the knowledge that Rubix would never have another chance to lay a hand on me—either way, Rubix had screwed up and it would cost him his life. There was no other path for him and I meant to be there when it ended.

Arthur will kill him. And we'll both be safe.

My attention zeroed in on his injury. He had to get better and quickly. I had no intention of us ever being apart again. No wound or disease could deny us a happy future.

I won't let it.

It was his responsibility to protect me and look after himself, just like it was mine to tend to him and love him unconditionally.

"We should go back to the hospital. I think you need to be seen by another doctor, Art." I tucked my arms beneath my makeshift clothing. "You're hiding something from me. You're not as well as you say you are. And I won't let you hurt when you can get help."

His nostrils flared. "Always so damn nosy and bossy." He narrowed his eyes. "Hospitals are public places. Anyone can get to us there. I agree, I need another doctor—we both do. But I'm not going to the hospital."

"What are we going to do, then?"

"I'll get the hospital to come to us."

"Ah, yes. Money can do that."

He scowled. "You come from wealth, so I don't know why you're suddenly uncomfortable with it."

That's true.

Why bicker about something so useless? Was it because of what he planned to do with his money? Or deeper distrust that wealth couldn't buy happiness?

Arthur asked, "Was your family in England poor?"

I paused, my mind skipping back to the movie nights with fish and chip takeaways and the occasional treat at Corrine's favorite Indian restaurant. "No, my foster parents weren't poor. They drove midrange cars and worked in clerical jobs. I was comfortable in their home and what they lacked in monetary wealth they made up for in love." I smiled, thinking how lucky I was to be cared for by a family who didn't mind I couldn't remember and who put up with my years of quiet sadness. They'd been exactly what I needed and Corrine...she was the sister I'd never had.

A pang of misery hit me hard. I missed them just as much as I missed my biological parents. And I missed Corrine a ton. I missed our chats. I missed the studio apartment we shared.

"You loved them," Arthur whispered. "I can tell."

I met his eyes in the mirror. "They were all I had. They put up with me sullen and uncommunicative. They healed me even when my mind remained broken."

They were good people.

I wanted to see them again—to tell them how much I appreciated what they'd done for me—to show them how happy I was now that I remembered.

I gasped. Oh, my God. "We could go to England after this. Go and see them. I'd love to introduce you and tell them I remember."

Corrine would finally understand why I had a thing for green-eyed heroes in movies. I could show them my past and bring them fully into my future.

Arthur snorted. "You think they'll still look at you the same way when you say you're the daughter of a biker president and dating the man who murdered your parents? You think they'll welcome me into their house?" Looking at the ceiling, he laughed. "Like that's going to fucking happen."

"Stop being so pessimistic."

And I'm not dating you. Dating was temporary. What we had was permanent. As permanent as ink on skin or fossils in stone.

Arthur growled, "I'm being a realist."

A slither of panic worked down my spine. Arthur was hot tempered...but never this argumentative. I couldn't seem to say a thing without him jumping down my throat.

Is it his concussion? Did people suffer mood swings from a head injury?

Silence settled like dusting snowflakes as we sped down the motorway, following the long journey back home.

Arthur threw the car into fifth gear, then activated cruise control. His large hands held the steering wheel as he glanced at me in the mirror again. "I'm sorry."

I tensed. "It's not just a concussion you're suffering...is it?"

He pinched the bridge of his nose, then rubbed his eyes. "I'll tell you. Just...let's get home first, okay?" A shadow cast over his face.

"You do know the only way this will work is if we have complete honesty between us?" I didn't shout. He needed to hear how serious I was without volume.

He froze. In a single breath, he switched from angry and invincible to deflated and terrified. "I know." His eyes met mine. "If you can find some way to stay with me after what I did, I promise I'll make it up to you. Give me a chance…to make this right. To give you more. To give you so much fucking more than I have."

Once again that panic of him keeping secrets swarmed me.

"You don't owe me any more than you've already given. And I'm not going anywhere. How many times do I need to tell you that?"

He sighed wearily. "For so long I've been driven by an obsession. To create more wealth. To create more power. Only those with more than others can ever hope to win. But now that you're back in my life—the obsession is even worse. Instead of being satisfied, I feel as if I don't fucking deserve you unless I continue to gather more of everything."

His knuckles tightened around the steering wheel. The motorway was a blur of lights and concrete. "I never wanted to go to war. But sometimes we have to become something we hate in order to get what we want."

My brain hurt. *What does he mean now?* There should be a warning about falling in love with geniuses. Riddles to him were conversation. Equations and patterns were punctuation.

I wanted simple—if only to unscramble the puzzlement of the past.

Reaching behind his seat, he stroked my thigh still swaddled in the blankets. "You're my more, Cleo. But it's still not enough. It won't be enough until the end."

Chapter Ten

Kill

I was going to hell.

I knew that now. She'd turned thirteen last week. I'd told myself she was old enough to be accountable for all the frustration and need building inside of me. I'd believed my own rationalizing that she was mature enough to know what she offered.

So . . . I'd kissed her. I'd stolen her first kiss on a swing in the park. And again when we'd arrived home.

I'd taken her behind the Clubhouse and stuck my tongue down her throat. And fuck if it wasn't the best thing in my entire life. —Kill, age sixteen

Home.

Nothing in the world could beat the welcoming embrace of safety and sanctuary.

The gates around my property rolled open and the smooth Merc needed only the gentlest coaxing to slide into the awaiting garage. The car fit perfectly with the black Mustang and Land Rover. It was as if the last remaining spot was made for it.

My custom Triumph rested like a mythical beast in the center, waiting to come alive and hurtle down roads. Its matte black framework sucked light from the space like a black hole—there was no chrome—unlike Grasshopper's decaled extravaganza.

As I parked and wrenched up the handbrake, I admitted my garage of vehicles was complete with this latest machine.

If Grasshopper had stolen this, then I would return it to the owner with a thank-you gift. But if he'd bought it fair and square, then I was keeping it. Fifty-fifty chance. I supposed I'd have to wait to find out.

Cleo rustled in the back. She'd fallen asleep in the last thirty minutes. The moment her eyes closed and her face slipped into slumber-softness, I'd freaked the fuck out. Should she sleep after what she'd been through? Should I keep her awake until a doctor examined her?

But watching her rest, I didn't have the heart to wake her. I didn't have the strength to fight with her again over something that had the power to smash us apart.

How can she even look at me? How can love still glow in her gaze?

I couldn't understand how she'd come out of my father's madness and not only remained strong and stubborn, but also remained the same Cleo who I thought I'd lost forever. She was something unique and so damn priceless.

"We're here, Buttercup."

Her eyes cracked open, awareness slowly animating her face. With a soft groan, she touched her head and sat up. "Sorry, I didn't mean to leave you alone."

My lips twitched. Even now with her own pain, she was more worried about mine.

Fuck, I loved this woman.

Swinging her legs to the floor, she went to open the car door.

"Wait!"

Her eyes popped wide. "Why? What did I do?"

"Don't move." Without waiting for her reply, I shot from the car and opened her door. The world shot upside down. My brain sloshed in my skull and a rush of sickness hit the back of my throat. *Shit, I shouldn't have moved so fast.*

Holding on to the car door, I breathed hard through my nose. The pressure throbbed with every heartbeat but slowly eased.

I didn't want Cleo moving on her own. The doctors said movement only worsened the swelling on my brain. If Cleo had a concussion, too, I would rather move for both of us so only one of us had severe side effects.

I've already lost most of my IQ... what's a few more lost points if I can fix her?

When I opened my eyes, Cleo's face was stark with worry. "Arthur, you need to sit back down. You look like you're about to pass out."

"I'm fine." I ducked to her level in order to grab her.

"Wait. What are you doing?" She swatted my hand away as I gathered the blankets. "I can walk, you know."

I didn't bother replying.

Scooping her behind the shoulders and knees, I plucked her from the leather and hoisted her into my arms.

Oh, fuck me.

Nausea slammed into me. My brain felt as if it would ooze from my ears like spaghetti.

"Good God, Art, put me down. You're shaking like a crack addict."

"Give me a sec," I muttered through gritted teeth. She hung in my embrace. A second turned into a minute, but my brain finally decided today wasn't the day it would explode and the pain receded to a tolerable level. "See, all good."

She huffed under her breath as I kicked the car door closed and strode away from the Mercedes.

One foot in front of the other.

I'd forgotten a shitload of important information but walking wasn't one of them.

Carrying Cleo through the connecting door and into the two-story-high foyer, I suffered a spasm of rage at the thought of men infiltrating my home and hurting us. They'd tainted this place and proven I'd been far too arrogant.

Cleo squirmed in my arms and placed a delicate kiss on my scruffy chin. "It's so nice to be home with you."

A wash of comfort and contentedness settled, easing with familiarity and a promise that things would be dealt with once and for fucking all.

I stared into her moss-green eyes. "I agree."

Her lips parted, conjuring the always present lust and desire that seemed to infect us. There was no cure for what we suffered. There was no pill to dampen our tempers or simmer the violent hunger for each other.

And I was glad. I wouldn't take such a medicine even if it did exist. She made me *alive*.

Too alive.

Stupidly alive and prone to mistakes and disastrous errors all because she preoccupied me.

"Nothing seems to be taken," she added, glancing around the grey painted walls and black and white wall hangings.

"I wouldn't care if they did." Possessions didn't mean a thing to me. Apart from the Libra eraser that I'd had for so many years, of course.

This house didn't hold precious mementos such as photographs and love notes written when we were teenagers, but it did have a part of Cleo already in its walls. My blood had seeped into the grout of the tiles in my office while she'd sewed me up. My sweat had dripped into the carpet as I fucked her and loved her before I even knew she was the girl from my past.

We'd started afresh here, and soon...we would leave and never come back.

That was part of the plan. Formulated and agreed upon by Wallstreet and myself.

My time is almost up.

"Come on. I need to get you comfy so I can call a doctor." Striding forward, I aimed for the staircase with the idea of putting her to bed.

My knees turned to useless water with every step. Now that we were home, my strength rapidly siphoned away.

Someone clapped me on the back.

Fuck!

I spun around ready to tear whoever it was to fucking pieces.

Grasshopper grinned, holding up his hands. "Whoa, just me."

My heart slammed like a sledgehammer. "Goddammit, Hopper. What the hell are you doing sneaking in here?"

"Not sneaking. Arranging." He smirked. "Besides, two wheels always outrun four." His eyes dropped to Cleo. "You feeling okay, Butterbean?"

I growled under my breath. "It's Buttercup, asshole. And I'm the only one who's allowed to use it."

Cleo giggled. "What did you say you wanted to call me back at the diner? SC or CS—something like that?"

Grasshopper nodded. His mohawk was no longer floppy and covered in fire extinguisher foam but straight and bristling thanks to the hair wax he kept in his bike. "Sarah-Cleo." He rubbed his chin. "Or was it Cleo-Sarah? I've forgotten. No matter, I think I'll stick with Butterbean."

"Only if you want to end up dead," I muttered.

Grasshopper laughed, slapping me again. "You know I'm only yanking your chain." He turned serious. "The doc is here. I called ahead. Figured you wouldn't want to go back to the hospital after what happened." He snickered, obviously remembering the incident with the nurse and stolen clothes. "Even if they let you in."

"Why wouldn't they let you in?" Cleo frowned. "What happened?"

"Nothing," Grasshopper and I said at the same time.

I grinned slightly at my VP. He was a lot of things, but he trumped it all by being a friend first. "You're a good man, Hopper."

Grasshopper puffed out his chest, grabbing the lapels of his leather cut like some pompous ass. "Aw, shucks. Probably now is the good time to mention it's going to cost you a fucking fortune, though. Triple callout fee for the late hour and the rumor of your not-so-nice-patient manner back at the hospital."

I groaned.

Grasshopper chuckled. "But she's the best in her field and assures me she knows her shit."

"I don't care about the cost. If it means Cleo will be okay—"

"And you," Grasshopper jumped in. "Can't forget about you."

Cleo suddenly grabbed his cut, dragging him close. I stumbled as she sandwiched herself between the two of us and pressed a fleeting kiss on Grasshopper's rough cheek. "Thank you for keeping him safe all these years."

What the hell?

Grasshopper froze.

I took a livid step backward, breaking Cleo's hold on his jacket. "What the fuck, Cleo? No kissing other men—*especially* my fucking VP."

She laughed, waving off the infraction as if it were nothing. It wasn't fucking nothing. She was mine, goddammit. Her lips weren't supposed to touch another man. *Ever.*

"Art, calm down. You know you're it for me." She smiled at Hopper. "I'm just thanking Wallstreet's son for taking such good care of you when I couldn't."

The house seemed to exhale. Furniture gathered in ringside seats for whatever spectacle was about to begin. The air turned thick as fucking molasses.

What is she trying to do?

I'd only just come around to the idea that the man who'd served beside me all these years was related to my benefactor. I didn't want it blurted out. Information like that had to be carefully controlled. Measured. Dealt with on the lowdown.

Grasshopper's eyes widened. Smacking his lips, he rubbed the back of his neck. "Eh..."

Nervousness darted over his face, but he didn't run.

He was a secretive bastard but he wasn't a snitch and he wasn't a pussy. I had to give him that.

He looked at me, guarding his thoughts before dropping his attention back to Cleo. "You know?" Running a hand over his face, he lowered his voice. "How?"

His eyes met mine again. Decisions collided in his gaze. Should he be scared of me or honest? I couldn't give him an answer because I didn't know, either. I had no idea how I felt about this mess.

All I knew was my body was shutting down and if I didn't put Cleo in bed soon, I'd drop her.

Cleo shifted in my arms, choosing her words. "I guessed."

"You *guessed*?" Grasshopper's face fell into shock. "I've been waiting for someone to connect the dots for fucking years and no one ever did, yet you're here for two seconds and *guessed*? How the hell did you do that?" Looking between us, he shook his head in disbelief. "What gave me away?"

"Can we talk about this later?" I growled.

Cleo ignored me, squirming in her blankets until they tightened like a python around her. "It was your eyes. And then your mouth."

Grasshopper blinked. "Huh."

"When Arthur took me to meet Wallstreet, I connected the dots. He reminded me of someone. He reminded me of you."

Grasshopper snorted. "Well, fuck me."

My arms burned and the smudginess in my head only grew worse. "No matter how much I'm enjoying this entertaining conversation, there's a time and place for this, and this isn't it."

Wanting nothing more than to crash in bed beside Cleo, I snapped, "Enough. When I can think fucking straight, *then* we'll talk."

Grasshopper nodded. "Sure thing. My bad."

"Wait. You can't think straight?" Cleo's eyes zeroed in on mine.

I groaned.

Damn woman.

Grasshopper clucked his tongue. "Doctor first, then questions, Butterbean."

My stomach snarled with possession, but I let the nickname slide. He'd helped divert a line of questioning that had no right to be discussed tonight.

Mo appeared in the foyer from my office. His jeans were dirt-scuffed and his jacket reeked of booze from creating bottle bombs. "You guys ready to be poked and prodded? Doc's waiting." He tapped a nonexistent watch on his wrist. "Minutes are like fucking gold with the rate she's charging."

I hoisted Cleo a little higher. "Lead the way."

"She's worth every penny, Kill." Grasshopper nudged my shoulder. "Majored in brain and neurological synapses. Done a few papers on the lingering effects of concussions."

My heart turned from a crawl to a run. It wasn't just the short-term effects scaring me shitless—it was the long-term problems I might face.

Of course, hoping Cleo didn't put two and two together and get a million and fucking four was like wishing for a damn genie to grant three wishes.

"Neurological expert?" she asked, her voice wobbling with worry.

"Don't worry about it." Hugging her closer, I asked Mo, "Where is this mystical practitioner?"

Mo pointed toward the lounge. "That way."

I moved as straight and as streamline as I could with the walls bowing and swaying.

Leaving the foyer, I stepped into the open-plan lounge. The lights were dimmed, highlighting abstract artwork. The large space was both designer and comforting with sliding doors all along one side, a kitchen equipped with every mod-con a person could need, and an area for dining and entertaining.

The blackness outside made the glass doors act like a mirror, reflecting Cleo and myself as I marched across the carpet in muddy boots.

The dining table was my destination, along with the stranger waiting in a pristine white coat.

The woman watched as I stopped before her.

Her coiled brown hair, basic makeup, and wide blue eyes hinted at intelligence and no-nonsense.

The moment I stopped, she smiled professionally and pushed off from the table. "You must be Mr. Killian. I'm Doctor Laine." Her attention dropped to Cleo in my arms. "Please, if you'll put the patient on the table, I can begin tending to her."

The thought of putting Cleo down was a lance to my fucking gut.

Cleo stroked my chest, soothing me. "Thank you, Art. Thank you for bringing me home safely. You can let me go now. I won't break."

"You heard the girl," Doctor Laine said softly. "Best if you leave the rest to me."

You better know what you're fucking doing.

The doctor never took her eyes off me as I very carefully deposited Cleo on the table. She winced as I transferred her weight onto the hard wood.

Taking a few steps back, I murmured, "I'm right here."

My arms felt empty and weightless after carrying her. I ached to pick her back up again and keep her safe.

The black duvet slipped from one of her shoulders, revealing the translucent beauty of her skin marred by shiny scars that would never disappear.

Her flaws could be called ugly—an imperfection to be hidden. But it only made me fall deeper in love with her. She had the strength to bare them—even using them to define how others saw her.

The doctor peered at the blood covering Cleo. Urgency sprang into her tone. "Are you bleeding?"

Cleo shook her head. "No, it's not mine." Touching the large bump on her temple, she added, "The only injury is from when they knocked me out."

My hands curled into fists. My fucking father would pay. *He'll pay a hundred times over.*

Turning to face me, the doctor looked over my shoulder at Mo and Grasshopper loitering in the background. "You can go now, gentlemen. If I need anything, I'll call."

"Sure thing," Grasshopper said.

They shuffled immediately to the exit.

I was glad. I didn't want them seeing Cleo if the doctor asked her to remove the blanket.

I crossed my arms, bracing my legs against the pain, and waited for the doctor to tend to my woman.

Doctor Laine cleared her throat. "You, too, Mr. Killian. I'll call when we're done here."

I scowled. "I'd rather not."

When I refused to budge, the doctor narrowed her eyes. "Privacy would be appreciated. She'll be perfectly fine with me. I want to do a full examination."

"If you're asking me to leave behind the only thing of value I have left and trust you with her life—well, you don't know me very well." Grasshopper lingered over the threshold, not entirely leaving as I'd requested. I asked him, "You checked her credentials?"

Grasshopper frowned. "Of cour—"

"Arthur...it's fine," Cleo interrupted. "Just go. I'll come find you when it's your turn."

My heart clobbered against my ribs. Why did the thought of being away from her break me out in a cold sweat?

Because the last time you were apart, she disappeared for eight years and then became a toy for your fucked up father.

I swallowed hard.

The doctor glowered. "I'll pretend I didn't hear you discussing my skill set." She pointed at the door. "I'm not asking you to trust me. I'm *telling* you to. She's in better hands with someone experienced in medicine. Now leave. I need to tend to your wife."

Cleo's face broke out in an adoring smile, her eyes locking with mine.

Wife.

My legs threatened to topple like a hurricane-lashed tree. I'd never heard anything I wanted more. There'd never been any doubt that Cleo would end up becoming my wife, but hearing it spoken by a complete stranger made it entirely real.

I couldn't help it.

Crossing the small space, I captured Cleo's cheeks and kissed her on the lips.

She froze, then softened in my hands. A soft moan escaped her as the tip of my tongue flickered over her bottom lip.

Wife. Mine.

The feverish lust sprang into being—a ghost that could never be exorcised.

Her mouth parted, welcoming me to take more.

Doctor Laine coughed loudly.

I smiled against Cleo's lips. "Will you be okay without me... wife?"

Her entire body deliquesced, her green eyes glowing. "I'll be fine." She kissed me one last time. "And for the record, I love that word."

"Time to leave, Mr. Killian. My patience isn't infinite." Doctor Laine tapped her foot.

Grasshopper appeared behind me and tugged my ridiculous stolen Hawaiian shirt. "Come on. Let the women heal in peace. I think you deserve a drink."

Ignoring his pulling, I couldn't tear my eyes from Cleo. "I'll be back soon."

She nodded. "Can't wait."

"Drink, dude. Let's celebrate the Dagger Rose bonfire."

There would be celebration but no alcohol. I would abstain until I fixed the mess inside my brain.

Stealing one last kiss from the woman who kept my heart beating, I allowed my VP to drag me from the room.

Two damn hours.

Two interminable hours of waiting.

I sat with a single shot of untouched whiskey, staring at the wall. All I wanted to do was slip sideways on the couch and slam into sleep, but every time my eyes closed, Hopper was there with his damn annoying voice and his pestering rules.

Don't fall asleep.

You can't go to sleep until your concussion has been assessed again.

No sleeping.

Over and fucking over.

I was ready to knock the motherfucker out just so *he* would go to sleep and leave me in peace.

Even though I was ready to wring the guy's neck, it didn't mean I wasn't grateful. Even as I called him a cocksucker and a nag, he knew I appreciated his attempts to keep me alive. I would never admit it to him, but the way my brain throbbed and my vision flickered, I honestly didn't trust in my ability to wake up.

Grasshopper was a reliable friend. Wallstreet was my savior, mentor, and advisor. I trusted both men explicitly, but at the same time, I always understood that my partnership with Wallstreet was for mutual gain. Wallstreet wanted me to transform and rule the Corrupts—which I did. He wanted me to become friends with senators, journalists, and police—which I did.

He wanted more.

Always more.

Same as me.

Everything he asked me to do, I did.

Everything he requested had a reason.

A reason bigger than just Pure Corruption. Bigger than trading. Bigger than both of us.

We both wouldn't stop until we brought about a revolution, and that revolution was on the horizon.

Wallstreet gave me a dynasty to oversee.

Mo came into the room after completing another patrol around the grounds. "Brothers are in place, Kill. I've set up a rotation of three Pures to stake out the house—they'll share the workload. No other asshole is breaching this place."

My head was the weight of a damn skyscraper but I nodded in thanks. "Appreciate it." I trusted Pure Corruption far more than the hired security firm from before.

Bastards.

They'd get an ear-bashing and a lifetime of bad press after what they let happen.

"In a few days, we'll arrange a better alternative." Mo stalked across the small sitting room where we'd taken up residence while waiting for Cleo. "Perhaps you could move to the Clubhouse for a bit—until this is all done and fucking dusted?" Helping himself to the open bottle of whiskey, he poured a generous shot and knocked it back.

Glancing at Grasshopper, he shook the bottle. "Another?"

Hopper shook his head, wiping his mouth. "Not for me, dude."

Turning to face me, Mo said, "No doubt the next few weeks will be full of war. Best to rest where you know you have reinforcements."

My blood thickened. "Not war..." I grinned coldly. "Genocide."

Grasshopper reclined in the single leather chair he'd commandeered. Tipping his glass in my direction, he cocked his head. "Exactly. Genocide."

An utter bloodbath.

There would be no more waiting around. No more putting chess pieces into play and striking off a never-ending to-do list. That had been systematic and time-consuming. This would be swift and archaic.

And at the end of it, my revenge will be sated. Wallstreet's goal completed. And Cleo cemented in my future.

If she forgave me, of course.

My stomach contorted into a knot.

Wallstreet's plans meant I inherited larger and complicated tasks the more successful I became. In the scheme of things, my father was a fucking fly needing to be swatted with my shoe. *He's inconsequential.*

Nothing would tax me more than what Wallstreet and I'd been working toward all these years. I couldn't afford to be ill.

"By the way. We found him." Mo fisted his glass.

"Who?" I rubbed my temples, hoping to dispel some pain.

Mo took a swig of his drink. "Adam 'Alligator' Braxton—the cocksucking snitch who infiltrated us and started this fucking mess. He was staying at Dagger Rose."

The asshole had bolted before we'd had time to apprehend him. But running and hiding wouldn't save him.

Nothing would save him.

He's already dead.

Mo ground his teeth, dragging a finger across his throat in the sign of execution. "He'll pay when we catch up to them."

The door cracked open and Doctor Laine entered. Her eyes skimmed over the wall where a blown-up map of the world hung. I'd stood for hours at a time staring at islands and cities, wondering where Cleo might be if she hadn't died that night.

Her gaze drifted to the small cluster of seats all placed on a deep turquoise rug that looked like an oasis in a sea of white tiles.

"How is she?" I asked, leaning forward to place my glass on the kidney-shaped coffee table. The distance wasn't much. My arm span was more than enough to place the glass safely on the table. But somehow...I missed. The lip of the wood caught the liquor, tipping the entire thing upside down and drenching the carpet.

"Fuck!"

"Hey, it's okay, dude. I'll grab a rag." Grasshopper leapt to his feet.

The damn man had guzzled copious amounts of whiskey over the past two hours but still looked completely sober. Me, on the other hand? I hadn't touched a drop and I was the one fucking spilling things.

Damn this headache!

The doctor cleared her throat, her eyes taking everything in. "She's fine. She'll have a headache for a few days, but her vitals are good and eye dilation perfectly normal." Moving toward me, she added, "She also took a shower. Without the blood covering her, I was able to assess and make sure there were indeed no lacerations or wounds." She smiled gently. "She'll make a complete recovery, and I've sent her to bed."

I slouched in my seat, no longer caring about the spill. "Thank God."

Grasshopper came back with a rag, throwing it on the carpet and stomping on it with his dirty boots. Dried mud rained every time he trampled the absorbent cloth.

I was too exhausted to care.

The doctor peered at me. "Your impairment is worse than I thought. Your friend said you checked yourself out of the hospital a few hours ago—but I wasn't advised how bad you are."

My forehead furrowed. "What do you mean? Just 'cause I spilled a bit of whiskey?"

"No, because you're slurring."

The world stopped still. "What?"

"Shit, man. You are," Mo muttered. "Thought you were just tipsy, but you haven't touched a drop."

Fear wrapped itself around my throat.

I'm not slurring. Am I?

I shook my head, trying to realign my disobeying tongue. "Just tired." Swallowing, I peered at the doctor. "Time for one shmore—I mean one *more* consultation, Doc?"

Shit, I am *slurring.*

What the fuck did that mean?

She smiled. "Of course." However, her calm bedside manner couldn't hide the sudden worry in her gaze. "Come into my office and climb up on your dining table."

I tried to crack a smile—I really did. But everything was such an effort. Shit, even standing felt as if I fought the couch for centuries before I managed to climb unsteadily to my feet.

Shuffling forward in shoes filled with concrete, I passed Mo and gripped his shoulder. Holding on to him, I played it off as a goodbye when in reality he was my damn crutch to stop me face-planting to the floor.

"Make sure this kind shlady is paid, won't you, Mo? After this, I plan on shleeping and I've completely forgotten the combination to my safe." I laughed as if it was the funniest thing I'd said. "I'm broke until I remember."

It's not fucking funny.

I couldn't stop laughing.

It's fucking terrifying.

Nothing could sober me up. I'd well and truly lost it.

Lost everything.

My mathematical ease. My carefully trained conscience. Shit, every bank code, password, and trading algorithm had flown free, leaving my brain a forsaken wasteland.

I was...*empty.*

Mo shot a worried look at Grasshopper. "You got it, Kill." Grabbing me around the nape, he guided me like a dog leads a blind man to the door. "Go get better, Prez. The war can wait. But your health and woman can't."

Without another word, I followed the doctor to her temporary examination room and passed the fuck out on the table.

Chapter Eleven

Cleo

Crap, I was in so much trouble.

Dad had caught us. He'd seen Arthur kissing me. Or rather, me kissing Arthur. God, it'd been so embarrassing. Why couldn't Mom have caught us? She'd delivered the "sex talk" like an automated textbook with no giggling or embarrassment. But Dad...ugh. The fact that he'd sat me down and told me that Arthur had a penis and that I was to never—under any circumstances—let it come out of his pants was the singular most mortifying thing that'd ever happened to me. Only thing was...instead of being horrified at teenage pregnancy, now all I could think about was Arthur's penis. —Cleo, diary entry, age thirteen

Funny how sleep had the power to erase the trauma of the previous day.

How dreams wash away grime and heal wounds in a way water and medicine never could.

I'd gone to bed achy, wrung out, and fretting myself stupid over Arthur.

Now I woke stiff, lethargic, and fuzzy—but revitalized enough that past concerns no longer gnawed so deeply.

The clock still ticked.

The world still spun.

We were alive and that was all that mattered.

Glancing around the room, I reacquainted myself with the space I'd slept in before I was stolen. The carpet was still the same. The layout hadn't changed. The drapery hung open and inviting eager Florida sunshine to act as our alarm clock.

I waited for a flutter of panic at having a safe place breached. But it never came. I remained centered and content.

Stretching and sucking in a replenishing breath, I rolled over to face the man who'd been beside me when our safety had been compromised. My heart pattered with horrible memories of him being whacked over the head and left bleeding.

I hurt more for him than myself, and I cursed the world for damaging him yet again. The injustice he'd lived through—the betrayals he'd suffered.

But life doesn't play favorites.

Just because I loved him didn't mean he was exempt from bad things happening.

Life went on. Waited for nothing and no one. It was up to us to put the past in the past and grow stronger.

Looking at the world in such a way made me feel very insignificant, but at the same time, relieved. Relieved because no matter what atrocities happened, they could all be forgotten if we allowed the magic of a new day to wipe the slate clean and begin anew.

I smiled slightly, thinking about my progress from blankness to remembrance.

The doctor last night had been one of the best I'd ever talked to. Not only had she discussed the symptoms I'd suffer over the next few days as the swelling in my brain went down, but also put my fears to rest about my amnesia. She'd studied psychogenic amnesia at length as part of her thesis and promised to catch up to discuss possibilities of me ever having a relapse and how to patch up the final holes in my past.

She made me trust that I could be fixed...that I could become completely whole once again.

When she'd finished with me, I'd headed upstairs to wait for

Arthur. I'd had good intentions, but the moment I climbed into bed, I was out.

I should've stayed up to make sure he was okay.

I bit my lip, guilt clouding inside. *What if he's worse and I didn't notice?*

Snuggling closer to Arthur, I feathered my fingers over the dark circles beneath his eyes. I held my breath, waiting for him to wake from the slightest touch.

He'd always been a light sleeper—explosively coming awake if he heard a noise or, as he used to say, "a disturbance in the force." He wasn't a *Star Wars* fanatic but he'd seen the movies enough in his youth to quote it at the strangest of times.

But...nothing happened.

Arthur...

His breathing hitched but he didn't flinch away or open his eyes.

Ice entered my heart.

Wake up!

I slid my fingers over his cheekbones, moving to trace his mouth.

Still...nothing.

Oh, God.

Sitting upright, I swallowed back a rush of nausea and nudged his shoulder. "Arthur."

Old wounds caused by eight years apart ruptured inside me, bleeding, drowning with panic.

I tapped his cheek harder. "Art. Wake up."

My wounds continued bleeding, flowing with no tourniquet, filling me with horror.

"Arthur." I shook him. "Wake up."

His large body twisted, a lethargic arm swatting at me. He mumbled something, then slipped back into slumber.

He's still alive at least. He could just be super tired from the stress of finding me and everything else that he refused to share. *Or he could be slipping from me.*

I would never let that happen. My veterinary training kicked in. I searched for vitals, sought out his pulse and temperature. What was the proper medical attention for a concussed man who couldn't wake up?

My brain rushed with textbook solutions while my heart fisted and pained.

I shoved him hard. "Arthur Killian, wake up this instant!"

I couldn't shake the concern that he was far worse than a simple concussion. I hated him so quiet, so lifeless. "Arthur!" He couldn't leave me. Not now. Not *ever*. Why would life be so damn cruel? To let us find each other again and then tear us apart?

Grabbing his cheeks, my hair fell over my shoulder onto his chest. "Arthur, open your eyes. *Please*, open your eyes."

He moaned, his forehead furrowing into deep tracks.

"Yes. That's it." *Come back to me. Don't leave me.* "Arthur, wake up!"

His eyes cracked open.

My world ended and began again. Jitters hijacked my muscles; oxygen refused to stay in my lungs. The greenness of his gaze was just as vibrant, just as stunning.

He's okay . . . please let him be okay.

Confusion flickered, followed by alarm. "Wh-what?" He grimaced, shuffling higher against the pillows. "What's so important?"

His voice was a blanket, putting out the flames of my panic. *Oh, thank God.*

My insides stopped bleeding but my heart galloped like crazy. "What's so important? I'll tell you what's so damn important. How about the fact you wouldn't wake up!"

My temper replaced the feeling of helplessness and my healing knowledge took over. There was strength in becoming a nurse rather than a grieving spouse. It was comforting to go through the motions of checking his pallor, counting the beats of his heart, reaffirming that the soul I loved so much was still firmly anchored in his body.

"Buttercup, what the hell are you doing?" Arthur smiled, his voice sleep-soft.

He wasn't slurring; his eyes weren't unfocused, but I didn't trust he was fine—not after the struggle to wake him. "I want to call the doctor. Something's not right."

He scowled. "Just because I slept like the dead doesn't mean you have to go all iron-handed."

"It does if you should be in the hospital."

He groaned under his breath.

Needing to test, to make sure he was okay and fully with me, I arranged my shaking hand into a Girl Scout salute. "How many fingers am I holding up?"

"Eh." Arthur blinked. "You know, homework first thing in the morning isn't exactly my idea—"

"Just answer me. Humor me. Laugh at me if you must, but answer the damn question." I shoved my hand in his face. "How many?"

Rolling his eyes, he winced and jammed his thumbs into his sockets, rubbing sleep away. Yawning, he took his time—deliberately antagonizing me.

He narrowed his gaze. "Seeing as my multiplication skills so interest you, I'll put you out of your misery and say three." A smile played on his mouth. "Want me to recite the three times table while I'm at it?"

Relief slammed into me. I dropped my arm, growing numb with delayed shock. "That might be an idea."

Prove to me you're whole and maybe I can relax.

He chuckled but a shadow suddenly crossed his face; he shook his head. "On second thought, it's still too early." Tossing his arms above his head, he stretched. "How about you quit pestering me and come back to bed." He looked like a giant jungle cat. All he needed was a palm tree as a scratching post.

My tummy clenched but I still couldn't shake the fear. "How are you feeling?"

Tell me the truth.

Yawning again, he rubbed his temples. "Surprisingly, better than yesterday."

I collapsed against my pillow. "Oh, thank God for that."

"Don't worry about me, Buttercup." He rolled onto his side, throwing his arm over me. "I'm fine, really." His words said one thing, his voice another. He wasn't fine—his tone just admitted it.

But what could I do? Time would fix him—and if it didn't, I just had to hope doctors would.

We stayed quiet for a while. I feared he'd gone back to sleep, but then his voice trickled into my ears. "You can't keep worrying, Cleo." He nuzzled closer. "The doc last night was really great. She gave me some painkillers and anti-inflammatories. Did a few tests that I have no idea the purpose of, and arranged to pop by in a few days for a checkup."

Propping myself up on my elbow, I looked down at him. "Did she say you'll be okay? No long-term effects?"

He looked at the ceiling, avoiding my eyes. "Of course. What else would she say?"

A tremble quaked down my spine. *He's lying again.*

I didn't know how to reply.

Arthur suddenly rolled onto his side and spooned me against his hard, bed-warmed body. "Like I said, stop worrying. I'll be fine. Yes, I'm not a hundred percent yet, but I will be."

Kissing the top of my head, he threw his leg over mine, capturing me possessively. "However, I do want a bit more sleep." His long length rippled like polished stone, his hard edges intoxicating.

My heart skipped as he pulled me closer and rocked his hips against my butt.

"Just…lie here with me for a little longer." His breath caught. "And then we have the matter of settling a bet about money bringing happiness."

Money doesn't bring happiness. You *do. And right now you're hurting me by avoiding what's important.*

I wanted to deny him. I wanted to force him from the bed and call the doctor to check him over again. Something wriggled in my heart, urging me to uncover whatever he kept hidden.

"Cleo, stop," he breathed. "Your thoughts are so loud."

I stiffened, unable to relax when all I thought about was him passing into a coma if he went back to sleep.

"I'm okay." He pressed the sweetest kiss on my shoulder. Heat spread like blooming tendrils, disappearing down my back.

I shuddered and sighed, unable to hide the watery sound of my concern.

Arthur squeezed me closer, his strength undiminished even if his head was broken. "Honestly, Cleo. I'm fine. Just need a few days to rest, that's all." Kissing me again, he whispered, "Now, can you please stop thinking and let me hold you without fearing a panicked rabbit lives in your chest?"

I laughed halfheartedly. *He's right.*

My heart raced to a supersonic beat while Arthur's pounded slow and sure behind me. I forced myself to take comfort from the strong, steady tempo.

He's alive.

That was all I needed—for now.

"Just another hour, shokay? Then...we'll..." His voice slurred a little as he slipped quickly back into sleep. He drifted.

"Okay, Arthur. I can wait another hour before interrogating you."

Counting down minutes in my head, I lay still and silent.

I should've been comforted in his embrace, but instead all I suffered was fear.

A day passed.

One moment it was dawn, the next it was dusk.

How did one hour turn into ten?

I'd remained unyielding and unsleepy in his arms for his requested hour. Once time had run out, I'd tried to rouse him but failed—he'd succeeded in swatting me away like an annoying bug, rolling himself up in the blankets. He was out again before I could poke him from his greedy dreams.

Another hour had passed.

I'd learned from my past mistakes and didn't make the same again. Rolling him onto his back, I'd given him no room to hide. I'd slapped him. Gently at first, but harder until he rose from the clingy existence of sleep and opened his eyes.

And there, I'd trapped him.

I didn't let him sink again. I caught him in my net and chatted and questioned and became so annoying he laughed and shoved me playfully.

Even when he climbed from the covers to shower, I followed and gossiped and became a hyped up version of the weather channel, shopping network, and self-help station all to keep his mind here with me and not in the abyss of concussion.

And it worked.

After his shower, he was alert.

We snuggled back into bed after raiding the kitchen for cornflakes and fruit, and spent the day side by side. We didn't move far from the bedroom, but we turned the space into our haven, and for the first time since I'd woken tied in the back of the van with a scary biker battle as my welcome, I found a slice of ordinariness.

I adored it.

Arthur lost the argumentative snappiness from last night and we both ignored our unfinished argument in favor of pliancy and togetherness.

By the end of the day, my headache had faded to a gentle throb and with the aid of a few painkillers it disappeared entirely.

I'd never spent a full day in bed before. I could never stay still long enough or tolerate my own company for long, as it only highlighted my lack of a past. But the movie marathon we indulged in, laughing at others' misfortune and relating to lovers in the midst of trouble, was rare and cherished.

Occasionally, Arthur would roll over and gather me close. His nose would nuzzle into my neck and we'd watch the flickering scene with nothing between us.

Those were my favorite times.

The brief moments when we were nothing more than a man and woman snuggled up in bed watching other people's lives for a change. It made me glow and ache all at the same time.

To have this with him, after all this time was…indescribable.

But to have missed out on this for so long was…*unbearable*.

The last episode of the show we were watching ended and Arthur turned his green eyes on mine. The strain hadn't left and he looked hollow almost—empty from the vibrancy I was used to.

He looks lost.

Cupping his cheek, I willed my panic to remain hidden. If he wanted to talk to me about his symptoms, then he would. I couldn't force him. I didn't want to make him face things he might not be ready to face. But at the same time, it was all I could think about.

The longer we stared, the more lust thickened. My nipples hardened and his arms bunched on top of the sheet.

My fingers moved from his cheeks to his lips. His mouth parted, eyes shadowing from bright green to forest. I leaned in to kiss him. Eager for his taste. Desperate to connect.

Then…his stomach rumbled.

Loudly.

The noise turned a sexually charged moment into a comedic one.

I laughed.

Dropping my hand from his face to his stomach, I rubbed his sculptured abs. "Hungry?"

He smirked, looking younger than his years and nowhere near as scary as he did in leather and windswept dust. His perfect teeth were sharp and dangerous against his tanned face. "I've been hungry for the past five hours."

"Then why didn't you say something?"

"Because I didn't want to get out of bed again." His leg rubbed against mine. "I enjoyed having you in my arms too much."

My heart melted. "And you were willing to suffer starvation for me?"

His gaze turned serious. "I'd be willing to suffer anything for you, Buttercup. I thought you knew that by now?"

I gasped.

His fingers trailed down my side, then skated across my chest. "I'm hungry for other things, too." He rolled my nipple with delicious pressure.

My head fell back onto the pillow, delivering myself into his control. The ravenous need to have him inside me overrode hunger for physical food.

I groaned as he scooted down the bed and sucked the same nipple into his mouth. Clutching his head to my chest, I tangled my fingers into his hair. "Um...you can eat me. I don't mind."

He chuckled, his breath tickling my cleavage. "If I eat you, you'd be gone."

I pulled on his hair. "But if you eat me, then I become you."

He paused. Climbing my body again, he captured my chin, holding me firm. "You *are* me. And I am you. We might have separate thoughts and minds, Buttercup, but we have the same heart and soul."

I couldn't speak.

How could he go from violence and bloodshed to sprouting such tender, heartfelt things? He was the perfect man—prepared to do anything to protect me, while not afraid to be soft when it mattered.

Pushing at the sheet covering us, I glanced at his rapidly hardening erection.

We'd been naked all day. A fort of blankets protecting us from what'd happened and what was to come. I loved the sensation of being adrift in our own world.

His eyes burned mine. "You're looking at me as if you would happily devour every inch of my body."

I smiled wickedly. "Depends how many inches of you there were."

His eyes widened, then hooded with need. "Goddammit, you tempt me."

"If I tempt you, then don't resist me." I reached for his cock, ignoring food in favor of having him.

But I never managed to grab him.

He moved too swiftly. Pushing my shoulders, he pinned me to the bed and pecked a kiss on the tip of my nose. "That's not yours to play with. Not yet, at least."

I stuck out my bottom lip. "It is mine. Just like everything of me is yours."

His eyes wandered down my front. He swallowed a groan. "You're right, but I need to eat. I need energy so I can give you what you deserve."

I love his train of thought.

His denial heated my blood until I was lava and fire. "And what do I deserve?"

His breath caught as he bit his lip and squeezed his eyes shut. "Fuck, that sounded sexy."

I arched upward as much as I could—submitting myself to a kiss—or whatever else he wanted to give me. The sheets tantalized my flesh. The warm air licked around my nipples. Everything was an aphrodisiac.

Suddenly, he growled and rolled away.

What the—

Climbing off the bed, his legs planted wide on the floor. My eyes trailed to his heavy cock as he scooped a pair of discarded black boxer briefs from the end of the bed and stepped into them. His muscles flexed and bowed, looking part fantasy, part illusion. Nobody should be that divine. Nobody could be that divine and be *mine*.

He looked like a demi-god ready to carry me off into the heavens only to corrupt me with decadent sin.

"You can't stand there looking like that and expect me to behave," I whispered, rubbing my thighs together.

Leaning down, he captured my wrist and pulled me toward the edge of the bed. Lifting me from the mattress, he plopped me onto my feet, then wrapped me in the tightest embrace. "Never stop being you, Buttercup. Never stop being bold or bossy or brave."

The swift change from erotic to endearing left me stranded and swimming to catch up. My fingers latched on to his narrow hips, stroking the cotton of his underwear. "I'm bossy?"

Unable to help myself, I nipped at his pectoral, tracing the pink scar and tiny puncture holes left over from my stitches.

His back tightened but his chuckle echoed like a chorus inside my ears. "Very." Holding me at arm's length, he smiled. "But I like bossy women."

Coldness entered my lava-blood, delivering once again the fear that he wasn't as well as he made out. Tilting my head, I peered at him, hoping to read his secrets.

Why was he making such an effort to distract me?

Distract me from what?

"Wrong, Mr. Killian. You only prefer *one* bossy woman."

Capturing my cheeks, he placed his lips against mine. "Only one. Only you." His tongue slipped past my lips, tasting me, encouraging me to let go of what'd happened and allow myself to be swept away in this new cascade of togetherness.

Obeying his command, I did my best to let go. I did my best to live in the moment where his kiss was as fleeting as a comet and as precious as a falling star.

The kiss stopped as sweetly as it'd begun. Arthur brushed a fiery strand from my cheek. "Let's go rectify the problem of my starvation. Savory first, then dessert." Pinching my butt, he smiled. "And if you hadn't guessed by now—you're the dessert."

Chapter Twelve

Kill

Genius was a gift. But obsession was a curse.

Problem was I'd never been able to have one without the other.

When I wanted something—I'd go after it. I'd chase it until I'd either solved it, or it no longer interested me. That sort of single-minded determination was fine—to some degree. But in some cases, it was the worst kind of punishment because I was never satisfied. Never content. Always driven for more. —Kill, age seventeen

I left Cleo in the bathroom as I threw on a T-shirt before descending the stairs.

The steps remained where they should and my eyes judged distances like normal. The reprieve after last night's agony made me weak at the knees with gratefulness.

It wasn't intentional to keep the seriousness of my condition from Cleo.

Who are you fucking kidding?

Okay, I *was* intentionally downplaying the agony in my head and the terrifying sludge where my intelligence used to be. But I couldn't handle hurting her even more with a weakness I couldn't control.

She didn't need to fret. And I had the power to stop her worrying by simply withholding tiny details.

It was a worthwhile trade.

I stepped into the foyer with strong convictions that I'd done the right thing keeping her in the dark. My body wasn't nearly as tense as it was yesterday, my eyes not nearly as bruised.

That was until I saw the letter.

Then I tensed up like a fucking fist.

The mail had been delivered.

Hardly a life-changing event, if it wasn't for the very common and familiar envelope sitting on top of my utility bills.

Moving calmly, I stole the mail as if it was any other day.

My hand stayed steady as I took the correspondence into my office and sliced the paper with a letter opener.

The stationery brought back so many memories. Memories of scribbling equations after equations, committing to memory Wall-street's famous trading sequence. Memories of jotting down names of newspaper editors, friendly police officers, and most importantly eager politicians—all so I would know who to contact when I found freedom.

Looking over my shoulder—never able to shake off the feeling of being watched—I unfolded the note from Florida State.

Wallstreet's swift font indented the page.

Kill,

All plans change and ours have done just that. You received the one thing you thought you'd never see again and in return I want you to finish our ultimate goal.

It's time.

Up until now you've been playing with inconsequential affairs. That was your training. Consider this your graduation.

You know what to do.

Wallstreet

He was right.

I *did* know what to do and I'd been expecting this letter for months. Having Cleo come back from the dead only expedited the inevitable.

And regardless of my concussion, I was ready to take on a new challenge. Ready to complete my final task. Ready for *more*.

To the outside world, I was just a biker.

To my brothers, I was just a president.

To Cleo, I was just Arthur the mathematician from her past.

But everyone was wrong.

Only Wallstreet knew the real me. He knew me because he'd groomed me into what I'd become.

We both knew I had bigger dreams, loftier goals. It wasn't that I didn't value my success or ranking within my Club—it was just...not entirely what I wanted.

I wanted retribution. I wanted to live in a world where evil and corruption didn't win over love and togetherness.

I wanted a great many things and not all of them achievable in the lifestyle I lived now.

And that's why I need to become someone else...someone more equipped to deliver my promises.

My obsession for *more* had threatened to cripple me with my never-ending desperate drive. The pressure for more money, more security, more freedom.

More. More. *More.*

Wallstreet had seen that. He said that was what made him choose me—even over my intelligence and gift with numbers.

To him I was an entrepreneur, harbinger, and founder all in one.

Because inside me resided not a man who could take orders and make them a reality, nor was I employee who obeyed what his commander told him.

I was so much more than that.

I had a goal. A goal that mirrored Wallstreet's. One that made us a match made in heaven.

He wanted more, too.

In fact, he wanted everything.

And the only way to get everything was to rule everyone.

And who ruled everyone?

The men who made the laws.

The motherfucking government.

Chapter Thirteen

Cleo

Would he ever be satisfied?

I'd never admit it aloud, but I was afraid I wasn't enough for him. I wanted to give him everything. He already owned my heart and soul—I had nothing else to give. Most of the time, it seemed like enough. But then there were the other times. The times where I'd catch him watching me with hunger in his eyes. Hunger that had nothing to do with lust or friendship. Hunger that I didn't understand. —Cleo, diary entry, age fourteen

"Where did you learn to cook?"

I perched on the marble countertop in a singlet and panties as Arthur moved swiftly and surely around the pristine kitchen. His boxer briefs left his legs naked and seductive—the redheaded mermaid inked into his thigh twitched her tail with his every step. I couldn't tear my eyes away from the delicious sight he made with shaggy, bed-mussed hair, tight boxers, and the charcoal T-shirt he'd thrown on highlighting his toned chest.

As much as I loved his mermaid tattoo and the Libra star signs hidden in the whitewash of a wave, I was glad his T-shirt covered his full-back tattoo with its Dagger Rose emblem drawn over by Pure Corruption. It spoke of two responsibilities and oaths. Two sentences and obligations. The ink cast a terrible premonition that Arthur wasn't free—that he was bound to others.

He's bound to me, no one else. Even if Arthur is so loyal to Wallstreet.

I didn't know why, but whenever I thought about Wallstreet I grew temperamental. Arthur explained a little about why he was so steadfast to that man, but to me it seemed like Wallstreet was the biggest user of all.

I won't stand for it.

Especially after everything Arthur had done for him.

"I never learned. Self-taught I suppose," Arthur replied, pulling out bowls and chopsticks. "I don't do it often. Too busy." His eyes darkened. "And what's the point of cooking when it's only for one?"

Throwing me a look twisted with levity, he couldn't hide the hint of self-pity.

He's been so lonely.

Redirecting the conversation to lighter things, I joked, "I assumed you couldn't even boil water."

"Why?" He chuckled. "Because you still see the boy who burned everything his mother tried to teach?"

My mind filled with images of Diane Killian laughing hilariously as smoke spewed from her oven for the thirtieth time. Arthur was never destined to follow her and become a baker. Not with his track record.

Kicking my legs, banging my naked heels against the glossy cabinets, I smiled. "No, I assumed because of all the fancy delivered meals. Those weekly menus are fabulous but not exactly conducive to getting someone in the kitchen."

Grabbing a strainer, he plopped steaming hot water and rice noodles into it, letting the water sift into the sink. "I'm hurt that you have such little faith in me." He spun around to splat the noodles into a wok filled with soy sauce and other spices, but he stumbled and grabbed the counter instead.

Immediately, my heart skyrocketed. "You okay?" I gripped the marble edge, ready to hurl myself across the space and grab him.

A second ticked past before he moved—slower this time. "I'm

fine. Stop fussing. You'll drive me crazy." With measured strokes, he turned on the gas and tossed the now glistening and fragrant rice noodles, before folding shallots and bean sprouts into the mess.

Biting my lip, I didn't say a word as he kept his back toward me and cooked. I didn't know if his reluctance to face me was due to his concussion or just concentration on his culinary masterpiece.

Either way, I didn't take my eyes off him the entire time he cooked.

Finally, with the scent of exotic dinner making my mouth water, Arthur divided up the portions and presented a perfect Pad Thai.

My mouth popped open. "Wow, Art. It looks scrumptious."

"Oh, wait." He headed to the pantry, grabbed a packet of crushed peanuts, and scattered a pinch over the steamy noodles. "Now it's ready."

Lifting his bowl to my nose, he said, "Sniff. Does it smell authentic?"

I inhaled deeply, instantly recognizing the spicy allurement of chilies and the mouthwatering aroma of garlic. "Yes. It smells exactly like a Pad Thai from my local takeout."

Arthur scowled. "Takeout? Really. You never got to travel with your foster family?"

"No." I looked away. "They tried to take me to Corfu once, but I refused."

"Why?"

I shivered as the old lostness and fear of my mind-black-hole came back. "Because I was afraid of going somewhere where I might've been before. Afraid of running into people who..." My eyes trailed to my scars. They were answer enough.

Arthur sighed. "Even apart we were still living with the same trials. Both alone—just in different ways."

We slipped into silence as I accepted a pair of chopsticks, then scooted off the countertop to sit at the breakfast bar. Sliding onto high stools, we sat haloed in light from three glass-domed Edison bulbs.

Arthur waited until I'd sat and devoured a few mouthfuls of his incredible dish before saying, "So...tell me. What have you been up to the past few years?"

I was mesmerized by his expert use of chopsticks and the way his throat tensed as he swallowed.

I laughed even as my heart thundered. "We're truly doing this?"

He frowned. "Doing what?"

"Getting to know each other."

Putting down his chopsticks, his forehead furrowed. "Not getting to know you, Buttercup. I already know your soul. It's been mine since I set eyes on you. But I want to know the type of existence you had when I wasn't there. I want to decide if I should be pissed off with your foster family for keeping your memories hostage, or silently grateful that they gave you a better life than the one you would've had if you'd remembered."

The ache returned full force. I rubbed my chest with the heel of my palm. "Every time you do that I feel terrible."

"Do what?"

Our banter dissolved, showing black and white beneath the colors of where we'd been living. We loved each other. It was undeniable. But where our souls remembered and adored, our personalities had evolved due to circumstances beyond our power.

We're strangers.

"Remind me that it was *me* who left *you*." My skin flashed with heat. "I know you don't mean it, but it hurts to think it was my fault—"

Arthur slammed his hands on the marble. "None of this is your fault, Cleo."

I hung my head, poking my noodles with no appetite.

How had this happened again? Could we not talk about anything without bringing up the past and ruining our simple fun?

Taking my hand, he rubbed his thumb over my knuckles. His eyes were strained and hollow. "Forget all of that. I want to know about you. Just you."

"There isn't really much to tell." Bravery strengthened my resolve as Arthur smiled encouragingly.

Okay ... I guess we're talking. Truly talking. For the first time in eight years.

Trying to tame my heart from kicking with first date nerves, I sucked in a breath. "I suppose, in a nutshell, I achieved the dreams I set for myself. I graduated and earned my veterinary degree. I—" Cutting myself off, I waved my hand. "You know all this. I feel like I'm repeating myself." I stabbed the chopsticks in his direction. "What about you? I want to know about you."

He shrugged. "Prison. Revenge. That's all there is to know about me." His words were simple but his eyes were complicated.

Shaking my head, I smiled sadly. "Not true. Where did you learn to cook like this? Did someone teach you?" My heart fisted as I asked. I knew he hadn't slept with other women for affection but there might've been someone—*a friend*—someone who'd replaced me in some capacity, if not all.

Arthur took another bite, taking his time to chew. The longer he made me wait, the worse my suspicion grew. *Oh, God, he* does *have someone close to him.*

His eyes darkened. "You're asking if a woman taught me this, right?"

I flinched. *Yes.* "No. I just—there's so much about you that I missed out on. Tell me something—anything." *Tell me that no one else mattered but me.*

He ran a hand through his hair, wincing as his fingers found the bump of his concussion. "Okay ... I'll put your mind at ease." His lips curled, deliberately leaving me hanging.

"And ..." I leaned forward, panting for his next word.

"I took a Thai cooking class." He popped a bean sprout into his mouth.

"You took a *class*?" *Huh. Not quite what I expected.* Tilting my head, I waited for him to carry on. "When?"

"A few years ago." Shifting under my reproachful stare, he continued. "When Pure Corruption was operating smoothly and my trades were finally paying dividends, I had this insatiable need to run. Everything was moving forward, life was getting better, and I fucking hated it because I felt like I was betraying your memory." His voice thickened. "I often found myself at the airport, staring at the flight departures, wondering if I just switched off my thoughts I could somehow chase your ghost around different continents."

My heart demolished into dust. "Arthur."

He didn't hear me. Throwing me a self-abasing smile, he said, "That day, I couldn't return to Pure Corruption or the brand-new mansion I'd bought with cash. I felt like a fraud—like my life wasn't my own anymore. So, I jumped on the next departing plane."

My tongue was a brick.

His gaze met mine, his face heavy with the past. "I didn't even know where I was headed until we touched down in Bangkok, Thailand. I had nothing packed and only a newly minted passport in my pocket..." His voice dwindled off, reliving those moments of exploration. "I'd wanted to feel excitement, *freedom*. But all I felt was loneliness." His head dropped, his long hair curtaining his eyes. "I was so fucking lonely, Cleo."

The sudden torture in his voice froze my blood and every inch of me needed to hug him. He sounded as if he believed that loneliness could come again. That what we had would disappear, leaving him destitute.

Nothing could be more wrong.

"I ended up staying for three weeks. I did the usual stuff. Traveled around, faded into one of the world's busiest cities, but no matter what I did or saw, I was still alone with no one to enjoy it with. I finally had to accept that no matter where I was, how much wealth I had, or who I associated with, I would never stop the one thing I couldn't change."

"And what was that?" I asked quietly.

He took a sip of his water, a lone droplet sliding from his lips and over his chin. "That you were the only one with the power to fix me and because you were dead I had to come to terms with always being broken."

This time I couldn't stop myself.

Screw Pad Thai. Screw food.

Slipping from my seat, I moved like a river, slinking around chair legs and melting into his lap. The moment I sat on his knee, his large arms laced around me. He shuddered, holding me eternally close.

We both sighed hard.

"Take me there. Show me," I murmured. "I want to put our life in a suitcase and never look back."

He sucked in a breath. "I'd love that. So much." A long hiatus lasted, before he buried his face in my hair. "I sound like a fucking sap. Shitty headache is making me admit things you don't need to know."

I struggled in his arms. "Never feel like you can't tell me anything."

He kept me imprisoned. "What you *do* need to know is I'm no longer broken, Buttercup. Don't feel like you have to mend me or that I'm going to be a burden. Because it's my fucking responsibility to look after you and I'll do a damn better job than I have in the past. I promise."

"I'm not your responsibility," I said. "I'm your equal."

The air switched from past pains to current agonies and Arthur's arms twitched harder around me. "We need to talk about what happened that night."

Somehow, the time between our argument at Dagger Rose and our current dinner vanished, leaving us exactly where we'd been— tense, frustrated, and confused.

My pulse thickened, feeding my cells with adrenaline in preparation. "Why didn't you believe him?"

His question was so quiet it was almost nonexistent. And it made no sense.

"What?"

He flinched, forcing himself to continue. "My father. He must've told you why I was in prison. He must've shown you the police report." He glanced at me. "You would've seen it with your own eyes."

"You still think I'll hate you, don't you?" Taking courage from his body heat, I said firmly, "I told you. I know everything. I saw everything."

His shoulders hunched. "Then how can you honestly forgive me? No matter how I look at the situation, there is still me and my unforgivable crime." His jaw clenched. "Your conviction that I didn't do it—that you can absolve me—is bullshit. It makes me fear for your state of mind even more than when you were amnesiac."

"Gee, thanks."

"None of this makes sense anymore."

My mind charged over the memories that were still so raw. How did we have such different versions of that night? And what would I have to do to make him see the truth? "There's nothing to forgive. But obviously you need to forgive yourself."

"Goddammit, I want so badly to believe you." Arthur squeezed me tighter. His eyes were wild as if he couldn't stomach the strained silence that followed whenever we stopped talking.

"You don't have to believe. It's the truth."

When he didn't say anything, I whispered, "Are you going to listen this time?"

Are you going to believe me unlike when you ignored my every proof that I was Cleo?

Arthur nodded slowly. "Yes. I'll listen." The entire day had been leading toward this conversation. "I need to know. Why do you think I'm innocent? Why aren't you threatening to kill me for what I've done?"

Looking into his green eyes, I brushed unruly hair off his forehead. "I'll tell you why." Taking a deep breath, prickling with the ghosts of my slain parents, I did my best to offer absolution. "You *did* kill them, but it wasn't your fault."

Arthur stiffened—trading flesh and bone for steel and rebar. His large hands clamped around my hips. "What do you mean?"

"I mean exactly that. It's not a riddle."

His eyes turned brittle, disbelieving. His face filled with guilt, consumed with self-hatred. He had it all wrong.

For him to understand, I had to take him back further than just that night. I had to prove to him why everything he recalled was wrong. "Do you remember the first time I walked in on you and your father? That night after the Club meeting when Thorn disciplined Rubix in front of the brothers for leading an unauthorized raid on a bank?"

His face scrunched in irritation. "What does that have to do with—"

Pressing my finger against his lips, I shook my head. "Answer the question. I'll make you understand."

With his forehead deeply lined, Arthur's gaze turned inward. Colors and shadows of the past clouded over his face. He nodded as the night solidified. "Yes." Then his features fell as if plummeting off a high-rise building. "Shit, I hated you seeing that."

My heart beat faster—just like it had the evening I'd witnessed domestic violence for the first time.

Oh, God. What was going on?

Arthur was curled up and bloody on the carpet in the middle of the lounge. Diane wailed from the kitchen as I dry heaved and clung to the windowsill outside with all my strength. I wanted to call Arthur's name, to let him know I was there. I wanted to scream for help.

This wasn't okay. Abuse was never okay.

But I couldn't move from my secret spot as Rubix and Asus delivered kick after kick into Arthur's stomach.

"Family doesn't snitch, boy. I know it was you. You told Thorn about the raid."

Coughing up blood, Arthur moaned, "It wasn't me. I swear."

"As if I'd listen to you." Another vicious kick as if Arthur were a football and the goal net was miles away. *"Do it again and this will seem like a fucking picnic."*

Goose bumps sprang up over my arms. "You were telling the truth. You never told my father. Thorn found out some other way but it made no difference to Rubix."

Arthur laughed coldly. "Believe me. By that point, he didn't need a reason." His gaze was flint and hardness, but his tone slipped into tender. "You made it better, though. You patched me up and made me so fucking embarrassed."

I shook the memories free of wiping away his blood and listening to his excuses for his father's wicked temper. "It wasn't the last time, either."

Arthur shook his head. "No, not the last."

"Now you remember how they punished you for doing nothing wrong, do you also remember how good they were at getting you to give in?" This was the part I feared bringing up. Arthur had a heart of pure gold, but like any precious metal it had impurities—imperfections that could be exploited and twisted to condemn its own molecular structure.

He sighed heavily. "Which downfall are you talking about? There were many."

I traced the ropes of muscles in his forearm, not making eye contact. In a way, by not looking at him, I gave him an element of privacy. "Not that many. And I'm talking about the night they got you so drunk, you almost single-handedly exterminated the smaller MC just out of our boundaries—just because they lied that I'd been hurt by one of the prospects. You didn't kill anyone, Art...but you were close."

Do you see what I'm saying?

He froze. "I always wondered why I woke up to being reprimanded in the Club meeting and having dried blood on my fists."

Shock turned me cold. "You mean...you don't remember that, either?"

He smiled, but it wasn't jovial or free. It was a trap, a cage—a self-inflicted sentence he couldn't unlock. "No. It's a blur. I know what I did. I felt their noses crack beneath my fists and I remember the taste of wretched bourbon as my father held my head back, making me drink." He strained for more, but gave up. "That's about it."

"Well, my point is made, then." I sat back, studying his face with anxious eyes.

He frowned. "What point?"

"You wanted so much to fit in with your family that you were at their mercy. You were manipulated first with kicks and harsh discipline and then encouraged by promises and kindness. They got you drunk, told you lies. They drugged you, told you more lies. They scrambled you up so much inside, Art. You had no idea what you were doing half the time."

His mouth hung open. A beacon lit behind his eyes as a shred of hope ignited. "What…what do you mean?"

Taking a deep breath, I held my bleeding heart. "I mean you were drunk the night you shot my parents. Beyond drunk. You slurred and stumbled. You had a terrible black eye, blood on your lip, and could barely move. You were probably drugged, too. You couldn't walk unassisted—let alone aim and shoot."

Arthur scrambled to his feet, shoving me away from him. Pacing away, his fingers dived into his hair. "I don't understand. That doesn't make any sense. I remember everything so clearly."

I stood. "Do you, though? What do you remember?" When he didn't stop patrolling or chewing on his lip, I tensed. "You remember what they told you. You recall what they said happened. Believe me— you weren't in any state to recall anything but a raging hangover."

"But—I shot them. I remember that." Spinning around, his words spewed forth in a confession-torrent. "I'd pumped myself up to do it. I had no choice. My father threatened you. He said he'd rape you in front of me, then kill you in front of Thorn. He said if I didn't do it, he'd make me wish I was dead but never give me that freedom."

My heart stopped beating. "You're saying you went along with it to *save* me? You would've killed my parents all because of something your father said—even after a lifetime of lies?"

I couldn't believe it. How could he have been so gullible?

"Yes. Of course I would. I loved your parents, Cleo. So damn much. They were so nice to me. Accepted me into their family. But by loving me, they ruined me. My father would never have permitted us to be happy because then I would've ruled and never him. Just like he took you from me the second time—he didn't do it to rape or kill you, even though he had every opportunity. He did it because he *could*. Because once again he's shown that he's better than me."

He kicked a cupboard. "He was teaching me another fucking lesson!"

My knees locked in place. "What lesson?"

"That he can still take whatever he damn well likes! My happiness. My goodness. My freedom. He can screw me over and there's nothing I can fucking do about it."

"But don't you see—let him try! He'll never succeed now that you understand how he controlled you. He's worthless, Arthur." Moving around the breakfast bar, I went to him.

He darted out of my reach.

"For once and for all, you need to forgive yourself." I braced myself. "Yes, you killed my parents. Yes, you pulled the trigger. But, Art, you were dead on your feet. You were bleeding, you didn't aim—Rubix did. You didn't squeeze the trigger with your lifeless, drunken fingers—Asus did."

My mind cartwheeled back to that night.

My heart was lead and wings, sinking and fluttering all at once.

His footfalls were so familiar but for every stagger of his, there were two other sets that sent terror to my bones.

I crawled from beneath my covers, blinking away sleep. Something urged me to follow, to hide, to see.

Moving from one puddle-shadow to another, I swallowed my gasp as I saw Rubix and Asus carrying a mumbling Arthur between them. I trailed behind, unable to leave as Rubix whispered atrocities in his ear.

"You have to do this, Art. Thorn raped her as a little girl."

"They deserve to die, Art. Her mother sells her to other men for pleasure."

"They must be destroyed, Art. Her soul is doomed unless you free her from them."

When Arthur groaned and didn't believe his lies, other monstrous things fell from Rubix's lips.

"Kill them or I'll rape her."

"Kill them or your brother will rape her."

"Kill them or the entire Club will rape her."

Tears streamed down my cheeks as Arthur stumbled and stuttered, finally positioned at the foot of my parents' bed.

I couldn't watch.

I couldn't look away.

Rubix laughed as my father woke up. In slow motion, Asus raised Arthur's arm, even as Arthur screamed and fought.

But it was too late.

Bang!

Tears escaped unbidden as I sniffed back the past. "You were just the pawn they used so their hands weren't dirty. They made sure the gunpowder was on your skin. Your fingerprints were on the murder weapon. They killed them and framed you. They destroyed both of us."

Our breathing acted as knives, smashing the stagnant silence into smithereens.

That night replayed over and over again, but I remained in the present. I didn't need to relive how the fire began or how I screamed as the flames found me.

Arthur moved toward the marble-topped island, gripping the ledge with his fingers and bowing as if the weight of the past was too much.

Seconds ticked endlessly loud. We didn't move or speak.

Finally, I couldn't stand it any longer.

I went to him.

Lashing my arms around his middle, I squashed my cheek against his spine and willed him to feel my heart beat. To understand the forgiveness in its rhythm, to finally come to terms with the only crime he was guilty of: of being a puppet for his heinous father and brother.

Slowly, Arthur linked his fingers with mine. My skin sparked where he touched me and my knees trembled as he unlocked my iron-fast grip and spun around to face me.

His emerald eyes were pools of despair and desire.

With hitching hesitation, his body swayed into mine and his mouth hovered a whisper away from taking. "Can this be true? Not only can you absolve my sins, but also give me even more justice when I end his fucking tyranny?"

I nodded, standing on tiptoes to finish what he'd started.

I kissed him.

I expected a sweet surrender, a gentle sweep into bliss. Instead, something that'd been brewing in Arthur since that night unleashed.

He shed the pain of his concussion.

He shed the agony of being incarcerated unfairly.

And he shed the unhappiness of being betrayed.

His lips claimed mine; his loud groan entered my lungs. His tongue wrenched past my lips and the kiss I'd envisioned wisped into smoke as he drove us from lust into mania.

His hands clutched my backside, lifting me up and swinging me around to land on the countertop. My panties weren't enough material to slip and slide and my naked thighs glued me to the cool surface, wedging me at the perfect height for Arthur's questing hands.

Imprisoning my knees, he opened me wide and settled his large bulk between them. His lips nipped and caressed their way down my neck. The small tank top I wore didn't stand a chance against his teeth and a vicious tug. The white cotton shredded like a flag of surrender, baring my breasts and throbbing nipples.

"I'll never be worthy of you." His mouth suckled my left breast, his hot, wet tongue swirling until I gasped and writhed.

"I'll never understand how I stole your love." His lips found my other nipple, granting it the same treatment. His voice never rose past a caress, lulling me into him with every syllable.

My back bowed and I grabbed his head, holding him against me. He devoured every millimeter of skin, rising over me to trail wet kisses from my cleavage, to clavicle, to mouth.

I gasped as his lips claimed mine again, bending my neck with a fistful of red hair until I moaned and handed myself completely into his control. He was merciless while I was meek. He was dominant while I yielded.

He took everything and I let him.

Demanding.

Feral.

Consuming.

Arthur was everywhere at once.

In my mind.

My heart.

My soul.

His taste.

His scent.

His heat.

He planted a hand on my sternum, forcing me backward until my spine met marble. My rib cage strained against flushed and sweat-misted skin. My breathing was wild and loud.

"Fuck, Cleo. You're so goddamn beautiful." His fingertips trailed my exposed skin. My tattoos glowed beneath the Edison bulbs and my scars shone with disfigurement. I was both inked and ugly but in Arthur's eyes, I was exquisite.

"I'll never tire of looking at you." Something hungry and dangerous flashed over his face; his fingers dug into my multihued skin. "You're my miracle."

I tried to rise—to grab at his T-shirt and jerk off his boxer briefs. But he shoved me back roughly, pinning me in place. I didn't care that he was brusque. I didn't care that my back twinged with pain.

I was in pleasure heaven.

I need him.

He commanded, "Don't move. I need to look at you. I need—"

I moaned as his hand fell down his front, cupping his hard length and squeezing. "Goddammit, I want you."

"Take me, then," I whimpered.

Arthur yanked my hips forward. We groaned in perfect unison as his hardness molded with my damp panties. I couldn't stay still as he grinded unashamedly. I was stuck between cold marble and the hard heat of him.

My breath caught as his hands moved from my thighs to scrape against my naked rib cage, slinking upward. His thumb grazed the underside of my breasts.

I moaned again. "Please, Art. Stop teasing me. Take me."

"God, I love it when you beg." He thrust against my panties. "Tell me what you want." His voice was deep and gruff, threaded with lust and need.

Heat was everywhere. My head fell back as he cupped my breast, tweaking my nipple with dexterous fingers.

"I want you to fill me. I want you to bite me. I want you to do anything you want to me."

My stomach melted; my core grew wet. I'd never wanted someone this much before. Never found utopia in a simple touch echoing with unspoken adoration and power.

I tugged his T-shirt. I needed skin on skin.

Arthur got the message. Grabbing the material, he ripped it over his head. His chest was broad and tanned. His muscles created grooves and shadows, leading toward a perfect trail of hair disappearing into his boxer briefs.

My mouth watered.

I reached out and traced the shape of his erection, barely contained by the black material.

He shuddered; green fire blazed in his eyes. "God, you drive me insane."

I had no reply. I was past speaking.

Arthur fumbled with my panties. His fingers brushed against my damp core.

I shot off the counter at the barest pressure. The spindles of an orgasm twisted and teased.

Arthur wrenched my panties down, tugging angrily as they caught around my ankles. In his rush, he ripped the delicate lace. "Oops." His face transformed with a grin even as lines feathered around his eyes from his never-ending headache.

I beamed, falling deeper into love with this complicated man. "You're rich. You can buy me another pair."

"If it were up to me, you'd never wear underwear again. I could slink my fingers inside you whenever I damn well pleased."

I suffered a full-body convulsion. "Consider it done."

With a harsh growl, he tossed the tattered lace away. It was a beast of a sound, not from a man, but a lusty male who was past the point of reason.

His eyes dropped, feasting on my exposed, glistening sex.

Soaring upright, I grabbed his biceps, digging my fingernails into his flesh. "Please... Arthur." His flesh was on fire. "Come here." My skin missed his skin. My lips wanted his lips.

He pounced on me, mouth crushing mine. I tasted urgency on his tongue, the metallic tint of desperation. He needed this as much as I did. Something drove us. Something primitive.

It was my turn to fumble with his boxer briefs. Spearing my fingers through the waistband, I pulled them with no finesse. The tip of him escaped, then his girth, until finally his tight and drawn up balls were revealed.

Without moving away, he shoved the tight material farther down his legs and kicked them away.

Naked, I spread my legs wider, beyond ready for him to take me.

But Arthur had other ideas.

Bending over me, he scooped me from the unforgiving marble and carried me from the kitchen. My legs wrapped around him, pressing my core directly against his erection.

We both gasped. Arthur paused in his stumble to kiss me—savage and swift. Then we were moving again, swaying with sexual need and lurching with lust.

I rode him. I didn't care. I rubbed against him like a cat in heat. I had to find some relief from the bonfire in my blood. The flames that'd marked me now lived inside, whipping around until I boiled with desire.

"Arthur, I have to have you inside me." Sinking my teeth into his shoulder, he groaned as I bit harder than I ever had before.

We'd passed soft caresses and tender touches. I wanted to be bruised and to bruise. I wanted to mark him while seeking beatific pleasure.

"God, Cleo. You've poisoned me. Your lips are fucking venom. I'll never get enough of you." His voice was thick as he stumbled toward the couch. The sliding doors were wide open, the dark evening hiding onlookers and witnesses.

Before I could worry about being watched, Arthur dropped me. I sailed through the air, then hissed as my back connected with the sofa. The ache from being thrown was nothing to the way it amplified the fire inside. I loved that he was so far gone to be gentle with me. I loved that he felt the same way I did—dangerous with desire.

The moment I was horizontal, he climbed on top of me, smothering me into the cushions. He gave me no time to adjust to his weight or heat.

"Oh, God!" I cried out as one long finger disappeared into my heat.

"I want to crawl inside you and never fucking leave." His voice and the way he hooked his digit inside hurtled me toward a searing orgasm.

My back arched; all reasoning shot out of my head. Holy sex on fire, his finger was amazing. Slow and firm, curving and stroking. He pushed another finger deep. I bit his shoulder, piercing his skin, my nails scrabbling at his back.

I had to have him. *Now.*

Reaching between us, I squeezed his cock. With my other hand, I grabbed his ass, trying to guide him inside me. I shivered as his butt clenched beneath my touch, his hips pulsing with need just as strong as mine.

He didn't stop touching or kissing me. It was as if his new mission in life was to make me insane. "Now," I demanded.

He laughed, shaking his frame, causing unique sensations with his fingers inside me. "Always so bossy."

"Do it."

"What if I want to lick you first? What if I want your taste on my tongue?"

"Later. Please, God, later."

He chuckled, loving my unraveled behavior. "Do you need something, Buttercup?"

"You know I do!" Frustration wobbled my voice.

My skin blazed as he kissed my neck. He cupped my core, grinding the heel of his palm over my clit.

Shit.

"You can have me, then, woman." The animalistic lust on his face tore a moan from my lips. I pumped his cock, working him so his eyes snapped closed. He shuddered in my grasp.

I wiggled closer, guiding him with my hand. My world ceased to spin as I pushed his tip inside me.

His eyes flew open.

He swallowed a curse.

Then he gave up and thrust into my heat.

I cried out.

I welcomed completely.

My skin enveloped him, sucking him deeper until there was no space between us.

Arthur froze as I moved my hips.

He felt so good. So thick, so long, so mind-shatteringly *good*. My entire being was full, every nerve ending sparking. Frustration built. I needed a release. *Why isn't he moving?*

"Art—take me. Fuck me. I'm begging you."

His breathing turned heavy and noisy, his face scrunched up.

He's in pain.

From holding back his orgasm?

I didn't care if he spurted inside me with no other movement than a quick rock. I could come. My release would obey my summons to explode the next second he thrust. I was achingly sensitive.

But...he didn't.

He didn't open his eyes or thrust.

I scratched his back, bit his ear, yet he stayed frozen. His biceps bunched as he clutched the cushion behind my head.

"Arthur?" I raked my nails down his back. "I'm begging you to fuck me, President Kill."

He gave a half chuckle, half choke. "I...I can't. I'm on the edge as it is." His hand stilled my hips, stopping me. "Give me a second."

My core screamed for release. This wasn't fair. He promised me something he couldn't deliver. He was the one to grab me. He was the one to bring us to this point with no conclusion.

I twisted beneath him. "Yes you can. I want to come together. I don't care if it doesn't last long."

I didn't think he'd obey. But with a furrowed frown, Arthur pressed his hips into me.

Once.

Twice.

My vision glazed over. *Yes.* Something built incredibly fast. It gathered and congregated. It hovered hard and determined in my belly. *Yes.*

Arthur stopped. He inhaled as if he'd run miles. His face shone with sweat. "Cleo...wait."

No, don't do this to me. "Don't stop." I bit his ear. Needing this orgasm, needing to feel connected to him—to let go of our tension through pleasure—I grabbed his ass and sank my nails into his flesh. "Take me."

He cursed and lost control. He thrust into me, pressing me deep into the sofa.

He dropped his walls and gave in.

We rode each other as if any moment one of us would disappear. We claimed each other. We adored each other.

"Yes!"

His strokes lost all sophistication and turned downright dirty.

I *loved* it.

With each stroke, I panted faster and faster. I was so focused on where we joined, his lips on my neck, hands on my breasts, and cock driving inside me that everything else ceased to exist.

My release began with a pleasure-pain I'd never experienced before. Building, building. Seeping energy from my cells and centering them in one part of me screaming with feeling.

Arthur grunted. Skin slapped against skin.

And that was it.

I screamed and shattered. I was delirious with sharp spasms, swept away by passion, completely besotted in the way he made me explode.

I didn't hear the agonizing moan from Arthur.

I didn't see the whitewash of his skin.

I was far, far away.

I was spiraling into bliss.

I was self-obsessed, self-absorbed, self-consumed as my lover slipped away from me.

I didn't notice.

How did I not notice?

Arthur never did come with me.

His elbows buckled, his body crumbled.

And he fell into unconsciousness.

Chapter Fourteen

Kill

I'd died today.

I hadn't meant to. Not that anyone meant to die. I'd drowned at the beach when I'd lost my footing and became a wave's plaything. I wouldn't be alive if it wasn't for my brother. He'd been the only one there. Despite our strained relationship, he'd risked his life to bring me back to shore. He'd given me CPR. He'd saved my life. I owed him. But Cleo didn't like my newfound tolerance for my brother. She'd tried to warn me. Tried to distance me from my family. But they were my family. I couldn't turn my back on them. —Arthur, age fifteen

"Will he be okay?"

Will who be okay?

"He'll be fine."

Who will be fine?

"I told him last night to avoid rigorous exercise. The swelling in his brain hasn't diminished enough to raise his blood pressure to such extremes."

"It wasn't planned . . . it sort of just happened."

A sniff, then a condescending quip. "Yes, well. Next time, don't let him break my rules and no sex."

Sex!

Everything came tumbling back. Shit, the last thing I remembered was the sensation of champagne bubbles building at the base of my spine. That feeling was common and known: I was about to come. My heart was racing. My thoughts were spinning. My cock was thrusting.

And then... *nothing.*

What the hell happened?

The pain inside my skull invaded the rest of my body. My neck throbbed with crippling aches. I felt as if squeezed with a vise, my back crippled with aches. I felt as if someone had taken an axe to my spinal column.

Cracking open my eyes, the lounge came into focus, along with the smell of cooking, stickiness of sex, and nausea of concussion.

My limbs took a while to register ownership, and I twitched as I came fully awake. A blanket over my hips tickled as it began to slide downward.

Snatching it quickly, I cupped the area of my body that'd gotten me into this mess.

Doctor Laine's warning last night came back.

"You'll be fine if you take it easy. Rest. No exercise or stress. Take these tablets three times a day with food and drink plenty of water."

I'd always been stubborn; ignoring doctor's advice was a forte of mine. Pity it'd backfired so completely.

Tilting my head on the pillow, I assessed who was in the room with me.

"Holy fuck." I grabbed my chest, trying to keep my heart from seizing as Cleo and Doctor Laine suddenly loomed over me from the back of the couch. They had twin expressions of concern.

"Ah, good, you're awake." Doctor Laine bent over and pressed cool fingers against my clammy forehead. "You haven't been out for too long, so you shouldn't suffer anymore side effects."

I flinched away from her touch, scowling. "How long?"

"I got here within ten minutes of receiving Mrs. Killian's call." She looked at Cleo. "So, what? About fifteen minutes would you say?"

Cleo nodded. "No more than that." Her hair crackled with static, her cheeks painted with worry. "Arthur, do you remember where you are?"

At some point in my snooze, she'd slipped on a black knee-length dress. Everything about her yelled sex—from her wild hair to her pink and kiss-swollen lips. My eyes drifted to her chest; her breasts were braless, taunting me with pebbled nipples.

I clenched my jaw as my cock came back to life. "Yes. I remember where I am, who you are, and what we were doing before..."

Doctor Laine snorted. "Typical man. What did I tell you last night?"

When I didn't respond, she stood upright and listed on her fingers. "No exercise, no stress, no sex, and under no circumstances, no strenuous activities such as heavy lifting." Narrowing her eyes at the kitchen and discarded clothing leading toward the couch, she pursed her lips. "I think everything I told you not to do—you just did." Planting her hands on her hips, she snapped, "Feel happier knowing you aren't superman and should've listened to the woman you paid a fortune to ensure you heal?"

A grin tugged at my mouth. Who knew? The doc had a temper.

Cleo moved to sit beside me, patting my leg through the blanket she'd draped over me to protect my decency. "We won't do it again, Doctor."

My eyes snapped to hers. *Like hell we won't.*

"No, you definitely won't." Doctor Laine wagged a finger in my face. "Because if you do, you might not get up again, or you might kill off more brain cells and wake up a completely different person."

Ice water joined the rocks inside my head, freezing me solid.

Wallstreet would have a fucking fit if he knew what I'd done. The upcoming battle with my father was only half the war. The other half didn't rely on fists and bullets but negotiation and public speaking.

I have to be personable and quick—not a fucking dim-witted buffoon.

How could I risk being such an idiot when my livelihood was on the line?

I shivered as Cleo gripped my thigh. Her fingers landed so damn close to my cock.

That's why I played roulette with my brain. Her.

Buttercup was my Achilles' heel—a witch who made me hot, hard, and so fucking weak.

Her green eyes flickered from me to the Doc. "Um, excuse me if I'm slow to catch up, but what do you mean? Kill *more* brain cells?"

I stiffened. "Nothing. She meant nothing." Digging my hands into the soft cushions, I propelled myself upright. The room spun, but I deliberately kept the vertigo and throbbing pain from showing on my face. "Thank you, Doc. I feel ten times better and would like to get dressed."

The doctor looked at me with far too much understanding in her gaze. She knew I was embarrassed, pissed, but, most of all, scared shitless that this seemingly simple thing had the power to strip me of everything I knew.

Is this how Cleo felt with amnesia?

I shook my head—that hurt far too much to even consider.

"Yes, thank you for coming again." Cleo stood. Her face was gentle but her eyes burned with questions—no doubt preparing to spit them in my face the moment we were alone.

"I'll see you out." Planting my feet on the carpet, I tugged the blanket tighter around my waist.

"No, just stay there." Doctor Laine pressed my shoulder. "Rest, remember?" Letting me go, she cocked her head toward the kitchen. "I've left some higher dose anti-inflammatories for you on the counter. Take four in the next twenty-four hours, then stop. They'll destroy your stomach lining and you'll have more problems to deal with if you don't."

I nodded. "Got it."

Rolling her eyes, she nodded at Cleo. "If you need me again, you have my number on speed dial. Goodbye, Mrs. and Mr. Killian."

Cleo flushed.

My heartbeat picked up, imagining an existence where we became irrevocably joined. My insatiable need to make it a reality almost had me dropping to a fucking knee right there.

With one last disapproving look, Doctor Laine disappeared briskly from the lounge and the faint click of the front door was the starting gun for Cleo's impending tirade.

She spun around, her soft flush transforming to bright anger.

I tensed in preparation for her onslaught.

I waited...

Only, it never happened.

I glanced at her from the corner of my eye. My heart splintered as a single tear rolled down her cheek. "Ah, Buttercup...don't."

She swiped at her cheeks, backing away from the couch. "Don't 'Buttercup' me." Dragging hands through her lust-tangled hair, she bared her teeth. "You passed out while inside me, Arthur! Do you have any idea how *terrifying* that was? How scared I was when you wouldn't wake up? How much I screamed when I had to roll you off me and felt you slip out of me like you were *dead*?"

She wrapped her arms around herself, trembling. "It was awful! And what's worse—it was all *my* fault!"

I sat forward, clutching my head in my hands. "It wasn't your fault."

"Yes, it was. You wanted to stop. You kept trying to go slow and I forced you."

My own temper unfurled. "This isn't about you, Cleo. I knew better, but I have no fucking control when it comes to you."

"See, my fault again!" A sob existed behind her sharpness.

Standing, I moved toward her. I had to hold her. Had to apologize. Holding out my hand, I murmured, "I'm sorry."

She stumbled away. "What is going on with you? Why won't you tell me?" Taking a shaky breath, her voice turned cold. "I'll tell you why. Because you're pigheaded and arrogant and think you're invincible. You've hidden your pain all your life. You never trusted me to help you."

Her face twisted but she didn't break down. "Well, newsflash for you, Killian. *You are mine.* If you're not well, I need to know. If you're keeping things from me, I deserve to be informed. Now that you're awake, I need…I need some time alone. I can't deal with your secrets anymore."

Her voice disappeared to an axe-sharp whisper. "You can't keep things from me. I won't let you. You've always had every part of me— but I never had all of you. And that…that hurts me so much."

Before I could argue, she ran.

I'd never shared a house with a pissed off female before.

It officially fucking sucked.

Cleo somehow managed to fill the house with her outrage, spreading it in every room. Everywhere I moved, her petulance followed me. It redecorated the entire place, successfully making me feel like a jackass.

I didn't know if I was meant to go to her or wait until she came to me, but by eleven p.m. I'd had enough.

I'd taken my prescribed drugs but my head was no better. I'd spent a few hours trading—which was absolutely fucking useless. And all I wanted to do was sleep again.

She'd had five hours to stew. It was time to get over it and let me make it up to her.

You're banned from sex.

As much as I wanted to, I couldn't afford to be so reckless again. I'd sensed the entire time I held her on the countertop and seduced her that I wouldn't last. Every pump of blood that'd disappeared into my trousers had clanged warning bells behind my eyes. The lance in my brain grew to epic proportions the more I gave in to her spell.

And you fucking passed out while inside her.

I groaned.

Turning the lights off downstairs, I climbed the stairs with one heavy footfall after another.

I held the banister—which I never normally did—just to be on the safe side in case my brain decided tumbling to my demise would be worthwhile.

"I missed you," a soft whisper sounded in the dark.

I stopped short, willing my eyes to acclimatize to the lack of light. That was another thing I noticed from this fucking concussion. My eyes weren't quick to adjust, remaining fuzzy on the outskirts despite my immense concentration.

Doctor Laine had said she saw no reason why my intelligence wouldn't be the same as it was before—if I graced my body with enough time to do what it needed to do.

Only problem was, I had shit hanging over my head. My future was as complicated as a demolition building in a highly populated area. I only had eyes on one destruction but if I didn't manage it closely, it could end up taking out entire blocks of innocents.

Cleo finally came into focus. I frowned at the way her knees were drawn up to her chin, her arms wrapped around her shins. She looked lost, afraid, and uncertain.

I did that to her.

Squatting before her, I kept hold of the spindle of the banister. "What are you doing sitting on the stairs?"

"Waiting for you."

My headache twinged. "Why didn't you come get me?"

"Because I'm mad at you."

I smiled. She was too damn cute pouting and pissed off. Tucking a cascade of hair over her shoulder, I trailed my fingertips along her cheekbone.

She shivered, sucking in a breath.

"Don't be mad at me. I hate it when you're angry."

"Then don't keep things from me." She moved her face from my touch, her green eyes the only color in the darkness.

I sighed heavily. "I was only sparing you from the details. I didn't want you to worry."

"How about giving me those details so I can be prepared? Having you just black out while making love to me hasn't exactly given you a gold star."

I chuckled. "I didn't know I was on a rating system."

She pursed her lips.

Moving to sit beside her, I nudged her shoulder with mine. "Okay, you want to know? Fine. My brain is swollen. The doctor gave me some rules that I should've followed, but I didn't." I shrugged. "I paid the consequences. Simple as that."

She turned to face me, her gaze sparkling with new sprung anger. "No, not simple as that. What else. You're keeping something else from me. I want to know. Right now."

What do you want to know?

The fact I will murder my own flesh and blood in a few days?

The fact I made a promise to hand my life over to a cause that I believe in completely but now feel as if it's controlling me?

Or the fact that no matter what I do with my life, it's never enough? That I always second-guess—think I could've done better—done more?

I massaged my temples. *She doesn't need to know any of that.* "I'm having trouble with certain parts of my life."

"Like what?"

"Like trading and mathematics," I said quietly, knowing the moment I said it aloud, Cleo would pity me. But it was the easiest detail to give.

"Oh, God, Arthur."

And there it was.

Fucking pity.

"But you've always relied on numbers."

No shit.

"I know." Forcing myself to sound optimistic, I said, "But the doctor assured me there's no reason why it won't come back, so...I'm not gonna dwell on it."

Cleo didn't respond.

Instead, she stood up and held out her hand. "Come on."

Eyeing her cautiously, I stood up and placed my hand in hers. She was so tiny, so delicate, so *breakable*, yet strong enough to put up with me and my mess. And my life was a fucking mess. With more on the horizon.

Her green eyes remained glossy and deep, but the pity I feared faded into conviction and courage.

My cock twitched, setting fire to every bruise and twinge.

Stop that.

No sex. No orgasm. No pleasure until I got this under control.

Closing the distance, her arms wrapped around me.

My heart clenched, then drowned in love for her.

I squeezed her close. Goddammit, it'd been a rough few days. All I wanted to do was slip inside her again, make her shatter, and then sleep. Preferably in that order.

But she wasn't on the menu.

Her tiny fingers landed on my chest. "Remember when I first arrived? You tried to climb these stairs with that knife wound bleeding you dry and almost passed out on the first rung."

I kissed the tip of her nose. "I was trying to run away from you."

"Why?"

"Why do you think?"

Her face fell. "Because you hated me."

Christ, no.

"Wrong. It was because you made me feel something I never wanted to feel again. I wanted you—fuck how I wanted you—but I hated that I wanted you, too."

She inhaled hard. "Why?"

"Because by wanting you, I was being a traitor to your memory."

I held her away from me, staring into her eyes. "Guilt is as much a part of me as breathing. Every damn day I suffered with it, knowing I'd ruined us, your family, myself. Every time I craved company, I drowned in guilt because I couldn't have you. I could never have the woman I loved because of what I'd done."

She stretched on her toes and kissed me. "How many times do I need to tell you? You didn't do any of that." Her fingertips circled my heart. "Cut out that guilt. It has no reason to be there anymore."

Unable to speak, I tucked her into my side and together we climbed the last step and headed toward the bedroom. Once inside, I spun her around and undid the zipper holding her black dress in place. She didn't argue as I slid the metal teeth apart and let the material slip from her shoulders.

Her gorgeous body of scars and ink stole the remaining intelligence I had left. I morphed back into the boy I'd been—a boy who'd never forgotten his perfect soul mate and now somehow had her for all eternity.

Gathering her close, I kissed her shoulder, slinking my hands to massage her back. "I never let anyone else into my heart, yet the second I saw you bound and gagged and covered in mud, I fell in love with you all over again. I cheated on you with you. I found comfort from missing you with you. And it fucking killed me to think I was moving on when all I wanted to do was live in the past."

She captured my face. "I hate that I left you behind. I hate that I caused you so much pain. But I can say that even though I didn't remember, I never stopped loving you. Your eyes haunted my dreams. Your touch and smell were phantoms in my life—tugging me back to you." She kissed me, her tongue hesitantly licking my bottom lip. I opened for her, welcoming her taste into my mouth.

She relaxed into the kiss. "There was never anyone else for me."

"You could've moved on," I panted, never tearing my lips away from hers, kissing her and feeding words directly into her mouth. "You had a choice."

Her fingers dug into my cheeks. "I *never* had a choice, Art. Never."

Her soft kiss turned demanding—a need to confirm we were both still alive. My cock swelled and as much as I wanted to break the rules, I couldn't.

I wanted to grow old with her.

I wanted her all the days and all the nights I had left on this earth.

I wouldn't risk her—not now I had her back.

"Wait here," I whispered, kissing her one last time.

Moving before she had time to quarrel, I disappeared into the bathroom and turned on the taps of the large bath. Waiting until the water temperature was perfect, I slipped out of the jeans and T-shirt I'd shrugged into after Doctor Laine had gone and prowled back to the bedroom.

Cleo stood gloriously naked exactly where I left her. Her flat stomach was smooth and perfect while the shiny scars licked her right side and the pretty blue flowers and hidden star signs decorated her left.

She's like a colorful constellation.

Her mouth parted as I looped my fingers with hers and guided her toward the bathroom.

My headache pounded harder, keeping up a rhythm with my racing heartbeat and throbbing dick.

Calm down.

No fucking way did I want to pass out again.

This wasn't about sex or lust.

This was about *more*.

A purging of sorts—washing ourselves free from the past and embracing the present.

Stepping over the rim of the bath, I gently guided Cleo into the warm water until it lapped around our waists. My breathing becoming faint as my vision stuttered. The sound of gushing taps and steam spirals filled the bathroom as Cleo melted into the heat and reclined against my chest.

Having her surrender to me, with her breasts floating and breaking the film of the water and her eyes at half-mast sent my heart racing for an entirely different reason. And when her head lolled dreamily and rested between my shoulder and base of my neck, I crushed her to me with far too much strength.

She squeaked but didn't complain. I didn't do anything but hold her wordlessly. Her vulnerability gave me power. Her submission gave me peace.

Words weren't needed.

Conversation not required.

The soft mist and condensation did a much better job, drenching us in silent feelings.

I'd never known how she could make me feel invincible one second, then hopeless the next. Her love did that—it was an elixir and a curse. Something that would be forever at odds with my world and everything I currently stood for.

Reaching for the expensive soap that my maid stocked, I slowly washed her chest.

She purred as I massaged her shoulders, touching her all over. Ungluing her head from my shoulder, she looked lazily into my eyes. Without a sound, her tiny hand disappeared behind her and wrapped around my cock.

What the hell is she doing?

"Cleo—" I hissed as she held me tighter. "You heard the doctor; you need to stop."

She would have to be the one to pull away.

I couldn't make her. I had no willpower. None. My life as well as my dick was in her hands.

She didn't let me go, nor did she stroke me either—just continued to hold me as if I were a possession. "I have a point to make." Her fingers squeezed. "Hopefully, I have your utmost attention this way."

My balls twitched. I swallowed hard. "You have my undivided concentration."

I groaned as she tightened her fingers again. "I've always belonged to you, Art. Only you."

My blood pressure pinged, screaming like a kettle about to explode.

"I know." Blissful sensation gathered stronger. My head thickened. "And you know I've always belonged to you. But by Christ, Cleo... you. Have. To—"

"Not yet."

I gritted my teeth.

I couldn't stop her. Even though she didn't move, her grip felt too fucking good.

"Shit...it's too much." The room went dark. "You have to stop."

"It's always too much with you," she breathed. "Everything about you is too much. Your size, your love, your generosity, your wealth." She tilted her chin, her lips grazing mine. "But no matter how much I get of you, it's never enough. I can't even stay mad at you because I understand the way you think. And I can't punish you even when you hurt me so much by hiding."

Her other hand rose from the water, raining droplets over my chest as her fingers twined into my hair. "You terrified me, Art. You cut out my heart when you passed out inside me and I'll never forget the feeling of losing you in my embrace." Holding me hostage, her lips pressed against mine.

I grunted with pain. My vision went completely black. I had no idea where I was or how to fucking stay sane. "Goddammit, Buttercup. *Stop*."

My hips twitched. My cock wanted every squeeze and stroke she gave, even as my brain wept at the thought of passing out again.

I hoped she'd ignore me and straddle me.

I hoped she'd obey me and grant me mercy.

I hoped for so many things.

And I ached with bitter disappointment when she finally surrendered and let me go.

Blood rushed into my balls; my vision stuttered into pieces.

"Consider that a warning, Art. Hurt me by hiding important things again and I'll make sure you know firsthand how it felt."

My heart struggled to calm.

In that moment, I saw the firecracker teenager who I fell so fucking hard for. I remembered why I'd been equally enamored and terrified of her. She turned me on, excited me, but ultimately ruled me with just one touch of her tiny hands and one reprimand of her perfect voice.

I understood why she'd ignored the parameters I'd been set. I knew why she'd done what she had and I didn't blame her.

I hurt her. And she needed me to see just how much.

"I'm sorry."

Her hands fell away; a single kiss lingered on my lips. Her voice wrapped around me as gently as the steam from our bath. "I love you, Arthur Killian. I would do anything for you and I promise to adore you forever. But if you *ever* cut me out to protect me again. If you keep secrets or hide, I won't be the sweet girl you remember."

I know.

Her green eyes sparked. The atmosphere changed to electric. I didn't need to ask who she'd become if I hurt her again—I recognized the fiery girl from my past, now transformed into a woman in my arms. But I wanted her to know I took her seriously. That she'd proven her point rather eloquently. "Who will you be?"

She stroked my thighs beneath the water, her nails skating threateningly. "I'll be the woman who will make you pay."

Her words echoed in my heart, heavy with warning.

How did I think I could continue to live a singleton life? How did I think I would ever get anything past this woman?

I've been a fucking fool.

Hugging her close, I vowed, "No more hiding."

Her body melted into mine. "No more hiding."

Her head turned, her mouth inviting.
A kiss sealed our vow.
She was mine. I was hers.
Our problems had to be shared.
Our successes equally celebrated.
I would have to tell her ... everything.

Chapter Fifteen

Cleo

Were love and hate the same thing?

They must've been because I had no other explanation for how I felt about Arthur. One moment, I wanted to smother him in kisses, the next I wanted to steal my father's gun and shoot him in the leg. He was so strong but sometimes so stupid. Couldn't he see what I was offering? Couldn't he see what his father was doing? His mother saw it, but she was too frail to intervene. Well, I wasn't frail and I wasn't afraid. And I wouldn't put up with idiotic behavior any longer. —Cleo, diary entry, age thirteen

Three days.

That was the allotted prescription that Doctor Laine advised.

Three days of rest and recuperation.

Needless to say it wasn't easy to get Arthur to submit. He kept growling about time frames and battle dates. Mo and Grasshopper were constant visitors, locking themselves in a room with their president, cooking up plans and discussing war.

Every day I henpecked Arthur like the bossy woman he claimed I was. I made sure he ate, drank, took his pills, and even took to watching him at night to ensure he was dreaming and not unconscious.

I couldn't shake the fright I'd had when he'd squished me against the couch and passed out. The sensation of having his body inside me, then feeling the withdrawal of his intelligent mind as he slipped away scarred me for life.

I meant what I said. I would hurt him if he kept anything from me again.

He'd turned me into this neurotic mess. He was responsible for putting me back together again.

I jumped at the smallest noise—fearing he'd fallen. I eavesdropped on conversations—scared that he might suddenly start slurring.

I was a wreck.

And facts were facts—Arthur was a *terrible* patient. He tolerated me hovering, but he finally put his foot down on the third day.

He was in his office, busy placing trades on foreign currency pairs that he'd tried to teach me about but gave up when my eyes glazed over. The way he delivered his endless wealth of knowledge was stilted—punctured with awkward pauses and hovering with quavering confusion.

The fear in his eyes belied his true thoughts and I didn't need to ask what scared him the most.

I believed he used those teaching sessions for himself to recall what he knew—not to teach me what I didn't. I didn't want him overthinking that those skills were lost. I believed in Doctor Laine. He would remember.

He will.

It would just take patience.

I placed the meat lovers pizza beside his keyboard, and he looked up, jerked from whatever world he existed in while staring at the four glowing screens. Swiveling his chair to face me, he watched as I flipped open the box. "Lunch is served. As you can imagine, it was a mammoth effort to hunt and slaughter something as wily as a pizza."

"Thanks."

My heart fell. I willed him to crack a smile. The more hours that passed, the more he acted as if he was under house arrest. Couldn't he see I was only trying to heal him so he could be whole once again?

Looking back at the screens, he distractedly handed me a piece of meat lovers.

Arthur might've killed bare-handed, controlled a Club of anarchist bikers, earned millions trading countless stock markets, but he was still the boy I knew from all those years ago. Still fixated on math—to the point of unhealthy obsession.

I eyed him while taking a bite.

The temperature in his office seemed determined to rival an Amazon rain forest, yet Arthur wore low-slung black shorts and dark grey hoody. He looked like a young college professor on a sabbatical with messy hair, five o'clock shadow, and tomato sauce smearing his lips, whereas I wore a blue maxi dress and cursed the heat.

Why was he wearing a sweater? Was feeling the cold another symptom of his concussion?

He said he felt much better, but the shadows in his eyes hinted that he was lying.

Again.

Seemed my threat in the bath three days ago wasn't working.

I almost wished I'd gone to medical school, rather than veterinary college—then I might be better equipped at healing him. Being in his office reminded me of stitching him up, leveling a gun at him, and suffering bone-deep knowledge that he was more than just a trafficker—I'd known.

And I hadn't given up.

Just like I won't give up now.

Taking a seat in the extra office chair, I chewed a mouthful of pepperoni. "Perhaps we should get the doctor back? Make sure you're okay?"

Arthur swallowed, wiping his mouth with the back of his hand. "You don't trust me?"

The air sparkled with a sudden argument. "What's that supposed to mean?"

Oh, God. I don't want to fight.

I put my pizza down. "I just mean I don't want you pretending you're better when you're not."

"And who says I'm not?"

I looked away, hiding the fire in my soul. "Whatever, Art. It's your head. Your pain." Snatching up my pizza, I waggled it in his face. "But if you suddenly pass out or drop dead, I'll curse you forever." My voice dropped with conviction. "Your life is now mine and it's your responsibility to make sure you look after it, because if you don't...I'll be..."

"You'll be what?" His voice was heavy and soft.

My heart did a little skip as he swallowed another mouthful.

"I'll be pissed, all right? I love you far too much to let you leave me."

Suddenly, the pizza slice went flying and he tackled me against my chair. His mouth smashed against mine. He swept me away with a consuming kiss tasting of passion and oregano until I forgot why I was mad and gave in to his command.

My legs parted, my nipples tightened, my core melted.

Then a little bell chimed, wrenching Arthur's mouth from mine and stealing his attention.

I *hated* that little bell.

"Fuck!" He shoved away the pizza box, clicking his mouse furiously as a red dot on one of the screens swooped out of its little quadrant and shot past a blue line.

"What? What happened?"

"The fucking pair bombed. Ran straight through my stop loss in a matter of seconds. Christ, how I did I screw that up so badly?"

My heart raced at the rage and fear in Arthur's tone.

"Perhaps it's a bad day for that currency?"

He shook his head. "My system was foolproof." His eyes met mine, full of panic. "I just lost a hundred grand. That's the most I've ever lost since I began trading the fucking markets." Fisting his hair, he tugged hard. "Damn brain injury. Damn fucking Rubix!"

"Hey, it will be okay."

"Will it?" he roared. "Because I'm at the end of my fucking rope,

Cleo. I can't…I can't stay here anymore. I need to be doing something. I can't keep letting Mo and Hopper run my last plan for vengeance."

Standing, he hit a key that blanked out the screens and stormed to the door.

"Wait! Where are you going?"

Spinning around, he snapped, "I'm done wasting time. We're going to Pure Corruption."

Grasshopper looked up from a ledger as Arthur barged into the common room with my hand clasped in his, dragging me in his wake. The main space at Pure Corruption was quiet and welcoming, its polished floor-boards and spotlessly clean surfaces so different to Dagger Rose's filth.

Grasshopper beamed. "If it isn't the prez and his old lady."

Arthur threw him a look.

The coolness of the room was welcome after the heat of the late afternoon sunshine. My retinas still had imprints of tire scuffs and slick oil stains from the bright concrete outside Pure Corruption.

Brushing down my jeans and white T-shirt, I gave up trying to hide the dampness of my skin or the sheen of sweat. I missed my maxi dress, but it wasn't exactly the most practical thing to wear on a motorbike.

I tried to untangle my fingers from Arthur's calloused ones. The bike ride here and the bristling tension between us was enough for me to need some space.

After I managed to get free, Arthur threw me a quizzical glance before marching toward Grasshopper and sitting gingerly in a black single-seater beside him. "I need some fucking action, Hopper."

Inching away, I beelined for the blown-up magazine covers on the wall. The high-resolution pictures of the man I loved glared down from their pedestals.

Arthur today looked nothing like yesterday's smooth, sexy, corpo-rate man who'd been primed and photographed.

The subtle backgrounds of the magazines harmonized the juxtaposition of shadowy president with vibrant accents. He looked like an underworld emperor reigning over his lowly minions.

My eyes trailed over the one of him in a tailored suit.

I've never seen him dressed that way.

My heart flurried at the thought.

To run my hands over the silk of a freshly laundered shirt. To coyly remove the cuff links from his wrists before helping him shrug out of the expensive material.

Yes, I would like to see him in a suit.

My mind skipped back to when I'd first arrived. He'd blindfolded me with his tie. He'd trussed me up and took me from behind.

A cocktail of jealousy and nostalgia wedged like a pebble in my tummy. I never got to see him develop from boy to man. Would I be lucky enough to be there while he grew from vengeful to peaceful?

God, I hope so.

Grasshopper and Arthur mumbled too low for me to hear. I let them talk. There was no point interrupting when I had nothing to offer or contribute. They would kill Rubix and Asus. And I didn't object to that plan, but the thought of full-on war frightened me tremendously. Arthur's love for me might be immortal but he was still dangerously human.

His name is Kill. And in return, he's killable.

I had no intention of losing him a second time.

I continued gazing at the covers until Grasshopper stood up and clapped his hands. "I'll arrange it. Leave it with me."

Arthur nodded, running his fingers through his hair.

The silence was like diesel-laced smog, stinking up the room. Unable to stand the murky thoughts or horrible conclusions of what Arthur and his men would embark on over the next few weeks, I said, "I want to know why you're in the *Wall Street Journal* and the *Times*."

Art's head snapped up. The same pain he'd had in his eyes for days glowed bright. Heaving himself out of the chair, he came toward me. His black jeans and T-shirt silhouetted his figure while the brown leather cut glittered with the silver thread of their MC. "It was a way to get my name out there. Wallstreet's idea. Definitely not mine."

Grasshopper followed, pointing at the magazine picture of Arthur sitting behind his desk, glaring at the camera. "That one was taken the morning he surpassed five million—all earned from trading the FX market."

My eyes snapped to Arthur. "Five million?"

Arthur frowned, glowering at the collage of triumphs and downfalls decorating his Clubhouse. "It was the beginning of everything. With money came power and with power came freedom." Forgetting where he was—or perhaps not caring—he hesitantly wrapped his arms around my waist, hugging me close. The tension of our minifight finally dispersed like raindrops on a hot road. "I'm sorry."

Grasshopper kindly gave us some space, drifting away and texting furiously on his phone.

I leaned into Arthur, hugging his forearm around my middle. "Me too."

"I don't want you to worry, Cleo. Whatever is going on inside me will get better. I just need to know you won't hate me while waiting for me to heal."

I flinched. "You think I could do that?"

He shook his head. "The way I'm feeling right now, I keep fearing you'll be gone when I wake, or realize what a liability I am and break my heart." His voice dropped to a tortured strangle. "No matter what you say, I live with the memory of what I did to your parents every goddamn day. I'm worthless and selfish and so damn thoughtless."

My chest throbbed.

"I've sent the message. The Club will rally. Told them to get their asses here in thirty minutes," Grasshopper announced, dimming his phone and returning with his gaze pensive and full of planning. He looked between us, sensing unfinished business but in a way, I was glad he'd interrupted.

Until Arthur found salvation in himself, there was nothing I could do to make his guilt go away.

Arthur nodded. "Good."

"Also Wallstreet called. Told me about the other thing." Grasshopper's eyes told a complete story that I couldn't follow. But Arthur did.

"Great. Tell him the journalist who covered the last leak can have the scoop on this, too. Tell him to set up a meet next week and it's all his."

"You got it."

I looked between the two men, chewing my lip. "Care to share?"

Arthur pinched the bridge of his nose. "I know I promised to tell you everything, but this is complicated."

"You'll find out soon enough, Butterbean." Grasshopper winked. "You'll be freaking proud of him when you do."

I frowned. "Why? What are you planning?"

Arthur kissed the top of my head, clearing his throat. "Something huge. Now, change the subject 'cause we don't have time to get into it."

Grasshopper shifted. The silence became awkward.

Dammit, why can't he just spit out everything and let me decide what's important or not?

Needing to dispel the festering quietness, I asked, "Do you trade, Grasshopper?"

Hopper shook his head, his body unyielding as a brick wall but somehow warm and friendly. "Nope. Too much risk for me. However, I trust Kill to manage a few investments on my behalf."

Arthur chuckled. "A few investments? That's what we're calling it these days?"

"Hush, dude. I like having cash but I don't like people knowing where the decimal point falls." His blue eyes flickered to mine. "No offense. Still not used to never having to worry about money."

The entrance slammed as men trickled in, summoned by Grasshopper. They didn't stay, making their way briskly to the meeting room and disappearing.

My forehead furrowed. "But Wallstreet was rich—wasn't he?" I'd wanted to check online and research Arthur's mentor but hadn't found the time what with being stolen and used as a pawn in a decade-old game. But I listened to my gut and my gut said he was rich—some people just wore money as if their clothing glittered with newly minted dollars.

"You're asking if my father gave me any of that wealth he 'lost'?" Grasshopper highlighted the word with air quotes.

Arthur didn't move, just kept his eyes on the magazine covers.

More men entered the Clubhouse, stomping in boots and leather, being respectful not to interrupt our conversation.

"The answer," Grasshopper said, "is nope. Not a dime. I wasn't exactly Mr. Responsible when I was younger. I don't begrudge him keeping away temptation."

"And you don't hate Arthur for being the chosen one, as it were?"

Art and Hopper sucked in a harsh breath.

What are you doing, Cleo?

"Sorry." I dropped my head. "I didn't mean it like—"

"No, I understand." Grasshopper leaned against the wall, crossing his arms. A relaxed smirk decorated his lips. "Without Kill, the Corrupts would've murdered each other and brought an end to our Club. I always knew what my role would be."

Arthur stiffened, his hard stomach flexing against my back. "Oh really? And what was that?"

Grasshopper's mohawk swayed as his head whipped to face his president. "Wallstreet told me to be by your side at all times. To give you support. Make sure you weren't hurt."

Arthur made a noise in the back of his throat. "Did that include spying on me and reporting back to him?"

Whoa. Where did that come from?

Grasshopper froze. His eyes were the only thing that changed from narrowed to wide. "Wow. Can't believe after all this time, we're finally having this conversation."

More bikers arrived. Somehow, they recognized the tense atmosphere and beelined for the meeting room. Only once they'd disappeared did Arthur let me go. "I've wanted to ask for a while. Now's a good time as any."

I stood adrift, waiting for one of two things: a fight or acceptance. Testosterone thickened the air. It could go either way.

"Yes, I reported to my father, but only on how he'd chosen the right man. He picked you out of everyone, Kill. You're like another son to him and I would never betray you by speaking behind your back."

Arthur didn't make a sound.

Hopper added, "With what you'd lived through you deserved a lot more than suspicion and control. Wallstreet saw that and left you completely in charge. I was nothing more than a friend to you."

Never-ending moments ticked past before Arthur finally nodded. "You've been a good friend, Jared."

Hopper beamed. "And you've been a good leader." Swiping his thumb across his phone, he looked at the time. "Some of the brothers are here. We ought to head to Church, see who's gathered. The rest can join us." Turning to leave, he rubbed his forehead. "Minus the four men on patrol duty and the two shadowing Night Crusaders' every move, of course. They'll have to be updated later."

Arthur grunted in thanks. Yanking me close, he kissed the top of my head. "Ready for your first Pure Corruption meeting, Buttercup?"

Wait. Church is men only . . .

"Yeah, Butterbean. Top-secret stuff." Grasshopper shoved his hands into his pockets, grinning. "What is said can never be revealed—just like that movie with those rules."

Arthur snorted. "You mean *Fight Club*?"

"That's the one."

Cupping my elbow, Arthur guided me toward the back of the large room. "I learned a lot from your father, Cleo. Let me know how I do when compared to Thorn."

I wanted to scream that he should stop comparing himself to anyone. He was Arthur. He was perfect. *He's mine.*

Instead, I asked, "You're taking me to Church?"

Arthur didn't reply as Grasshopper opened the door in invitation. He bowed in my direction. "After you, Butterbean."

"Quit it with that fucking nickname." Arthur cuffed him around the back of his head.

Nervousness tickled my insides with effervescent bubbles as I entered the large oblong room where I'd been taken the day I'd almost been sold. Instead of pizza boxes and beer littering the large table, now it was empty with neatly clasped hands of groomed and gnarly bikers.

I wanted to ask Arthur again if there was some mistake. Surely, I wasn't allowed here.

"Kill!"

"Hey, Prez."

Men shouted out greetings, friendship, and respect.

Oh, God, what am I doing here?

It wasn't that I was afraid of being in a room full of men. It wasn't even that I had no urge to listen to plans about vengeance and mayhem. It was the fact meetings were never done in the presence of women—I was out of place, an infiltrator.

This is a man's domain.

Holding up his hand, Arthur waited until gentle murmurs and sporadic laughter died down. "I'll discuss every facet and answer every question, but prepare yourselves for hard work over the next few days." His green eyes pinned each brother into his seat, glowing with authority. "I want riders sent out to all the Clubs who have agreed to back us. I want memos and emails sent to the Clubs overseas to arrange additional support if required. And I want gossip to spread how fucking raging I am. How unstoppable I'll be. How disastrous things will become for those standing in our way."

The twenty or so Pure Corruption brothers nodded, their fists clenching in preparation. "We'll shout far and wide, Prez. By the end of next week, we'll own this fucking country and everyone who ever betrayed us will be alligator chum."

A shiver shot down my spine.

Arthur suddenly grabbed my wrist and pulled me closer. "As you know, this is Cleo Price. Her father was Thorn Price of Dagger Rose. She's mine. And I want you to welcome her into our family with open fucking arms."

Smiles split leathered faces. Laughs bubbled from mouths.

"I take it your name was never Sarah, then."

My eyes fell on the biker who'd joked and pried for personal information between Art and I the first time I'd been in this room.

I shook my head. "It's a long story."

"Too long, and it's time to begin." Arthur moved away from me, stomping in large black boots to take his appointed throne at the head of the table.

Grasshopper moved, too, yanking out a chair before throwing himself onto the hard seat and tossing his phone onto the table.

Lost, I stood like an out-of-place toy.

Men bowed their heads together, conversation sprouting from all corners in one loud hum.

My ears rang with their masculine deepness, revealing innermost secrets and tales of Pure Corruption.

I wasn't a patched in member. Prospects weren't allowed and definitely not women.

I wasn't even Arthur's officially.

I shouldn't be here.

Inching toward the door, I pressed on the handle and cracked it open.

No one paused in their river of conversation, and I prepared to slip silently through.

"Where the hell do you think you're going?" Arthur asked, planting his palms on the table. Even from here the color of his eyes was muddy and pain-riddled.

I shrugged. I thought it was obvious and what was expected of me. After all, I owned a vagina, not a penis. "Um, giving you guys time to talk."

Men laughed as if I'd quipped the funniest joke in history.

Mo came into the room, striding past me with a smirk. His blond shaggy hair was windswept and sunshine compared to Arthur's brooding darkness. "You're too cute."

I scowled. "*Cute?* Why am I cute?"

Mo laughed. "Because you're still hung up on old Club rules. Haven't you learned anything these past few weeks?"

No, because Arthur refuses to share anything!

Arthur crooked his finger. "There's a seat over there. Take it."

"But I thought you're going to discuss Club—"

"Business—exactly." Arthur pursed his lips. "You have as much right to contribute as every other member here."

My eyes popped wide. "Even though I'm a girl?"

Grasshopper laughed. "After everything you've seen of Pure Corruption and the weirdo that runs it, you still believe meetings are just for guys?" Looking around, he added, "That's a point, where are those two-bit hussies?"

"Don't you fucking talk trash about my old lady, man." A biker curled his fist, waving it dramatically at Hopper. He laughed, showing a grill of gold teeth and softening his threat to a joke. "Wait till you have your own ball and chain—then you'll watch your fucking mouth."

"Can't tie me down, boys." Grasshopper chuckled.

What on earth is going on here?

The joking between these men was so refreshing—so different to the anger and hierarchy of Dagger Rose.

"They've been dealing with the books. Melanie's also been working on befriending more reporters for when Kill decides to make the final move," a biker with a bald head and long beard said, looking at his wristwatch. "I reckon they're only minutes away."

"Oh, and Jane's been typing up that report you asked for, Kill. On the leaked files you handed to the local gossip column last month," another middle-aged biker said.

"Did it get traction?" Arthur asked.

The biker nodded. "Turns out, it did pretty good. Might be a good avenue. Enlighten the housewives first and they can badger their husbands. Then when they hear it mainstream—least the seed's already been planted, if ya know what I mean."

I have no idea what you mean.

My concussion headache had disappeared but listening to this code brought it right back.

When the bikers spoke of these unknown women—working side by side in Club business—my blood blistered with pride. However, my mind couldn't comprehend this fundamental change. What had Arthur created here? Equality for men and women? A true family rather than women simpering to every whim of their men?

"That's a good angle." Arthur nodded. "Let's do more of that. Mo, whatever else we have low-key, leak it to one of the cheap rags. Let's see what sort of unrest we can begin by low-balling it. If we can unseat the current democrat, all the better."

What on earth is he up to?

I'd expected conversations about war and massacres but here they were talking about media, housewives, and God knew what else.

I looked with fresh eyes at the Club. I'd been brought up in a life-style that held no bearing to this new existence. I was lost...but also strangely liberated.

Arthur's eyes landed on mine. He smiled softly. "You're jumping in when we've been juggling these things forever. You'll catch on."

I shook my head in amazement. "What are you doing here?"

"Making the world a better fucking place, that's what," a biker with a topknot replied.

Arthur grinned. "That's about the gist of it." His eyes were bright and reminiscent of the intelligence I was so used to. "I learned everything of what *not* to do in a Club, thanks to our upbringing. I fashioned Pure Corruption on things that didn't work in theirs. And made it my oath to create something unbreakable." He waved once again at the vacant chair. "Sit. Take your place. Time to get to know your new family and learn all our secrets."

Chapter Sixteen

Kill

I wished I was lucky enough to have a father like Thorn Price.

He'd taken me to get my exam results. He'd sat outside the school without any argument, then taken me out for a beer to celebrate earning the highest scores the school had ever seen.

He didn't pry about my fresh bruises. He didn't tease me about how I felt about his daughter.

He was a class fucking act and I was jealous that he wasn't my father.

But then again, I was glad he wasn't mine. If he had been, Cleo never could be. —Arthur, age seventeen

I hid my smile as Cleo edged away from the exit and made her way to the empty chair.

Her features couldn't hide the confusion or questions. She looked amazed and also slightly awed.

I hadn't stopped to think how strange this would be for her. How lost she'd be in our long-term goals. How scrambled she'd feel when she finally learned the truth.

What she saw was still so small. She wasn't ready yet to understand the big picture. Shit, I'd worked on this for four years and still had moments where doubt stuck a gun in my gut. We weren't just taking on cartels or rivals. We weren't just bloodthirsty and violent. We were working for the greater good—only nobody but us knew it yet.

The rule-makers—the stinking government—looked down upon us as lowlife scum on the fringes of society.

They had no idea what was coming.

I mean to change everything.

Once again, I'd dragged Cleo into my world without taking her feelings into consideration. She might not want the level of commitment and lofty aspirations shared by my men. She might not like the goal of reform we'd all been working toward. Shit, for all I knew, she might prefer the way things had always been done—just like the idiots who'd tried to steal my leadership the night Cleo came back to me.

All my worries could've been extinguished with a simple question. But once again, I'd barreled forward with no time to think.

I have to stop doing that.

She had to be first in my life—that was the way love was supposed to be—but in order to do that, I had to finish what I'd started.

We'd lived separate lives and now we needed to find common ground—to learn to coexist.

"It's okay, Cleo. Sit. Stay."

Her eyes flickered to mine.

Our entire childhood, we'd been taught that only full-fledged members were allowed in Church. No wives. No prospects. No children.

Yet here I was ripping up the fucking rule book and treating the meetings like family get-togethers where *everyone* had a voice. And I did mean everyone. Kids were allowed to join if they'd had an issue with school. Parents of members were welcomed if they needed a favor or loan.

We turned no one away and that was why we all fought together. Because we fought *for* each other first and foremost.

Fisting the gavel resting on the table, I rapped it once. "Matchsticks, you're taking notes." I looked over at the potbellied biker. Another thing I'd abolished was set duties. The only three positions were president, VP, and master at arms. I had no time for secretaries or treasurer. We worked better if we were all equal with the barest authority overseeing.

"Sure thing, Prez." Matchsticks pulled the large binder that sat in the center of the table toward him and turned to a fresh page. His stubby fingers curled around a pencil, ready to begin.

I sighed. My head was a motherfucking pickax, but being here... putting things into action helped my temper and soothed the overwhelming helplessness I'd suffered sitting at home.

"Everyone know what happened the past few days?" I glanced around the table. The jokes and gossip halted, everyone ready for business.

"Yes. Details have all been shared," Mo muttered.

The door suddenly swung open, spewing forth the female equivalent of my motorbike-riding soldiers. There was no hint of sequins or perfume. They were business. They were ruthless. They were Pure Corruption.

"Nice of you to join us, woman." Dodge, an excellent mechanic with only nine fingers from a bad factory accident, eyed up Molly as she sashayed into the room. Molly had been with us from the beginning, running the many businesses our Club owned.

More females entered behind her.

They were soft and sexy—but there was an undeniable hardness about them. Something no amount of working in an office or climbing the corporate ladder could achieve. They'd seen evil. They'd married men on the fringes of society. And they helped run our empire with utmost loyalty.

They were also the perfect weapons in spying and covert operations. Secrets were rarely divulged when pried by a gun-slinging biker. But deliver a pretty smile and feminine charms...answers flowed like fucking candy.

"Nice to be here, husband." Tossing her blonde curls, Molly held her head high as she made her way to the chairs ringing the edge of the room. "Did you miss me so much? Or was it because I left you passed out from that thing I did last night and went to work without saying goodbye?"

Men chuckled.

These women were different from ordinary gigglers or whores. These women had been rigorously questioned, chosen, and tested to become patched members as much as their men. And they provided invaluable feedback on certain missions and trades.

However, just because they lived and breathed this place, it didn't mean they knew *everything*. They weren't privy to the recent trafficking or the greyish areas of our life. I protected them from things they wouldn't understand.

The back of my neck throbbed as the room swarmed with members.

There was no space with the new arrivals; the air turned claustrophobic. The entire fucking Clubhouse needed an overhaul—we'd outgrown the building—but until we secured our future goals, we couldn't move or renovate. Wallstreet's orders.

The four women threaded around the room, smiling at their husbands and nodding respectfully in my direction. They all knew the rules: *If you swear allegiance, you behave accordingly.*

In a few moments, the women sat in their designated chairs and trained a menagerie of green, brown, and blue eyes on me.

"Sorry we're late, Prez." Jane, a mousy brown–haired woman, who, according to Muffet was a fucking dynamo in the bedroom, smiled.

Cleo never took her eyes off the newcomers, looking as if she'd never seen a woman before.

Silly Buttercup.

Didn't she know me by now? Of course I would run my Club differently. How many nights had we stayed up late, switching the rules and brainstorming ways to improve this livelihood we'd been born into? Ultimately, I'd designed this Club in her memory. I'd created a place of peace for others, all while I lived a life of torment without her.

"Right, back to the meeting. You all know what we've been work-ing toward. None of what we're about to discuss will be new. However, we do have a new member and it's up to us to inform her."

The wives all turned their attention to Cleo. Interest and friend-ship sparkled in their gaze. Jealousy and pettiness was not allowed—they knew that. It was the one thing I was fucking strict on.

"Cleo." I looked at my woman. My heart fucking swelled until it thrummed against my ribs. "What you're about to hear is everything we've been working toward for four years. Not only was it put into effect to avenge your life, but also to save the lives of so many others."

"Damn straight," Mo said, tense with retribution.

"Eh, Kill?" Piebald's wife, Melanie, piped up.

I cocked my head. "Yes?"

Her blue eyes landed on Cleo, her eyebrow raised. "You can't hon-estly expect us not to focus on the first woman you've ever brought to a meeting. Who is she?"

The other women nodded. "It would be handy to know."

Molly flicked her hair over her shoulder. "Kill doesn't have to answer, girls. That is Cleo Price. Dagger Rose princess. Amnesiac sur-vivor. Long-time lover of our president."

Cleo's jaw hung open.

I wasn't surprised. Molly had an IQ to rival mine.

Not that that's hard with how fucked up my brain currently is.

She was also sharp and quick-witted and kept the small business owners in line with just one stare.

"And now you're one of us." Feifei smiled. Her dusky skin and Chinese origins made her look like a perfect doll. She'd been an ulti-mate temptress, stealing Dodge's heart and joining our family.

"Eh…" Cleo glanced at me, seeking help.

Our eyes locked.

I couldn't hide my desire that Cleo would find happiness within this group. If she was to become completely immersed in my world, she had to become accepted and loved by the Club.

She was it for me. She needed to realize that—along with everyone else in this room.

I smiled. "This is our brotherhood, sisterhood...family. The sooner you get to know them, the better." It was up to her to set rules and boundaries. I wouldn't do it for her. I was her lover, not her fucking jailer.

Looking around the room, I knew some of us might not survive the upcoming war. Death wouldn't take us easily, but nothing was guaranteed in our world. We all knew the risks. We all accepted them in order to do what must be done.

The room was packed with leather and humans—the sooner this meeting was over, the sooner I could get some fresh air. The pounding in my skull only grew worse the stuffier the air became.

Rapping the gavel on the table again, I cleared my throat. "Now that we're all here. Let's begin."

Chapter Seventeen

Cleo

*H*e loved it.

It was worth the excessive price tag. The moment I'd given Art the Libra-shaped eraser, something had changed between us. It was as if his eyes were opened, like he'd finally noticed me after all this time. He wanted me as much as I wanted him. I knew that now, and I wouldn't stop until he was mine completely. —Cleo, diary entry, age thirteen

"Rubix and Asus Killian, along with every member of Dagger Rose who won't repent, will be slaughtered with no fucking mercy."

The room instantly lost its friendly buzz, heading straight into cut-throat. Arthur's voice—as deep and comforting as velvet—switched to a savage scrawl. "You always knew this day would come and I prepared you for it. You know what is expected of you and I also know what a sacrifice it might be. But they deserve to fucking die again and again for what they've done."

The men sat taller.

The women shuffled closer.

This was no longer about wealth or company or comfort. The Club—with just a few sentences from its leader—switched into a machine I recognized. A machine evolved to fight, murder, and pillage. Bikers lived on the outskirts of the law for a reason. We made our homes in the grey, impervious to right and wrong.

Arthur had achieved the impossible by turning people who fought against authority into a close-knit team, but at the same time they were still ruthless, still terribly dangerous.

"Over the past three days, Grasshopper has been collecting intel on where Rubix and his Club fled to." Rubbing a hand over his face, Arthur dispelled some of his pain but not all of it.

The telltale sign that he wasn't coping sent my heart racing.

Residual agony glittered in his eyes like shards of green glass. "I admit I was arrogant and paid the price." Arthur glanced at me, guilt glowing in his gaze.

Glancing back at his members, he said, "At least our plan no longer includes petitioning the state to relinquish Dagger Rose land to us." Arthur threw me a conspired look. "We have the rightful owner sitting among us, and the bastards fled, so that aspect solved itself."

"What do you mean?" Mo asked. "How did it solve itself?"

Arthur smirked. "Cleo can tell us."

My lungs stuck together. "Um, I can?" I had no idea how.

Arthur spun the gavel in his fingers. "Did your father ever tell you what he did?"

I blinked.

Time stopped. The feeling of being overwhelmed increased at the mention of Thorn Price—my kindhearted, lovable father. "What he did?" I tried to remember, but there was nothing. Whatever shields were in my mind still kept that part captive. I'd hoped I wouldn't be prisoner to amnesia anymore, but there were certain holes waiting to be filled.

Just ask him.

Arthur would tell me.

But wouldn't that be cheating? I had to do this on my own—otherwise, who was to say what I recalled wasn't his version of the events and not mine. I might be tainted and not remember the truth.

Arthur nodded. "He did something rather extraordinary."

The Club watched us, their heads volleying from side to side with who spoke.

"Remind me," I said. "Tell me something and I'll see if I can remember the rest."

His gaze turned cloudy, looking into the past like a seer. "We'd just come back from the beach. It was mid-summer and you'd just turned—"

"Thirteen," I gasped, hurtling headfirst into the memory.

"Happy birthday, Buttercup."

I threw my arms around my father once he put down the castle cake and thirteen candles stuck into the turrets. "Thank you, Daddy."

He grinned, motioning behind me.

Hands came over my eyes and the familiar scent of spicy deodorant and grease bombarded me. "Art, stop it." I laughed, unsuccessfully ignoring the tingles his touch caused.

"Wait a second." His voice was a soft caress.

"Okay, she can open them now."

Arthur dropped his hands, letting me blink and focus at a piece of paper in my father's hand. It looked like the most boring birthday present ever. But somehow, I knew it wasn't.

This was precious. To my father. To me. To my future.

Capturing it, my father tapped the bottom where a signature had already been scribbled and a blank space for another. "You have to sign here."

My eyes scanned the title. "Deed to property Forty-Seven Hundred."

Arthur came from behind me, grinning broadly. "It's yours, Buttercup."

"Mine? What's mine?"

My father passed me a pen, tucking a wayward strand of hair behind my ear. "You're my only child. I own Dagger Rose outright. The land, the holdings. There's acres of land that will only keep growing in profit the more the world expands. I want you to have it."

I shook my head, the piece of paper trembling in my hands. "But... I don't want it. It's yours."

My father smiled, but his eyes were guarded. "Sometimes, Butter-cup, it's best to prepare for the worst when everything is at its best. You're young, but it doesn't matter if I give you this now or when you're eighteen or twenty-five. It doesn't change the fact that I want you to have it."

Taking my wrist, he guided the pen over the piece of paper. "You're old enough to know the value of what I'm giving you. Sign it, sweetheart. Let me know that I've given you a present that will provide for you until you're old like me."

I slapped a hand over my mouth. "Dagger Rose . . . it's mine."

Arthur nodded. "Every shrub, tree, and piece of dirt is yours."

"But—"

Arthur held up his hand. "You want to know how my father was still living there with the Club? After destroying your family?"

I nodded, unable to comprehend such an asset or that I'd forgotten something so life-changing.

And we burned it to the ground!

Had that been his plan all along? Was that why he gave me the torch—because it was my land to destroy?

My mouth hung open.

"Because there was a clause. The land and buildings all belong to you, but as long as Dagger Rose remained, it was a commune for all to enjoy."

His lips pulled back into a cold, vindictive smile. "However, the land has just been vacated and the remnants of such a history demolished. They have no more claims. It's yours to sell if you wish—I know big developers are looking for parcels of land to build housing. You could sell it at a fortune, Cleo. Or keep it and do what you want."

I sat dumbfounded. I wanted to ask so many questions, but Grasshopper jumped in. "Did Rubix know? That the moment he left he'd be homeless?"

Arthur laughed. "Probably not. That's what makes this sweet as well as frustrating. He ran like a fucking pussy—thinking he could outsmart me and prepare for his next attack. But in reality, he just gave me a winning hand. He's out in the open at the mercy of other Clubs. He thinks they're in on his schemes. I admit I underestimated him, but soon...they'll all be exterminated."

The ghost of the deed tickled my fingers as I remembered my father folding and sending the contract to his lawyer the moment I'd finished signing. How awful was it to think only a year later his inheritance would be forgotten and his life stolen?

We could've gone home. Once all of this is over, we could've taken back the compound. But now we couldn't because it was rubble.

I didn't know how I felt about that. The more I thought about it, the more I figured I should be angry that Arthur hadn't told me it was mine before we burned it to a crisp. Instead, a strange relief settled over me, almost as if by burning it we'd erased the atrocities done to my parents—purging it from Rubix.

Everything was gone now.

Fresh for a new beginning.

"One less thing to worry about, then," Matchsticks said.

Melanie typed something on her phone. "I'll go to the records office. Get a copy of the deed and add it to our acquisitions and future developments."

My heart suddenly swooped. "It won't be valid anymore."

All eyes turned on me. In one second, I learned I'd inherited acres of prime property. And in another, lost it all over again.

"Fuck, you're right," Arthur muttered.

Grasshopper ran his hand over his face. "You're dead."

"What—" Molly stopped herself, nodding with understanding. "You were taken into state care."

"A death certificate was issued," Arthur said. "I saw it with my own eyes."

Mo slapped his hands onto the table. "Add to the to-do list. Hire a fucking resurrectionist."

Chuckles broke the tension.

I smiled tentatively. Fear billowed like smoke in my lungs. Being dead on paper had protected me. Being Sarah Jones had been a safety net. Not only had I stepped into harm's way but now I also faced endless questions and debriefing, and whatever else the FBI would require closing my case. Not to mention the reprimand for leaving without a word.

"We'll deal with that later." Clapping his hands, Arthur changed the subject. "Did you call him?" His green eyes swooped to Grasshopper. "Arrange the next meeting?"

"Sure did. Two nights from now. His place. All arranged."

Arthur nodded, pointing at Matchsticks to make a note of whatever had just unfolded.

I sat there still reeling about Dagger Rose but also just as lost. However, beneath my confusion was pride—a lot of pride for everything Arthur had accomplished.

Glancing at Mo, Arthur ran a hand through his dark hair. "The interviews arranged? Like I asked?"

Mo crossed his arms, reclining in his chair. "All done, Prez. Ready and waiting for a few days from now."

What the hell do interviews have to do with killing a few bikers?

The more I learned, the more worried I became. I should've known that a battle over betrayal was too small for Arthur's unwavering attention. I knew what he was like—always striving for more, never happy. *What is he chasing this time?*

My brain continued to clog up with information that I couldn't compute as Arthur shot off questions and gathered answers that I supposed made sense to them but definitely not to me. It didn't matter I was immersed in this new Club. It didn't matter I slept beside the president every night. I couldn't decipher their secrets no matter how hard I tried.

Time trickled past as the meeting grew more and more involved. Arthur was in his element. A born leader.

And all I could do was follow.

Chapter Eighteen

Kill

I'd said it.

I'd told her I loved her. It was too late to change my mind. All I needed to do was wait until she'd finished school and then I could officially date her. Yes, there were a few years between us. Yes, I was sure her father didn't approve. But none of that mattered. Cleo was mine. And the world finally needed to know it. —Kill, age seventeen

"Come with me. I have a surprise for you."

The members of Pure Corruption had filed outside, slowly trickling like water through sand until it was just Cleo and me in the room. The meeting had gone well. Things were in place. It was time to relax and regroup like we always did.

Tonight would be something normal and common, but for the first time I'd have my woman on my knee and that just made everything fucking brilliant.

Cleo's eyes met mine, her long red hair looking like living fire down her back. "A surprise?"

I nodded, moving around the table to pluck her from her chair. Her body moved like rigid plastic, no sway or buckle toward me.

My heart stuttered as I cupped her face. "Everything okay?"

Biting her lip, her gaze searched mine—trying to tear whatever she needed to know unwillingly from my soul.

"Buttercup, whatever it is. You can ask me. You don't need to search for answers when I'm ready to tell you anything you want to know."

"Anything?"

I kissed her forehead, dragging her into an embrace. "Anything."

Her small arms wrapped around my waist. My body wanted to give in to her. My legs were sick of holding my weight. My head was pissed off with existing with lousy vision and pain. But a simple hug from her crippled me.

"For over an hour, I've listened to plans that you've had in place for years. I've witnessed passion, intelligence, and a ruthless determination shared by all members. But I'm completely lost."

"Lost?"

She pulled away. "What are you planning on doing? What interviews are arranged for a few days from now? Who are you meeting?"

A smile tugged my lips. "That's a lot of questions."

"There was a lot of information."

I caught a handful of hair, curling the long strands around my fingers, forcing her to come closer. "There was a lot to plan for."

Her lips parted as I dragged her closer. "Arthur, I've been in the dark for eight long years. Don't blot out my light now."

My heart flip-flopped. My fingers slipped from her hair, dropping to secure around her hip bones. Jerking her forward, I spun her around and pressed her against the table. "I would never do that. Never."

The tip of her tongue ran along her bottom lip. "I know. You're not deliberately keeping me confused, but I need to understand."

"And you will understand. But there's only so much I can tell you before it sounds impossible. I have to show you—mainly to prove to myself that I haven't been wasting my time all these years planning this."

She laughed quietly. "In that case, show away. You have my undivided attention."

My fingers trailed from her hips to her rib cage, feathering lightly, skating over the cotton of her top. "Undivided, huh? Just like you had mine when you squeezed my cock in the bathtub?"

Her head lolled back as my thumbs caressed her nipples. "Uh-huh…" The sensitive flesh instantly budded beneath my touch. "Exactly like that," she moaned as I switched from caressing to pinching.

Scooting backward onto the table, her legs parted, beckoning me closer. Accepting the invitation, I wedged my thighs between hers and rocked the fly of my jeans on her denim-clad pussy.

"Oh, God." Her skin flushed a flamingo pink as my lips kissed a path from her throat to her mouth.

"Kiss me, Arthur."

My cock swelled; I couldn't disobey. Her lips were silk and softness as I took her mouth.

I didn't rush. I didn't take.

Time slowed down as we breathed slow and deep, both keeping hold of the straining leashes of our desire.

Her tongue chipped away at my self-control, licking me sweetly.

I parted my lips, letting her taste and guide.

Her small hands landed on my chest, sweeping down my front to catch on my belt. We both sucked in a breath, standing on the edge of stopping or giving in.

Doctor Laine's warning came back to mind.

No exercise.

But that was fucking three days ago. Surely I'd healed enough to handle sex. I wasn't that much of an invalid, was I?

Cleo kept kissing me and there went my conscious decision. There was no way to know if I was better—unless we tried.

And fuck I wanted to try over and over again.

Her fingers went from still to swift, unbuckling the leather and tugging it from my hips. I kissed her harder as her touch dropped lower, popping open the button before following the metal teeth of my zipper and unlatching each tooth with a tease.

Damn her for changing before coming here. If she still wore her dress, I could've just pushed up the material and thrust inside her. Now I had to fumble and wait. And I couldn't wait. The desire to take her almost buckled me.

My headache pounded as I cupped her hot core through the denim. Her legs opened further, sensual and sexy.

Blood flowed faster to my cock, leaving my damaged brain gasping for help. The smog I couldn't seem to shake clouded thicker, pressing on the back of my eyes.

Keep it together.

I couldn't pass out again. I had no doubt the next time Cleo would admit me to a hospital. I'd wake up to countless tests on my horizon rather than the final pieces of my intricate puzzle.

No. I had to stay whole for a few more days—then I could relax.

Then stop this.

I paused, testing my self-control.

My hands moved on their own accord.

I have no self-control where she's concerned.

Undoing her jeans was nowhere near as quick and streamline as she'd undone mine. A small laugh escaped her as I finally fumbled and won, yanking both her jeans and panties down her legs.

"Wait—what if someone walks in?"

I kissed her again, unable to look at her wet pussy without shuddering with need. "They won't. They'll all be busy organizing tonight."

"What—what's going to—"

I interrupted her question by brushing my thumb against her clit and slowly sliding a finger inside her.

Her hands clutched my shoulders. "Oh."

I groaned as her inner muscles clenched around my finger. I bit her neck, forcing her body to arch and her hips to ride my hand.

"Wait—"

I pressed another finger inside her.

"We shouldn't do this. You're still concussed."

My cock was past fucking caring.

The way she gasped and flinched—I couldn't stop now. I wanted her so fucking much. "Stop thinking," I commanded, licking my way down her throat and nuzzling my face into her cleavage.

"But, Art—I'm worried about you." She sucked in a breath as I sucked her nipple through her T-shirt. Her fingers threaded through my hair, holding me tight against her breasts. "We...we should stop."

I chuckled.

Her words said one thing but her body entirely another.

"You sure?" I twisted my fingers, rubbing her G-spot.

Her legs went bowstring stiff; a small cry escaped.

"Yes..."

I did it again, moving my fingers and rubbing her clit in the way I knew she loved.

"Yes, we should—ah..."

"Stop?" I smiled against her mouth. "Is that what you're trying to say?"

She nodded drunkenly. "Yes. We really need to—" My touch switched from teasing to demanding. I thrust my finger inside her, grinding my aching cock against the table ledge.

Fuck, I need her.

Her head flopped backward. "Oh, don't stop. Please..."

Her beg completely undid me.

Stroking her slippery wetness, I never stopped coaxing her orgasm, massaging her clit, and playing her body to the music I so badly needed.

"I...I need you inside me, Kill."

Kill.

All this time she'd called me Arthur—ever since I stopped being an asshole and finally believed the truth, of course. I couldn't lie that having her call me Kill turned me the fuck on.

I didn't say a word as she grabbed the waistband of my boxers and jeans and pushed them to mid-thigh. Her eyes opened, blazing with forest fires. "I'm begging you. I need you inside me."

I gritted my teeth as she rode my hand. "If I take you, I won't last long."

"I don't care. I just need you." Wrapping her legs around my thighs, she slid closer. Her hand latched around my length as she leaned forward, pressing her forehead against my chest.

Withdrawing my fingers, I shoved her top up, rolling the weight of her breasts as they swung like sinful pendulums.

Does she have any idea the effect she has on me? Her commanding presence, her effortless grace and courage? It utterly fucking destroyed me.

Bending my knees, I allowed her to guide my cock to nudge against her entrance. We both stopped breathing as the tip of me slid into her wetness. Her eyes fought to close but we never looked away as her body slowly welcomed me.

We quivered as inch by inch her body melted with pleasure. She was born for me. This perfect fucking woman was born for me.

My Sagittarius.

Her Libran.

"I love you," she whispered as I sheathed to the root inside her.

My heartbeat exceeded all rhythm. My head throbbed in perfect harmony but all I could think about was the joyous feeling of home.

I groaned as she leaned back on her elbows, giving herself up to me like a brilliant sacrifice. The view of her—with her T-shirt pushed up, her legs spread, and me deep inside her—almost sent my vision skittering into the void again.

Her fingers darted between her folds, and, locking eyes with mine, she rubbed her clit. "I'm so close. So close. Don't hold back."

A growl echoed in my chest. Watching her touch herself threatened to shove me over the edge without moving.

My head bellowed but I slammed my hands on the table for an anchor and thrust.

She cried out, her fingers working faster as I drove again and again.

There was no ease into this. No tease.

I went from stationary to fucking.

The tightening of my balls built exceedingly fast. The heavy swing of them heightened to tingling pleasure as I rode Cleo hard.

"I love fucking you," I growled. "I love knowing you're mine."

She tensed, her cheeks flushed. "God...I adore it when you talk dirty."

I chuckled, thrusting deeper, harder, quicker. "Oh, yeah? I can say much filthier things."

Her cheeks pinked, her lips damp and skin glowing. "Oh, really?" The glint in her eyes urged me on. "Like what?"

I searched my broken brain for something dirty but the damn headache tarnished everything.

"I love how you make small noises when I'm inside you but they act like fucking cannons in my chest." I thrust again, staying in the moment and not thinking about the overwhelming pressure in my skull.

Fuck, everything was an effort. My tongue was fuzzy and twisted. Consonants and adjectives played hide-and-seek in my despairing grey matter.

"I love your pussy. I love the size of your tits. And I love your scars."

She twitched. "My scars?"

My hips never stopped rocking as I traced her burns, feeling the strange ridges and smoothness of skin that'd been through so much. "I love them because it shows how strong you are. That you're a survivor. That you're so fucking brave. And pure. And sexy. And mine. All fucking mine."

My hips quickened. My balls ready to spurt and mark.

My touch went to her tattoo; my voice dropped to stone and smoke. "I love your ink. I love the tale you painted. I love that your heart never forgot me, no matter that your mind tried to hide."

"Never." Her backed bowed, forcing the colorful patterns deeper into my palm. "I could never forget you." Her fingers worked harder on her clit, her breathing tattered. "God, don't stop. Don't stop."

I was past the point of stopping.

We both were.

The table creaked and the legs scraped against the wooden floor but nothing else mattered.

Dragging her upright, I cushioned her back as I brought her face to mine.

I kissed her. Hard. Our tongues linked, our breathing synced and it was just us—just *this*.

I couldn't hold off any longer. I needed to come. I needed to fill this woman. Her body arched in a shameless silent plea.

Her body turned from liquid to lava as her release detonated around me.

"Oh, shit!" Her curse flowed onto my tongue.

Waves of her inner muscles gave me nowhere to hide as my orgasm shot into existence. *Shit, shit. Don't pass out.*

The pain was agonizing, threatening to split open my head with pressure.

I groaned as Cleo massaged the back of my neck—almost as if she understood my torture.

I gave in to her magic.

I let go.

Exquisite agony shot up my cock and splashed inside her. My thrusts became erratic, driving into her slick pussy, plunging over and over again.

Her stomach tensed. Her lips devoured. Her legs spasmed around me.

We came together.

We finished together.

My orgasm bulldozed through my headaches and bruises, turning me boneless.

We didn't move.

Shit, I *couldn't* move.

I would've stayed forever in her embrace, glued together with sticky pleasure and concreted with love. But my phone rang, vibrating against the back of my knee still in my jeans pocket.

Cleo laughed softly. "Thank goodness whoever that is had the decency to wait and not interrupt." Reclining on the table, she smiled. "I don't think I could've stomached two instances where you stopped midway."

I winced. "When will you let me live that down?"

She smiled. "Never."

The lull of serenity and pleasure made my pain fade considerably. Fisting the base of my cock, I pulled out from her and ducked to pull up my boxers and trousers. "I didn't want to stop. I passed out. There's a difference."

The phone rang louder, shrill and piercing.

"Are you going to answer that?"

"Probably not." Scooping the peace-ruining device from my pocket, I looked at the screen.

Shit.

"On second thought, I have to."

Cleo narrowed her eyes as I patted her knee and moved away, trying awkwardly to do up my jeans with one hand.

"Kill speaking."

"Mr. Killian. We have a Mr. Cyrus Conners on the line. Do you accept the charges from Florida State?"

I flicked a look at Cleo. I didn't really want her to overhear, but there was nothing I could do. "Yes. I accept."

The god-awful hold music assaulted my eardrum as I waited. I'd called Wallstreet yesterday to tell him the new timeline of our plan. I'd been expecting his call—just not straight after having fucking sex.

"Kill, my boy."

The old-world charm and perfect pronunciation of Wallstreet's voice trickled down the phone.

"How's it going in there?" Continuing to pace around the meeting room, I gave up trying to secure my pants and focused on the conversation. "You hear any more about your parole hearing?"

Cleo jumped off the table and shimmied back into her jeans.

"Yes, as a matter of fact. Some good news on that front. The appeal went well. I've been told a positive verdict might be forthcoming. However, I could be waiting months for their conclusions, so I won't be ordering balloons or fireworks just yet."

I chuckled. "Well, you've served enough. Time to get you home." Along with vengeance, our long-term plan would also benefit Wallstreet and every other man and woman who'd made a mistake and paid—the reformed criminals, the forgotten soldiers, the rebels of society, right down to the hardworking poor and middle-class citizens who had no skeletons in their pasts, only the bad luck to be born into a system that sucked them fucking dry.

The way this country—this *world*—was run made me bloody rage.

That was what his letter was about.

It would be fitting if he was freed in time to help me finish—to stand before everyone and announce that there was another way than the one we'd been spoon-fed by dirty politicians.

"Grasshopper informed me that you have a meeting with Mr. Samson in a few days."

"Yes."

"And you've dealt with Dagger Rose?"

I rubbed at the slight scruff on my chin. "Not exactly dealt with. But soon. The fuckers ran."

"I know where they ran to."

My blood frosted with retribution. "Perfect. Tell me."

Wallstreet went silent for a moment. "Night Crusader compound.

Most of the Club are holed up there, but others have split and gone alone."

"What?! We paid them off. The whores, the cash. How fucking dare they go back on their word!"

"I know. I expect you to severely discipline them." Wallstreet's voice was black.

My fists clenched. Oh, they'd be severely taught—lesson after fucking lesson. Breathing hard, I flinched against the pressure in my head. "Do I need to worry about the others?"

"No."

I spun to face Cleo, sensing her presence behind me. A hesitant smile flickered across her lips, her eyes full of concern from my outburst.

Looking away, I calmed down. "Look, I've got everything under control. I'll give you an update when I've seen Samson."

"I have no doubt you'll pull it off effortlessly, Kill. You always do." Cleo came closer.

I wrapped my fingers around her wrist, pulling her against me. She snuggled into my chest, her warm body acting like a painkiller for my head, calming my temper at yet another fucking betrayal.

"Grasshopper also told me about the concussion. Has it affected your trades?"

Shit. He always knew. I could never keep anything from him.

Grasshopper's information highway.

Squeezing my eyes, I mumbled, "It's getting better. Every day, it's easing."

Bullshit.

Cleo squeezed me, her small inhale echoing with relief.

"Well, keep an eye on it. That brain of yours is too precious to risk."

Temper swarmed and I clutched the phone harder. "Anything else? I have to go." I released Cleo, moving away. "Club's having a get-together tonight. We're late."

Wallstreet cleared his throat. "Nope, nothing else. I'll keep you informed if I get the good news I'm hoping for. And I'll look forward to your call about Samson."

I nodded. "Will do."

"Oh, one other thing. Tell Cleo I look forward to meeting her again soon. You've chosen a fascinating woman, Kill."

My spine shot straight. "What do you mean?"

Wallstreet laughed. "Nothing, my boy. Only that I want to get to know her better. After all, she's now in equal command in my Club. Bring her to see me again soon."

I gritted my teeth. As much as I loved Wallstreet and as much as I adored Cleo, having them as anything more than long-distance acquaintances wasn't a good idea.

"Sure, will do." Before he could say anything else, I hung up.

"Everything okay?" Cleo asked, dragging the tip of her finger along the grooves of the tabletop.

"Yes, fine."

Her eyes lingered on my phone as I strummed the keypad. A thought shadowed her face like a passing cloud before dispersing with a gust of wind.

"You all right?" I moved forward, pinching her chin with my thumb and forefinger, forcing her to look at me.

She smiled. "Yes, of course. Why wouldn't I be?"

The thought might've disappeared from her face, but it lingered in her eyes. "What is it?"

She dropped her gaze to the phone again. "It's nothing...silly really."

"Nothing you want or need is silly, Buttercup. Tell me and I'll make sure you get it—whatever it is."

She sighed. Gathering her hair into a twist, she draped it over her shoulder. The stalling didn't calm my nerves, but I let her decide when to tell me.

"I miss her," she suddenly blurted.

"Miss who?"

"Corrine."

When I stared blankly, her lips quirked. "My foster sister. I didn't even say goodbye to her properly when I came here. Rubix's letter sort of wrenched me from my simple world and didn't give me time to decide if I should cut ties or just treat it as a vacation."

Without a word, I placed the phone on the table and nudged it toward her. "Call her."

Her eyes popped wide. "Really?" She looked at me with such gratefulness, such love, that a fucking sledgehammer mangled my heart. Is that how she thought of me? That she was still my captive? Cut off from the people who'd taken her in and kept her safe when I couldn't?

Taking her hand, I grabbed the phone and placed it into her palm. Curling her fingers over the device, I smiled. "Call her. I'll be outside with the others." I kissed the tip of her nose. "Take all the time you need. I'll be waiting."

With one last kiss, I left.

Chapter Nineteen

Cleo

Arthur said he wasn't a romantic.

I told him he was a liar.

Last week, I'd found daisies stuffed into my sneakers when I went to put them on. They'd been where they always were—haphazardly kicked off and abandoned on the porch, but they'd transformed from shoes to vases.

Yesterday, I'd found a little note stuck in my window frame. It was soggy and smeared from the recent rain shower but I could still make out his neat penmanship. All it'd said was, "As You Wish," but being that it meant "I love you" from my favorite movie . . . my heart almost burst.

And tonight, he'd given me a ring. A mood ring with a Sagittarius archer guarding the stone. It was a gimmick. A child's toy. But to me it was so much more. —Cleo, diary entry, age fourteen

"Hello?" a sleepy voice crackled in my ear.

The moment Corrine's feminine, flirty tone came through the phone, I wanted to laugh, cry, and spew out every single wondrous and horrendous thing that'd happened since we'd last been together.

So much to say.

So much I couldn't say.

I'd stared at the phone for minutes before deciding to call her. Arthur didn't know the gift he gave when he left.

He's so good to me.

"Corrine."

A shocked pause, followed by a squeal. *"Sarah?"*

The name felt wrong—like a pair of shoes I'd been trying to wear in but never could. Sarah pinched and confined, whereas Cleo was comfort and home. *No, wrong name.* "Yes, it's me."

Rustling filled the line before a short curse was uttered. "Shit, what time is it there?"

I slapped my forehead. *Of course, time zones.* "Crap, I'm so sorry. Did I wake you? It's only early evening here."

"You did, but only 'cause I pulled an all-nighter last night with a kitty who wasn't doing so well giving birth. I crashed when I came home."

Instantly, my mind filled with sterile surfaces of the veterinary clinic we both worked at. The stench of antiseptic and wicked glint of scalpels. My heart warmed to think of the timid licks from animals thanking us for saving their lives, or the terrified yips of those who didn't understand we were on their side and not to be feared.

I missed that vocation. I missed the rush of cheating disease. I even missed the crazy owners who provided endless entertainment.

"How many?"

"Eight babies, can you believe. Poor thing didn't make it, but we did manage to save six of the kittens, so it wasn't as tragic as it could've been."

I looked at a chair, debating if I should sit or pace. The amount of nervous energy sparking through me preferred to walk.

Patrolling around the room, I asked, "How are you? Did you find the rent money I left for my share of the studio?"

Corrine snorted. "I found it, but I didn't use it. This place was too small for the two of us anyway. I can more than cover it." Her tone was reserved but warmed. "Plus, Nick has been staying over a lot, so in a way, you did me a favor."

I smiled. "I'm glad things are working out with you two."

"What about you, hairball? Did you find that guy who wrote you the letter?"

My old nickname—earned from being vomited on by a cat with a wicked case of undigested hair—made me laugh. The happiness didn't last, however, as my thoughts turned instantly to Rubix and what'd happened at his hands. "I found him," I hedged.

"Uh-oh, that doesn't sound good. You okay? Need me to call Scotland Yard or MI6? How about James Bond?"

I giggled. "No, I'm safe. It was just a bit scary to begin with."

"He didn't hurt you, did he?"

I swallowed. How much could I tell her and how much was appropriate on a phone call? Not to mention the cost of the international call and the fact Arthur was patiently waiting for me.

"Believe me, I have so much to tell you but now is not the time."

"Well . . . why bother calling me, then, spoilsport?"

I laughed. "Because I couldn't let you worry about me. I owed you that."

Corrine snorted again. "As if I was worried about you. Why would I worry about the girl who sat through weeks of tattooing without a single tear? You're like She-Woman, or one of those Viking people who don't feel pain." Another rustle of what I assumed were bedclothes. "So . . . tell me the most important part."

"Oh? What's that?"

"Did you find your hero with green eyes?"

Her question transported me back to the movies we'd watch together, always grumbling over swoon-worthy heroes who had blue or brown eyes but never green. My heart twisted with love as I thought about Arthur.

"Yes . . . I did."

A squeal forced me to jerk the phone away from my ear. "Really? Oh, my God. That's awesome!"

"His name is Arthur and I'll introduce you once a few complications are ironed out."

"Arthur? As in King Arthur of the Knights of the Round Table? Does he have Merlin conjuring spells for him by any chance?" Corrine snickered.

The picture of a wizened old man wrapped in mystique and secrecy was the exact summary of Wallstreet. I rolled my eyes. "Funny enough, he does have someone kind of like that."

"Whoa, now I have to meet him."

For a second, I wished I were back in England, curled up on the couch and sipping dirty martinis while plotting our future and fawning over ideals of future husbands. The only thing was, every trait I ever wished for in a future lover was everything Arthur was and had been in our youth.

"Oh, by the way, your case worker called last week. You forgot about the regular check-in."

I slapped my forehead. "Shit."

"I covered for you, but I don't think she bought it. I'd call them if you don't want some angry FBI dude chasing you down. Mom and Pop have been chatting with someone, too. They're not happy that you upped and left. Going to have some explaining to do."

"Thanks." An awkward pause followed. There was so much to say and not enough time. Sighing, I said, "I have so much to tell you, Corrine, but I have to go."

"Aww, that sucks. Just when it was getting juicy." Her tone lost its joviality, sliding into serious. "Sarah...everything is okay...isn't it?" A pregnant pause. "Do you remember—what happened to you, I mean? Do you know how you got the scars?"

I held my breath. How could she ever understand the world I'd been born into and the circumstances that forced me out of it? She was smart, sweet, and strong but so innocent at the same time.

"Yes. I did remember. I know how I was burned and I know who did it."

"Are you safe? What can you tell me? Give me something—*anything*."

Flicking through my revelations and problems, I decided on the issue raised thanks to Dagger Rose. "I inherited a large estate. But I can't claim it."

"Why not?"

"Because I have to come back from the dead."

A shiver ran down my spine. On paper I'd died years ago. How did one come back from the grave?

"What do you mean?" Corrine's voice trembled.

"I mean my name isn't Sarah, it's Cleo. I've fallen back in love with the boy who stole my heart when we were young, and I'm about to help him end the man who killed my parents before trying to murder me."

The silence was long and deafening.

When Corrine didn't respond, I said, "You still there?"

Corrine said, "That's a lot to dump on a girl."

We didn't speak for a while, finally Corrine whispered, "So my sister's name is Cleo and she's a ghost."

Smoke and soot and sausages.

The scents shot up my nose, igniting hunger and welcoming me outside.

Corrine had understood when I said I truly had to go. She'd assured me she would let her parents know I was safe and I promised I'd call again soon. I meant what I said about taking Arthur to visit them. My foster family could never replace my real parents but they'd been so good to me and I loved them.

The door behind me swung closed as I crossed the threshold from Clubhouse to backyard. I hadn't explored the expansive grassy lawn leading to a fence cutting off the everglades. The grass was thick and lusciously green.

The sun had put itself to bed, and the stars had decided to break all bedtime rules and pepper-sprayed the rich velvet of the sky. Constellations twinkled brightly, the perfect backdrop for the gathered members and the relaxing embrace of an evening of laughter, good food, and great friends.

"Holy shit, it's alive!" someone yelled. Followed by, "Didn't know we had a damn dragon!" Men abandoned their beers on strewn tables or on the ground by chair legs as they raced toward billowing black smoke.

Three men with vests marking them as prospects fanned tea towels and dueled the morphing blackness with cooking tongs.

"Christ's sake." Mo jogged across the grass and slammed the lid down on the flaming barbeque. Coughing and wafting at the smoke cloud hovering over his head, he growled, "What the fuck are you doing to our steaks?"

Grasshopper stomped over, snatched the tongs from the closest prospect, whose eyes ran red with soot, and shoved the other two aside. "What kind of man can't barbeque without setting the fucking place on fire?"

A prospect with a large gauge in his ear shrugged. He looked completely happy to give up control. "You told me to get the chow ready. I tried to tell ya that I've never cooked in my life. Not my fault you didn't listen."

"How hard is it to work a fucking grill?" Mo asked, hoisting up the cover of the barbeque and assessing the damage now the flames were out. The smoke lazily dispersed like spirits summoned back to the underworld.

The two other prospects, one with long ratty blond hair in a ponytail and another freshly shaven, snickered. "Yeah, Mo. You should know not to trust Beetle with anything."

Shaking my head, I ignored the instruction on how to cook a perfect steak and focused on the rest of the gathering. A chain-link fence barricaded us in and kept trespassers out, while a few sparse trees had been layered with fairy lights by some overzealous old lady.

The ground vibrated with footfalls beneath my ballet flats and I spun to face him. Somehow, I knew it was him. The hum of my skin, the glow of my heart. His cells spoke to mine in a way I would never understand. "Hi."

Arthur stepped closer, an imposing statue of muscle and authority. He shook his head, his lips twisted in wry amusement watching his dinner go up in smoke. "Can't trust anyone these days."

I swayed into him as his arm brushed mine. "Who names the members here? Matchstick, Beetle? They're hardly scary."

His green eyes smoldered in the gloom. "I was the one who gave Beetle his name, actually." He smirked. "I found him shoplifting at one of my businesses." His eyes clouded, recalling the past while I'd been curing puppies and dreaming of him. "His getaway car was a dinged up Beetle. Needless to say, I outran him on my bike and put an end to that fucking nonsense. After a bit of a rough-up—so he would remember the lesson of 'thou shalt not steal'—I gave him a choice."

"A choice?"

He nodded. "Stop stealing and make money *my* way or I'd report him to the law and see how he liked jail." His gaze glinted. "I might also have provided insider knowledge on just how much he *wouldn't* enjoy captivity."

My mind reeled. There was so much to unscramble, but the most important slapped me in the face. "I heard Molly mention other businesses in Church. What do you mean?"

Arthur smiled, his teeth white and perfect in the night. "Oh, didn't I tell you?"

I scowled, not appreciating his obtuse merriment at hiding yet another thing about himself. "No, you didn't tell me." Putting my hands on my hips, I looked him up and down.

Arthur had evolved from boy to businessman with endless connections and wealth to bring everything to life. No wonder Wall-street chose him—he saw the potential, even after Arthur had been destroyed.

"Well, I can tell you now." He gathered me close, tucking me against his side. "Believe me, Buttercup. The only things you need to know about me—you already do. The rest of it—the businesses, the trading, the Club—none of that makes me who I am." Leaning closer, his eyes tripped into mine. "Only you can do that. And I'm the man I am because of the girl you were."

My heart pounded. The gentle warmth of him softened my every molecule. After the meeting, I'd been tense and slightly unnerved about what plans were about to be implemented. And after calling Corrine, I'd been homesick and—if I was honest—guilty for how I'd run away. But all of that disappeared—that was the magic of his embrace.

Somehow, with just one touch from him, energy, excitement, and most of all lust rejuvenated me all over again.

"Besides," Arthur said. "Everything I've created belongs to you anyway."

Following the silver thread of the Pure Corruption logo on his breast pocket, I bit my lip. "I don't want it. Everything belongs to you—not us."

Arthur chuckled. "Buttercup, I earn a fortune with one click of my mouse." Tapping his temple, his smile faltered just for a second. "This machine up here has meant I've been able to fulfill everything Wallstreet has ever asked and create a buffer for myself so if anything changes in the future, I'll be able to survive."

I cuddled into him, hating the sudden bleakness in his voice at the thought of things changing. Yet another family torn from him. Another choice taken. *Of never having his full capacity back from the concussion.* His thoughts led him somewhere dark; I needed to bring him back to the light. "You're a mathematical whiz. I always knew you were destined for great things."

His eyes shadowed. "Try telling that to my father back then. He thought I was a fucking pussy."

I tensed. I couldn't talk about Rubix without wanting to murder the son of a bitch. Forcing him out of my mind, I rested my head on his chest. "You're changing the subject so I don't find out just how wealthy you are and then cook up plans to divorce you and take half."

He went still.

The whoosh of air in his lungs echoed in my ear. I flinched. Did he take it the wrong way? I hadn't meant it—not at all. I would never do that to him.

"To divorce me means you have to marry me first."

Slowly, I untangled myself from him, staring into his eyes. "Not these days. De facto counts as marriage in legal purposes."

His face fell.

God, why did I say that? Why did I say such a stupid thing? It made it sound like I didn't want to get married. That my heart hadn't selected him since I was born. "I didn't mean it like that. I'm..." I glanced away. "I'm nervous, I guess."

Arthur's fingers pressed against my jaw, guiding my eyes to his. "You're nervous because you're worried I'll think you're after my money, or you're nervous because I might ask you right here, right now to marry me?"

The world stopped spinning even as my heart started whizzing in my chest. "Um, both."

Bending slightly, he pressed the sweetest of kisses against my lips. "Riches come in many forms, Buttercup, and you've made me beyond wealthy." His mouth moved to my ear. "And rest easy. When I propose, it won't be in the middle of a smoky barbeque with a bunch of drunk-ass bikers."

I swallowed. My heart floated. My body was weightless.

"You know me. You know I've always had that desire to better myself. To provide for people I care for." His tone was strained rather than proud. "To make a mark in the world."

"I remember," I murmured. "But what does that have to—"

"Nothing. I'm just glad you're here. You can tame me. Bring me back to what matters and stop me chasing things I don't necessarily need."

Like what?

A patter of fear disappeared down my spine.

"Take that, motherfucker." Grasshopper danced around like a

lunatic, holding up a perfectly charred piece of meat. The barbeque was now tamed and behaving after imitating a fire-breathing demon. "You can all refer to me as master chef from now on."

The men and women mingling around laughed.

The interruption ceased our conversation and Arthur let me go, moving away to slouch against a spindly looking tree. He shoved his hands into his pockets. I liked to think he just wanted to relax, but the pain darkening his eyes squeezed my chest. The tree wasn't just to lean against—it was for support.

I let him recuperate in silence.

I went to his side, and we watched the commotion for a while. Beetle came forward and handed Arthur an icy beer. When he offered me a bourbon, I turned my nose up and accepted a bottled water instead.

Sipping quietly, my heartbeat calmed and I soaked in the happiness of such an evening.

I didn't know how much time passed while we relaxed in each other's company.

I wanted to ask questions. I wanted to know everything there was to know, but I kept my thoughts to myself.

However, Arthur must've sensed my desires, because he took another pull of his beer and said, "When I gained my freedom from Florida State, I had nothing to my name—not even the T-shirt on my back. Wallstreet made sure I had a home to go to, a bank account to utilize, and friends to trust."

His voice was thick and delicious as honey. "The money trickled in at first. I wasn't confident in what Wallstreet taught me and it took a while for me to start trading large amounts." His eyes connected with mine. "Wallstreet gave me two million dollars to use to get the Club back in order and to trade with."

I blinked. "Wow. That's a hell of an investment."

Arthur took another sip. "It was the strangest thing to be treasured for the same gifts that I'd been shunned for all my life." Stroking his weeping beer bottle, he continued. "Like I said, I didn't feel comfortable trading with his money—what if I lost it and couldn't get it back? I owed him my life, my world." He shook his head. "No, I couldn't do that."

"How did you make your fortune then?"

Arthur kept his eyes on the chaos of bikers and their women as the Club prepared the garden for dinner. Three large foldaway tables appeared and were put in a mismatch of places. Chairs were slammed into the grass and firewood was brought by the armful to slowly create a teepee of logs and tinder in the central fire pit.

"I allowed myself one hundred thousand of Wallstreet's money. I figured if I lost it, I wouldn't be in debt all my life trying to pay it back. And it was enough to trade large amounts that meant my rewards swiftly grew."

I stayed silent, willing him to tell me more.

"I came pretty close to losing it. One trade wiped me out because I hadn't put a fucking stop loss." He scowled. "A dumbass mistake—just like the one I did today. I should've known better then and I definitely should've known better now."

Taking a deep breath, he ran a hand over his face. "Stop loss, Buttercup. The ultimate requirement in any trade. I'll teach you that. Don't worry."

I jolted to think of ever having the intelligence Arthur did. Trading with money terrified me. It seemed as dangerous as gambling if not taken seriously and approached with logic and formulas.

Arthur pushed off from the tree. "When I'd doubled the hundred grand, I started to look at other means to make money. I used some of my profits and bought a local business."

My interest piqued. *Keep going.* "What did you buy?"

He chuckled. "Don't laugh, but a salon."

"A *salon*?"

"I bought it because the owner was being harassed by a small Club on the outskirts of town. I also bought it because the woman who owned it looked a bit like you." He sighed heavily. "She was older, but her hair reminded me so much of your red curls that when she burst into tears knowing she'd be broken into and destroyed the moment I withdrew my protection, I couldn't walk away." His lips curled into a self-conscious smile. "I gave her cash."

My heart flipped over at the kindness inside him. "And it was a loss?"

"No, not at all. It's rather profitable considering the small investment I made." Smiling coldly, he muttered, "Not to mention the small Club who'd been raiding shops and raping girls walking home from work was suddenly torn apart and never seen again."

A chill worked down my spine. "You stopped them." It wasn't a question.

He glared past the chain-link fence to the everglades beyond. "Yes, I stopped them."

I shuddered to think how many bodies the local alligators had devoured over the years. But if they were evil men disrupting a peaceful city—was there harm in that? To take a human life in order to save countless more? What would karma say to such a decision?

I changed the subject from death and carnage. "What other businesses do you own?"

Arthur finished his beer, dropping it by his feet to tick off on his fingers. "Well, there's two bars, a burger joint, and another salon. Oh, and there's also a sushi train and I'm part owner in a security firm that does neighborhood watch pro bono."

My jaw fell wide. "Holy crap." Was that all he did? Trade and save and invest into people he believed in? He gave so much to others, all while living a bare existence in comfort and connection. "Arthur, I'm—" *Blown away.*

He cocked his head, his forehead furrowed with yet more pain from the headache that never left. Pointing at Grasshopper and Mo, who were now the main chefs of tonight's dinner, he grinned. "Grasshopper owns a pet groomers and donut shop, while Mo manages to split his time between three pubs and a yacht that's a floating restaurant on the bay." He laughed. "We're all very entrepreneurial."

"I can see that." I laughed quietly. "Who knew? Not all men dressed in scuffed leather and riding around on custom-designed Triumphs prefer girls, drugs, and rock 'n' roll."

He frowned. "Those things have never been in my repertoire." His eyes blazed. "I almost became a monk because every other woman paled in comparison to you."

I rubbed at my chest where a sudden unbearable pressure swarmed. "I'm glad you're not a monk."

He chuckled. "Me too."

We stared at each other, wrapped up in so much said and so much still to learn. I wished we were alone again—so I could show him just how amazed I was by his accomplishments.

"I'm proud of you. So proud." I couldn't contain the awe and pride. I hugged him. Hard.

He tensed, then relaxed in my hold, hugging me back. His leather cut creaked, smelling of lanolin and masculine musk. It was the best smell in the world.

"All right, everyone. Grab some plates and form a queue. Dinner is finally served," Grasshopper yelled.

The men clapped and women paraded from the Clubhouse with salads, pastas, and breads in their arms. I should've been helping them, but tonight I permitted a bit of laziness—after all, it meant Arthur and I finally got to enjoy something so simplistically precious.

Someone switched on a radio, turning the cicada-laced air into a jive of sixties music.

"Come on. Let's eat." Arthur guided me forward and together we joined our new family.

Chapter Twenty

Kill

Why *was it that people seemed the happiest on the cusp of disaster?*

It was like clockwork.

My mom had been happiest before her cancer diagnosis. Thorn had been happiest before my father decided he had to be removed. Even I'd been at my happiest just before my life ended.

Cleo made me happy.

But ultimately, she was the one who made me want to die. —Kill, age eighteen

Sitting in the darkness with my brothers and sisters around me granted the same kind of happiness I'd seen infect others. It was dangerous. This type of joy made people lazy. Unaware. Close-minded.

Happiness was a drug. The strongest of all because it made life seem friendly, open, and kind.

That was bullshit.

I'd forgotten that lesson when I was younger. Believing that everything would work out and my dreams would come true.

And I'd paid the price.

I'd paid the price for my blindness and almost sacrificed everything to despair.

So, even though I wanted more than anything to believe in the happiness spread before me. To open up my heart to the warmth. To bask in the glow of companionship...

I couldn't.

Wallstreet was still in jail. My father was still alive. And the world was still the same stinking pile of corruption and lies it'd always been.

Until those three things changed, I had no space for intoxication on dreams and fantasy.

Only once I'd achieved what I promised could I find any hope in trusting again. Only once I'd eradicated the lies and treachery could I be free. And only once I'd put into place something so much bigger than myself could I stop chasing that ever-elusive *more*.

Then...perhaps—just fucking perhaps—I'd let myself be happy.

Chapter Twenty-One

Cleo

*A*rthur had made me promise something strange.

He'd stopped marking my homework and went silent for ages. I thought he'd leave, but he'd stolen my hand and made me promise that I would run away with him. I knew his family was cruel, but this was our home. Only, he didn't feel that way. He said we were dying slowly—being strangled by lies. I didn't agree, but what could I do? He needed me...so, I'd promised. I'd promised that I would run when he told me to. —Cleo, diary entry, age fourteen

Early evening turned into early morning.

The cicadas had retired, the radio continued its scratchy tunes, and the jokes became sloppy and crude.

However, I'd never had such a good time. Never been so relaxed and contented.

With my foster family, I'd always held back at gatherings or parties—afraid of forgetting something important or saying something wrong. No matter how much Corrine made me laugh, I'd never really made peace with the emptiness inside. I'd tried filling the amnesia-hole with new thoughts, but it was bottomless...devouring everything, throbbing with urgency to have me jump into the pit and remember.

However, there was one thing shadowing the ease and pleasure of the evening. The sense that this wasn't just a bonfire to bond and gossip, but to hang out one last time before war broke out.

In the past few days, I'd been kidnapped, Arthur wounded, and the house broken into. That wouldn't go unpunished. We were all on the precipice of something huge and it added a strange edge to the celebrations.

Could this gathering be the last time everyone was alive? Could this be the last time I witnessed Pure Corruption as a whole?

Arthur stared into the fire, his green eyes slightly unfocused as he relived things I could only guess. I slinked my arms around the back of his neck. "You okay?" I'd been on his lap for hours, my back nestled against his front, cocooned by his heat and smell.

He nodded, pressing his lips against my shoulder. "Never better."

Pushing away my morbid thoughts, I sighed with contentedness. More time passed; we stayed poised in nothingness, hypnotized by the fire, and rocked into a lullaby of safety and serenity.

"What are you thinking about?" Arthur asked softly.

I smiled lazily, surveying the churned grass, discarded napkins, and strewn bottles around the roaring open fire. The majority of men were drunk. In fact, so were the women. But there was no aura of violence or suspicion like the occasional functions at Dagger Rose. No jealousy or resentment.

I just hope they all survive whatever is coming.

"I'm thinking how happy I am. Here with you." Twisting on his lap, I pressed my mouth against his in a tender kiss. "I missed you so much, Art."

His eyes shot to a dark green as lust sprang strong. "I missed you, too."

The buzz in my blood from alcohol layered my vision with a romantic haze as I turned my attention back to the gathering. Chairs had been pulled from the tables and ringed around the large fire. Women perched on their men's knees, their arms—bare in the Florida heat—draped over them. Affection was visible: pink strands joining ruffian men with their significant others.

Cuts had been removed and littered the backs of chairs while others puddled on tables. The orange glow of the fire sent stencils over their tattooed skin, marking all of us with its warmth.

"They're a great group," Arthur said, lifting his beer to his lips. The sound of him swallowing sent a shiver of need through me. As delicious as it'd been sitting on his lap all evening, eating morsels of barbeque from his fingers, and sharing a plate of dessert, I ached with desire.

Not only was I fascinated by this man but I was also in shock, in love, and most of all in wonderment of him. I needed to have him naked. I needed him above me, inside me, bared to me—so I could finally uncover every facet of who he was.

I need him because all of this . . . it's fleeting. We were in the eye of the storm—whipped by unseen winds just waiting to tear our happiness away.

"They have a good leader." My eyes fell on Grasshopper. He'd entertained us with bad guitar playing, awful lyrics, and terrible ghost stories once we'd all slipped into a food coma around the bonfire.

Now he sat alone.

Unpaired with a woman, he was one of the few single men, sitting in a fumigation of smoke, sucking on a cigar and nursing a beer. His long legs were spread in front of him, the heels of his black boots indenting the dry dirt below. Despite his aloneness, he seemed happy. His gaze was warm and slightly glazed as he took in his Club.

"What's his story?" I asked, sighing deeper into Arthur's embrace.

"Hopper?"

I nodded. "Despite being related to the man who sprung you from jail."

Chuckling, Arthur shuffled me higher on his lap. The warmth of licking flames slowly turned the liquor in my blood into a sedative.

The strawberry daiquiris Melanie had concocted subdued noise and light—making everything dreamlike.

"Jared is loyal, loyal, and hardworking." Arthur finished his beer, placing the empty on the ground. "He's been with women, but no one ever sticks."

"Why not? He's good-looking, well spoken, got a good position." *Not to mention a rich family.* Being Wallstreet's son meant he would inherit a lot. If Wallstreet had hidden away his assets before going to jail, of course.

Arthur shrugged. "At the time, I thought he might have the same issue as me: heartbroken in the past and unwilling to move on."

"You don't think that anymore?" I jumped as Arthur's fingers spread over my belly possessively.

"No, I don't think that anymore."

I bit my lip as his fingers inched downward, teasing the delicate skin above my waistband. Without a word, he popped the button and pushed his large hand past the restriction of my jeans and into my panties.

Oh, God.

"Art, what are you doing?" My eyes grew heavy with need, but the awareness of being on display itched my skin. I tried to halt his hand. "Stop it. They can see."

Arthur didn't seem to care, unaffected by my scrambling fingers. "I'm touching you, Buttercup. And I have no intention of stopping." His cock thickened behind me, his hand hot on my core.

"But—"

"No buts." His touch dominated my nerves, making me obey.

My head fell back, resting on his shoulder. My hands fell away reluctantly. Every part of me tensed, unwilling to be on show, but unable to fight him.

"Good girl." He sucked in a breath. "I love it when you give in to me."

"I'd prefer it if we didn't have an audience." I had no choice but to permit his control. However, I couldn't deny that his possessive hold clenched my tummy.

It's...intoxicating.

In a weird, naughty way, I liked it—enjoyed showing a secret part of ourselves.

"They're not watching. Besides, there's something fucking hot about touching you in public."

My core rippled, liquefying with desire. I struggled to stay coherent and not drift away with his magic touch. *What were we talking about before?*

It was an impossible task to carry on conversation, but I tried. "Grasshopper. We were talking about Grasshopper."

He chuckled, his touch dipping farther. "In case you hadn't noticed, I really don't want to talk about Hopper anymore."

My mouth parted as he rocked his hips into my spine.

"I want to talk about how damn delicious you are." He licked my throat gently. "In fact, I'd much rather it was my tongue between your legs and not just my hand."

I gulped. "You're not playing fair."

"Who said anything about playing, Buttercup?"

My eyes fluttered closed. The bonfire faded; the gathering disappeared. It was just me and him and tantalizing sensation.

My legs fell open, inviting him to take more. My heartbeat accelerated as I opened my eyes. *People might see.*

A flush at doing something forbidden made me blurt, "But you said you didn't think it was heartbreak keeping him alone. I want to know what you think it was."

I didn't care—not really. I just couldn't get too carried away; otherwise we'd end up having sex right there by the fire.

Arthur groaned, "God, you're determined to distract me." His thighs bunched beneath me. "Fine, I think he just hasn't found his best friend yet, that's all."

I sucked in a breath as his fingers stretched lower, gracing ever so teasingly over my clit. "A man needs a woman. A man needs to fuck, love, and protect, but he also needs an equal. And you don't get an equal unless you have respect. And you only get respect if you have friendship."

My breathing stuttered as Arthur stroked me. "That's why I was fucked when I thought I'd lost you. You died. You took more than just love away—you took away belonging, home...*trust*. I'd seen how good a partnership with the right person could be. No fucking way could I settle after you."

My heartbeat clanged like a church bell, dispelling cobwebs and ghosts, and filling up the hole inside me forever. "You really know how to melt a girl."

His teeth nipped at my ear. "I'd say you're melting pretty quickly, Buttercup." His fingers worked faster. "You're wet and it's turning me the fuck on."

I couldn't deny I adored him touching me but I couldn't shed the nervousness of being on display. "We should stop."

"Why?" His breath was hot on my neck.

"Because people might see." I peered into the gloom. Members surrounded us, but each was in their own perfect world—consumed by drink, laughter, and friendship. No one looked over—giving the illusion of privacy.

"I don't care." Arthur hooked his finger, dragging more pleasure from me. "Let them watch. Let them see how fucking gorgeous you are. How your inked skin flushes and how your scars glitter when you pant." He buried his nose in my hair. "God, I want to be inside you."

I moaned.

Somehow, he stole all my inhibitions.

"You're far too good at loving me," I groaned, giving myself completely into his power, neither caring people might watch, nor worrying about inappropriate behavior.

Arthur growled, "I'm only good because I've fantasized about touching you for eight long years. Every night, I dreamed how I'd push my fingers inside you and make you come. Every morning, I imagined dropping to my knees and making you writhe on my tongue."

His voice turned deep and raspy. "And now that I can, I can't help touching you every second of every damn day."

My hips arched toward his fingers. "I hope you never stop." The more time I spent in his arms, the more whole I felt. I was no longer hungry for knowledge or harassed by endless questions.

I could live in the moment.

Right here.

Right now.

And not constantly compare it to the past or fret over the future.

I'm home.

Arthur's finger feathered harder over my clit.

"You said you could never settle after me." I tilted my head, seeking his mouth. "I know exactly what you mean." Pressing a kiss on his five o'clock shadow, I tried so hard not to rock against his hand. "We were young, but we knew. The day you helped me back home from falling off my bike, I knew."

He laughed; the sound quaked through me. His finger decorated my swelling flesh with tiny circles. I clenched with sparkling waves as Arthur became both seducer and pyrotechnic—whenever he touched me, I turned from human to orgasmic fireworks.

His voice was rough and strained. "What we have is so goddamn special. So strong and consuming...but it's also not unique. We aren't the only ones who found our significant other."

His hand moved faster inside my panties, the tip of his finger entering me.

I cried out, scissoring my legs against bliss. "Wait!"

He panted. "I don't want to wait. Fuck, I never want to wait again now you're back in my life." His hand widened my legs, giving me no room to disagree.

"We should move. We should find a dark corner." *Put us out of our misery.*

"I agree. I'm so damn hard."

My heart flew drunkenly. I was entirely caught in his web—wrapped up in lust and fire and seduction.

His voice caught, his thoughts turning dark and dismal. "But to move, I have to let you go. And I never want to do that. You're mine forever. *I* know that. *You* know that. Shit, we knew that when we were kids. But we aren't the first or the last to find this."

I frowned, trying to keep up. "What do you mean?" I rolled my hips, despite my shyness, enticing his finger to slide deeper.

Oh, God…

"I mean everyone has someone designed for them, but very few people recognize it before it's too late."

I nuzzled into his delicious body. "It was never too late for us. We were never apart. Not really." My nipples pebbled as he ran the tips of his left hand down my exposed arm. Having him touch me so sensually, surrounded by murmurs, stagnant humid air, and serenaded by the hum of insects, I'd never been more alive.

My skin prickled with heat. I wanted to wriggle out of my jeans and welcome Arthur into my body right here in front of the fire.

"You're right. We were never apart." Arthur nibbled my ear. "I think it's time for us to leave, don't you?" His finger dived inside me. I couldn't help it—I moaned.

"Yes. I think leaving would be a very good idea."

Kissing my cheek, his finger withdrew, drawing my wetness over my skin until his hand slinked from my jeans. "Screw goodbyes. We're sneaking out of here."

Sitting upright on his lap, I ran shaky hands through my hair. "Okay." All I could think about was licking, joining, and coming. My eyes rose, locking on to Grasshopper's.

Tapping ash from his cigar, he tilted his head, a smirk on his lips. The glow of the fire danced over his glossy mohawk and his expression said he'd watched what Arthur had just done.

I blushed, looking away. "Oh, crap."

"Oh, crap, what?" Arthur asked. His eyes shot to where I'd been staring and a cocky smile spread his lips. "I get it. Horny bugger watched. Well, he knows he can call any woman on his speed dial and get laid tonight if he wishes."

I narrowed my eyes, risking another look at Hopper. His baby blue gaze spoke of a man who had a lot to give and the intelligence in which to protect what he had.

"Perhaps he should get calling, instead of leering."

Grasshopper raised his glass in a toast, a chuckle shaking his chest. *Pervert.*

Then again, it was us who'd put on the show.

Blushing, I placed my bare feet on the grass. I'd kicked off my shoes a few hours ago and had no idea where they were. I pushed off from Arthur's lap.

Arthur cleared his throat, his hand trapping my hips. "Give me a second. Fucking hard-on is refusing to deflate."

I laughed, looking over my shoulder at his crotch. "You started it."

"I had no choice. Your ass is too fucking perfect in those jeans. I've been hard all night thinking of peeling them off you." His eyes dulled with pain and my desire faded a little.

"Are you sure you're okay? Don't you think the pain should've lessened by now?"

Arthur scowled. "Well, you picked a good subject to make me lose my fucking boner."

My heart thudded at his sudden temper. "I'm only worried about you."

"I don't want you to be worried. There's nothing to be worried about. Got it?" Breathing hard, he plucked me from his lap and placed me on my feet. I stumbled forward a little, landing straight into Mo's arms.

"Whoa," he said, grabbing my bicep as I balanced. One hand was wrapped around the neck of a bottle of Jack Daniel's and he'd shed his cut so his black T-shirt showed off strong muscles.

"Thanks." I pulled away, aware of Arthur climbing to his feet behind me. Mo was another singleton at tonight's shenanigans. He'd been drinking all night, but he didn't look intoxicated.

Actually, he looks sniper ready and focused.

He smirked, running a hand through his shaggy blond hair. "You guys can't leave yet."

"Why the fuck not?" Arthur growled, swaying a little beside me. His arm draped over my shoulders—not out of possession but support.

My heart went wild. Was his temper hardwired to the amount of pain he was in? Why had he suddenly switched?

Trying to be inconspicuous, I wrapped my arm around his waist and tucked my hand up the back of his T-shirt.

I froze. *Oh, no.*

His skin was slick with cold sweat. How long had he been in agony, ignoring his body's need to lie down and relax?

Gritting my teeth, I said, "We're leaving." My voice shocked me with how curt it sounded. "I'm tired and want to go." Hugging Arthur close, I wanted to help him but at the same time I wanted to hit him over the head for being so stupid. "Let's go, *Kill.*"

Do you hear that I'm pissed with you?

I dug my fingers into his slippery side, trying to pull him forward. His large bulk stayed wedged to the ground.

His green eyes darkened. "See, Mo. My old lady can be pretty controlling when she wants to be." He threw me a pissed off look, but beneath it I detected thanks. Thanks for giving him an out where he didn't look weak, only indulging a fickle woman who suddenly wanted to go.

That's fine with me.

As long as I could get him home, feed him painkillers, and watch him sleep, I didn't care if he made me seem like the worst controlling woman in the Club. "Exactly. What I want, I get."

I smiled coolly at Mo. "It was lovely spending the evening with you guys, but it really is past my bedtime."

Letting my arm untwine from around Arthur's back, I captured his hand instead. The large palm squeezed mine. "Come on."

"See ya tomorrow, Mo." Arthur grabbed his cut from the armrest of the chair we'd abandoned and made our way slowly around the fire.

Mo dashed in front of us. "Fuck you're both so stubborn. Least you can do is stand there." Pointing a finger in my face, he ordered, "Don't move." Tossing his drink onto the grass, he jogged to the Clubhouse and disappeared inside.

"What the hell was that about?"

Arthur's face glistened in the fire. "No idea. Whatever it is, I'm not waiting here like a trained fucking poodle. I want to leave. We're leaving."

All thoughts of having him the moment we were away from the crowd disappeared in favor of getting him into bed and healing. Arthur followed my train of thought. "I'm well enough to fuck you tonight, Buttercup. Don't think you're getting out of it that easily."

Untangling my hand from his, I crossed my arms. "You know what the doctor said. No sex or strenuous exercise until you're better."

"We had sex before. Therefore, I am better."

I snorted. "No, you're not."

Anger painted his face. "I don't have time to be sick. I have a shit-load of stuff to do—once it's done, *then* I can focus on taking a few days off."

I rolled my eyes. He needed a good punch to realize how stupid he was. "If you die on me, I'll curse you forever."

He chuckled. "You already died on me, so I guess fair's fair, right?" He meant it as a joke, but it was the worst, most tasteless punch line I'd ever heard.

It *killed* me.

I gasped. "Seriously?" My voice turned to a thread. "Did you seriously just say that?"

Instantly, his anger and temper disappeared. He jerked me close. "Fuck, I'm sorry. I didn't mean it like that."

I squirmed in his arms, trying to get away. But he held me tight. "Look at me, Buttercup."

I refused, staring at the ground instead.

How could he even jest about something like that?

"I'm an asshole." His fingers trembled around my hips. "Forgive me, please. I can't do this without you."

I looked up. His nostrils flared, his eyes wide and full of turmoil.

I didn't have time to accept his apology. His lips planted on mine and his tongue tore into my mouth—almost as if he wanted to steal the past few seconds and replace them with something so much better.

I tensed in his arms. But then ... I opened for him—how could I not? Despite my hurt, I kissed him back.

As our tongues met, our bodies relaxed and forgiveness webbed around us. My heart fluttered with affection and frustration.

By the time Arthur pulled away, my bruised feelings dismissed and only the rawest form of love remained.

Arthur's eyes darted over my head, a frown furrowing his fore-head. "Where the fuck did everyone go?"

I looked around. *Uh, that's strange.*

The garden, where multiple couples had been making out, whispering, and staring entranced into the fire, was empty. The evening was late, but no one had made moves to leave before now.

Movement by the door caught my eye. "There." I pointed to the Clubhouse as Grasshopper appeared, a large grin splitting his face, something hidden behind his back.

"What the hell are they up to?" Arthur tilted his head, never taking his eyes off the procession of bikers and their women as they emptied out from the Clubhouse, coming to ring around us.

"Whatever you're up to, quit it," Arthur growled.

Grasshopper and Mo joined us in the center of the ring created by Pure Corruption. My muscles vibrated. I couldn't understand what was going on. Was this a mutiny? A double cross?

You only think that because you've lived through an uprising. Not all Clubs go against authority—especially the Club Arthur has created.

Crossing his arms, Arthur stood to his full height. "I'm not into séances or whatever shit this is." His voice bordered on aggression and amusement.

"Calm your fucking tits, Kill. Let us do this." Mo grinned.

The Club traded their fussy, foggy drunkenness and sobered with secrecy. Everyone beamed, conspiring as one entity to deliver earth-shattering news.

Mo clasped his hands together as if preparing for a sermon. "See-ing as tonight is the last night we have until all of this is done—a war waged on both bikers and politicians alike—we thought it was a good opportunity."

"Hopper?" Mo moved to the side, giving Grasshopper lots of room to swing his hidden treasure from behind his back and present it. The parcel rested heavily in his raised hands.

My eyes widened as I looked at Melanie.

She winked.

I think I know what this is...

Grasshopper closed the last few steps and shoved the item into Arthur's chest. "It's all you need to make an honest woman out of her."

I covered my mouth with my hands.

At Dagger Rose, I'd been too young to appreciate the bonds of love and the tether of a family group—even though I'd loved Arthur with all my heart. But this...this was more than just love for one person. This was a welcome, an initiation—an acceptance into a world I knew and forgot for so long.

I belonged here.

I was no longer a stranger.

"Fuck." Arthur glanced at me, understanding slowly smoking his eyes. He looked at Mo and Grasshopper, then the rest of Pure Corruption. His hands shook a little as he tore open the package.

Forgetting the circle of gawking people, I drifted closer to Arthur, never taking my eyes off his strong fingers as he tore at the cello tape and scrunched up the paper. Tossing the wrapping in the direction of the fire, he revealed a tan leather jacket.

My heart stopped beating.

Grasshopper laughed. "Couldn't have a Dagger hanging out with us. No offense."

Arthur cleared his throat as he shook out the jacket, dangling it in his arms. The back faced me and I gasped at the perfection.

Reaching out, I traced the emblem for Pure Corruption with its skull and abacas. Peering closer, I noticed the filigree circle encompassing the logo, threading with Sagittarius and Libra star signs.

And above it all were the words *Property of Kill.*

I trembled. I never expected to be accepted the way I had been. Never expected to find such a place after being adrift for so long.

Resting my hands on his, I sensed the pressure of his headache, the joy of his excitement, and the sharp tang of his lust.

If we were alone, I would've grabbed him and kissed away the lingering worry in his gaze. I would've shown him just how much I was already his, regardless if I had a ring, jacket, or marriage license. None of that mattered as long as I got to sleep beside him at night and rise with him in the morning. We were equals. We were each other's.

"Cleo—" Arthur cleared his throat, his voice scratchy and coarse.

The group surrounding us gathered tighter.

I stood stiffly in front of Arthur. My heart was a runaway rabbit. My body a vibrating engine. I wanted it over with so I could sink into the new leather and find home.

Arthur's body heat battled with mine. Pressing a swift kiss on my mouth, he murmured, "Turn around."

Drinking in his green eyes, I struggled to obey. Pirouetting, I faced Pure Corruption.

A rustle, a footstep, then a heavy, welcoming weight fell across my shoulders. "You are no longer a Dagger Rose, but a Pure. From this day forth, you belong to this family, you will honor our rules, you will protect our members, and you will forever be welcome within our walls."

Arthur wrapped his arms around me, kissing my hairline. His large hand imprisoned my breast, dragging my attention to the glitter of silver. "See...it's real, Buttercup. Written in thread. You're mine forever."

I sucked in a breath as I looked down at the front pocket.

"It's official now," Arthur whispered. "The Club has spoken."

Tears swelled as I read four embroidered words:

Cleo.
President's Old Lady.

Chapter Twenty-Two

Kill

Everything of value had always been taken from me.

If I showed the slightest affection toward anything, my brother would steal it or my father would ruin it.

That was what they'd tried to do when they'd seen the Libra eraser from Cleo.

I could've yelled and demanded they give it back—but I'd learned to ignore them. I'd adopted that habit with Cleo. Whenever my family was too close—I pretended I didn't care. I hid the fact that I loved her and hurt her instead. I did it to keep her safe. —Kill, age sixteen

It was getting worse.

The pain.

The fucking excruciating pain.

The drugs the doctor had prescribed weren't doing shit, and it took every inch of strength and energy to hide the extent of agony I was in. I fooled most people, but not Cleo. I'd never been able to fool her.

I took a huge gulp of air as we entered my home. The bike ride over here had been a blessing and a curse. The wind had helped blow away some of the hot pressure in my skull, but the concentration to lean into corners, brake for traffic lights, and keep an eye on the speedometer taxed me.

Tonight should be the fucking happiest night of my life. Instead,

I battled with sadness. And, if I was downright honest, self-pity. I was done feeling like this. Done feeling so fucking weak.

Tomorrow, I would see the doctor again. I couldn't go on this way—despite the upcoming war and meeting with Samson, I had to face facts that I needed help.

And I needed it now.

Cleo walked backward, heading toward the stairs. The foyer chandelier glittered, drenching the space in light and committing treachery to my brain.

Her fingers toyed with the zipper of her new jacket. The soft tan radiated against her flawless skin. Her green eyes popped from the mess of fiery red hair and her legs looked so damn tempting in her tight jeans.

I rubbed my thumb and forefinger together remembering how wet she'd been at the gathering. How her hips had rocked on my lap as I touched her.

My cock swelled, stealing some of the pressure from my skull.

"Where are you going?" I asked as she licked her bottom lip.

"To bed."

I cocked an eyebrow at her lust-filled tone. "To sleep?"

She laughed softly. "What do you think?"

I think another orgasm would help a lot.

One thing that did seem to work on the pain was a release. If I could ride out the overwhelming agony to get to the point of explosive orgasm, the relief and endorphins afterward gave me much needed respite—almost as if the blood erupted from my body, allowing the swelling in my head to recede.

My eyes remained fixed on Cleo's hands as she fiddled with the zipper. "Come to bed."

Fuck, she looks amazing in that jacket.

I couldn't stop staring. She was mine. All deliciously mine.

Her voice lashed through the air, licking straight around my cock. She was like a siren...like the mermaid inked on my thigh, grasping me around the balls and coaxing me wherever she wanted me to go.

Crossing the small distance, I cupped her face. My mouth watered to kiss her, but I couldn't. Not yet. If I did, I'd end up fucking her on the stairs and I didn't think I'd survive a breathless rutting. I wanted her. I wanted to come in her. But I needed it to be...quiet.

"Give me ten minutes. I have to do something first."

Her eyes narrowed. She stopped playing with her zipper and pulled her face free from my hands. "Do what?"

I tensed. How could I explain that all through the meeting, all through the gathering and socializing all I could think about—all I could focus on—was the fact I'd lost a trade today.

Not because of the money.

Not because of screwing up.

But because it symbolized something so fucking scary.

I should never have fucked up something so simple.

How could I hope to create world anarchy and put things into place when I couldn't even handle a basic trade?

The answer was simple: I couldn't.

And I had to.

This was what I was born to do.

I'd lost the affinity with numbers. I missed thinking in algorithms. I felt lazy and dumb and unhinged.

I needed to find a way back. And if it meant retraining, then so be it.

"I'll be up in ten." Catching her shoulders, I spun her to face the stairs and tapped her ass. "Go up to the bedroom and wait for me. I want you naked with just your cut on." Gathering her masses of hair, I kissed the back of her neck. "Understand?"

She shivered. "I understand."

"Good." I pushed her gently, and she didn't look back as she scurried up the stairs.

I watched as the last flick of red hair vanished around the corner.

The minute she'd disappeared, I sighed.

I'd do anything to protect her. I'd become anyone to ensure she had the life she deserved.

But the more I thought about what I had to do in order to formulate the future I wanted, the deeper the fog of ennui I lived in became.

My limbs were listless. My brain lethargic.

Pain made everything so fucking hard.

Turning, I marched into my office. Closing the door—something I never bothered doing—I made my way to the four screens and powered them up.

The moment the glare from the screens glowed blue, I squinted and popped two painkillers from the bottle in my desk drawer.

From mastermind to defunct has-been.

I had to find a way to reboot myself before it was too late.

My heart stuttered as the failed trade flashed in red, determined to never let me forget the fuckup this afternoon.

Stop focusing on the past. Just fix it.

I corralled my remaining wits and concentrated. Gritting my teeth, I closed the charted history and opened a fresh window.

With a barely there tremble, I selected a new foreign currency pair, checked to see if there was any news in order to go bearish or bullish, and entered the trade into the software.

Cross-referencing the pair with my trusted candlesticks and technical indicators, I wiped away my nervous sweat and committed.

My mouse clicked.

The computer chimed.

And I hoped to fucking God I could remember how to do this.

Chapter Twenty-Three

Cleo

He'd been mean again today.

Honestly, he was like a bloody yo-yo. One minute he'd let me touch him, laugh with him, let me get close. The next, he treated me as if I had a disease. He belittled me in front of his father; he ignored me in front of his brother. I wasn't stupid. I knew Dax was a liability waiting to happen. But I just wished ... I just wished everyone would butt out. Why couldn't things be simple? Why couldn't the world be safe? —Cleo, diary entry, age twelve

My nipples tingled beneath the supple leather. The hair on my arms stood up as the sleeves cocooned my naked skin. And my belly tightened as I inhaled the tanning chemicals and newness.

I'd never worn something so sensual or so strict. Sensual because it heralded me as taken, belonging ... *loved*. And strict because it meant I was one of them. I had responsibilities to uphold, people to answer to, duties to honor.

Lucky for me, Arthur had always held that hierarchy in my life. Yes, we were equals, but I was happy for him to protect and cherish me because I did the same in subtler ways. He was brawn and brash brutality while I was the soft drizzle after a harsh summer's day.

Stroking the patch over my breast, my heart squeezed.

I'd done exactly as Arthur told me.

After scurrying up the stairs like an eager church mouse, I'd had a quick shower. Afterward, I'd moisturized, pampered, and padded naked across the room. I'd made sure the bedside lights were on romantic glow rather than interrogation brightness, and curled up in the middle of the bed wearing nothing but my new jacket.

And there I'd waited...growing wet with anticipation and breathless with desire.

Every rustle I made, the new jacket sent another wave of need through my blood. The silver thread glittered, reminding me time and time again who I loved.

The small jacket fit me perfectly.

Riding on the back of Arthur's bike from the gathering had filled me with a mix of joy and justice. Any motorist who saw us growling past knew I wasn't one of them—I wasn't from a normal nine-to-five society—I was a member of something *bigger*. A sister, wife, and friend to people who understood the meaning of togetherness.

The skull and abacas logo teased fear into some people, believing we were lawlessness and terror. What they didn't see was an extended family, and I'd just been handed the keys to their home.

I sighed, staring at the ceiling.

How much longer will he be?

My ears strained for any noise of his boots on the stairs. My instincts fanned out for any prickle that he might be close.

I was tempted to go down to find him—it'd been forty minutes, not the ten that he promised—but something inside me hesitated.

I didn't want to interfere.

Losing the trade this afternoon did something to him I couldn't understand. And unfortunately, this was one time I couldn't help. He had to fix it. He had to come to terms with whatever injury shadowed him. All I could do was be there for him when he healed.

The house breathed around me, hugging me with its white

painted walls. So many memories already existed in this place: the trials of convincing Arthur I was the girl from his past. The fear of being sold. The blankness of amnesia.

The echoes of everything that'd passed hovered in the air, twisting and twining, waiting for new memories to play with.

And tonight I plan on making new memories.

I planned on doing something for Arthur that had never been done before.

The bedroom door suddenly swung wide.

Arthur appeared.

His boots were off, his feet bare as he moved silently over the carpet. His eyes feasted on my nakedness and I deliberately wriggled, letting the front of my jacket gape, hinting at nipples and flesh. "I missed you."

His lips quirked as his eyes blackened. "I can see that."

Unashamedly, I spread my legs a little. "I missed you a lot, in fact." The color of my tattooed leg looked almost garish against the white of his bedspread. I was a splash of color on a simple cloud.

He didn't reply, only stared. Taking his time, he drank in my scars and ink—once again making me feel as if I was the most unique woman in the world.

"You were gone awhile." My skin warmed beneath his gaze. "Are you okay?" I flinched as the question crashed between us. I didn't want to keep hounding him, but I couldn't stop my worry.

I'd long since given up trying to forecast the future—guessing what would occur tomorrow, next week, or next year. Life had taught me that things could go disastrously wrong within moments. But I also wasn't prepared for chaos to win. There had to be structure and Arthur's head injury was ruining that structure.

He'll beat it.

We just had to be strong enough to weather all triumphs or tragedies that rested on our timeline.

Arthur ran a hand through his dark hair, pulling it back from his face. "I'm…better." He smiled gently. "I made back the money I lost this morning. So yeah…I'm okay." His voice was achingly soft. If I didn't know him, I would believe his words. But I did know him, and his tone said he was still afraid.

Sitting upright, I scooted onto my knees. "Is there anything I can do?"

His eyes blazed with love. "You're doing it. Just by being you." His hands went to his belt. "I couldn't ask for more." His gaze latched on to my inner thighs as his fingers pulled the buckle aside, then unhooked the button of his fly.

I stopped breathing.

An electric storm brewed around us, tingling my scalp.

Drifting from my knees to all fours, I prowled to the bottom of the bed and stopped before him. Beckoning him closer with my finger, Arthur obeyed, coming to stand within touching distance.

We didn't speak as I reached out and stilled his hand.

His skin scorched mine.

He sucked in a breath, turning to stone. "Cleo…"

Shaking my head, I pushed aside his grip.

His large chest rose as his arms dropped woodenly by his sides.

Silence wrapped around us like a blanket as I sat higher on my knees and ran my hands over the planes of his chest. The warm cotton of his T-shirt guided me under his cut, muscles bunching beneath my fingertips.

We match.

My heart skipped.

We wore the same emblem. A perfect mirror image. I was marked forever with his protection and commitment.

Never looking away from him, I bit my lip and pushed the heavy leather off his shoulders. The dense material slipped down his arms, catching on his large hands.

His lips parted as I tugged his hand forward, carefully freeing him so the cut fell to the floor.

We flinched at the soft slap of leather on carpet—the noise seeming to reach out and stroke us with hungry greed. Our breathing ratcheted as I followed the contours of his chest. Hills, valleys, indents, and ridges. Every inch of him impenetrable.

My mouth watered, intoxicated on his perfection. His five o'clock shadow, the long length of his hair, the way his eyes glimmered with acuity.

I never wanted anyone else. For as long as I lived.

Working my way downward, I sketched his stomach, loving the way he gasped and shivered.

He held his breath as my fingertips found his zipper. Ever so slowly, I tugged it south, never looking away from his eyes.

His trousers flared open—a welcome invitation. Sliding my hands around his narrow hips, I pushed the heavy denim down his legs.

His hands fisted by his side.

The urgency and need in his eyes crackled the air, but he didn't reach for me. Didn't try to touch me. Somehow, we wordlessly agreed that I was in charge. That I was in control of our tempo.

I wanted to take from him.

I wanted to give him something he'd never had before.

A secretive smile tugged my lips as I captured the hard length of his erection through his boxer briefs.

My breasts swelled, my nipples pebbling even harder. My knees wobbled as I ran my thumb over his crown, drawing a low groan from his chest. The sharp Vs of his stomach tightened as he gave himself into my power.

"God, Cleo…" His eyes snapped closed as I continued to press against the highly sensitive tip. Growing bold, I squeezed his girth. I wasn't gentle. I was demanding.

My heart liquefied at the gift of touching him. "I want you, Art. So much."

"You have me." His voice was gravel.

"Don't move."

His eyes connected with mine, a slight question forming in their depths. But then... he nodded.

He sighed, relinquishing total control. The weight on his shoulders disintegrated; his worries fading by letting me rule.

I was a goddess.

I was a witch.

The thrill at having his utmost trust feathered through my soul.

He didn't twitch or smile as I tugged his boxer briefs from hips to knees. His nostrils flared as I left the tight material around his legs, imprisoning him where he stood—cutting his tattooed mermaid in half.

My heart beat faster at his perfect length and thickness. I couldn't ask for a better lover. Even when I was fourteen, I'd wanted him. Wanted to know what existed in his trousers. Wanted to touch him. Lick him.

He wouldn't let me then. But he will now.

Rising up on my knees again, I grabbed the hem of his T-shirt and raised it over his head.

With half a smile, which was so damn sexy it hurt my heart, he ducked and raised his arms. With a sharp tug, the T-shirt flew over his head. I dropped it to the abandoned clothing on the floor. They were like leaves from a giant tree, shedding for another season.

The moment Arthur was naked, a delicious sparkle effervesced through me. He was chocolate and Christmas all at once.

He's mine.

Having him so exposed, while I wore his jacket claiming me as his property, made me feel powerful—invincible. I wasn't owned—*I* owned *him*.

I loved the aphrodisiac...the knowledge he would let me do anything.

His hand captured my cheek, his thumb rubbing over my skin.

My fingers tightened around his cock, tugging him closer to the bed.

He groaned, his eyes fluttering to half-mast. "Christ, you undo me, Buttercup." His hand fell away and I licked my lips at the thought of bringing this warrior, this incredible biker, to his knees.

My new jacket creaked as I shuffled closer, never letting go of his erection.

I grew wet.

I grew eager.

Stroking him, I ran my thumb once again along the tip.

The muscles in his neck stood out as he hissed between his teeth. His eyes remained closed while every inch of his powerful body stiffened.

He knew as well as I did what I was about to do. His hands fisted by his sides, humming with impatience and joy. We hovered on the knife edge, waiting to explode.

With one hand squeezing his length, I cupped his balls with the other.

"Shit," he breathed as I tugged the soft skin and trailed my touch upward to press against the erogenous zone behind his cock.

He staggered. "Fuck me. What are you doing to me, Cleo?"

"Giving you pleasure."

I wanted to draw the moment out but my legs trembled and my mouth ached to fit around him. With the way he shuddered, I doubted he had the self-control to let me postpone much longer.

I want to taste.

Taking a deep breath, I stopped torturing and gave him something he'd never let any other woman do.

I'm taking this from you.

I'm the only one who will ever lick you this way.

I felt as if I cast a spell, binding him to me forever.

Leaning forward, I breathed on him, letting the heat cascade over sensitive flesh.

He froze, gulping in air.

"I want to suck you," I whispered.

"Fuck . . . ," he groaned.

Tugging his balls, I positioned my head above him, and with the flat of my tongue, licked him for the very first time.

My heart banged against my ribs.

"Oh, *shit*." His hands shot upward to fist in my hair.

He was sweet, musky. Hot. So hot.

His thighs trembled; he dug his toes into the carpet. His scent instantly wrapped around my soul and squeezed.

I licked him again, relishing in the way he quaked and shivered.

"Fuck." He shuddered again, his hands yanking on my hair. The mermaid with her red hair and green tail danced on his thigh as he braced himself. Her strands wrapped around his balls, inking the end of his shaft as I opened my mouth and guided him inside.

A grunt—half pleasure, half pain but complete submission—wrenched from his lungs.

I smiled, stretching my lips around his thickness as I licked the underside, sucking his length with deep pulls.

I didn't move quickly or slowly. I didn't take him hesitant or boldly. I took him peacefully, reverently—both of us adjusting to the power switch of me taking, not submitting.

His body never stopped vibrating. He growled and cursed, littering the air with passion. Slowly, his tension bloomed into need as he grew accustomed to the foreign sensation of being sucked.

My jaw ached as I sheathed my teeth and sank over him as far as I could go. My lips wrapped around him, claiming him as my own.

"Fuck!" His hands wrapped harder in my hair. He didn't try to control me, but his hold was firm, fisting the long strands into a ponytail, steadying himself as if he'd topple at any moment.

I was hot.

I was cold.

I was wet.

So wet.

Unconsciously, I fell into a rhythm. My right hand moved up and down, spreading the slipperiness of my saliva.

Keeping the sharpness of my teeth away from his delicate flesh, I dragged my tongue up the silky steel and down again.

Up, down.

Lick, swirl.

"Fuck, you're incredible." Arthur's hips moved to match my pace, thrusting in time, but never taking more than I offered.

His fingers slowly started to guide me, forgetting everything but seeking the final reward. Pinpricks of pain danced over my scalp, sending washes of desire through my system.

I never knew I could become so wet by doing something singular for him.

He made me feel adored.

Worshipped.

Indebted to my gift.

Withdrawing him from my mouth, I swirled my tongue around his tip before swallowing him in one swift sweep.

"Ah, shit." He jerked, bending over me. "Goddammit, Buttercup." His voice was unrecognizable—brittle and strained.

With a racing heart, I kept going. I dedicated myself to giving him the best blow job I could.

His balls tightened, tensing against his body. Ripples of pleasure worked along his shaft beneath my tongue.

He was close.

Switching from languishing to quick, I sucked harder, wanting to steal every control from him.

He cried out as his hands moved with my head, bobbing up and down on his cock.

His hips twitched faster.

His breathing came quicker.

His body unraveled with every second.

Together, we found a perfect waltz. Every swallow down his length he thrust forward, using my mouth but giving so much in return. He gave me his soul. His undoing. His vulnerability.

Then, he froze. "Fuck, I'm going—"

I swirled my tongue faster, squeezing him harder in answer.

I want you to come.

I wanted to taste everything he could give me. Maybe then he would be mine for eternity.

His fingers yanked on my hair with urgency. "Stop. Fuck, I'm going to—"

I moaned low in my throat. The vibrations of my voice amplified the slick heat and wetness of my mouth and Arthur lost the battle.

"Shit!"

He grabbed my head, his strong fingers digging deliciously into my scalp as he roared and gave himself over to me.

I bobbed faster, unsheathing my teeth to scrape the sharpness down his satiny length, highlighting his pleasure with a threat of pain.

He combusted.

His balls throbbed in my touch; a wave of pressure escaped the base of him, rippling past my tongue and shooting into my mouth.

The first splash caught me by surprise. Hot. Thick.

Squeezing my eyes, I kept sucking, kept stroking.

His hips rocked faster.

I moaned again as another salty spray coated the back of my throat.

Another wave.

I kept licking, kept taking until he shuddered in my hold.

His body crumbled, losing its strength and giving in to gravity. With an endless sigh, he ran his fingers from my hair to my chin, prying me upward and forcing me to let go of his cock.

Raising my head, I smiled and swallowed the remainder of his orgasm.

The glow in his eyes utterly undid me.

I got chills at the fathomless affection and awe blazing on his face.

Crashing to his knees, he captured my cheeks and kissed my lips with utmost humbleness. "Thank you," he panted between kisses.

"Thank you for exploding my world and showing me heaven does exist."

I laughed softly, pulling away from his mouth. "I'm so glad I was the one to show you."

He shook his head, his hands never leaving my face. "There's never been anyone like you. Never. You owned me since I was a boy. And you completely consume me now that I'm a man."

Tears pricked my eyes as he struggled to hide the sudden glassiness of his own. "Cleo…" His voice broke. "Fuck, Cleo. I love you so goddamn much."

He launched himself at me. Syncing our heartbeats, plaiting our minds—ensuring we were soldered together.

Wrapping long arms like a cage around me, he squashed me against his chest. The rapid *thump-thump* of his heart echoed from his body into mine and I felt something I'd never felt before.

A link.

An intrinsic otherworldly link that bound me not to this world but another.

Our world.

Our home.

Our harmony.

I woke to the rays of golden sunshine and the gentlest stroking of my lover.

My mind was soft and floaty. My body warm and toasty.

It was the best wake-up call I'd ever had.

Turning to face Arthur, I smiled. My vision cast everything in a sleepy haze. "Morning."

His smile lit up my world. The strain around his eyes remained and the tightness around his shoulders hinted he still suffered, but for now…he looked radiant.

"Morning." He kissed the tip of my nose. "Did you know you moaned in your sleep?"

Rolling onto my back, I threw my arms over my head and stretched. "I did?"

He nodded, his eyes glued on to my bare breasts from the sheet sliding down. "You did. It was long and loud and..." Without another word, he bent over me and sucked my nipple into his mouth.

I gasped at the sudden shock of heat and wetness.

"I think you were dreaming of me. Am I right?" His mouth trailed over the swell of my breast, licking my other nipple as if I were a melting ice cream and he needed every drop.

My mind emptied apart from the intoxicating lick. "I...I don't know." Slinking my fingers into his hair, I murmured, "I might need some coaxing to remember."

He chuckled, cupping my breast and squeezing with a possessive tantalizing hold. "Coaxing? Are you certain?"

I arched into his touch, luxuriating in the way my body warmed. "Very certain. My memory is terrible."

He flinched, his eyes glancing up my torso to connect with mine. "You can say that again."

Pain shadowed. My faux pas tainted our fun.

It wasn't the best joke. Should I apologize?

But then I burst out laughing. If we couldn't laugh about the past, what could we do? "I suppose it is a little ironic for a recovered amnesiac to say she has a bad memory."

Rolling his eyes, he muttered, "Only you could laugh about something so painful." His smile returned. One eye was obscured by his inky hair, decorating his sexy features in a way that made me want to flip him onto his back and repeat what I did last night.

"Come here." I held my breath as Arthur obediently propped himself up with a straining bicep and hovered over me.

Pulling him down, I tilted my head and trembled as his mouth met mine. Our tongues danced in unison, listening to the same silent tune.

It began with me kissing him.

But it didn't end that way.

Arthur submitted, then dominated, switching the kiss into a soul-searing possession. His tongue dueled with mine with slow, deep sweeps—trading the sine wave of bliss for something filled with dark overtones. His hunger and need smeared my senses, until all I craved was sex.

Rough, dirty, delicious sex.

I whimpered as he sucked my bottom lip; my hands tangled deeper into his hair.

His answering groan quavered through me, tightening my nipples and sending sensitivity scattering over my skin. I melted into opulence.

"I'll never forget you again," I whispered as he pulled away and pressed butterfly kisses down my neck.

"I'll make sure you never can." Swirling his tongue around my nipple, he bunched the sheets toward the end of the bed. His fingers landed on my knee, pressing, teasing, moving in infinitesimal increments up my inner thigh.

"You'll never forget how it feels when I touch you." He pinched me, wrenching a breathy moan from my lips.

"Never."

His teeth graced over my breast. "You'll never forget how it feels when I taste you."

I smashed my face into a pillow as he sucked greedily. "Never. I promise. I promise forever."

His fingers crept higher up my thigh—they were the epicenter of the quake he'd conjured inside me. Aftershocks radiated upward to my core and downward to my toes. I shivered.

I froze.

I waited.

I wanted.

I need him so much.

When his finger finally found my folds, I bowed off the bed, only to be slammed down again by his lips on my chest.

My mouth parted as he pressed inside me, inserting two long fingers in an effortless slide. "You'll never forget how it feels when I fill you."

I ceased to make sense of the desire fogging my head. Every inch of need from last night rushed back, compounding lust upon lust.

I cried out as Arthur's hot mouth landed on my throat, sucking and biting, driving me insane with sharp teeth. His fingers stroked my inner walls, twitching in the perfect way to draw slipperiness and sensation.

"Is this my payback?" I asked, squeezing my eyes against the new onslaught as he rubbed my clit.

Laughing quietly, he worked his way along my collarbone and dropped farther down my torso. Kissing each rib, he replied, "You controlled me last night. You took what you wanted from me and I didn't complain."

I snorted. "I took nothing. I did it for you—to give you pleasure."

He shook his head, the dark strands tickling my belly as he scooted between my legs. "You did give me pleasure, but you also enjoyed dominating me." Blowing a breath on my exposed pussy, he whispered, "It's my turn."

Pressing me back on the mattress, he shoved the sheets onto the floor and sat on his haunches.

My heart stopped.

His cock stood straight up from between his sculptured legs. The mermaid tattoo seemed to have an extra twinkle in her eye, just like Arthur.

"I'm going to show you how much last night meant to me, Buttercup."

I shivered, raising my hands above my head on the pillow. Boldly, I spread my legs, displaying everything I was to this man. My breasts—

one burned, one inked—my stomach with its color and scars. I let him drink me in. "I'm not going to argue."

He smirked. "I'm glad about that; otherwise I'd have to get my tie."

I clenched. "On second thought..."

Shaking his head, mirth suffusing his gaze, he imprisoned my hips. His fingertips bruised my skin, sending flares of heat through me.

Arthur Killian was polished ruthlessness and savage lawlessness. He camouflaged himself with an urban gloss that fooled no one; he was never fully able to hide the untamed animal inside his heart. But where an animal was vicious and controlled by instinct, he was also loyal, affectionate, and kind. An animal had no secrets—it bared its soul, loved unconditionally, and had no defenses when it came to its mate.

I'm his mate.

And I was helpless to resist him when he drugged me so completely.

His vivid green eyes gave me no room to hide as he inspected every fraction. His fingers toyed with the trimmed curls between my legs. His lips seduced me with a lazy smile speaking of carnality and destruction.

"You're breathing very fast, Buttercup."

"I can't help it."

His eyebrow rose, willing me to go on—to divulge secrets of my own. I had no more walls, no more black holes in which to fight for answers. I owed him every memory, every thought. "The way you're watching me. The way you're touching me. It's driving me insane."

He bit his lip, eyes darting between tattoos and scars. "Having you in my bed is more than just a miracle; it's a goddamn phenomenon. Forgive me if I look at you as if you aren't real." His voice dropped, filling with awe. "It's because I keep thinking none of this *is* real. That the headaches are a sign of my insanity. That I've left reality behind and found salvation in hallucinations."

His fingers floated over my belly, through my folds, along my inner thighs. Everywhere he touched me, I erupted and smoldered.

His pain fisted my heart.

He was too much.

Too deep, too pure, too perfect.

"Could a hallucination give you what I did last night? Could a ghost lick you until you came?"

His smile was crooked and cheerless. "You don't know how many nights I woke to a dream so similar to what you gave me. You don't know how many times I woke cursing and raging because I didn't want to leave a world where I had you only to lose you day after day."

My chest splintered. My rib cage became firewood for the incinerating flames inside my heart. "Arthur..."

I loved him too much. The way he spoke terrified me that I wouldn't be able to keep him now that I'd found him again. Would we always be shadowed by the past?

My shaky sigh webbed around us. "Let it go. You have to let it go."

The pain.

The torture.

The driving need for revenge.

He needed a fresh start—away from here. He needed to let the future take us forward, rather than let the past drag us back.

Raising his hand, he squeezed the bridge of his nose. "I'm sorry. I have no idea how this turned from pleasure to..."

Wedging myself upright on my elbows, I whispered, "I know why. It's because you don't believe in us."

His eyes flashed open. "How can you say that?"

"Because it's true. Until you accept that life has brought us back together and stop reliving the pain of being apart, you can't believe in what we have."

"I know what we have and I *do* believe in it." His voice was a whip, slicing through the melancholy. "I'll show you."

Knocking away my elbows, he forced me to lie back down. In a swift move, he switched from haunches to stomach, positioning himself between my spread legs.

His hands clamped down on my thighs, gluing me to the mattress. "I'll show you until you trust me." His dark hair framed his extraordinary face as he looked up the length of my torso. "I'll prove to you that I'm yours, no matter what."

"I know you are." My heart skipped a beat at the determination on his face and the dark shadows beneath his eyes.

He was stunning. Masculine but caring. Possessive but loving. The complete perfect package.

I grabbed handfuls of linen as his head bent. His breath fanned hot and steamy on my pussy. His lips hovered, trapping me in the acute moment of anticipation.

My pulse turned into a geyser, wanting to burst. "Please…" I braced for the slippery incredibleness of his tongue.

Another breath, the billowing heat condensing on my skin.

Another.

I couldn't stand it any longer.

"Please!" I cried.

"Be my fucking pleasure." He licked me.

I shot upright, hurling straight toward heaven. "Oh, God!"

His hands captured my thighs, holding them down and spread. His tongue dashed over my clit, lapping quick and sharp. Then he flattened the strong muscle and swept it from bud to entrance.

I spiraled.

The pleasure…it was too much.

My mind swam as he nibbled and speared inside me with no warning.

"Oh, hell. Arthur!"

He growled, thrusting his tongue again. "Goddammit. Believe me."

"I believe you. I believe you!"

His five o'clock shadow rasped my sensitive inner thighs. "No, you don't. Not yet." He tasted me thoroughly, moving back to suck on my clit.

It was too good.

I'll explode.

"I do. I do believe you!" My legs tightened until every muscle cramped. "Please... I can't stand it. Stop."

But he didn't stop. Again and again he dipped inside me, dragging his tongue to lap and lathe.

I lost myself to him, bobbing away on the tide of bliss he created. He was Poseidon and I was an unlucky ship about to be wrecked on the shores of a detonating orgasm.

My pussy tightened, reaching for the promised shoreline, wanting nothing more than to decimate into tiny shards.

"Yes..."

"Not yet," Arthur growled. "You're not allowed until I say so."

My eyes flashed open, half in rage, half in obedience. "I can't stop it."

"Yes, you can." Letting me go, he crept up my body. His lips were swollen and damp, my wetness glistening on his chin. I waited for him to smother me with his body, but instead he urged me to roll onto my side. "You're not to come until I'm inside you."

Every inch of me was alive, crawling and begging for a release.

Lying down beside me, he lassoed a strong arm around my belly and yanked me into the hard muscles of his body. My back to his front. My softness against his hardness.

I flinched as he ground his throbbing erection against my lower back.

"I'm going to fuck you now, Buttercup. I'll prove to you that I can love you while using you. That I can trust you while riding you. That I can believe in you."

I moaned as his hand ran over my hip, grabbing my thigh and wrenching it back to entwine with his.

"Take me," I mumbled. My body undulated, my core empty.

With my legs open, he maneuvered his hips and fisted his cock, guiding it to my entrance.

The moment the tip of him entered me, I gritted my teeth and fought off the relentless orgasm.

"Don't come. Not yet," he ordered, thrusting inside me with one slippery impale. "Do. Not. Come."

I stopped cataloguing how my blood boiled, how my skin itched, and how my mind sang for freedom. I focused only on the thickness stretching me. The overwhelming delight of accepting my soul mate into my body.

He was what I craved. His tongue had been a perfect entrée, but this...this was the main course and dessert all in one.

Keeping me pinned against him, he rocked into me, rolling me from my side onto my stomach. My arms splayed out. I moaned, biting a pillow as he rode me. His thrusts were slow, then quick, gathering speed faster and faster.

"God, you feel amazing," he grunted. One hand clamped on my hip, keeping me imprisoned beneath him, while the other wrapped around my nape.

The primitive way he held me undid the floodgates and I cried out louder and louder with every thrust. I couldn't move. I could only take what he gave. Every stroke sent me higher into the spindling promise.

His teeth razored my ear. His breath scalded my skin. "Come. I need you to come." He thrust hard. "Now, Cleo." His voice was no longer controlled.

His divine rock gave me no room to argue. I was trapped. He was above me, around me, inside me. He was me. I was him.

My orgasm would be his. We would share our release in some cosmically charged way.

His hand drifted down my front and pinched my clit. "I said I need you to *come*."

I moaned as his fingers rubbed in perfect circles, blending in empathy with his rapid pace.

"Oh, God. Yes, don't stop." My body gave up trying to make sense of where to rock or flow. I stopped trying to hold off and gave myself over to the inevitable combustion.

I screamed as an intense orgasm sliced through my body. My core clenched with devastating pressure. The ship I'd become destroyed itself over and over again, splintering against the battering of his storm.

It was staggering. It was paralyzing.

I turned into a puddle of delirium.

Arthur groaned, "Goddammit!" His rhythm lost its perfection and he slipped from making love to fucking me ruthlessly.

My orgasm only strengthened and continued. I crashed harder knowing that even as he used me, he worshipped me. His violence and craving blazed with truth.

"Fuck, yes." His release erupted deep inside me. His pleasure resounding in my ears.

On and on, he spilled inside and I took every drop. I was no longer a ship floating on his tide, but drowned and consumed in his wake.

By the time we opened our eyes, we were both sticky with sweat and overheating in the patch of sunlight streaming through the window.

Slowly, we uncramped our toes and fell apart with a boneless sigh.

"I believe you," I mumbled. "Ten thousand times, I believe you."

He chuckled, tucking me into his side. His warmth spooned me and I'd never been so safe or contented. "Finally." He nuzzled behind my ear. "Things are going to be wonderful. You'll see. Once I've taken vengeance and things are dealt with, it will all be over."

A shadow fell over my heart that no amount of sunshine or love could diminish. Would it, though? Would we find a happy balance? Would his headaches fade and leave him unharmed?

My eyes fell on the silver thread of PROPERTY OF KILL on my jacket tossed on the floor. It glittered in the sunlight. I stroked his forearm still wrapped around my chest. "I hope so, Art. I truly do."

"This is our fresh start, Buttercup. You'll see."

My mind darted back to the night I'd arrived. The battle, the trafficking. Our reunion hadn't been ideal but we'd made it work. We would make whatever the future delivered work, too.

"I'm so in love with you, Art."

He sucked in a breath, pressing a kiss on my temple. "The same for me, Cleo. I've always loved you and I always will."

Chapter Twenty-Four

Kill

What was I supposed to do?

I'd finally come of age to be inducted into the Club. I'd sworn my oath, wore my cut, and promised to obey Thorn Price as my president. A party had been thrown in my honor. Yet later, once the men had passed out from drunkenness, my father had reminded me of one important clause. The Club came first. The Club was my life. But I was the loophole because my father was blood and demanded ultimate fealty—even over my president. —Kill, age sixteen

"Are they here?"

Grasshopper looked up as I strode into the Clubhouse. I'd had a hell of a time getting Cleo to stay behind, but I'd finally been able to reassure her enough that I needed to complete some business and it would be boring as fuck.

I'd lied to keep her behind.

Having her in my life was personified ecstasy but I couldn't have her knowing everything.

Even though you promised you would tell her.

Scowling, I shoved those thoughts away. She'd begged to come with me, but tough luck.

I knew she wanted to keep an eye on me with my headaches, but this was a part of my life where I didn't want her.

Revenge.

It was a lonely obsession. And should remain a lonely obsession.

She didn't understand, couldn't contemplate the overwhelming drive to make my father pay. She seemed content to let fate or karma deal with him—even after everything he'd done.

She didn't believe in retribution or taking payment for past sins.

But I do.

Wholeheartedly, and luckily, so did Wallstreet and Pure Corruption.

"Yep, all the men you requested. Ten in total." Cocking his head toward the door leading to the meeting room, Grasshopper added, "We've got your back on this, Kill. Everything's in place."

Nodding, I ran a hand through my hair. It hadn't been easy and we still had much to do, but it was almost over. Once my father was dealt with, all I had to focus on was becoming the poster boy for world revolution. My eyes shot to the blown-up magazine covers. For years, Wallstreet had built my "brand." Through TV and newspaper interviews, he'd ensured people with money and influence knew my name. So when the time came to call on their network, our message would spread far and wide.

I'm one of them through careful scripts and fabrication.

I snorted. To some, waging war on another Club would seem more than enough to stay occupied. But to me—it was nothing compared to our main strategy.

Only once it was executed could I relax and focus on getting rid of this motherfucking headache.

"Good. Let's go."

With a smirk, Grasshopper saved an email on his phone and shoved it into his pocket. "You're the boss."

Together, we strode across the common room. Grasshopper reached the door before me, twisting the knob and ushering me into the meeting.

Ten pairs of eyes met mine, including Matchsticks, Mo, Beetle, and a few other original members of Corrupts who were dead-fast and loyal to Wallstreet. These men I trusted and these were the ones who'd been carrying out my plans over the past few years, building up our reserves, planting doubt in our enemies, and arranging a worldwide takeover.

We weren't after small control anymore. We were after *global*.

Mo stood up as I circled the table and took my seat. The gavel fit perfectly in my hand as Grasshopper took his place.

"All ready to begin, Kill. They've been debriefed on the upcoming meeting with Samson, and the majority know of what is expected of them tonight."

Rolling my wrist, enjoying the weight of the tiny hammer giving me so much authority, I smiled. "Perfect." Looking toward the men, I rapped the table and narrowed my eyes. "Let's start."

Grasshopper was the first to steal the floor. "I'll go first."

The men grinned, already knowing the order in which they'd go. It never deviated. We were all equals, but in Church we followed a hierarchy.

"I've been in touch with our other chapters in San Francisco, Los Angeles, New Mexico, and Arkansas. They're all aware of what's in the pipelines and ready to bowl into fucking town at the slightest request."

"Did you ask them to come?" Mo asked.

Grasshopper shook his head. "I figure, with our reinforcements from Green Clovers up north, we should be sweet. They've proved themselves in the past and won't fuck up an opportunity to shed their Irish authority and come into the Pure fold."

This wasn't news to me. Lucky himself had been in touch with me over the years. He'd been hankering for a challenge to prove himself worthy of wearing our patch. Word had got out that being a Pure meant wealth. Being a Pure meant safety, brotherhood, and living a long fucking life, rather than turf wars, discipline, and a one-way ticket to Hades.

Men were sick of being controlled by a drunken mob still living in Ireland. They wanted home roots. They wanted a faction large enough to spread out and grow.

It was a win-win.

"Mo, how's it going with what I requested?" I looked to the messy blond biker who wore his battle scars like fucking jewelry. In the garish overhanging light, tiny silver scars glittered on his face, neck, and hands. They played peekaboo—almost invisible until illumination shone in just the right way.

It made him a scary motherfucker.

"I've got three back so far. That leaves one more. Seeing as that blonde bitch was killed back at Dagger Rose."

My eyes widened. "Shit, I didn't expect you to be so quick about it."

He smirked. "I'm a fast worker, Prez. The three are still in our custody."

"What? Here at the compound?"

Mo shook his head. "Nope. Got two in drug rehab and one is safe in a halfway house out of town. Thought I'd take the initiative 'cause that's what you'd have done."

Once again, Mo proved I had no reason to micromanage.

I leaned my elbows on the table and clasped my hands.

With all the carnage I planned, it was nice to have done a good tiding for once.

The women who'd been trafficked with Cleo when she first arrived had been reclaimed. Reclaimed and rejuvenated and heading back to health and normalcy—it was a damn sight better than being whores for men who didn't fucking deserve them.

The girls had been "gifted" to other presidents in turn for their loyalty. It'd been Wallstreet's idea: pussy and money—a fail-safe for fealty—but I hated that Cleo had seen me stoop so fucking low.

I didn't trade in skin. I didn't deal drugs. I didn't sell guns. I wasn't out to hurt anyone. I was out to reform the wrong and uphold justice. I couldn't be such a goddamn hypocrite by selling women for my own purpose.

"Good to hear. Let me know when they're detoxed. Need to know if we can do anything else."

Mo raised an eyebrow. "Do *more* for them? Shit, Kill. You've given them a life they didn't even have in the beginning. They were the ones who caught their idiotic asses with bikers and spread their whorish legs."

"I know. They joined this game, but I sent them deeper. It's on my fucking head."

Topic closed, I turned to the next speaker and cleared my throat. "Next agenda, Matchsticks. Did you hear back from Black Diamonds in England?"

Matchsticks sat higher in his chair, his large belly squashed against the table ledge. "Yep. Jethro Hawk said he'd provide use of his diamond shipping routes for anything we need transferred and also mentioned a face-to-face meeting with you next time you're in the UK."

I cracked my knuckles. The English tycoon who outweighed my bank balance by almost double—which was no mean feat—had been of great assistance over the past few years. I'd met him at his diamond-processing plant and been so fucking jealous of the son of a bitch for what he had. Not because of the wealth or glittering rocks all around him, but for the woman standing by his side.

There'd been so much fucking tension between them, but all I could think about was Cleo. Cleo rotting in a grave. Cleo burning alive in her family's home. I'd wanted to wring his neck for being so lucky. But I never got the chance, because we ended up forming a grudging respect.

Along with respect, I also found a kinship I never expected. He had a strict father—a family that expected far too much of him. I recognized the trap he lived in and our similar family issues strengthened a bond I knew I could trust. To be honest, my circumstances were a damn sight better than his. At least I had the freedom to kill my father and brother. Jethro? I doubted he'd ever be free.

"That'll work. Pass on my thanks. Fingers crossed we won't have to call on him, but it's good to have everything in place."

Looking around the table, I racked my brain to see if I'd scratched everything off the list. *Wasn't there something else to discuss?* My fucking headache still wouldn't leave me alone. It'd eased a little, thank God. Mainly thanks to the two releases I'd had inside Cleo.

My lips twitched remembering her head bobbing between my legs. She'd been so fucking pretty.

I grew hard just thinking about her.

Beetle announced, "By the way, our snitch has been busy."

Everyone's attention shot to the youngest member, waiting for him to continue.

Playing with the gauge in his ear, Beetle said, "The snitch in Night Crusaders. He said Dagger Rose is overstaying their welcome. Making plans to move due to a fight they had last night with the Crusader prez. A few men got hurt. They've been told to fuck off before the end of the week."

"Shit!"

Grasshopper slammed his palms on the table. "But that's in two fucking days."

Beetle shrugged. "I know. We need to move fast on those assholes. Already told the boys; they've stockpiled more guns and prepped the bikes." His eyes fell on me. "I'm on it, Prez."

My heart raced. *Two days.*

The timing didn't really matter; in fact, I'd planned on ambushing them this week regardless. We couldn't afford to let them fuck off. Not now.

But two days? Could we be ready?

"Is Alligator with them? The fuckwit who hurt Cleo?"

The men shifted in their chairs. The bonfire last night had firmly rooted Buttercup into our family. The men wouldn't be fighting just because I said so, but because she was theirs now. We had a joint interest. An investment into her future.

"Sure is," Lance muttered. The biker was a weathered man with faded tattoos of his beloved Yorkshire terriers on his forearms. He was an enigma but was fucking brutal in war. "Been spotted with Rubix. He's there. Ready to be executed."

Excitement inched through my veins. Despite my weakness, fuzziness, and occasional dizziness that made me stumble like a freak, I was able enough to fight.

I want to fight.

I've been waiting eight long years for this.

I had every intention of enjoying it.

Fisting the gavel, I brought it down onto the table with a smack. "Good work, boys. You know what else you have to do. We attack in two days. Gather ammo, clear the roads of local police, stockpile everything else we might need."

Standing, I growled, "In two days we wipe Dagger Rose from existence and put this fucking treason behind us."

Thirty minutes later, I straddled my Triumph and slotted the key into the ignition. Twisting my wrist, the silent machine evolved into a rumbling beast.

Sunshine sliced slivers off my eyeballs and made my brain bleed. I wanted to get home. I wanted shade. I wanted Cleo.

But as I turned the handlebars for home, I paused.

I had one last thing to do and I didn't want to do it where Cleo could listen in.

Pulling my phone from my back pocket, I dialed the number I knew by heart and waited for it to connect.

"Florida State. Please dial the extension you require or hold for assistance. Our visiting hours are between eleven a.m. and two p.m. Monday through Friday and require a prior arranged booking."

Pulling the phone from my ear, I pressed the five-digit extension to be put through to the petitionary wing I'd been housed in and suffered the familiar fisting around my gut as I waited for it to stop ringing.

"Florida State," a female voice answered. "How can I direct your call?"

"Prisoner number FS890976. Wallstreet, please." My tone was curt.

"One moment."

The line switched to god-awful music and I stroked the matte black of my gas tank while I waited.

It was never a quick turnaround calling Wallstreet.

The line crackled, cutting off the music. "You have ten minutes."

I waited for the additional click as the operator connected me to a line in Wallstreet's cellblock.

"Kill, my boy. You got my message, then?"

I still hadn't figured out how he managed to send text messages in his predicament, but he did. On a regular basis. "Yep. Received and noted. It's going down in two days."

Top rule when speaking on prison lines. No details. *Ever*.

"Good, good. I thought as much. At least I'll have something to celebrate when I get out of here."

My hand tightened. "You heard back?"

"Sure did."

When he didn't elaborate, I pressed, "And?"

He laughed, sounding twenty years younger and fucking spritely. "I'm done, Kill. Served my time, paid my price. I'm gonna be a free man again."

"Fucking hell." I stared ahead, reliving those days when I first came out. The fear of open spaces, the constant questions of "Can I go there? Who do I need to check with to make sure I'm allowed? What's my curfew?" Even breaking the habit of going to bed and getting up—set by the warden's hateful alarm clocks—took time. "Shit, Wallstreet, that's fantastic."

"They're letting me go early due to good behavior and proof of conforming to the necessary requirements of a rehabilitated criminal."

I knew for a fact that was the truth. He hadn't had to bribe anyone. He was an exemplary prisoner. I had no doubt the warden would've kept him forever if possible—just for the respect and peace he wielded. J Block would never be as calm the day he left; I was fucking sure of it.

"Do you have a date?"

"Not yet. The sentencing was just confirmed yesterday. Paperwork and all that jazz is always a holdup, but I'll let you know when to pick me up."

My heart raced to think of him coming home. This man had done so much for me. Made me who I was. Built me up when I was down and all that fucking sob-story bullshit.

I made a mental note to throw him the best damn party he'd ever seen.

"I'll be there, Cyrus. You can count on it."

Chapter Twenty-Five

Cleo

I'd gone to a high school dance last night.

I'd attended with a boy I didn't like.

Arthur had refused to take me. My mom said he wouldn't have been allowed anyway. He was too old for me. But what did they know? He wasn't too old. How many times did I need to tell them that he was the boy I'd end up marrying?

I knew what I was and I was happy with that. And I'd be ecstatic when Arthur finally understood that our future wasn't with others but together. His family, my family—they didn't count. He was my family. —Cleo, diary entry, age thirteen

Two worlds.

Two identities.

When Arthur disappeared to deal with Club business, I'd fretted. When he said he'd be back before dinner but never showed, I'd panicked. And when a mysterious package arrived with instructions, I'd freaked.

I never expected this.

I never expected Arthur to be such a master juggler with so many moving parts flying unseen above my head or to be left so far behind. Sure, he'd always been a planner, crossing t's and dotting i's, but to this extent...I would never have guessed.

My heart fell thinking how much had changed since we'd matured into adults and formed our own existences.

I just have to trust that he'll tell me when he's ready.

My eyes focused as I shoved aside my thoughts and concentrated on the now.

The gloom welcomed me and I turned to face the man who held my heart.

"Arthur...where on earth have you brought me?"

He grinned, wrapped in shadow in the expensive limousine's interior. His teeth were white, his face rugged and handsome. "You wanted to know—I'm showing you."

I blinked, trying to make sense of everything that'd happened today. My mind skipped backward, reliving up to this moment.

The package.

It all started with the package that'd arrived a few hours after Arthur had left.

"Yours, I believe." A Pure Corruption brother stood on the stoop, hold-ing out a large box. *Dressed in his uniform of jeans and cut, he looked the part of a biker but seemed too baby-faced to be dangerous. However, his nickname Switchblade said he wasn't exactly as cherub-like as his features suggested.* "Deliveryman just left. I signed on your behalf."

"Uh, thanks." Taking the package, I closed the door and scurried up the stairs to open it. What on earth was going on? Where the hell was Arthur?

As I sat on the bed and stroked the black silk ribbon wrapped around the large white box, I suddenly felt as if Arthur were beside me—an appa-rition waiting for me to open the mysterious parcel.

Slowly, I undid the bow and cracked open the lid.

Inside was a simple note.

For you. For tonight.

My heart skipped, trying to keep up. I'd made a mistake believing I knew everything there was to know about Arthur. I knew the boy, but not the man. And I'd forgotten one very important thing: Arthur was a plan-ner. An arranger. He never stopped orchestrating or plotting.

I can't believe I forgot that.

And this was a prime example how his body might be in my arms, his heart might be nestled snugly beside mine, but his mind...that was off busily constructing world domination.

I had no clue what would happen tonight.

But that wasn't new. Being with Arthur was always a surprise. From daisies in my shoes to impromptu picnics on the Clubhouse roof. Every-thing was always a shock. But a nice shock, nevertheless.

Inside the box, sleeping in decadent purple crepe paper, was the most incredible dress I'd ever seen. I'd never been a dress-wearing girl. I favored jeans and T-shirts. A no-nonsense wardrobe when dealing with puking puppies and scratching kittens. But this...wow.

I didn't feel worthy pulling such resplendent material from its bed of crepe. Holding the strapless gown toward the window, I fell in love with the intricate turquoise beads on the lacy bodice, flowing down the front to form a jagged lightning bolt teasing with the black tulle of a full-bodied skirt.

Along with the dress, there was a strapless bra and matching G-string in black and turquoise.

"Where on earth did he get this from?"

With serendipitous timing the phone rang, and, with infinite careful-ness, I tucked the dress away and ran to answer.

"Did it arrive?"

I beamed as Arthur's voice pooled into my ear. "Yes. It's stunning."

"Good, I called a local boutique. They assured me it would fit you after I gave them jumbled descriptions on your height and weight."

I giggled. "Well, I think they're mind-readers, because it's perfect." *Silence fell. I asked,* "Where exactly are we going?"

A masculine chuckle sent my heart skipping. "No questions. We have to work tonight and I need you looking astonishing so I can gobsmack the men in the room."

I plopped onto the bed, fingering the crepe. "So you're pimping me out? Have you no shame?"

"None when it comes to you. Is it bad that I find you fucking incredible and want to show you off? I want other men to stare at you and know that you'll never be theirs because you're mine."

I sucked in a breath.

"I have to run another errand. I'll be home later. In the meantime, have a bath, do your hair—do whatever you womenfolk require to get ready for a party. I'll see you later."

Before I could say goodbye, he hung up.

"Cleo? Cleo, for God's sake, are you listening to me?"

I jumped, skipping from the past and back to the present. Bringing Arthur into focus, my eyes trailed from his chiseled jaw to the exquisite sight of him wearing a dark grey suit, complete with the tie he'd used to blindfold me. My core melted at ensnaring someone so beautiful—both inside and out. "Sorry. You were saying?"

He laughed softly. "I was saying what to expect tonight, but seeing as I was boring you, let's just go in, shall we?"

I swallowed hard. "Go in where?"

With glowing green eyes, he shifted in his seat. "Not my fault you weren't paying attention."

I pouted. "It's entirely your fault that you're far too distracting and delicious. All I want to do is tear off that tie and put it to other uses."

His knuckles turned white, clutching his thighs. "Don't." He sent me a warning look that sent electricity scattering to every cell. "I'm struggling to keep my cock in order without you saying things like that."

Sliding over the glossy leather of the backseat, I fluttered my eyelashes. "At least people can't tell what I'm feeling."

His breath turned shallow. "And what are you feeling?"

Boldly, I captured his wrist and brought his hand from his thigh to mine. The rustle of my skirts sounded excruciatingly loud on my over-sensitive nerves. "Put your hand up my dress and find out."

He let out a strangled noise. Yanking his hand back, he growled, "You're playing with fire, Buttercup." The word "fire" sent his eyes darting to my scars—prominent and unashamedly on display. There was no mistaking that I wasn't just a girl in a pretty dress. I was a woman who'd lived a story and wasn't afraid to tell it.

"I like to play with dangerous things."

He groaned, staring at the limo ceiling as if begging for deliverance. "You don't know what you're doing to me."

I whipped out my hand, ready to wrap around his cock.

I'll find out.

In a flash he trapped my fingers, holding me millimeters away from touching him. "You're going to pay for what you're doing."

I shivered. "How much will you make me pay?"

He smiled like a scoundrel—a rogue who was exactly in control even when he looked wildly out of it. Dragging me forward by my hand, he murmured in my ear, "Your payment will consist of whatever I deem worthy." He pressed a kiss on my powdered cheek. "Until then, you can live in anticipation of what I'll make you do."

In a second, he was gone—springing from the car as an unseen chauffeur opened the back door.

I blinked. It'd been eerie being driven to an unknown destination by an unknown driver. The limo had magically appeared the moment Arthur returned home—already immaculately dressed and smelling divinely like woodsy smoke and seaside.

There was a few seconds' delay as the driver came around to my side. With a flourish, he opened the door and revealed the most immaculate villa in all of the Florida Keys. My mouth fell open at the stunning façade of the stone home with sweeping porticos and pastel accents. Strategic lights illuminated shrubbery and pathways, turning night into starlight.

"Wow," I breathed as Arthur appeared, holding out his hand. "This is the party?" I couldn't stop staring.

"It is indeed." His fingers clamped around mine, pulling me from the car.

The moment I tottered on insanely high turquoise heels—also courtesy of Arthur's chosen boutique store—I self-consciously smoothed down the thigh-length strapless dress.

"Who owns this place?" Up till now I thought Arthur's mansion was slick and beautiful, but it looked clunky compared to the feminine beauty of this timeless villa.

Arthur smiled secretively. "A friend."

My hackles rose at the thought of any friend living in such a place. "A *female* friend?"

Placing his hand on the small of my back, he pushed me down the glowing path. "No, jealous Buttercup. A man."

"Oh."

"Yes, oh. His ex-wife is an architect. Built this place, decorated it to rival any interior design magazine, then left him for a younger version."

"Ouch."

Arthur shrugged. "That was a while ago. Samson is now happily remarried and even has a brat or two, I believe."

Carefully keeping my eyes on the decoration of white pebbles latticing the black pavers leading to the doorway, I asked, "You believe?"

Arthur's touch turned protective as we scaled the three steps and stood poised at the front entrance. "We don't talk about personal things. We're friends because of mutual goals, but we aren't about to go to each other's birthday parties."

Who was this unknown Samson? If he wasn't a friend, why was he important in the scheme of things?

Standing on the threshold, I suffered nerves and butterflies. Was I enough? Had I done the best I could with my hair? My makeup? I'd taken the longest I'd ever done applying just the right amount of mascara and dusky pink lipstick, and I'd never fussed so much over my hair.

I'd even watched some online videos to attempt a fishtail braid, draping the tamed hair over my shoulder and finishing it with the black ribbon from the dress box.

But no matter how much I'd primped and painted, I still felt like a fraud—someone who looked the part but beneath was absolutely unprepared and a sham.

Arthur squeezed my hip, sensing my anxiousness. "Relax, Cleo."

"But what if I say the wrong thing? I've avoided parties and social gatherings all my life. I'm always terrified of meeting someone I once knew and not being able to place them, or making small talk only to find amnesia devoured that piece of information, too."

Sweat rolled down my spine, spreading my panic. I didn't know why I was so close to freaking out. It wasn't like I didn't have my memories this time, and I had Arthur by my side.

But that inescapable fear still clutched me.

Looking into his calming emerald eyes, I begged, "Please don't leave me alone tonight. Promise you'll stay by me?"

With a gentle smile, he dragged me into his embrace, cocooning me in his arms.

Instantly, I relaxed, feeding off his peacefulness, his capable, unflappable ease. "I promise I'll never take my eyes off you."

I exhaled in relief. "Thank you."

Arthur's jaw-length hair was swept off his face in a slick ponytail. From the front, he looked like a distinguished businessman in a tailored charcoal suit and tie, but from the side—with his rugged jaw, roguish hair, and bulging arms threatening the seams of the suit—the truth was visible.

He was dangerous.

He was a man not to be messed with.

He played with the ribbon in my hair. "You know me so well, Buttercup. You know my thoughts, my heart, my past. But you're still blind to what my life truly entails." He pulled me tighter against his body. "Tonight, you'll see the truth. You'll see the other world I exist in, the one run by politicians and democrats rather than bikers and gasoline." Kissing my forehead, he magically smoothed away my final nerves. "This is yet another facet of my life."

The door swung open, revealing a butler dressed all in black with combed balding hair. "Welcome, Mr. Killian."

A security guard I hadn't seen ghosted from the shadows behind one of the pillars. His eyes were shielded by dark glasses—even though it was far too gloomy to need them.

Why was there security detail for a simple house party?

Because this isn't *a simple house party.*

I wasn't stupid. Even though my lack of memory often made me seem that way. Whatever Arthur was coordinating relied on something to do with this evening's success.

I don't mean to ruin it for him.

"And who shall I say is accompanying you tonight, Mr. Killian?" The kind-faced butler smiled in my direction.

Arthur stood taller. "Cleo Price."

My heart winged at the possession in his tone.

The butler looked at the guard who shifted on his toes and peered intensely behind smoky lenses. A clipboard magically materialized in his hands. After a quick glance, he nodded curtly.

I guess I'm approved.

The butler sidestepped into the grand entrance, beckoning us inside. "Please, come in."

I mumbled thanks as Arthur and I stepped into the extravagant foyer and feasted on the oversized modern artwork and the three-meter-high driftwood horse dominating the space.

"Do you have any jackets or coats you wish me to take?" the butler asked.

Arthur shook his head. "We're good. Thanks." His height gave him an advantage, easily browsing over the milling guests in distinguished suits and bright dresses. The men were punctuations to their pretty wives decorating the space like sugary confectionary.

"Mr. Samson is awaiting your arrival." The butler pointed across the room where a punch bowl and delicate sandwiches rested on side tables. "He requested you speak to him first."

Arthur stole my hand. "Will do."

Leaving the butler in our wake, we weaved our way through the crowd. Bubbles of perfume and clouds of aftershave popped and swarmed as we brushed past men and women who would never step foot inside a biker compound, let alone mingle with one.

Squeezing Arthur's fingers, I asked, "Are you going to tell me what this is all about?"

He looked down, his face cordial and cocky. "Soon."

Happiness filled me to think he might be on the mend, but then I stared harder and saw past his walls. Whatever headache he suffered, it hadn't dispersed yet. It was there with its fingers of agony and heart-beats of pressure.

A waitress appeared with champagne flutes. "Drink?"

I raised my hand to say no, but Arthur released me and plucked two sparkling glasses from her silver tray. "Thank you."

She nodded, cast an appreciative glance at Arthur, then glided away to provide liquor to other parched individuals.

I scowled. "You're not going to drink that, are you?"

His eyebrow rose. "Uh, I'd thought about it, yes." Offering a flute to me, he added, "And you, too. Unless you've stopped drinking after being spoiled by Melanie's concoctions last night?"

I took the glass, rubbing my thumb through the icy condensation. "No, I'll sip one. I just don't think it's a good idea that you do."

He scoffed, deliberately taking a swig. Somehow, he made sipping golden champagne from a dainty glass rough and tough and utterly masculine.

My throat turned dry.

Licking his lips, his eyes shot to a forest green. Desire sparked, lacing around us and shunning everyone else in the room. The unfinished business in the limo only grew more intense. "You were saying."

All I could focus on was a glistening drop on his bottom lip. "I was saying?"

Taking a step toward me, Arthur twirled the ribbon from my braid, gracing my décolletage with his knuckles.

I shivered.

"You were saying I shouldn't drink. If your concern is because of my head, I told you—stop worrying about me. I'm fine."

I twirled the stem of my flute. "I'm worried that you aren't taking this seriously. Alcohol can't be good for your condition."

His shoulders braced. "I drank last night and it didn't bother you."

"That was different."

"How was it different?"

My knees wobbled beneath his scrutiny. "We were surrounded by people who care about you. Plus, you only had two beers all evening. I watched you."

He scowled. "Can't get anything by you, can I?"

"Nope." I swallowed hard. "You're still in pain. I can tell."

His jaw clenched but he forced himself to relax. "It's nothing, Buttercup." Kissing me swiftly, he whispered, "Forget about what happened. Forget about what's about to happen. And let's just enjoy tonight, okay?"

I nodded but I didn't agree. How could I forget about what'd happened when his father had started this mess? How could I forget when it was all I thought about?

For the first time, I let my thoughts slip through my iron control.

My worry wasn't just about his concussion. Or his pigheaded belief he could extract revenge without being hurt. It wasn't even about him living a life still shackled so heavily to the past.

It's because I'm worried he'll die. That he'll arrange a war and perish because of it.

I threw a mouthful of chilled wine down my throat. I hated worrying. I hated not knowing. I'd lived for far too long not knowing and I wouldn't do it any longer. Arthur was mine—therefore he was my responsibility and I would be damned if I let him get hurt again.

"We could just leave...," I whispered, twirling the stem of my glass.

Arthur froze. "You want to go home?"

Home. Where was home? Dagger Rose was gone. Pure Corruption was still too new. *We can start a new home.*

Looking into his eyes, I begged him to understand. "We could go somewhere, just us. We're together again. We always said we were each other's home." Urgency filled me. I grabbed his wrist, sloshing his champagne. "We could just go. Move overseas. Start again."

Like I did.

Become new people.

Hide.

Arthur stiffened. His eyes hooded. "You want me to just *walk away*? After all this time? When I'm so fucking close?" His voice never rose above a whisper but the steely tone whipped my heart.

"Why would that be so terrible? You're beyond wealthy. You have no reason to stay—"

"No reason?" Arthur ran an agitated hand through his hair, disturbing his ponytail so he looked even more untamed and unpredictable. "I have so many fucking reasons."

How on earth had this happened? All we seemed to do these days was go from closeness to clashing.

Then again, I had just asked if he'd drop everything and run away with me—in the middle of a war and who knew what else. Not exactly fair.

Whoops.

I only did it because I'm petrified.

"Forget I said anything." I laid my hand on his sleeve. "It was selfish of me. I know you have responsibilities here. I'm just—you can't be mad at me for loving you so much that I want to keep you safe. To never share you."

The fib rolled off my tongue and I let the truth sink into darkness. I loved him; that was real. But I was also worried that he would go too far. That his thirst for vengeance overshadowed everything—even me.

He sucked in a breath, his eyes never leaving mine. He knew I offered an olive branch, but at the same time he was wary that I wasn't entirely happy.

Sighing, he nodded. "Buttercup, you have my ultimate word. When this week is over and everything has gone to plan, we'll go away. Just the two of us. We'll go wherever you want. England to visit your foster family, or some tropical hideaway in the middle of nowhere. Whatever you need, I'll do." Bringing me close, he breathed, "Okay?"

I swooned into him, pressing my cheek against his tie. "Okay."

Just please let this week go smoothly. Please don't get hurt.

The tension between us disappeared as quickly as it'd arrived. Arthur let me go, taking another sip of his drink.

His throat tensed as he swallowed and once again desire thickened my blood. His chest rippled as he moved, every inch of his tailored suit hugging his incredible physique. Women watched him, interest sparking in their gaze despite wedding rings wreathing their fingers.

I'm completely out of my depth.

And completely possessive.

"You're far too handsome for your own good dressed in that..." I waved at him as if his perfectly sewn suit offended me.

My petulant voice rose Arthur's eyebrow while a sexy smirk twisted his lips. "What did you just say?"

I narrowed my eyes. "You heard me."

A sly glint glowed in his gaze. "You're right. I did hear you." Taking a step, our bodies aligned like colliding asteroids. "Are you jealous of them looking? Doesn't it turn you on knowing you're the only one who gets to see what's under my suit? That you're the only one who holds this." Stealing my hand, he placed my fingers over his heart.

He brushed his lips against my ear. "Because I get hard seeing the way men look at you, knowing you belong to me and only me."

His breath sent goose bumps splattering down my arms.

Chuckling, he let me go and I took a reinforcing sip of chilled bubbles. "Let's just say I prefer you in mud-stained jeans and weathered leather."

"Why?"

"Because a biker president scares the bejesus out of everyone."

My lips parted as Arthur wrapped his arm around my waist, pressing me hard against him. The rapid thickening in his trousers made my insides melt. "I'm still scary...even if I'm wearing a tie."

I struggled to continue with the conversation. We'd bounced from lust to anger and back again. And now all I wanted to do was drag him away from this hoity-toity crowd and prove to myself that despite his plans and headaches and stubbornness he was still the boy from my past.

Nothing was complicated as long as we remembered that.

I whispered, "Not to me."

His eyes burned deep emerald holes into my soul. "No, not to you." He kissed me quickly. "The minute I've spoken with Senator Samson, I'm having you."

Having me?

As in sex?

"What, here?" I squeaked.

He inhaled deeply, dragging my spritz of perfume—orchids and summer sunshine—into his lungs. "Here." Laughing softly, he looked around the room as if seeking a dark corner in which to carry out his threat. "I'm going to sink inside you somewhere inside this house and prove to you that it doesn't matter what I'm wearing or what situation we find ourselves in, I'm still yours." His eyes shadowed. "For some reason, I think you need reminding of that."

My heart expanded with love.

Letting me go, his hand disappeared into his trouser pocket. Opening his fingers, he said, "See?"

My muscles locked. The worn Libra eraser rested like a talisman in his palm.

I couldn't take my eyes off it. "Do you take it everywhere?"

Tucking it away safely, Arthur nodded. "Every day. It started off as something I hated because it reminded me too painfully of you. But every time I went to throw it out, I couldn't. I couldn't remove you from my life." He shrugged. "It became a good luck charm and I grew superstitious that if I didn't have it with me, my luck would run out and I'd end up even more alone."

Right there. What he just said. *That* was why I was petrified of the future, of what he planned to do. That after all this time apart we would end up more alone than before—all because he couldn't move on.

Closing my hand over his, I pushed aside my worries.

With a ruthful smirk, he linked his fingers with mine. "Come. I think it's time I introduced you to Samson."

Chapter Twenty-Six

Kill

Wallstreet *had taught me something invaluable.*

A lesson I'd never thought to consider. Cleo was dead and I was all alone. I drowned in guilt, festered in heartache. I was weak.

But in Wallstreet's eyes, I wasn't weak. I was perfect. Because without pain, I couldn't be strong enough to do what he truly needed me to do. He'd said I was the Armageddon that he'd been waiting for. And it was up to me to use my pain to deliver others' happiness. —Kill, age eighteen

Sometimes ignorance was easier than knowledge.

I'd been that way once upon a time. I'd been a child, believing in fairness and truth. I'd been a teenager, believing in togetherness and love. And I'd been a man, stripped of all hope by lies.

I'd witnessed what fellow humans would do for power. I'd grown up.

But despite what had happened, Cleo didn't see the world the way I did. She still believed in fairness, truth, and love. She was still gullible at heart and I envied her.

I envied her acceptance of a world steeped in deception. I wished I could relax. Just stop chasing this need to fix and tweak and change.

But I knew too much. I'd dug too deep and seen things I couldn't unsee. I had to do this. I had no choice.

Because if I didn't do it, who would?

It wasn't that I wanted to become someone I wasn't. It wasn't that I wanted public recognition or entitlement that came with my future placement. But I did want to right my wrongs—and this was my path to forgiveness.

All this time, Cleo thought I was the same math-obsessed boy from Dagger Rose. The same boy betrayed by those most dear and corrupted by a prison inmate.

True, parts of that boy survived, but the years had changed me, turned me into an entirely new man.

Tonight, she would see everything. She would finally know all of me. She would hear what I'd been working on. What the lawlessness, the trading, even the trafficking had been building toward.

I wasn't just a man with a vendetta. If I was, I would've killed my father years ago.

I was a man with a mission. A mission to eradicate this world of filth. To stop corruption. To end those who lie and cheat and steal.

I wasn't a vigilante.

I wasn't a crusader.

But I *was* a United States citizen and had a responsibility to deliver the truth.

Unfortunately, my eyes had been opened. I saw through bullshit and incorrect leadership all thanks to my father's treatment of his president and peers. *He* made me see. And he made me understand that he was nothing compared to the men in power. Lies were the backbone of our country. Men passed bills with no votes, they discarded doctrines, and shredded rules that had the potential to stop their reign.

My father was nothing in my overall scheme.

I was after more than just him. More than just Clubs who broke the faith of their brothers.

I was after the fucking top dogs. The men who ruined so many people's lives with no thought and decimated entire generations with a single signature.

That was my true purpose.

And when Cleo found out that I could never walk away from what I'd promised, then she would have to choose.

Choose to accept me and tolerate my obsession for equality.

Or steal the only happiness I've ever had and leave.

Chapter Twenty-Seven

Cleo

I don't remember."

It used to be such a flippant phrase. But now it was as if I scraped out my soul and handed it bleeding and screaming to whoever asked: Who was I? What'd happened? Who'd done this to me?

I hated those three little words. "I don't remember." I hated my brain for holding me hostage. But most of all, I hated being so empty. Memories were my enemies, judging me to solitary loneliness. —Cleo, diary entry, age sixteen

Arthur guided me across the large lounge. The house was pristinely decorated. Everything—from doors to trim—was lacquered in high-gloss white. Lights glittered with crystals and threads of a symphony orchestra dripped from ceiling speakers, sewing with the voices of expensively dressed guests.

"Who are these people?" I ducked around the train of a silver gown and smiled at a bushy moustached gentleman.

"People who run this country," Arthur said, never breaking his stride.

Government officials?

My eyes focused, searching strangers with deeper clarity. I didn't recognize anyone.

I couldn't align the two worlds correctly in my head. Here we were brushing shoulders with liberals and democrats, yet back at home *we* were the law. We penned rules and carried out justice—we were our own government.

But here, Arthur straddled two existences effortlessly. *Why?*

Last night we'd been around a campfire eating pork ribs, dancing in leather, and being entertained by awful ghost stories and cheap booze. Now I tottered on exquisite stilettoes, mingled with fashionistas, and became invisible at an exclusive cocktail party.

It doesn't make sense.

It was an eternity as we navigated the room and advanced on a small group of men by a bay window. The glint of a chandelier bounced off Arthur's wrist, revealing cuff links designed with the tiny skulls and abacas of the Pure Corruption logo.

Every step I fretted about what I would say and what was expected of me.

I don't remember.

Those three hated words from my past sat heavily on my tongue—just waiting for the questions to begin. My gut clenched. Cold sweat drenched. And I struggled to remind myself that I *did* remember. That I had nothing to fear. Nothing to forget.

The crowds parted, letting us cut through the masses of sequins and silk while they milled around like fattened carp. Bookshelves held treasured vacation artifacts, and the walls were adorned with family portraits of the man we were heading toward: the senator and his pretty wife with dark brown hair and two young boys who looked identical to their father.

I swallowed as the senator looked up. He paused mid-handshake with another gentleman and bent in to say something. A moment later, he excused himself and crossed the small distance to intercept us.

Without a word, he walked past, narrowing his eyes at Arthur.

Nodding at the unspoken instruction in the senator's gaze, Arthur turned inconspicuously and followed.

We chased Mr. Samson from the congested party, down a short

corridor, and into an office painted in maroons and dark greys. The ceiling had been decorated black so it pressed like a toiling storm—or a lid perhaps, a cap on all secrets and gossip shared.

The moment Arthur and I stepped inside, the senator locked the door, then made his way to the mirrored bar and topped up his goblet with amber liquor. Eyeing my half drunk champagne, he stole Arthur's empty flute, replaced it with a tumbler filled with what I assumed was whiskey or cognac, then clinked his glass to ours and smiled. "Welcome to my home once again, Kill." His hazel eyes landed on mine. "And you must be Cleo. I've heard a lot about you."

I froze, my glass half raised to my lips. "Very nice to meet you, Senator. Forgive me, but I've heard nothing about you."

But I'm beginning to suspect I've been stupidly naïve where Arthur is concerned.

Who was I kidding? Arthur was too complicated to remain fixated on revenge for so long. He would've grown bored. He would've set his targets higher.

But just how high?

Samson laughed, revealing a gold cap on his lower incisor. "That sounds about right." Cocking his head at Arthur, he grinned. "Secretive fellow, isn't he?"

I glanced at Arthur who sipped his drink. "If I'm so secretive, how do you know so much about Cleo, then?"

Samson toasted Arthur again, ice tinkling in his tumbler. "Got me again. Too smart for your own good."

I guessed the senator was in his late fifties. Trim body, stocky legs, haircut reminiscent of a soldier, hair flecked with grey.

Frowning, I asked, "Pardon my slowness, but if Arthur didn't tell you about me...then who did?"

Beaming a pearly white smile, the senator laughed. "From Wallstreet, of course. He keeps me up to date on all the latest chin-wagging." He tilted his thumb in Arthur's direction. "Wallstreet told me Kill had found something he'd lost long ago. That the main reason for the start of this campaign had reincarnated and that we were to work doubly hard to ensure the future is wiped clean of evil."

Is that supposed to make sense?

Patting my hand, Samson moved toward a cluster of chocolate-leather couches in the center of the room. "Besides, I'm trustworthy. Otherwise, I wouldn't be told shit. And yet another reason why I do what I do."

Drifting forward, caught up in his reticulation, I completely forgot about Arthur. "What is it that you do, Senator?"

Sitting heavily and almost disappearing in the supple leather of the couch, he smiled. "I like to think of myself as a fixer."

"A fixer?"

Arthur's body heat tingled my arms as he moved closer. "Samson has been a contact ever since I got out of Florida State." He gave one of his rare trusting smiles. "He's been crucial in getting our goal realized."

My high heels pinched as I moved forward, itching for information. "And what is the goal?"

Why do I feel as if this has all been there ... in the background, only I've been too blinded to see it?

Samson placed his tumbler on a glass side table. "The one that's about to be put into execution due to the recent events, that's what." He waved at the extra chairs. "By all means, have a seat."

I turned to the locked door. "What about your party?"

Samson snorted. "Screw 'em. Only here for the free booze and to kiss my ass. They can do that without me in the room."

Arthur placed his hand on my lower back and guided me forward. "Sit, Cleo."

The atmosphere in the room thickened with mystery. These men were schemers. Meeting in their private rooms, concocting plans as if they were princes rather than a politician and biker.

What the hell is going on?

Obeying Arthur, I sat stiffly. Biting my lip as the scratchy tulle of my skirts puffed around me in a loud rustle.

Arthur glanced over, settling into his own chair. His eyes trailed to my tattooed and burned legs, and for a fraction of a second they blazed with lust, then business and plans hijacked his mind and the lust was gone.

Spreading his thighs, Arthur leaned forward and nursed his drink between his knees. "Has the bill been drafted?"

My ears perked.

I'd been thrown in the deep end and left to swim in whatever information these two conspirators divulged.

Senator Samson nodded. "It's been drafted and delivered. I've enlisted the help of some local and stateside politicians. I see no reason why we won't be able to launch our attack full force."

"And the campaign? The advertising is all planned like we discussed?"

I kept quiet, nursing my warming bubbles.

Samson grabbed his drink, finished it, and discarded the empty glass. "The one-minute television advertisement is in place and ready to air. The radio, newspaper, and online targeting are also done. However, if you wish it to run frequently with a lot of impact to ensure people's attention, then we need more funds."

Arthur didn't hesitate. "Done. Email me the figure and I'll pay it. I told you before money is no object."

My mouth hung open. Only a few years ago this man had been a boy swatting me for incorrect decimal placement on my math homework. Now he was in league with millionaires and men who ran our beloved country.

I've been left behind.

My heart panged to think I might not be enough anymore. That soon Arthur would find me a novelty rather than precious treasure. What exactly could I contribute to this strange new world?

What exactly is *this strange new world?*

Samson ran a finger over his mouth, deep in thought. "In that case, I believe we'll be staring at a politically unrest nation by the end of the year."

Arthur shook his head. "I don't want unrest. I want reform."

Samson shrugged. "You can't have reform without unsettling them first. We need to make them think. Use their brains for once. Show them alternatives. Promise better solutions. Only then can they be open to new suggestions."

Arthur grunted in agreement, his mind taken hostage with whatever complications and issues he might foresee.

"Once we launch and offer transparent data on what we propose, then it's up to the public. We can only do so much before it's all up to them." Throwing me a glance, Samson pursed his lips. "The law can't be changed overnight."

"No, but it *does* need to be changed," Arthur grumbled. "And fast. I'm sick of living with the level of corruption. It's fucking insulting to think we don't see the level of cover-ups and bullshit they spread."

I swallowed, dying to ask questions but unwilling to interrupt. *Am I even privy to ask?*

Technically, I was in the private meeting at Arthur's request. Surely, I could ask—otherwise, what was I doing here?

Opening my mouth, I tried to formulate an intelligent question. But what could I say? What were the television campaigns on? What transparent data would they reveal?

However, just like so many times in the past, Arthur sensed my curiosity and twisted to face me. The simple act of turning his body to mine welcomed me into the conversation. "Cleo, I need you to understand what is about to happen. I need you to be on board because this rests on you, too."

I gripped my nearly dry glass. "I would like to understand." *What rests on me?* "I want to know."

Samson steepled his fingers, looking from Arthur to me. "What you're about to hear is top secret. I don't need to ask if you can be trusted." Pointing at Arthur, he smiled fondly. "He's proved himself time and time again. So I know you will as well. But until this begins you can't say a word, understand?"

I nodded. It wasn't a hard promise to make. My mind was a vault—even a master at hiding my own secrets from myself. Keeping them from others wouldn't be hard at all. "I give you my word."

"Perfect." His face was open and eager. The feathering lines around his eyes spoke of stress but also laughter and happiness. He looked stern but kind—the same type of look in Wallstreet's eyes and Arthur's. Wallstreet and Samson had taken a biker rapscallion and turned him into a precise weapon. I just hoped it was for good and not for wrong.

Samson settled into the comforting leather of his chair. "I'll just start from the biggest point and answer any questions you might have."

"Okay."

Cocking his head at Arthur, he smiled. "Kill here approached me a few years ago with a proposal to reinvent the United States government."

"What?" I blurted, my head whipping to face Arthur.

What the hell does that mean?

Arthur snorted, throwing back the rest of his drink and disposing the empty glass onto the coffee table. "That's not quite how it happened."

Samson laughed. "Fine. You want the complete story? I'll tell ya. About three years ago, Kill broke into my house with two of his biker buddies. Scared the living shit out of me and my wife."

My eyes narrowed.

He did what?

"Logistics," Arthur said, linking his fingers. "I did it for a reason."

Samson stole me away with his tale. "Instead of holding us at gunpoint and demanding money or favors or anything else you'd expect from a damn biker at three in the morning, he dumped copious amounts of paperwork at the end of my bed and made himself comfortable in a chair. He said something along the lines of—"

"'Excuse the intrusion; it's not my intention to scare you—only for you to take me seriously. Something drastic has to be done and someone has to have the fucking balls to do it,'" Arthur interrupted. His eyes danced with mirth. "Poor guy almost had a fucking heart attack, especially when faced with a night of paperwork in the form of every cover-up, scandal, and wrongdoing committed by the government since 1995. I could've gone further back, brought more evidence to light, but what would be the point? There was more than enough information to prove insane levels of corruption and put together a viable case for a revolution."

My eyes widened. The intrigue in this single room consumed me. "But how can you hope to take on the largest power in the world?"

Arthur sat back, his long legs spread before him. "Easy. We inform the people who gave them the power in the first place." Clearing his throat, his passion rose until the air vibrated with injustice.

This was what Arthur believed in. This was what he'd been working on. Not just revenge or thirsting for death of those who wronged him. *This*. He'd become a vigilante, trying to bring down a crooked government—the same government that'd sent him to jail for a crime he didn't truly commit, all the while letting the real sinners walk free. He'd been a victim—just as much as me.

I…I get it now.

It all suddenly made a lot more sense.

I trembled in my chair. "This…it's incredible. You're taking on something huge."

"Somebody has to," Samson said. "Why not us?"

"Why not people who made the government what it is? Don't they hold some responsibility?"

"Yes, but most don't want to change, and the others are happy with the way things are. It needs an outsider to begin something new. It needs someone like us," Arthur said.

"Someone like you?" My brain scrambled. "Why?"

Instead of answering my question, Arthur asked one of his own. "What draws people to bike Clubs? Why do men willingly turn their back on the law and embrace illegal acts knowing it could get them hurt, thrown in jail, or worse—killed?"

I shrugged, my skin prickling with chill. The tulle and corset of my dress imprisoned me, forcing me to listen to his huge ideals. Arthur's green eyes pierced mine, waiting for a reply. I tried to recall why men had begged for the opportunity to become a Dagger. But everything was polluted by Rubix and the lifestyle they preferred over the one Arthur granted. "Um... the love of lawlessness?"

Samson jumped in. "That's what I always thought, but thanks to Arthur, my eyes have been opened."

Arthur said, "I have my own issues with the government. The judicial system leaves a lot to be desired. They believed lies formed by my own father and let your attempted murder go unpunished, sentencing you to eight years with no memory, living all alone." His voice turned coarse. "Those reasons are personal and no one else's. Unless it hits them at a deeper level, no one cares about what I've been through, or you, or any other stranger. It took me a long time to decide if my reasons for doing this were purely selfish or warranted."

I shifted in the chair, completely absorbed by his righteous anger.

Arthur smiled, telling me with a simple look how deeply immersed he was. "I couldn't decide, even after soul-searching. So, I put it to a vote. I traveled to numerous biker gangs and spoke to many presidents. I asked them all one thing."

"And what was that?" I placed my unwanted drink on the side table and clasped my chilled fingers in the bushel of tulle.

Arthur smiled grimly. "Why do they do it? Why turn their backs on society?"

"And their answer?"

Arthur looked to Samson. "You want to do the honors?"

Samson ran a hand over his short hair. "The unanimous answer was: because they were sick of being stolen from by a system disguised as the law. They were sick of having their rights tampered with, their wives' rights, their future children's rights. They were sick of a future where obedience was punished and lies were granted rewards. *That's* why they sought a different kind of life."

Arthur nodded. "Sure, there are men who crave the forbidden, the danger, and the downright seedy aspect of living outside the law. Those men will never fit in with society, no matter how it conformed. Rape will never be okay. Robbery will never be okay. But the majority of men I spoke to are hard workers. Ex-army, ex-navy, and men who have given their lives to a corporation only to be royally fucked in return. Families live harmonious existences in the Club with laws that protect each other and their assets rather than penalize them. Sure, a few are still archaic with the way authority is run, but ultimately, they treat most members fairly and choose to live off the grid to protect their loved ones, not to boycott society."

I nodded, my mind swimming. "That sounds like the reasons why my father started Dagger Rose. He wanted a sanctuary for hardworking loyal people who were sick of being lied to by the men and women who were supposed to protect their livelihood and futures."

"Exactly." Arthur slapped his hand on his knee. "Once I took over the Corrupts and made them Pure Corruption, our main goal was to be honest and courteous but be ruthless to protect what we'd created."

Samson stole the conversation. "That's all we're trying to do. We're trying to show the country what they can have in a society that is out to *help* them again. Not focused on stealing their rights or taking away their future. I'm not saying the entire protocol is shady, but there are a few men in power that shouldn't be there. They have to be stopped. And sooner rather than later, before they pick another war or introduce yet another privacy invading requirement that strips all our rights away."

My heart raced. "You're talking about taking on the largest organization in the world."

"Not taking it on," Samson said. "Improving it."

Arthur took my hand, stroking my knuckles with a calloused thumb. "We aren't out to bring anarchy to the country, Buttercup. We're out to show the truth."

Chapter Twenty-Eight

Kill

What qualified another to dictate what I could and couldn't be?

What right did anyone have over another?

My father had given me life, but did that give him the right to beat me if I didn't obey?

My brother shared my blood, but did that give him the right to taunt and manipulate me?

I didn't need an answer. I already had one.

Nobody had the right to make another do what they didn't want to—especially when it was wrong. —Kill, age fourteen

It was done.

My ultimate plan was out in the open and Cleo knew everything.

My steadfast concentration over almost a decade was aired, admitted, and alive. Trading hadn't been for wealth or prestige—it was to finance the largest operation in reform we'd ever seen. Pure Corruption's overhaul wasn't for Wallstreet's enjoyment; it wasn't so small-minded to be about the members or our way of life—it was to show the world that communions who put their followers first thrived. It was to show that men voted into power had the responsibility to govern and direct without constant manipulation or supervision.

That was what the government forgot. It was so out of touch with its people. So blinded by kickbacks and bought by men through campaigns and under-the-table dealings that they'd become the enemy rather than the savior.

All of this had a purpose.

My revenge was multifaceted. Yes, I wanted my father's blood. But I also wanted payback. This was what kept me going in those pitch-black moments of missing Cleo and wishing for death so I could join her. This was what gave me energy to keep fighting. Keep believing.

Not to kill my father.

Not to extract revenge.

But to make the world better. So no one else had to suffer the betrayal I had.

"Say something," I finally murmured.

Cleo sat frozen, the blue beads on her dress twinkling every time she breathed.

"It's a lot to take in." Samson got up and poured himself another drink. "I was the same when Kill first explained it to me. But if you let it mellow, you'll see we're doing it for the right reasons."

Cleo swallowed, her hand opening and closing beneath mine. "I honestly don't know what to say. It's huge. I can't get my head around it."

I wanted to gather her close and chase away her dumbfounded fear. "I understand. I'm not asking you to follow everything we're saying, or even appreciate why it's up to us to do this. But I *am* asking for your support."

Please accept this part of me. Don't run.

I hadn't let myself acknowledge just how fucked I'd be if she said no.

Cleo's green eyes latched on to mine, blazing with honesty. "You never have to doubt that. You have it. Forever."

A huge weight dissolved.

I squeezed her hand. "Thank you."

"But why tell me now?"

I smiled. "A lot has come into alignment. I'd always promised

Wallstreet that I would take my time in the limelight when my father was dealt with. And..."

How could I tell her that the man who helped organize this—who gave me the confidence and skills to pull this off—would be released soon. He was the linchpin in all of this. He would become the spokesperson and it was up to me to have his throne ready for when he was freed.

"And...," Cleo prompted.

Scooting to the edge of the chair, my leg bounced with nervous energy. Talking about this sort of stuff never failed to energize and stress me out in equal measure. I knew the mammoth task we'd set. I also knew the lies and bad press that would come to light. Nothing about my life would be spared, and in turn—nothing about Cleo's life either. She was a part of this, even if she didn't want to be.

"Wallstreet has been pardoned. He's just waiting on the final discharge papers and he'll be a free man again."

Cleo's eyes narrowed. "And he thinks the world will follow him because he's a white-collar criminal who got done for what exactly? Tax evasion?"

I shook my head. "No, of course people wouldn't listen. He's not exactly an upstanding member of society. But in many ways, he's exactly what's needed. He's willing to donate the fortune he kept hidden from the government to aid those who need it most."

Cleo scowled. "So you're saying he's going to be a modern-day Robin Hood? Taking from the grubby paws of leaders and giving back to the penniless public?"

A grin broke my face. "It's a rather flattering analogy, but it sort of works."

Samson perched on the arm of the chair he'd vacated. "It's a lot more complicated than that. To pull off something of this scale, we need unlimited resources." Pointing at me, he smiled. "That's where the genius comes in."

A sharp lance in my skull reminded me that if I didn't fix my brain soon, all our plans might be in the fucking gutter. My ease and ingrained knowledge was still lost to me. The trades I'd placed yesterday clunky compared to before.

"And we need members on each side of the fence to be in accordance with one another. Politicians, bikers, journalists, squeaky clean businessmen, and convicted criminals. We all have a part to play." Samson raised his glass. "So you can see why it's been a long planned strategy."

My thoughts turned to all the other senators and men in power who'd agreed to work with us. Some had taken a lot of persuading with facts and figures. They didn't believe the blatant lies and forged documents from their departments were true. Others had been waiting for an upheaval like we offered and were only too happy to help. The biggest surprise had come from the local and worldwide MCs. Most of them had been only too happy to band together. For the first time in history, we weren't fighting against one another but working as one.

It was a fucking miracle.

Hopefully, Cleo would see now why I could never leave. When she'd died, I'd tried to replace her with this—given myself over to making other people's lives so much better than mine could ever be. Giving everything. Giving *more*.

And until it was done, I couldn't abandon it. No matter how much I might want to live a simple life. To have no worries or intricate plans. To have contentedness rather than obsession. What I wouldn't give to wake up in the morning and only have to care about what position I would take my woman in and for how long.

But this was global. This was infinite. This was my duty.

"Yes, but surely this isn't your fight? It's the responsibility of—"

"If we don't fight, who will?" I asked.

I'd started this journey with vengeance on my mind for both my father and the system that allowed him to destroy my life. But as time passed, my goals evolved. I became less selfish.

I wanted others to have the freedom and truth. And I had the means with which to make it happen. The global system was so fragile, so easily tainted by those who were out for themselves. And that was why I was an expert at foreign currency trading. All it took was one piece of misleading news, or mention of war, or market uncertainty by a politician in the pockets of some mega conglomeration, and the dollars fluctuated like crazy, allowing people in the know to swoop in, scoop up untold millions in the trade, and then get out. Insider trading was rife—and not just on the FX market but on everything known to fucking man.

Stocks. Fuel. Climate change. Property. Medical.

All of it was guided and directed by puppeteers who had no moral compass.

Corrupt.

The world was fucking corrupt.

Cleo never answered my question, so I did it for her. "If no one fights, it will only get worse. It's our duty to stand up now . . . before it's too late. People are desperate—just like I was before Wallstreet helped me. But I'll change that. If I can."

Cleo glanced between me and Samson. "And you *want* to be in the limelight? You want to be . . . what? A politician?"

My headache pressed harder. "No, I don't want that. The thought of being open to ridicule and scandal is the last thing I want."

"Then . . . why?" Her forehead furrowed. "Why put yourself forward? Why do something you don't want when you've been through so much?"

I smiled softly. "I started this when I had nothing to lose. I pledged my life to helping others, hoping to find value for mine since I no longer had you."

She gasped.

"I've been planning this for years, Buttercup. Regardless that I now have everything I ever wanted, I can't turn my back on something that got me through those darkest days. I can't give up on helping others find happiness and equality." Lowering my voice, I asked, "Do you understand?"

Her green eyes shimmered. The love shining there was infinite, decimating my heart all over again. "I ... I understand." Her shoulders squared. "I'm with you every step. What can I do to help?"

My soul lifted with thanks. I wanted to kiss her so fucking bad. "Nothing yet. I just wanted you to know what the future holds. Wallstreet will be out soon. And then it will be all over the news."

Samson cleared his throat, dispelling brutal honesty and changing the subject to less heavier subjects. "You're okay if I let Duncan and Spears know to begin?"

I nodded. "Go ahead."

Smoothing his trousers, Samson stood. He winced as his legs creaked. "Well, in that case, I'm heading back to my party. Don't think we need to confirm anything else, but if so, I'll send you an encrypted email."

I stood and shook hands with the senator who Wallstreet had told me to contact. My lessons hadn't ended when I'd been released from jail—they'd only just begun. I came out of Florida State despising the judicial system and everything to do with bureaucrats, but through Samson and Wallstreet, I'd immersed myself in men and women who wanted change, too—they just didn't know how to do it.

"Stay and mingle. Get a few more of these leeches onto your side." Samson laughed and bent over to kiss Cleo on her cheek. "Lovely to meet you, Ms. Price."

Cleo stood, looking as graceful as a fucking ballerina in her heels. "Thank you, Senator. I can't tell you what a relief it is to finally have some answers."

Samson's eyes softened. "No problem at all. And please, call me Joe. I think we're all on a first-name basis."

Moving to stand beside her, I asked Samson, "You'll talk to the other cabinet members? Tell them about Wallstreet?"

"First thing Monday, I'll go through what we've discussed and get the campaign started. The first advertisement will go live at prime-time viewing and then we'll be in for the long haul." Unlocking the door, he looked back again. "Once I have the extra funds, it's all systems full steam."

"Good."

Samson gave us a quick salute, then disappeared.

The moment he'd left the room, the air turned thick with questions—all originating from Cleo.

Grabbing her wrist, I said, "I know we have a lot to discuss. But right now, I need to do something."

My cock throbbed in my trousers—like it had the entire meeting. My headache compounded until I couldn't think straight and the alcohol hadn't done my hazy vision any good.

I needed pain relief and I knew how to get it.

"Do what?"

I gathered her close. "I meant what I said before. I'm going to have you here."

She trembled in my arms. "There's probably cameras everywhere." Trying to pull away, she fought a smile from her lips. "Can't you wait till we get home?"

I growled and bit her neck. "No chance. Not while you're in that incredible dress with your hair just begging me to fist it while I ride you."

She froze, her skin flushing with heat. "Well, when you put it that way."

Chuckling, I nipped at her ear. "You drive me fucking wild."

I didn't know how she felt about everything she'd learned. I didn't know if she was afraid, proud, or confused. But I did know she hadn't run. And by staying by my side she made me fucking invincible.

Lassoing my arm around her, I pulled her from the office. "Come on. Time to attend a different kind of meeting."

She trotted beside me in a rustle of skirts and smiles. "Are you doing this to avoid the huge cliffhanger you just left me with? Here

I was thinking all you cared about was math and brotherhood—I couldn't have been more wrong. I want to know more, Art. You can't dump all that on a girl and then seduce her, you know. "

I smiled. "Watch me."

She tried to act frustrated but she was just as hungry as I was. "If you won't tell me more now, shouldn't you at least mingle—like Joe told you to?"

Smiling at the odd democrat and not pausing to be roped into flowing conversation, I pushed Cleo toward the stairs. "I doubt they'll miss us for ten minutes or so."

"Just ten minutes?" she asked coyly.

I groaned under my breath as my cock grew harder with every step. "Stop looking at me like that."

A sexy glitter entered her gaze. "Fine. I'll let you hide your secrets about this revolution for a bit longer and play your game." She swayed closer. "Now, just to clarify, you don't want me looking at you *how*? Like I want to devour you? Like I want to pull your trousers down and kneel before you while I wrap my lips around your cock?" Batting her eyelashes, she laughed. "You mean that look?"

Shit, what was she trying to do to me? One minute she'd been the height of decorum and politeness and now she painted my mind with images of lips and tongues.

Yanking her to a halt, I pressed her against the wall. Her shoulders slammed against a family picture with Samson and his kids on donkeys in some mountain ranges. My fingers dug into her hip. "Yes, exactly like that."

Her body scorched my fingers. Her perfume made me drunk.

With smoldering eyes, she gazed at my lips. "Wow, I had no idea you had such big plans."

I captured her throat. "Oh, you have no fucking idea. I have huge plans when it comes to you."

Bigger than governments. Larger than reforms.

Her body tensed and melted all at the same time. "Oh really?"

"Yes, really."

Nipping at her bottom lip, I pushed away and captured her hand again. "Time to go upstairs. Away from curious bystanders."

She looked over my shoulder, no doubt catching some pervert's gaze. "Good idea."

I'd just admitted to wanting to topple the government. I'd just confessed to collaboration between bikers and senators. A fucking revolution. But all I could focus on was *her*. Everything else paled in comparison. It was work—something I'd been plotting forever. Cleo, on the other hand, was still so new. I had to reconnect—to make sure I hadn't scared her with my crazy ideals.

Weaving the final distance toward the staircase, I let her go ahead of me. She climbed the shallow steps in her delicate, danger-ous heels.

Every sway of her ass drove more blood to throb in my cock.

I could barely walk with needing her.

Halfway up the winding staircase, I spanked her through the puffiness of her dress. "You're going too slow, Buttercup."

Her hips wriggled, taunting me. "I'm going as fast as I can in these shoes."

"Not fast enough." Spanking her again, I grunted, "Get up there before I lose my self-control in front of these fucking people."

"So bossy," she breathed.

"Just wait till we get behind a locked door."

The climb took forever and I didn't let her stop when we finally crested the second floor. Wedging my hand against her lower back, we traversed the landing and entered a guest bedroom farther down the hall. It was a room I'd used once or twice when Samson and I would plot well into the night. My eyes would burn from reading for so many hours and I'd end up crashing here—having nothing to return home to but emptiness.

Cleo drifted inside, taking in the white rugs thrown over the dark brown carpet and the king-sized bed with hanging Morocco bedside lights from yet another one of Samson's travels. For a man who worked as many hours as he did, he did a lot of globe-trotting.

I locked the door, and my cock hardened. Every inch of my body reacted to the close proximity of the woman I needed. Even though she was across the room, watching me with anticipation and lust, our connection bound us—a powerful magnetic pull that only strengthened the longer we were together.

I would never be free of her power—orbiting around her for the rest of my life perfectly content.

It'd been that way with us from the very beginning. Ever since I helped her stumble home from falling off her bike, we'd been exquisitely drawn together. First by childhood fascination, then by aching teenage infatuation, until it had evolved into what existed today. A ferocious captivation of lust and love where every inch of her belonged to me.

All the rest … it could fucking wait until I'd had my fill.

My legs itched to cross the distance and drag her into my arms. I needed to feel her.

Touch her.

Love her.

The exquisite anticipation of what would happen made me rock hard. Fuck, it hurt. Everything hurt.

My dick.

My head.

My soul.

My hands fisted as I stepped closer. "I want you, Cleo."

She gasped, a delicate flush warming her cheeks. Her parted lips somersaulted my stomach.

"I need you so damn much." My voice was rough and ragged.

"I need you, too," she breathed.

My skin stretched across my bones, becoming hypersensitive and aware. I wanted nothing more than her fingertips on my arms, my face, my cock.

"Come closer, Art. You can't do too much when there's a whole room between us." Cleo tiptoed forward in her sexy high heels.

The svelte muscles in her legs dragged a groan from me. "Shit, you're beautiful."

Her eyes hooded. "And you're ridiculously handsome."

My fingers sparked, already drunk with expectation of stroking her. "You're killing me." I took another step.

And another.

With each one my headache pounded but it couldn't compete with the throbbing in my cock. Slowly, the distance shortened until the air crackled with intensity. For a second, I feared what would happen when we finally did touch. We would ignite, spark, and devour each other in a fit of carnal explosion.

There was another reason why I needed her right here. Right now. One that I would never admit aloud. Tonight was about paperwork and media. But tomorrow...

Tomorrow was about bullets and blood.

It's motherfucking war.

Rubix's time was up.

The battle was locked and my time with Cleo was fast ticking to either retribution or death.

"How?" she murmured. "How am I killing you when you're making me come so alive?"

Another step.

My heart clamored against my ribs. "You're killing me because without you, I'm so damn alone. I look back on the past eight years and wonder how the hell I survived without you. My fucking sanity depends on you. My self-worth, my happiness, my purpose in this life—all hinge on you."

What the fuck?

I hadn't meant to spew such debilitating truth. She didn't need to know just how broken I was with missing her. She didn't need to guess how close I was to losing it when faced with war tomorrow and no crystal ball on how it would go.

Before she came back into my life, I would've gladly died if it meant I had my revenge. But now...now I wanted to fucking *live*.

Running a hand through my hair, I yanked at the hair tie and destroyed the ponytail. I tried to get myself together.

Don't let her guess. Hold her. Fuck her. But don't let her guess.

She took another step, her face soft and eyes glossy. "You'll never lose me, Art. Not again."

An ache sucker punched me in the chest. "I wish that could be true." The constant headache that never left drained me suddenly. My ears ricocheted with the phantom sounds of bullets. I licked my lips. "Come here."

She obeyed.

We met in the middle of the carpet. We stared but didn't touch. We breathed but didn't speak. The tension sprung tighter until the hairs on the back of my neck stood up with need.

We were so close, but still so far apart.

"Goddammit, come closer." I grabbed her around the nape and smashed my lips to hers. The moment I touched her, the world incinerated.

There was no world rehabilitation. No upcoming battle. It was just us for eternity.

Her lips opened, welcoming me into my mouth as I walked her backward to the couch at the end of the bed. I didn't go for the mattress. What I needed wasn't long drawn out nakedness. I needed to be inside her now. Instantly. That very fucking second.

She was taller in her heels, her hands able to capture my cheeks without straining. Her warm touch sent my heart scattering and I groaned as her tongue massaged mine.

We didn't stop kissing even as the back of her knees hit the couch and almost sent her sprawling from my hold. Spinning her around,

I pressed her stomach against the high rolled arms of the settee and rocked my dick against her. "Feel how much I need you?" Trailing my fingers down her back, I traced the zipper, dropping to the stiff skirts below.

"I want you to submit to me. Let me take you this way."

Her head hung forward, her fingers digging into the purple fabric of the furniture as I swooped up beneath her dress and grabbed the thin lace around her hips. Tugging her underwear down, I fumbled with my trousers and belt.

It took me two seconds to unbutton, unzip, and yank out my cock. I gritted my teeth as I touched myself, so damn ready for a release.

My eyes bruised with the overwhelming headache, growing worse with every second. My heartbeat refused to tame, thundering faster and faster.

Cleo moaned as I tossed up the bottom of her dress, wedging my naked cock against her overheated thighs.

Her back arched. "Yes. Take me."

"Will you submit?" I drove against her again. Pre-cum shot up my dick, smearing on her perfect ass.

Will you give me this memory in case it's the last one I have?

"God, yes. I'll submit. I'll do whatever you want me to."

"You're incredible." I fisted my length, sliding deep inside her. No foreplay, no warning. The slickness of her desire let me enter smoothly with no restriction. Her body melted with welcome.

"Shit, you feel so good."

She folded deeper into the couch, giving in to me. Her hips rocked, forcing herself harder onto my length.

"Goddammit, Cleo." My fingernails pinched her hips, holding her still. "You do that and I'll embarrass myself in seconds."

She laughed quietly. "Embarrass away. I don't think I can handle too much of this." Her forehead bunched with pleasure. "It feels too good."

We were both still dressed in our cocktail finery, joined only where it mattered.

Looking down at Cleo's plaited hair and exquisite dress, watching her body press harder against the couch with my every thrust, I fell deeper in love. I'd loved her as a child, a teen, and a man. And now I loved her as if she was a dirty siren that didn't mind shedding her seraph wings and letting me take her dirty and wrong.

Massaging her lower back, I ordered darkly, "Spread your legs, Buttercup. I'm going to fuck you hard."

Cleo whimpered, obeying instantly. Her legs widened, her feet still encased in the delicious high heels.

The moment she moved, I didn't hesitate. With a powerful thrust, I drove deep inside her, stretching, claiming.

She cried out, bowing her head and biting a cushion.

Sparks shattered behind my eyelids as I thrust harder, faster, deeper.

Sweat glistened on her shoulders but I never stopped.

Moaning with delight, Cleo clawed at the sofa cushions, her nails indenting the thick fabric. "More, Kill. More."

Something switched inside me. I didn't know if it was her calling me Kill, or the deep passion in her tone, but I couldn't disobey. My cock grew thicker, and I drove inside her so, so deep.

I would mark her forever. I would imprint myself into her soul so even death could never part us.

My stomach kissed her ass while she bent like a wilting flower over the armrest of the couch. Folding over her, I planted a hand on the cushion by her cheek and captured the nape of her neck with my teeth.

"Ah!" she cried, arching in my hold, giving me better access to her throat.

We were no longer humans as I licked and bit with primitive claiming. We were savages intent only on one thing: destroying each other with bliss.

Her pussy clenched around my length, triggering my orgasm. "I love fucking you," I growled as pleasure spiraled through my system, shooting from my balls and through my cock.

I couldn't stop the release and threw myself headfirst into it. Leaning back, I planted my feet hard against the carpet and thrust.

"Don't stop. God, don't stop," Cleo panted. Her face was flushed and tense, every sense turned inward.

She cried out as I pounded into her with relentless rhythm.

"I'm coming!" Her voice tore through my haze.

I spurted inside her, over and over again.

Fisting her braid, I held it while my balls smacked against her clit with rhythmic slaps dragging on her orgasm.

The friction between us undid me. The grimace of tortured ecstasy on her face consumed me. She couldn't do a thing but endure my pace, my pressure—everything I gave her.

The last of my defenses toward her crumbled. I loved her so fucking fiercely.

The last band of bliss finished and I slowed down, running my hands down her back. Petting her, calming her. "That...that was—"

"Amazing," she breathed, her legs wobbling as I pulled out and tucked my cock into my trousers.

Smiling at how sated she was, I picked her up and sat on the couch, placing her on my knee.

Tomorrow, I would walk out without saying goodbye. I would go to battle without a backward glance, even though it would tear out my fucking heart.

I would do it to protect her.

I would do it to keep her safe.

But for now, she was mine and I meant to tell her just how much I loved her.

Kissing her ever so softly, I pressed my forehead against hers. "You're my home, Cleo Price. And through life or death, I'm never letting you go."

Chapter Twenty-Nine

Cleo

It'd been three years since I'd become Sarah Jones. Three years of living an imposter's life. Three years of emptiness. But now there was an itch inside my brain... begging for a scratch, craving the walls to fall.

Life had taken away my past and changed my future... I just had to hold on and see where the tide of change led me. —Cleo, diary entry, age seventeen

The next morning began like any other.

I woke on the left side of the bed with Arthur on the right.

We smiled and stroked and showered together.

We chatted and ate breakfast like any ordinary couple.

He skirted the topic of world domination, secret plans, and revolutionary reform. While I pried and inquired and tried to comprehend the magnitude of what would happen.

Then he announced he had business to attend to back at Pure Corruption.

I asked if I could go.

He said no.

He explained it was boring admin stuff. Stuff I wouldn't be interested in.

I didn't believe him, even when he assured me he wouldn't be long. That he'd be back for dinner. That I didn't need to worry.

He was downright lying.

When he walked out the door, I knew then that something was wrong.

It wasn't his overeager assurances that terrified me. It wasn't his curtness when I pried.

What petrified me were the words he *didn't* say.

The questions he refused to answer.

He was planning something.

Something huge.

And there was nothing I could do to stop it.

"What do you think of this one?"

Grasshopper's voice wrenched me from my thoughts.

I blinked, completely lost as to where we were and what the hell we were doing there. After Arthur had left, I'd paced the house, stewing with anger.

Once that proved unproductive, I decided to take drastic action. I threw on my jacket, tied up my hair, and stormed from the house—fully intending to drive over to the compound and demand to know what the hell was going on.

Only, I got as far as the garage before I was intercepted like some criminal.

Grasshopper had been put on babysitting duty.

And as much as I liked him—I wanted to tear him apart when he confiscated my pilfered car keys and threw me on the back of his Triumph with some halfhearted excuse of overseeing a few things.

The first half of the morning had been spent popping into the small businesses that Arthur, Mo, and Grasshopper ran—collecting income and records from the previous week.

But now it was late afternoon and I knew this rigmarole was intentional.

I was being kept away for a reason.

I could barely breathe with worry. Everything inside me screamed that something was seriously wrong.

Every time I sneaked into a bathroom and dialed Arthur's number, it went straight to voice mail. Every time I asked Grasshopper to elaborate on why Arthur had gone to the compound without me, he replied with the same annoying noncommittal response.

Once again I was in the dark and I hated it. More than hated it. Crushed by it. "Butterbean...earth to Cleo." Grasshopper snapped his fingers in front of my face, forcing me to focus. Another salon came into view. The third one today.

I scowled for the hundredth time.

The outside was pretty and cotton candy sweet. Decorated with golds and pinks, it enticed women—judging by the four clients currently in different stages of styling in the window—but set my teeth on edge.

I'd get a damn cavity just looking at the place.

I shifted on the back of the Triumph. The Florida sunshine hadn't let up and my jacket was stifling. All I wanted was a cold glass of water and some shade.

And the truth.

A cold dish of honesty.

Any other afternoon, I would've loved this. I would've jumped at the chance to get to know Hopper more—exploring all the avenues of Pure Corruption. But this *wasn't* any other afternoon.

Crossing my arms, I said for the twentieth time, "Give it up, Hopper. I want to go back."

Hopper twisted the accelerator; the bike rumbled between our legs. Avoiding eye contact, he glanced not-so-subtly at his phone. "Fine. I guess we can go back."

I tried to glimpse at whatever existed on his screen, but he cleared it and stuffed it back into his pocket.

"Take me to where Kill is."

He shook his head. "Nuh-uh. I'll take you back to his place."

My blood boiled. "I don't want to go back to his place—not unless he's there."

His back tensed, knuckles fisting around the handles. "Can't."

My blood turned to ice.

"Why not?"

Go on. Admit it.

The apprehension of a lie hovered between us.

"He told me to take you back, that's all. Meeting's almost over. He'll be back soon."

The fib threw sticky tar over my insides. It was so *obvious*.

Through his deception, he'd shown me the truth.

I know.

Hanging my head, I squeezed my eyes. "You just lied to me."

His leather jacket creaked as he turned to face the road, giving me his back. "I didn't fucking lie…" Sighing, he admitted, "I'm sorry."

My heart sank into the oily mess inside me. I knew why I'd been made to hop around town for no reason. I knew why Grasshopper had kept me distracted. "It's tonight, isn't it?"

Grasshopper froze, his strong muscles forming an unforgiving wall before me.

He didn't reply.

I sank into despair. "You don't have to tell me. I already know." The way Arthur had made love to me last night. The intensity in which he never let me go. He was saying goodbye—just in case he didn't survive.

No!

He can't leave like this.

He can't be so heartless to leave without saying goodbye.

Damn him! Damn his revenge. Damn his drive to avenge me.

Didn't he get that all I wanted was him to be safe? To live a life together?

What if he got hurt? Everything we'd been through would be pointless!

Tonight wasn't about business meetings or interviews. He was no longer a man in a suit but a biker in a cut. Last night had been the beginning of something. But today was the end of someone.

Today was war.

He hadn't even had the decency to tell me!

My heart fissured with a soul-destroying earthquake.

Grasshopper gunned the bike, taking his frustration out on the engine. "Don't hate the dude. He's doing the best he can."

No, he's doing what he's always done: not letting me share his problems.

Suddenly, it was all too much. I didn't want to be around anyone. I didn't want to be there. "Take me back, Hopper. I'm done."

Grasshopper stiffened and for the longest moment, I waited for him to crack and admit what he seemed too afraid to say. When he didn't, I squeezed his middle. "Take me wherever he is. Do it."

Grasshopper inhaled, his chest expanding beneath my touch. "I would if I could, but I can't."

"Why is that just a common phrase these days?"

He shook his head. "I can't because he's already gone."

No, no. No!

Everything inside became a fossil.

"What do you mean ... already gone?"

He cringed. "I was supposed to keep you distracted. You weren't supposed to worry. I'm sorry, Cleo, but he's already there."

My lungs ceased to work. "Where ... already where?"

Don't say it.

Do. Not. Say. It.

"He's gone to face Rubix. He's gone to finish a war."

Chapter Thirty

Kill

I'd always known I'd been raised to be a killer. Being the son of a murderer sort of defined my destiny. I'd been twelve when my father had taken me to witness my first homicide. Everything he'd done—boosting a car, trading coke, laundering a few rifles—was his side business. I'd been sworn to secrecy. Thorn Price never knew. I didn't like lying to Cleo's family. I'd hated blatantly hiding things from my president. But I'd had no choice. I'd lied to survive. —Kill, age fifteen

Grasshopper lied.

He lied for me. He lied to my woman. And he hated it.

Once more, I was a fugitive.

A liar.

A thief.

And I was about to become a murderer all over again.

I despised lying to Cleo. But I couldn't tell her my true plans. I couldn't run the risk of her following me and getting hurt again. I'd caused her enough suffering. These were my sins—not hers. And I fucking refused to have her pay another cent.

Lying was the only way I could keep her safe.

Sleeping beside Cleo last night, I'd ached to touch her one last time, to whisper in her ear and say that I loved her and would miss her—just in case tonight didn't go well.

But I couldn't do that.

I could only drink in the sight of her blazing red hair and hope to fucking God I survived.

Watching her sleep, I begged her not to dream of me. Not to dream of death and destruction.

And when the sun rose, I had to pretend that today was any normal day. I hid my rising anxiety and played the perfect part so I didn't raise her suspicions. Luckily, I'd had practice misleading those I cared about. First Thorn Price, then Cleo, then my own father as I fell more into Cleo and lied to protect her.

If I hadn't learned through habit and necessity, there was no way I would've succeeded. She would've guessed the moment I said good morning—her intuition far exceeded my ability to bullshit.

The minute we'd eaten, I sneaked away—like the fugitive I was.

I couldn't stand to be around her for another fucking minute in case my entire plan collapsed like a hopeless stack of cards.

The men had been informed.

The plan put into execution.

And Grasshopper was enlisted to distract her with monotonous businesses and pointless errands. Only once the brothers had been equipped, armed, and headed out to Night Crusaders could he return her home and come and join us.

Tonight, she would curse me. She would hate me for what I'd done. But I would take her hate gladly, as it would mean there was no way for her to chase us. We would vanish to do what was necessary, while she would be safe, far away from carnage.

If tonight worked—if the gods of fate had decreed I'd paid my toll and deserved my final retribution—then I would return a peaceful man. I would never raise arms again. I would have no need to. I would be content and redeemed. And Cleo would never have to worry.

I'd lived the past few years smelling nothing but blood. I'd existed craving nothing but revenge.

That was all at an end.

Tonight, I'll finally find closure.

My appetite for peace would be sated. My hunger for justice fed.
Salvation.

Shaking away the cobwebs of my thoughts, I centered myself. All thoughts of Cleo were silenced. All nerves that I might die deleted. All I needed to focus on was clearheaded anger.

The brothers around me throbbed with power. The night pulsed with sounds of engines and scent of gasoline.

I looked back at Pure Corruption's clubhouse one last time as I checked ammunition and pushed a revolver into my back waistband. My hands took stock, checking the sawed-off shotgun holstered to my thigh, the grenades gathered like a bunch of fucking grapes in my satchel, and the semiautomatic strapped to the back of my Triumph.

I bristled with war.

I dripped with weapons.

There was nothing left to do.

I gave the signal, and we pulled out.

"You ready for this, dude?" Grasshopper asked, his eyes trailing to the gate of the Crusaders' Clubhouse.

Three a.m. and it was a dead town. No security guard on watch, no trained dogs patrolling the perimeter. Just a squat, ugly brick building with rotting outhouses and overgrown weeds. Even the moon and stars hated this place, preferring to hide behind a belt of clouds.

It was child's play.

Undefended.

Unprepared.

Entirely fucking cocky.

Night Crusaders were new. Their MC hit four years old last month. When they'd encroached on our domain, we'd had...what should I call it? An *altercation*.

Egos were thrown, dominance asserted, and we'd taught them a lesson. We weren't a Club to be messed with. We had strict fucking rules and any newcomers were bound by those rules.

After spilling blood, we'd come to an understanding. They could stay, pay us our monthly due in order to receive our gracious hospitality, and promise allegiance whenever we called upon them.

My fists clenched around my handlebars.

Fucking traitors.

If I had known they would join forces with Dagger Rose, there was no way I would've ever fucking agreed.

They'd taken my money, accepted a whore, and lied to my face.

They'll get what they're owed tonight. Same as every Dagger.

Looking to my left, I nodded at Grasshopper. His silhouette was barely visible in the dark. "That question is irrelevant. I'm ready. Been ready for a long fucking time."

There was something to be said for just getting a job done. Dagger Rose had lived eight years longer than they were entitled. I should've slaughtered them the night I got out of the slammer. Why didn't I just do it? Why bother forming an elaborate scheme to destroy them piece by piece? Dead was dead.

Because Wallstreet had bigger plans and you agreed.

I gritted my teeth. That was true, but it'd also kept my mind off Cleo's death. If I hadn't had something so intricate to puppeteer, I didn't know if I would still be alive. I might've drunk myself into a coffin, or willingly been reckless, trying to follow her to the underworld.

Luckily, I had no wish to die. And Wallstreet's plans had finally aligned with mine.

It's time.

Grasshopper looked behind us. "We're ready when you are, Prez."

I swung my leg over my bike, unstrapping the semiautomatic and holding it high. There was no time for battle cries or courageous speeches. Each man knew what he was here for. We'd all done what was necessary to prepare.

The entire Club, minus two guards at the compound and one

watching over Cleo, was present. They all copied me, climbing off their bikes and arming their weapons.

"Say whatever prayers you need. Tonight there are no half measures. Got it?"

The men nodded, jaws tight.

Mo handed me a pair of bolt cutters. I felt like a fucking senator about to cut a city's ribbon. Handing Beetle my semi, I wedged the cutters through the metal links holding the flimsy gate together.

The chain snipped apart, slithering to the dirt, resting beside the pathetic padlock.

The gates swung open.

The Crusaders had tried to guard their home, but the barbwire on top of the fence was merely decoration when they chose to lock their gates with something as useless as a fucking chain.

I paused, glancing around the compound. We'd all studied blueprints, courtesy of a disgruntled Club bunny who'd been raped and left for dead by a prospect of the Crusaders. She'd spent a year as their slave before managing to escape. Now she wanted nothing more than revenge.

I understood her wish completely.

Pointing at the unprotected Clubhouse, I took the first step. Instantly, a ripple of action ferried through the men. We drifted forward as one.

Our boots crunched over twigs and dandelions. The moon remained hidden as if it didn't want to witness what would happen.

My eyes narrowed, seeking out weaknesses or problems.

This was no longer a Clubhouse but a battlefield. Luckily, there would be no civilian victims. The compound was out of the city limits, built illegally on an abandoned refuse site that no one touched due to chemical waste. Didn't they give a shit about their health?

I smirked in the darkness. *Not that they'll have to worry about their health tonight.*

Motioning in the air, I signaled the men to spread out.

Silently, our group thinned, forming a moving wall, ready to surround the building like gift wrap. Extra bullets were palmed, safeties flicked, and grenade pins pulled.

We'd come prepared for Armageddon.

Once we'd finished, there would be no Club, no compound, no *nothing*.

My father and brother would be pieces of meat.

I would finally find salvation.

Reaching the bricked wall, my men pressed up against it, fading into the night. Grasshopper's blue eyes narrowed, waiting for my next command.

Hefting the weight of my gun, I glared at my Pure brothers. "We all know the plan. Kill every motherfucker but leave the women and children alone. Anyone comes across Rubix or Asus, you leave those bastards to me."

Men smiled, pressing their fingertips to their lips in an age-old oath.

My word was their law.

Mo flanked me. "Perimeter check complete. No sign of life. Either they're all fucking high or complete assholes to not fortify."

"You take the left; I'll take the right. Kill can go in through the front door." Grasshopper slapped my leather cut. "After all, it's about the fashionable entrance."

Mo chuckled quietly. "You good with that, Kill?"

"Yep. You take a third, Hopper takes a third, and I'll meet you in the middle with the rest."

Mo didn't hesitate.

Slipping back into shadows, he darted down the lineup of bikers. Snapping his fingers, he summoned a third to go with him. His army disappeared around the side of the building in the first flank.

With a salute, Grasshopper summoned his third and moved in the opposite direction. We'd already discussed how we would attack: all at once from all fucking angles.

It would ensure swift victory. We would win.

I waited until Grasshopper disappeared with his group, before glancing at the remaining men. There were ten, eleven including me.

Each man bristled with armament, their eyes cold and focused.

They waited wordlessly, ready to begin. Looking at Matchstick then Beetle, I slinked forward.

I stayed hunched and low, fondling my semiautomatic. The safety was off. Tempers high. Adrenaline flowing.

Men deserved to die. My father deserved to die.

Boggy mud squelched around our boots as we inched around the building.

Beetle reached the front entrance first. He inspected the metal-reinforced door, seeking weaknesses.

I climbed the stoop. "Can you do it?"

Along with Beetle's past of shoplifting and anarchy as a kid, he was also a magician with locks.

Beetle squatted, eyeing up the mechanism. "It's an upgraded tumbler system. It'll take a minute, but I should be able to crack it."

Matchsticks hemmed us in. "Do it quick, else our edge will be gone."

The other men stood patiently, watching corners, weapons drawn.

Beetle unrolled his lock-picking arsenal and set to work. Matchsticks tapped his foot. My palms grew damp.

A minute screeched past, slicing my veins with impatience.

Beetle cursed, making a fucking racket with whatever tool he used.

"Enough," I hissed. I couldn't wait any longer. "What's the holdup?"

Beetle frowned. "Dunno. Something's jammed from the inside."

"I say we saw the fucking hinges or just blow it." Matchsticks pulled a grenade from his overstocked belt.

Christ.

I pinched the bridge of my nose. So much for a stealth entry. Grasshopper and Mo would've made their way around the building.

They'd seek other ways inside. But a bomb would give Dagger Rose and Crusaders time to mobilize. We'd planned on being quiet and dispatching as many people as possible before being noticed.

That idea was out the damn window.

"Any other way?"

Matchsticks shook his head. "The windows are barred. The only way in from this direction is through this door."

Shit.

Grabbing Beetle by the shoulder, I tugged him away. Matchsticks grinned, knowing what that meant.

"Blow it," I growled.

We had to get this done fast, otherwise our odds of a clean victory diminished.

Beetle didn't argue. We all moved back as Matchsticks unpinned his bomb and placed it at the foot of the door. Swinging his rucksack over his shoulder, he grabbed a few sticks of plastic explosive for extra insurance. Slapping TNT to the door handle and central hinge, he stuck a countdown device with a connecting wire between the two.

Once both were armed, he pressed a button and two red digits appeared.

20

19

18

Shit.

We stumbled for cover. *Damn asshole.* I thought he'd just use the one grenade, not an entire truckload.

17

16

15

"Move back." I herded Beetle and the men farther away. I wasn't afraid of gunfire the moment the bomb went off—but I was afraid of ricocheting shrapnel. The pressure of anticipation fogged around us. Men breathed hard, waiting to attack.

4

3

2

I tensed for deafening war.

Then, it happened.

The explosion tore through my eardrums. My eyes watered at the crescendo. The colossally loud noise cracked through the early morning sky, ripping at the once peaceful silence.

"Now!" I yelled, springing up and charging. "Go. Go. Go!"

We shot forward.

Smoking rubble and dust formed a barricade. Vision was shit as we bowled through the demolished door. There *was* no more door—only a cloudy pile of metal and smashed bricks.

Our boots clattered as we scrambled from night into reeking corridors. Marijuana, rubbish, and cigarettes punched us in the face as we streamed into the Clubhouse like an infectious disease, fanning out, clearing room after room.

Gunshots rang out, shouts, curses, screams.

It happened at mach speed.

Eight fucking years I'd waited for this and it felt as if the entire world fast-forwarded.

I wanted to *feel* this. To have my revenge.

But I turned into a machine, aiming, firing, shutting down to focus on staying alive.

Charging into a den three doors down, I ducked as bullets rained into the wall where my head had been. In a split second, I catalogued two bikers trying to kill me and three junkie whores on the floor.

I didn't think.

I fired.

A spray of bullets mowed them down, sending the two men face-first to the gross carpet.

The girls screamed, scrambling together as if there were safety in numbers.

I didn't check patches or discern who was what. Dagger, Crusader—it no longer mattered. All that mattered was finding my father and brother.

Where the fuck are they?

Ducking back into the corridor, I wheezed on brick dust and sulfur smoke. A barely dressed woman bolted toward me, her chest daubed in blood. I stepped to the side, letting her pass.

A biker charged after her.

I didn't give him a free ticket.

My finger squeezed the trigger.

He collapsed.

The Clubhouse was a fucking mess. Bikers, old ladies, my men, their men. It was an anthill with madness around every corner.

I lost count how many bullets I dispensed and how many lives I stole.

I didn't play favorites or hesitate.

No half measures.

This was what I'd been waiting for. I was *owed* this.

I shot without discretion, striking guts and legs, hearts and heads.

Every man I maimed didn't slate my bloodlust. Every room I entered didn't tame my heartbeat.

Only putting an end to my father and brother would do that.

Reaching the kitchen at the back of the house, where meth packets and bongs littered the countertops instead of cereal and milk, I bumped into Mo.

He grinned, a smear of blood over his forehead. "Sup."

I saluted. "Keeping score?"

"Too many to count." His lips twitched.

Mo was a seasoned fighter—he had the scars to prove it.

Tag teaming, we moved as one. Leaving the kitchen, we melted into bedrooms, dispatching men before they had a chance to shout and aim.

Mo grinned, completely in his element.

Turning my back on a massacre of Crusaders and Daggers, I slapped him on the shoulder. Sudden gratefulness and kinship swarmed me. He'd been a fucking dick when I first arrived, but ever since, he'd been a solid friend. "Morgan..."

He paused, his finger twitching on his trigger. "Yep, Prez?"

"Cheers—for everything."

He chuckled. "Didn't think carnage brought out the soppiness in you, Kill." His eyes glowed. "Means a lot, though, man. Thanks."

A bullet slammed into the wall, cutting our moment short. With no hesitation, he ducked, aimed, and slaughtered a Dagger.

Leaving him to it, I charged from the room and back into the corridor.

A shape barreled toward me. I raised my semi.

"Wow, Prez!" Beetle skidded to a halt, blood plastered all over his hair.

I pointed the muzzle at the carpet. "You seen them?"

He shook his head. "Not yet. Heard that Asus might be hiding in the john, though." He cocked his thumb up the corridor. "That way."

My gun grew heavier with retribution. "Perfect."

Without another word, he bolted away and disappeared in the hazy smoke.

I followed his direction, stalking past bodies and clearing suddenly silent rooms. Everywhere I looked, I saw men I'd grown up with—trusted and learned from—but no Rubix. No Asus.

My heart thundered. The longer I couldn't find my targets, the more my rage increased.

This was supposed to be their hideout. *So where the fuck are they?*

Slamming my shoulder against a toilet door, I bulldozed inside.

And fate finally smiled down on me.

Found you.

I stood in shock as I faced my brother.

"Shit." His eyes met mine, rage, fear, and surprise mingled in their depths. He sat on the dirtiest shitter I'd ever seen. A rifle pointed at my chest.

"Hello, Dax." My arm swung upward without thinking.

He snarled, every muscle locked. "Goodbye, Arthur."

The family reunion happened in a split second. Recognition, acknowledgment, anger.

He fired first.

"Fuck!" By some miracle, I ducked.

The bullet whizzed past my ear.

My brother, Dax "Asus" Killian, stood up, pumping his shotgun to fire again.

Too late.

I didn't bother aiming, just pulled the trigger. I didn't have time to make peace, or find an ending. The gun bucked in my hands, almost as if it knew this kill was different. This was the one I wanted more than anything.

"Motherfucker!" He collapsed sideways.

The bullet struck his shoulder, slamming him against the wall. Blood smeared down the dirty surface as he groaned in pain. "You fucking asshole."

Fumbling to get off another round, he folded forward on the toilet. "Fuck you! What do you think you'll do? Just kill us all and won't suffer any consequences?" He spat a wad of blood at my feet. "You'll go back to jail. Where you belong!"

I'd planned on dragging out his pain. I'd wanted to tell him why this had to happen. Why he had to pay for his sins. But staring at his betraying face, the agony of my childhood took me hostage.

The manipulation. The low-handed tactics.

It was no longer relevant—just like him.

I couldn't prolong it. I needed it over with.

"Just die, Dax."

This mayhem wasn't me. I wasn't a murderer by choice but by life's design. The sooner the past was in the past, the sooner I could throw down my weapon and live for the first time in eight long years.

His arm shook as he struggled to fire. "You first, brother."

Raising my gun, I pulled the trigger.

No remorse. No flinch.

My own flesh and blood existed, then…didn't. The hole in his forehead gushed with crimson as he slithered to the floor.

I waited to feel something. *Anything.*

He was my brother.

But there was only the glittering sensation of relief.

I'd turned my brother into a corpse and all I felt was solace. Endless solace to finally have payback. After what he and my father had done that night. After they'd drugged me, beat me, and made me believe I'd shot Thorn and Petal Price on my own accord—there was no other way this could've ended.

This was for her.

Grasshopper suddenly appeared. He favored his right side, holding two guns, fingers poised to shoot. His eyes darted into the single toilet. "Shit, you found him."

I didn't reply, only continued to stare at my dead relation.

He patted me on the back. "You did right, dude."

His touch snapped me back to the present. Clearing my throat, I backed away, throwing away the semiautomatic. I'd run out of bullets but I had plenty of other alternatives. Fisting the pistol from my waistband, I nodded. "He had to die."

Hopper's gaze was fierce. He knew what this meant but he also knew I wouldn't find complete redemption until my father was as dead as his firstborn son.

"Go," I ordered. "It's not over yet."

"On it." With a grin, he took off, charging down the dark, dusty corridor.

I looked left and right. Which way?

The screams and shots happened less and less. It'd been bloody and fast but the battle was almost over.

The adrenaline of war thrummed in my veins—not nearly satisfied. It'd been so long in coming but so short in ending.

Would I be happy with this? This quick conclusion after a decade of dreaming?

Turning left, I traipsed farther into hell. Rooms branched off like catacombs, all reeking of marijuana and sex. Cleanliness was nonexistent. The overall vibe derelict and sinful.

"Fuck, Mo!" Grasshopper's voice rang out.

My lungs stuck together in terror. My boots thundered against the carpet as I charged in the direction Hopper had gone.

Skidding into the laundry, where rank clothes hung in mildew humidity, Grasshopper clutched Mo on the floor. The minute he saw me, he cocked his chin at the back door. "There. That fucker just shanked him."

Leaving Mo in Hopper's care, I stormed outside. My eyes narrowed on to a fleeing figure in the dark.

Oh, no, you don't, you asshole.

My heart rate galloped but I forced my hand to steady. Closing one eye, I aimed at the traitor's back.

He didn't get far.

The shot rang out like a whip, ricocheting toward my victim. The bullet hit its target, halting him into death.

The moment he turned from running to face-planting into the toxic dirt, I forgot about him.

I didn't check if he was dead.

Mo.

He was much more important.

Hurrying back inside, I ripped aside a few shirts from the indoor washing line and ducked to my haunches beside Grasshopper. "How is he?"

Hopper's blue eyes glittered with rage. "Did you get him?"

I nodded.

Resting my hand on Mo's head, I muttered, "You okay, man?"

Mo winced, sucking air through his teeth. "Been...bet-ter." Black blood sopped his cut, puddling around Hopper like a morbid lake. "Ah, fuck it hurts."

Shit.

The bastard had got him good. Liver or gut...either way...Mo had a date with a motherfucking angel tonight.

Silent rage battled with grief. "He's dead, Mo. Got him for you."

He flinched, blood leaving his skin a ghostly white. "Go—good."

Trying to keep the knowledge that he was a goner hidden, I smiled softly. "You're all right. Don't stress, okay?"

Hopper met my eyes. I shook my head slightly.

His arms tightened around his brother, his mohawk quaking as he sucked in a breath.

Mo sighed heavily. "J-just my shitty l-luck."

I grabbed his hand. "Don't talk. We've got ya."

He smiled, fading fast. "You were a g-good prez, Kill. B-been a plea-pleasure..."

My heart fisted as his eyes suddenly lost their wicked loyalty and intelligence and turned to vacant film.

"Ah, shit...," Hopper choked.

Unfolding from my crouch, I looked down on the two men who'd helped me become someone better than a lost convict. "Keep watch over him. I'll go finish this."

Fisting my hands, I left before I gave in to the fucking fury building inside. Mo's death was my fault. His life stained mine.

I didn't feel worthy. Why did he have to die for me? What made me so fucking special?

Drawing my weapon, I sought enemies on which to take out my rage.

I craved something worthwhile—to prove he hadn't died for nothing.

Entering a bedroom, I didn't find what I wanted.

Instead of eradication of filth, I witnessed another murder. Only this one wasn't a Dagger or Crusader; it was a kid who was far too young to go.

"No!"

My vision stuttered as Beetle gasped, slamming to his knees before a man I recognized.

"Little twerp. I'll show you—" Sycamore laughed as a hole appeared where Beetle's heart used to be.

"Fuck!" I couldn't move as the youngest prospect's eyes shot blank, his body slithering into death.

It happened so fast. One second he was alive...the next gone. Just like Mo.

The cock-sucking-tobacco-chewing asshole who'd been there the day I was carted off in a police wagon giggled like a drugged-up slut.

Bastard!

"You fucking—"

Sycamore spun to face me, his arm raised to shoot. "You!"

He didn't get a chance to fire. I'd hated this fucking bastard all my life. My father's wingman. A devil within the ranks. He'd undermined Thorn and taunted Cleo constantly.

My gun swung up—so much lighter than my semi—and exploded in a spark of sulfur.

Sycamore stumbled backward, clutching his throat. The bullet tore out his windpipe, leaving him mute and gurgling as he smashed into a pile of worthless body parts.

My ears rang with injustice. I'd wanted him dead—but killing him wasn't nearly enough for the life he'd just taken.

Shit!

I turned to check Beetle's pulse. Poor kid. He was far too young to die. *I'm fucking responsible.* Two deaths now on my conscience.

A shadow appeared to my right.

I spun around, gun raised.

I was too late.

A sharp blade sliced through my side.

I bellowed, dropping my gun as a flash of agony scrambled my thoughts.

I staggered sideways.

Instantly, sticky wetness drenched my side. I flinched in excruciation. *What the hell—*

Then my eyes landed on *him*.

Thin lips, greasy skin, rampant greed, and diabolical ambition.

The one man I wanted dead above all others.

My father.

He smirked, darkness swarming in his green eyes. "Fancy that… you actually killed someone. After years of disappointment, I finally rubbed off on you." He came closer, weapon raised. "Any last words, son? Because I'm about to fucking slaughter you."

Chapter Thirty-One

Cleo

I'd found a dying bird today.

Its nest-mates had kicked it from its home, leaving it to die at the bottom of the tree. I'd wanted to tear apart the nest and see how the other chicks liked it—being bullied and left to wither alone. Instead, I'd scooped up the baby bird and took it home.

It was so easy to help. So gratifying to save another who needed saving. If I could change the life of a baby bird, perhaps I could change Arthur's life, too. After all, he'd been fighting to leave the nest for years. —Cleo, diary entry, age twelve

I was a prisoner.

For six long hours, I'd been barricaded in Arthur's home by Switchblade—the Pure Corruption security detail left to protect me.

Only, he wasn't protecting me. He was imprisoning me. And there was nothing I could do about it.

But then ... I felt it.

A snipping ... a slicing.

The link forged between Arthur and me through a lifetime of love suddenly ... severed.

My stomach plummeted.
My heart disintegrated.
And I gave up being calm.
I didn't know how, but I knew . . .
. . . something had gone terribly wrong.

Chapter Thirty-Two

Kill

*P*ain had layers.

I'd been wrapped in a layer for weeks—ever since Rubix had shown me how a creatively wielded baseball bat could be used.

But tonight, I was buried in layers.

Tonight, he'd beaten me so fucking bad, I swore to do anything just to get it to stop. That was when he'd laughed. That was when he'd told me what I had to do to make the pain stop.

Kill the Price family. —Kill, age seventeen

"Hello, Father." I gritted my teeth, holding my bleeding side. "I hoped I'd find you."

Scott "Rubix" Killian grinned. "What, so you could show me you haven't changed? That you're still a pussy?" His long hair was flecked with silver, messy and unkempt. His goatee held blood and dirt. "Or to learn about what I have in store for Cleo once I kill you?"

Every muscle stiffened. "Neither."

He cocked his head. "I suppose I should be proud that you found me—that you caught us unaware. Fuck, I'm even proud you got one over Sycamore. But then again, why should I be proud of a son that's always been a disappointment?" He chuckled. "All of this could've been pure luck."

That voice.

It crawled through my veins like a demon.

"Not luck. Years of preparation." The pain in my side disappeared under a torrent of adrenaline. I looked down briefly, clenching my jaw against the dark blood staining my T-shirt.

"You always were a slow-ass, Arthur. Surprised you're not wielding a math textbook or that tatty eraser you always carried." He took a step closer. "They were the only things you were capable of using."

Glaring at my father, I shrugged out of my cut, dropping it to the floor. The pain increased, sprouting sweat over my brow. "Little do you know."

I didn't have a weapon. I'd dropped it when my father's blade entered my flesh and he'd kicked it across the room.

Your knife!

My hands shot to my belt, unhooking the wicked hunting blade and brandishing it.

In a way, I was glad. A gun would've been too quick. Bullets weren't enough for this asshole.

I hadn't drawn out my brother's death. But my father? I would take great pleasure in extracting it.

"Oh, I know more than you think." Rubix glanced at the red river down my side. "I'll draw more before we're through, you'll see."

Bunching my fists, I advanced. "I guess we will."

His eyes widened, as if the memory of his browbeaten obedient son didn't compute with this pissed off president who'd served time for his sins. He back-stepped, moving toward the center of the room.

Beetle's corpse filled the space with seething retribution. Tonight, I wouldn't just kill my father for my sake, but for Mo and Beetle, too.

I have you now. I'm not letting you live another fucking minute.

Rubix ran a hand through his hair, clearing his vision from oily strands. "You really gonna take me on?"

A young girl in a torn nightdress and bruises all over her white skin sat upright in bed. The room was as filthy as the rest of the compound. Magazines scattered over the floor, tissues littered the bedside table, and the sheets looked like only a cockroach would find them sanitary.

"I'll take you on and win."

Rubix laughed. "As fucking if. You remember the past, don't you, boy? You remember the way I handed you your ass every fucking time?"

The girl whimpered, eyes bugging.

I tilted my head at the exit. "Leave."

I didn't want an audience and I didn't want collateral. If my father lost, he wouldn't hesitate to use her as protection. And I wouldn't hesitate to kill her if he did.

She scrambled off the bed, eyes dancing between Rubix and me.

Rubix sneered. "Get back into bed, baby."

"Do as I said and go," I growled.

Whatever loyalty she had to Rubix quickly vanished. Grabbing a disgusting bathrobe, she darted to the door.

Rubix glared. "Don't want a piece of pussy, Arthur? You always were a—"

"Were you the one to beat up that girl or just sloppy seconds?" I cut him off, taking another step.

He didn't back away this time, his bare feet stuck to the floor. He knew as well as I did that there was no more running—for either of us.

He looked older, eviler. His body wiry but soft around the middle. Dressed in low-slung jeans and no shirt, he exposed his Dagger Rose tattoo, which crept around his rib cage, merging with other ink on his chest and arms.

Time hadn't been kind to him—already making him bent and arthritic. His ink was an ugly faded green, while wrinkles lined his face.

He didn't look like a worthy opponent, but I'd been on the receiving end enough to not buy the feeble image. He was fucking vicious. He deserved to die.

We circled each other, staying out of punching distance. The knife he'd stabbed me with remained in his fist, dripping with tiny droplets of blood. *My* blood.

He smirked, unable to hide behind the mask he'd worn all his life. The truth shone: an evil bastard who truly didn't care about others.

I was doing the world a favor by putting him down.

"What's to say she didn't enjoy it? Bit like your piece on the side, eh?" Rubix laughed again. "Buttercup enjoyed her time with us. Didn't she tell you?"

My heart cracked open.

He'd die a thousand fucking deaths for touching Cleo.

My wound was a strange mix between hot and sticky, cold and damp. I didn't want the distraction, but at least the injury couldn't compete with the agony inside my head. My tolerance of pain had increased the past few days—no thanks to him.

I snarled, "She told me everything. It's only added to my conclusion."

Fury bubbled in my gut. I wanted to let loose and attack. But I couldn't afford to let anger get in the way. Emotions caused mistakes. This had to be coldhearted and calculated.

I would kill him. And I refused to die trying.

"Oh, and what's that?"

We continued circling, just waiting for the other to slip.

"That I'll kill you and never think of you again."

Rubix glowered. He suddenly threw the knife, lodging it into the mattress where his whore had been. "You never stopped believing in fairy tales, did you?"

I didn't answer.

"You want to kill me? Fine. Let's see you fucking try." He raised his fists. "No knives, no guns. We do this the old-fashioned way."

I cricked my neck, corralling my muscles to attack. "Fine by me."

A pause.

A single pause.

Then, war.

I didn't know who charged first. But in perfect sync, we stopped circling and met in the middle.

Everything inside me let loose. I'd dreamed of this moment—I'd begged for this chance. And now it was here.

I roared, clouting his chest.

He kicked and darted away, granting enough space for a brutal uppercut.

Stars burst in my eyes; blood coated my tongue.

"See, Arthur—you're still a pussy." Rubix darted away, fists raised. "Cleo will be such a lucky bitch to have me over you."

Red-hot rage combusted my veins like volcanoes. "You'll never touch her!"

We fell together again. Attacking, blocking.

The fight felt rehearsed. As if we followed some ordained path and choreography.

His fists connected. Mine connected.

His parries landed. So did mine.

We hurt each other but neither of us gained ground.

A purgatory of fighting where we both suffered to make the other bleed.

"Had enough?" Rubix panted, blood pouring from his nose.

I smiled, bordering feral insanity. All I wanted was his life to snuff out. I wanted him gone.

"I won't have enough until you've paid for what you've done!" I launched myself into him, fists flying—all uniformity scrambled in favor of granting as much agony as possible.

Each punch was cathartic. Each knuckle to his jaw healing.

Time lost all meaning as we chipped away at each other. For me, I only grew stronger with every strike—becoming weightless thanks to redemption granted piece by piece.

But for him, he faltered. Swing after swing, he lost his confidence, turning messy.

Breathing hard, he growled, "You're a waste of space, Arthur. Just give up already. Stop making a fucking fool of yourself."

I grinned, swallowing back metal and gore. "You're losing, Father." Every fumble and missed strike fed me like a beast. Rubix might've tried to turn me into him—but somehow, I'd become better. Stronger. Quicker.

Almost every night of my teenage years, he'd taught Asus and me how to throw a punch. He'd forced us to fight—cultivating hatred between brothers.

I'd loathed those nights, but I'd never forgotten the lessons. Never forgotten the way my father operated or favored his left fist over his right.

Energy poured into my tiring body. I used my trump card. "He's dead, you know."

Rubix's eyes widened, then narrowed. "What the fuck are you—"

"Dax. He's dead. I slaughtered the son of a bitch."

For a moment, grief clouded my father's face; then putrid anger replaced it. "You mother—"

I sidestepped his attack and let every lesson and memory guide my fists. He no longer scared me, controlled me, owned me.

Not this time.

My hand barreled into his face.

This is for Cleo.

My knuckles connected with his cheekbone.

This is for Thorn.

My boot thundered against his kneecap.

This is for fucking throwing me away like I was nothing.

My uppercut sliced through his jaw, spurting red rain from his mouth.

Rubix reeled away, groaning. He hurtled himself forward, going for my stab wound. He punched me right in the gaping slice. Nausea raced through me.

He dodged my retaliation to wallop my kidneys from behind.

I cried out, gritting my teeth against the whitewash of unconsciousness. Blood ran over my brow; sweat drenched my hair.

Rubix might've been a better fighter when I was younger, but the past had changed me.

He'd taught me to funnel my anger. When I'd been imprisoned at Florida State, his lessons had been a saving grace. I'd been able to defend myself—make a name for the barely adult convict and prevent worse tragedies.

My skills had been noted. I'd been recruited for the prison boxing team. For years, I served as entertainment for inmates and guards alike—learning, evolving, honing my skills for this very moment.

He didn't stand a fucking chance.

You see, Father. Payback is a bitch.

Pummel after pummel, we grunted and glared.

"Give it up, Arthur. You won't win."

I laughed because the words were false bravado from a dying man.

Accepting pain from his deadly aimed strikes only fueled me more.

I bared my teeth. "You're losing ground, old man."

I served an uppercut. Connecting with his chin, rattling his teeth like bones. He slammed to his knees, shaking his head. Before I could deliver another, he staggered to his feet, spitting blood in my direction.

My hands tightened. My heart lightened.

I'd made my father bow.

I'll make him do it again.

Breathing hard, I served a heavy slug, snapping his head back. He crashed against the bed, whirling away from me.

I'd never felt such freedom. Every punishment was medicine to my heart. His every cry soothed me, knowing I destroyed the monster of my past.

He deserved this and so help me God, I would *end* this.

Rubix slumped to the floor, shaking his head from dizziness.

I advanced.

We both knew who'd won.

It was schematics now. Inevitable.

For a moment, I paused. I could drag this out. I could wait for him to climb to his feet and torment him again and again. Memories of the past—of a childhood where firing guns, smuggling drugs, and assassinating business rivals was more common than barbeques or homework—I struggled to let go. To stop my tangled history having any sway over me—to stop pining for Cleo's teenaged ghost before she was scared and inked.

I hadn't been strong enough or cold enough to do what was needed all those years ago. I wasn't able to protect her.

But by fuck, I'd do it now. For as long as I lived, Cleo would always be safe, loved, and protected.

Rubix stood up. His nose was broken and his right elbow didn't bend correctly. My heart thumped to think of the agony I'd caused the man who gave me life.

Then I remembered his threats toward Cleo. I recalled his every torture and trickery, and nothing could stop me from exterminating him.

I was doing the world a favor. I was doing the only thing I could to finally find happiness.

Spinning in place, I roundhoused him. My boot landed squarely on his chest. The crunch of ribs cracked in the stagnant room as he folded to the floor. His scream bounced off the walls, sounding sickly weak.

Standing over him, I said goodbye to every hatred I'd carried for so long. I let go of what'd driven me and embraced a fresh beginning.

"Goodbye, Rubix."

He raised his hands. "You'll fucking regret it, boy. You're my son!"

I raised my boot. "Not anymore."

I kicked him. He rolled to his side, bellowing in agony.

Then I did something I wasn't proud of.

I stood over my father's body and kicked him in the head.

One last severance to end it all.

My father twitched and fell broken.

It's done.

The silence that followed didn't make any sense.

I was eerily empty.

Strangely calm and not entirely satisfied.

After four million minutes—eight long years—I finally had cessation. However, there was a part of me that didn't settle. It didn't feel *final*.

He's dead ... isn't he?

I bent to check his pulse.

There was a faint beat—his last attempt to cling to life.

Goddammit.

Why couldn't anything relating to my father be easy?

The fact he wasn't dead destroyed my inner calm. Even unconscious and barely alive, he still made me go into the pitch black to win.

Standing, I did the only thing I could. Grabbing the knife from the bed, I rolled Rubix onto his back and hovered over his unconscious body.

Hatred heated my blood, warming me despite the torrent soaking my T-shirt and jeans. Not only had I beaten him to a pulp, but I now had to murder in cold blood too. End an unconscious man—put him down like some sick dog.

Sucking in a breath, I wrangled my thoughts in order.

He's a monster.

He has to die.

Almost ritually, I pierced the blade between his ribs and plunged the knife deep into his heart.

He didn't open his eyes. He didn't flinch. There was no sign of him slipping from one world to the next. Only the barest stutter as his pulse ceased.

The room seemed to contract and exhale. Relief dripped down the walls and *finally* I felt a thawing inside me.

Everything I'd been carrying suddenly shot free.

The guilt, the fear, the betrayal—it all disappeared.

It was as if I'd somehow found my innocence that was lost that horrible night. Finally believed I deserved Cleo, even though I'd become a monster in order to slay one.

Everything was as it should be.

I'm finally free.

The only thing left was to drench the place in gasoline. To destroy the scene of carnage once and for all and say goodbye forever.

So much fire in my past.

So much destruction.

There would be no need for such violence ever again.

No need for revenge.

No need for hatred.

It's over.

The flames devoured the corpses.

The Night Crusader Clubhouse was nothing but ash, and the women left behind scattered like mice.

We stood there, retinas burning with bright orange and skin prickling with heat—each man closing this chapter of his life in his own way. Never again would I kill. Never again would I wear someone else's life on my soul.

The victory wasn't celebrated. We'd won, but lost. Mo's and Beetle's empty presence blemished the night.

No one spoke as we waited for the fire to fully take hold. Crackling and spitting echoed in the darkness as the fire chewed its way through filth. We waited until the evidence was consumed by the blistering heat before straddling our bikes and roaring for freedom.

The battle had been a success. However, there'd been casualties.

Terrible, terrible casualties.

My hands clutched around the throttle.

That ever-elusive happiness was finally mine.

I had my vengeance. I had my closure. And finally I had my woman.

But I'd also paid a heavy debt.

Two lives.

Two lives that'd belonged to me—that'd trusted me to keep them safe.

The wind in my face dried the streaks of blood, seeping the crimson through my skin to my soul. The slash in my side burned with agony. I'd torn up some sheeting to wrap around my chest, doing the best I could to stay conscious.

I needed a doctor—and this time, I would obey every instruction. Along with my body, I would fix my mind…I would get better—spiritually, physically, and emotionally.

The hum of my tires soothed my jagged nerves and for the first time in almost a decade, I could fucking breathe.

Breathe knowing I'd avenged Cleo.

I'd claimed what I was owed.

Even my headache couldn't take that away.

Everything would be better. I had a new future, new possibilities, new horizons.

My heart fisted as Mo and Beetle came back to mind. I couldn't shake off their sacrifice. I would never stop being grateful for the termination they'd given me.

Grasshopper looked over, his bike keeping pace with mine. He smiled sadly.

Tonight was a celebration and mourning all in one.

Our fallen comrades were with us on the road, even though their souls were not.

Their death would forever taint our victory.

Squeezing the throttle, I picked up speed, trying to outrun the sadness and enjoy the freedom just a little longer. I was selfish in a way—wanting to bask in the knowledge that my father no longer existed.

Mo had been a gruff, guiding force, invincible. And Beetle had been my protégé. They were good men.

I pushed my bike faster. Wind gushed harder and I shot forward from the crowd of my brothers.

No matter how fast I pushed the engine, it wasn't enough.

I wanted to see Cleo. I needed to be in her arms and bury my sadness for causing the deaths of two brothers.

But then . . . it didn't matter.

The concussion I thought I'd broken returned with a vengeance. Agony worse than the stab wound in my side splintered my skull.

I cried out.

The road disappeared before me.

Noise, touch, sight, sound—it all shut off as if I'd driven into a silent black hole.

The headache compounded. It didn't return with vise or needles, but with machetes and machine guns.

It tore through my head. It hacked through my thoughts. It careened me into agony.

One moment, I was lucid.

The next, I was falling.

Skidding.

Sliding.

The road came up to meet me.

My body tumbled to embrace it.

And that was the last I remembered.

Chapter Thirty-Three

Cleo

I knew what I wanted to be when I grew up.

I didn't want to teach or be a chef or fly the world. I wanted to heal animals. I needed to fix helpless creatures who suffered at the hands of sinners. I needed to put goodness back into the world. But mainly, it was because of Arthur.

He was fading before my eyes, withdrawing from me. He thought withholding information protected me. It didn't. It only made me worry more and no matter how hard I tried, I couldn't save him. —Cleo, age twelve

"Take me to Pure Corruption."

Switchblade looked up, his baby face wreathed in cigarette smoke, his jacket absorbing moonlight. His eyebrow rose, but he didn't have time to speak.

Charging past him, I straddled his bike resting in the forecourt. With my voice soft but lethal, I demanded, "I won't ask twice. Take me to the compound."

Switchblade shook his head. "You know I have orders to keep you here."

"I don't care."

"It's for your own safety."

"Think about your own safety if you don't take me to Pure Corruption this very second." My temper helped hide my fear, but once again the sinking, suffocating feeling of being untethered consumed me. It was like hurtling through space with no rope. Like jumping off a building with no parachute. Like amnesia for my heart.

It took all my power not to fall to my knees and scream. I squeezed my eyes. "Take. Me. To. The. Compound."

The unhinged beg in my tone sent alarm skittering through his eyes. Coming closer, he looked me up and down. "Whoa, everything okay?"

Tears were a diabolical enemy, doing their best to stream from my eyes. I wouldn't let them fall. Not until I knew. Not until I found Arthur and saved him like I should've done all those years ago. "No, everything is *not* okay."

Fear shadowed his face. Understanding animated his pudgy limbs. "What do you mean?"

Please, please let me be wrong.

Please, let this empty sickness disappear.

When my prayers went unanswered and the aching loneliness gaped wider, I choked, "Something's happened. We need to go. *Now.*"

It'd been too long.

Far, far too long.

I'd paced and fretted and gone out of my mind with worry.

For hours, I'd tracked paths through the Clubhouse, desperate for any news. We'd received nothing.

To start with, it'd just been Switchblade and me—rattling around in a space with my soul missing. Then, others trickled in. Melanie, Feifei, and more.

Cell phones had been called. No replies. Theories had been conjured. No answers.

We were back in the telephonic dark ages, waiting for our soldiers to return home. I had to hope the sickness inside me was wrong—that they'd appear any second and not some god-awful telegram with bad news.

The waiting was torturous. We suffocated on excruciating worry.

I could understand why women who lived through WWI and WWII signed themselves up for danger. Enlisted as nurses. Gave their services to sew buttons and build tanks. *Anything* would've been better than the endless waiting.

I can't stand it.

I felt helpless on the battle lines.

A mourning girl dying to tend but completely useless.

"Any news?" I asked for the billionth time, glaring at Melanie and Molly. They sat huddled on the couch in the main room of Pure Corruption.

"No, nothing," Melanie said sadly, never relinquishing her death grip on her phone. "No one has called and every time I dial, the connection fails." Her eyes met mine. "What if—"

"Stop it. Don't say it."

Molly curled her legs beneath her, looking dejected and lost. Gone were the capable businesswomen from Church. These women loved their men deeply. They felt their absence as deep as any wound.

In a way, I was grateful. Thankful that I didn't have to go through this alone. Thankful that I had others to hold up the curtain of grief so it didn't smother me entirely.

More time ticked by.

Slowly, anger chased away my concern. I filled with rage.

How could Arthur do this to me?

How could he invite me back into his life and then walk so easily out of mine? How could he leave me torn apart with no one to sew me back together?

Damn you, Arthur Killian. You owe me. Stay alive.

With nothing else to do, I slowly wore down the floorboards, making them gleam from my relentless pacing.

How much time had passed?

The Clubhouse was a prison drowning me. I couldn't stand it any longer.

Stumbling from the room, I made my way to the exit and wrenched open the door to the front yard. Barbed wire and high fences kept the world out but also penned me inside with my raging anxiety.

I'd gone through all stages of grief, cycling through them over and over again. I went from terrified to livid, from numb to sick. I'd passed the point of visualizing all the horrible things that could've gone wrong and forced myself to wait for answers. I even settled into acceptance—as if my heart couldn't handle the not knowing and would rather accept the worst than hope for the best.

My eyes were raw and strained as I stared at the waning moon above. It was pale and washed out as a new day dawned. Or perhaps it was merely feeling my pain and sympathizing.

Closing my eyes, I begged.

Please, let him return safely.

Please, let him be okay.

My knees wobbled; I couldn't take the worry anymore.

Moving around the front façade of the building, I slid down the wall and drew my knees up. Tucking my face in my hands, I tried to calm myself—to silent my concerns and stay strong.

Cicadas chirped. The honking noises of wild fowl in the everglades steadily grew more determined as daylight chased away the night.

Then…something hummed on the horizon.

My head snapped up, ears aching to listen.

It came again.

Louder than a cricket, more mechanical than any insect.

They're here.

Throwing myself to my feet, I charged inside. "Melanie! Molly! They're back!" I skidded into the common room. "Jane, grab the first aid kits. Feifei, you're in charge of getting food and water. Bring it all in here—just in case."

I went straight into triage mode. I didn't care if they all walked in thumping each other on the back and commiserating a fight well triumphed. I wanted to be ready.

Please, let them be fine.

The growl of engines grew louder as the women dashed off to do what I asked. Switchblade appeared from one of the offices, and, with a worried look in my direction, bolted to the garage to open the huge roller door.

The thunder of motorbikes boomed. Out of the gloom drove three, six, ten, then a torrent of bikers. They poured into the gleaming lights of the garage, parking haphazardly among resting Harleys and muscle cars.

I lost count as the last bike roared inside and Switchblade pressed the remote to cut off the outside world, protecting his brothers.

Engines were killed, helmets were tugged off, and groans of agony became the new cacophony rather than engines.

Dashing forward, I searched for Arthur.

Where is he?

Man after man I discounted as I searched for my soul mate. Blood and dirt and gore covered the returned warriors.

But there was no sign of their president.

A hand squeezed my shoulders. I spun in fright. My heart rabbited, already anticipating my lover, smiling secretively and full of life.

I froze.

Grasshopper cupped my cheek, his face smeared with grime and weariness. "Cleo..."

The world sucked into a terrible vacuum. My heart stopped beating. "Where...where is he?"

Hopper sighed; his mohawk bristled with debris and grease. His cut had a rip down the front and his boots were covered in mud. "He's not with us. He's—"

A screeching filled my ears, my head, my soul. Grabbing his lapels, I yanked him close. "Please. Please tell me he's okay!"

Grasshopper wrapped an arm around my shoulder, guiding me toward a hot, hissing motorbike. "We don't know yet. I came to get you. I'll take you to him."

With strong hands, he plucked me from the floor and placed me gently on the back of his Triumph. I didn't struggle. I didn't speak.

Am I in shock?

Am I broken?

Placing a helmet on my head and fastening the strap around my chin, he said softly, "He's alive, Cleo. Just hold on to that and let's hope the doctors keep him that way."

I decided something while waiting in the dismal, depressing waiting room of the hospital. In a way, I'd had my eyes opened and the last naïveté of childhood stripped away.

Being the one left behind—the one waiting to hear the news of a loved one's fate was the worst kind of punishment *ever*. I thought I'd understood Arthur's pain. Understood his grief to believe I was dead and never coming back.

But I didn't. Not really.

Dealing with amnesia was the easy part.

I'd moved on with nothing. No sadness to consume me. No guilt to enrage me. I'd had a clean slate.

Not Arthur. He'd been the one left behind.

My heart wouldn't stop aching to think of the intolerable agony Arthur had been left with. I'd waited for news of his surgery for eight hours. But he'd waited for me to be reincarnated for *eight years*.

He was so much stronger, braver, and more capable than me. Purely because he'd lived through that tragedy and continued on living. Me? I wanted to die and fossilize in this awful plastic chair, so I never had to hear the news that he didn't make it.

When we first arrived, Grasshopper had stayed close by. The nurses and orderlies all gave him a wide berth, eyeing up his bloody clothes and split knuckles. But gradually, as updates of Arthur's progress was delivered, more and more Pure Corruption members arrived.

They'd showered and donned fresh clothes but they couldn't wash away the stench of battle from their skin, nor banish the carnage from their eyes.

What they'd done last night hung around them like a thick aura and I made a promise never to ask what they did. Never to pry about the murders and torture that Dagger Rose deserved.

However, I couldn't block my ears from their whispered conversations.

That was how I found out Arthur wasn't the only casualty.

There'd been two others.

Mo and Beetle. A veteran and a prospect.

Dead. Gone. And all for what?

"Mrs. Killian?"

My head shot up. Doctor Laine frowned, taking in my ragged state and bloodshot eyes. "Everything okay?"

Seeing a familiar face threatened to break me. Digging my fingernails into the fleshy part of my palm, I stood. "There was a motorbike accident. Arthur is…" Taking a deep breath, I forced myself to finish. "He's in surgery."

I would've given anything to be in the room while they worked on him. My fingers itched to stitch and heal. But dealing with a dog or cat was entirely different than dealing with my lover.

Doctor Laine's face fell; her severe hairstyle made her look older than her years. "I'll find out what I can. But rest assured, he's in great hands here."

I tried to smile but nothing happened.

"Honestly, don't worry," she consoled. She tried to drag my thoughts from depression by distracting me. "I heard that you sewed up Mr. Killian when you first met."

My eyes widened. How did she get that piece of information?

Then they narrowed at the incorrect assumption. Having just met him implied he hadn't been mine all my life. I shook my head. "I stitched him up, that's true. But it wasn't the first time we'd met."

She cocked her head. "Oh?"

I frowned, struggling to focus on love when all I could think about was death. "The night I patched him up was the night we found each other for the second time."

Before Doctor Laine could reply, a male doctor with a receding hairline and lined eyes appeared. "Ms. Price?"

The tantalization of news hurled me forward, gasping for knowledge. But then the fear of bad news almost pushed me back, making me want to huddle in the vacated chair.

"Yes?"

He waved his arm, motioning for me to follow.

Doctor Laine squeezed my shoulder. "I'll catch up with you later. I have no doubt he'll be fine."

Grasshopper appeared from grabbing a vending machine coffee. His eyes softened. "Go on, Butterbean. It's better to know than not. I'll be here for you, either way."

Tears flooded my eyes but I didn't let them fall. Bracing myself, I chased after the doctor and waited.

"I won't beat around the bush, Ms. Price." The doctor hid behind his clipboard almost as if he protected himself from me and the family of bikers I ran with. "His injuries are pretty serious."

I wrung my hands. "What... what happened?"

"According to your, eh, friends, Arthur suffered a blackout from his previous concussion while driving. His motorcycle skidded out of control and he smashed into a highway barrier."

My heart stopped beating. "Oh, my God."

Hearing the truth after Grasshopper refused to tell me sucker punched my soul. Hopper had tried to protect me by hiding what'd happened—but it hadn't helped. I'd only come up with worse scenarios.

The repeating image of Arthur slamming into concrete tore at my insides.

"Arthur has suffered a slow bleed on his brain since he checked himself out from this hospital against my advice. Unfortunately, the pressure built and built until there was no more space to build."

"What does that mean?"

The doctor glanced away. "We had to operate. It was a delicate situation—always is when dealing with something as complex as the brain—but we were able to stem the internal bleeding." He cleared his throat. "The additional scans show promise. We hope with time, he'll return to normal functions."

What does that mean? Would he be the same man I knew? The same boy I'd fallen in love with?

"Will he be okay?" My voice was a tinny thread.

The doctor sighed. "As long as he listens this time and takes it easy, I have no cause to believe otherwise. Like I said, his injuries are serious, but the human body has repaired much worse. In situations such as these, it's common for a patient to wake and be in full capacity of their intellect, vocabulary, and show no adverse effects. Unlike other operations where healing is hindered with pain, the brain is different. Miraculous really."

I didn't know half of what he meant. But I didn't care. All I cared about was holding him and witnessing for myself he was okay.

My muscles vibrated, threatening to come apart. "Can I see him?"

"Of course." The doctor lowered his clipboard, waving down the corridor for me to follow. Silently, I trailed in his wake, feeling like I walked the pathway of death. Bright lights hurt my eyes; antiseptic stung my nose.

Planting his hand on a door, the doctor cracked it open and stepped back. "I'll give you two a minute. He's awake but groggy. We'll monitor him closely over the next twelve hours. Don't be alarmed. Half of his head is shaven and fully bandaged, and he's broken a couple of bones, but overall, he's strong and on the mend."

Broken bones?

Never-ceasing tears sprang to my eyes.

Oh, Art.

Unable to speak, I slipped past him into the room where a single bed hovered in the center, serenaded by gentle beeps and irregular humming.

My eyes drank in the man tucked tightly beneath starched sheets.

I blinked, staring at him.

Or at least, I stared at...*someone.*

Someone lay in the bed.

But I didn't recognize them.

Where was Arthur? My huge fearless Libran with arms roped with muscle and chest broadened with power?

This man was a stranger.

Covering my mouth, I drank in his injuries with horror.

His arm was at a right angle, encased in a fresh cast. His cheek scraped and raw, parts covered in gauze. And his head was covered in bandages. He looked so...lifeless. So broken.

My knees quaked as I crossed the short distance and went to him. "Arthur..."

He didn't respond. I stopped beside the bed, fingers trembling as I touched his cool cheek, doing my best not to look at the turban of white covering his shaggy dark hair.

The doctor had warned me.

His hair will be gone beneath that.

But no matter how much information I learned—no matter the statistics or in-depth detail of his operation and recovery—nothing could soften the blow of seeing the man I loved so bruised, crumbled, and pained.

Taking his hand, I squeezed his fingers. "Arthur...can you hear me?"

Nothing.

His face was white as the sheets, eyes ringed with shadow.

Urgency possessed me. He had to see me, had to open his eyes to know I was there...

I would *always* be there.

"Arthur. Please..."

I tightened my hold on his cold hand, wishing upon wishes for him to respond.

The fear of his concussion crushed me. The memory of him being a devil to rouse a few days ago caused a sob to build in my lungs. "Art..."

I rolled my shoulders, pressing my forehead on his chest. Wires and monitors covered him—some slinking beneath the bandage around his head—others snaking down the front of his hospital gown.

I wanted to rip them all away. To free him from suffering. To protect him.

"Arthur...please. I need to see that you're okay..."

He left me stranded for another long moment, but then something changed. A gathering of awareness—a coming to from deep slumber.

The first sign of life was a twitch, a breath, an extra beep as his heart woke up. The next was parted lips and color flooding to ghostly cheeks. It was like watching a butterfly escape from a chrysalis.

And then *finally*, his eyes opened.

They were just as green and brilliant as I remembered.

The color bowled into me, wrapping me in emerald hope and chasing away my clinging fears. "Oh, thank God."

I pressed a kiss on his cheek, inhaling him. His scent was faint, hidden beneath antiseptic but traces of leather and sea salt existed.

He still existed.

"You're okay...you're going to be okay." I peppered his face with love.

He groaned, shifting away a little.

Pulling back, I blushed. "Sorry, I didn't mean to attack you. It's just...God, it's been a horrible night."

He frowned, his eyes locking onto mine.

My heart stopped.

No…

Instead of love and affection, they were blank. Cold as rock and empty as a tomb.

Pain.

Pain I never knew existed splintered through me.

"Art?" A watery smile pulled my lips. "It's me…Cleo."

His forehead furrowed. He shook his head.

No. No, please.

Nightmares swarmed me with thoughts of him forgetting me. Of our roles reversing. Of amnesia tormenting me all over again by making me the forgotten not the forgetful.

I wouldn't be able to survive. I couldn't live in a world where Arthur didn't love me. Even while we were apart I'd felt it—some cosmic bond keeping me alive. He'd kept me strong. He was the reason I'd kept going.

If he's left me…

"Arthur…don't do this." The sobs I'd tried to swallow erupted. Tears flooded my cheeks. "You know me…remember?" I fumbled for his hand again. "I'm yours. Buttercup…"

He sucked in a breath. The blankness shifted like fog on a lake. "B-Buttercup…"

I shivered so hard my teeth rattled. "It's me. Please, don't forget me. I can't manage if you forget me!"

Suddenly, his lips twisted in horror. "Fuuuuck, Cleo…" The drugs cleared, his pain receded, and he truly *saw* me. His soul shone, glittering with agony. "Never. Oh, Christ, h-how could I e-ever forget you." His large body shifted beneath the sheets. His broken arm tried to wrap around my shoulders. He grunted in pain, breathing hard. "I kn-know who you are. I do." His voice cracked. "I'm sorry—I'm a little out of it w-with whatever they gave me. How could you ever t-think—"

"You didn't recognize me." I tried to hide my face. The lack of sleep and overwhelming worry gave me no room to hide. I became unhinged on a nightmare that wasn't true.

What if this was all in my head? What if the words I heard weren't real? Could he wake from brain surgery and start talking as if everything was fine? Is that what the doctor meant?

"Hey…" He managed to cup my cheek with his uncased hand. His rough thumb traced my damp tears. "You're t-tearing me apart, Cleo. Don't c-cry. I'm here. I'm still me."

Part of me didn't believe him. Part of me still feared the worst—that the doctors had chopped out the parts of his brain coded to me, the synapses that made him mine. I couldn't shake the debilitating terror that there was nothing I could do to stop him from leaving me—to keep him alive and in my arms.

Nothing!

Only fate. And fate had proven to be a merciless bitch.

I cried harder.

"Hey… Buttercup. D-don't." His hand wrapped around my nape, pulling me into him. "Christ, you'll make me c-cry in a moment, baby." His lips pressed against my forehead. "I love you. I will always l-love you. You're my world, Cleo."

His words were a balm to whatever terror held me hostage, slowly smoothing the more he shed his grogginess. My legs gave out, tumbling me into his chest.

He flinched, sucking in a ragged breath, but he didn't let me go. His arm banded tighter, crushing me with love. "I'm here. I'm still yours." His voice haunted with pain. "I'll *always* be yours. I p-promise."

I was a mess. He was the one in the hospital. He was the one on morphine and dealing with a brain injury. Yet *he* consoled *me*. He was once again the strongest, giving me sanctuary, holding me while I came apart.

"I'm sorry," I choked. "I c-can't. I just n-need—"

I couldn't do it any longer.

For so long, I'd pretended to cope. I'd painted on a mask and acted out the highs and lows of life. But I'd been dead inside. I'd missed more than just my memories. I'd missed *this*.

This wealth of emotion.

This undying affection.

This unswerving connection.

I'd been so alone. So afraid. And now...I was home.

A sob ripped itself from my soul, opening the floodgates of my tears. For eight long years, I'd never let myself come undone. I'd never undone the tight corset around my feelings to purge and heal. For eight years, I'd fought away sadness as if it was a plague trying to kill me. I couldn't fall apart because I had no one to glue me back together again.

But here...in a hospital, in my soul mate's arms, in a country I'd left behind, I jumped off the precipice I'd always clung to and fell.

I fell into sadness.

I fell into happiness.

I fell into love all over again.

And he caught me.

Arthur never stopped murmuring, his croaky voice the best chorus for my shattering psyche.

Tears streaming, I snuggled into him, inhaling the scent of him smothered with medicine. "You're a-alive." More tears. More sobs. "Thank G-God, you're alive."

He flinched as I kissed his brow, his eyes, his lips.

I wanted to kiss every inch, imbed myself into his every pore so he could never carve me out.

"Life and death don't mean shit to us, Buttercup. My love for you makes us immortal." His arm tightened, wrapping fiercely. "I get it. I get your pain." His kissed my eyelids. "Just let go, baby. Let me catch you."

More tears poured. I never knew I had so much liquid pain inside me. It all evicted, torrential waterfalls, unable to stop.

Time ticked past but I wasn't aware.

The door opened and closed but I didn't notice.

All I cared about was Arthur, his warmth, and his ever-steady heartbeat.

For a while, all I could do was hang in his embrace and sob.

I cried for everything.

For the past.

The present.

For good and evil.

And when I finally cried my last tear, I found completion. Every splintered piece realigned and for the first time since fire licked my skin and cast me from my world, I felt *whole*.

No more missing pieces. No more holey memories.

Exactly who I should be.

His.

My breathing slowly evened out, my hiccups fading in tune with the heart rate monitor.

Arthur settled into the single mattress, kissing my cheek. "Come here."

Kicking off my shoes, I climbed into the narrow bed beside him. Tugging me, he helped smuggle me into the sleepy heat of his bed. The heavy *thud-thud* of his heartbeat soothed me and I relaxed for the first time in years.

"Are we okay?" he whispered finally.

I nodded, rubbing my cheek on his chest. "Better than okay."

Smiling shyly, embarrassed from my breakdown, I looked into his eyes.

The green glowed with something I hadn't seen before.

Contentedness.

Gone was the harsh glow that never left. Gone was the rigid hatred in his limbs. He was free—just like I was. Healed and whole, truly living in the moment, not the past or future.

I sucked in a shaky breath. My eyes stung from crying and I wanted nothing more than to drift into a heavy sleep in his arms. But he'd given me safety to heal; I would do the same for him. "You found closure."

He nodded, the bandages around his head brushing against his pillow. "I did."

The promise I'd made not to ask what Pure Corruption did faded. I was happy he'd found peace, but at what cost? Would he be able to live with whatever occurred last night?

I looked away. "What happened?"

The words scattered around us like a jury waiting for a verdict. He tensed but his face etched with righteousness. "I did what had to be done."

I nodded, tracing a crease in the bedding. *He murdered them.* I didn't know how to be happy for someone's healing at the cost of another's demise—even if they deserved it.

When I didn't reply, anger decorated his features. "I ended it."

My heart spasmed. "You killed them."

Never looking away, not looking contrite or guilty or regretful, he nodded. "I did."

"Both Rubix and Asus?"

His good hand fisted on the sheets. "I delivered penance for the crimes they committed. *Both* of them."

I sucked in a breath, stroking the starched bedding. Part of me was horrified to be in love with a man who could steal a life with such precision, but the other part of me was proud. Proud of him for sticking up for himself. For finally putting this nightmare behind him.

Arthur's eyes locked onto mine. "My vengeance is complete, Buttercup."

I shuddered at the cold finality in his voice.

His lips softened. "Don't ask any more questions. What's done is done. And I'm *glad* it's done. But I don't want to talk about it. Do you understand?"

I understood. Whatever had happened last night had been harrowing and gruesome. I didn't want that knowledge tainting my thoughts. I didn't want to know what he'd done or the scars he would bear because of it.

I hung my head. "I understand."

Arthur breathed out heavily. "Thank you."

"I'm just glad you've found peace after all these years."

Taking my hand, Arthur smiled—a true smile—with no residue of past pain or suffering. My heart skipped as he kissed the back of my knuckles, gathering me close. "Life is going to be so much happier from now on, Cleo."

I smiled, melting into his embrace. "As long as we're together, life couldn't be better."

A few minutes passed with only the beeps and humming as conversation. Finally, Arthur murmured, "The past is dealt with. And soon the future will be, too." He kissed my head, muscles relaxing as he drifted with painkillers and sleep. "Stay with me..."

I nodded. "Always."

It didn't take long for him to stray into slumber. I didn't chase him into dreams. I lay awake for ages, hoping, fearing, praying that our future would be better than our past.

Last night had been one of the longest nights of my life. But it was finally over. Arthur was back where he belonged. He'd finally found peace instead of revenge.

We'd paid our toll.

Lived through sacrifice.

Life could be great again.

After everything we'd lived through, we deserved to be happy.

Chapter Thirty-Four

Kill

I couldn't remember the last time I smiled.

Death surrounded me in the form of rapists and murderers and thieves.

Life inside prison didn't reform me; it just made me more determined to find justice. Every day inside the festering cesspool reminded me that when I got out, something had to change.

And I would be the one to do it. —Kill, age nineteen

Life changed.

Not only was the world no longer polluted with my kin, but I also had to take a step back from the Club.

For twelve days, I remained chained to a bed inside a motherfucking hospital. Every hour, I badgered doctors to give me honest to God statistics on how damaged I truly was. Every day, Cleo would spend as much time with me as possible, keeping my mind distracted from the awful thought of losing who I'd been. And every other day, I submitted to rehabilitation therapy—making sure my basic accomplishments were still intact.

While I was healing, Grasshopper became more than just my friend and VP; he stepped into his upcoming role with ease. We'd both known this day would happen...I just hoped I wouldn't be a fucking invalid to celebrate it. He became a valuable second in command, and with me out of action, he postponed the interviews I'd had planned, kept Samson in the loop, and ferried funds where they needed to go. He kept Pure Corruption in order, ensured the books tallied and our turf remained protected.

Most of the day-to-day running he already knew, but occasionally I'd get a phone call asking my input on certain disputes or queries. He was no longer my helper but my equal and did his best to provide leadership as well as companionship for those who'd lost Beetle and Mo.

Wallstreet was almost out. It was time.

On the tenth night of being locked in an uncomfortable bed, Hopper came to visit.

I looked up from the *So You Think You're a Genius* book, fuming and fucking pissed that simple equations that'd been so easy once upon a time were still giving me grief.

Beneath my fear, I did acknowledge that every day the sludge inside my brain crystalized. I was getting better. But I didn't want to jinx myself. I wouldn't admit it out loud—I *couldn't*—not until I was back to full speed.

"You all good, dude?" Hopper came forward, his cut slung over his arm out of respect for terrified patients.

We shook hands. "Better."

"Sweet. That's great news." Patrolling my box of a room, he rubbed the back of his nape. "So...I did what you asked. Clubhouse is sorted, funerals ready to go, and paperwork in order."

I sat higher in my pillows. "We always knew this would happen. I'm still fine with it. You?"

He didn't meet my eyes. "Honestly, not really."

The past few years, I'd wondered how I'd react when it came time to honor my final vow to Wallstreet. I loved my Club. I'd devoted every waking moment turning it into a family. The men and women who served beneath me had given me something to fight for while I thought I'd lost Cleo.

They'd been my home.

But now I had another home and it didn't hurt me to move.

I growled under my breath. "This was always the deal. Wallstreet made me promise."

And I'd made Wallstreet promise in return. I'd had my own conditions when agreeing to his terms. This conclusion was a joint agreement—something benefiting both of us.

Pointing at him, I narrowed my eyes. "He made you promise. You, me, and Mo knew from day one that this was the plan."

Hopper stomped forward, his mohawk catching the spotlights around my bed. "Just 'cause it was planned, doesn't mean it's any easier."

Funny, it does to me. Always knowing this was my fate had given me structure and guidelines I needed.

I chuckled. "You'll be fine. You're more than capable." Closing my eyes, I visualized my upcoming future. I'd been both dreading and looking forward to this, but now all I felt was freedom. Complete freedom—a fresh start. "I'll be fine, too. It's the best thing...for all of us."

"Go head, Killian."

I looked up, squinting in the high noon Florida sunshine at the sprawling highway before me.

The concrete shimmered with heat waves, slick with tire tracks and gasoline. Out here was our Church. The roads were our sermons. The wind our vespers. There was no better resting place for one of our brothers.

Nodding at Grasshopper and the row of Pure Corruption behind me, I took the urn and tucked the remains of Mo into my chest.

The past three weeks had been a marathon of healing, saying goodbye, and attending funerals.

Beetle had been first. His send-off was a heart-tugging affair as we all paid our respects and laid to rest a loyal member. He'd chosen to be buried out of state with his twin sister who'd died when she was young. Together, we drove in a snaking entourage to say goodbye to the youngest and most promising prospect. He had no family left to compensate or to speak his praises, so we donated his income from serving the Pures to a local research fund dealing with infant deaths.

The last and absolute hardest was Mo.

The only surviving relative was his father who'd been estranged from his son for decades. He refused to come to the funeral.

Tristan "Mo" Morgan, the man who'd put me through my paces when I first arrived, who kept his secrets close, and never truly lost the bastard veneer, was sent off with our engines roaring and plumes of smoke sending his soul to heaven.

It hurt to think of him gone. I didn't realize what he meant to me until the moment he'd died in Grasshopper's arms. I wished I could do more for him. A bigger send-off. A more soul-healing goodbye.

But this was what he'd wanted.

No fuss. No tears.

Along with being a secretive prick, he'd also been organized. A will had been lodged with our in-house lawyer, along with instructions for his cremation, and his businesses had been divided between the members he bequeathed them to.

He didn't want to be eaten by fucking worms in a dark pit beneath the ground.

He wanted to ride the roads for eternity.

After dedicating his life to the MC, the least I could do was honor his last request. My own needs didn't matter.

I'll always have your back, man.

I'll see you on the other side.

The urn was heavy in my grip. With the cast still on my left arm, I couldn't open the lid. Glancing at Cleo who stood beside me looking fucking gorgeous in jeans and her jacket, I raised an eyebrow in request.

The past few weeks had brought us closer together. We were never apart. Never angry. The pain in my head had gone—replaced by incessant itching from the stitches in my skull as I healed from surgery.

Every day I completed the tasks set by doctors to ensure my healing continued uninterrupted. And every day I improved.

The doctors said I'd been a miracle. My IQ was on the rise, my intelligence returning at a rapid pace. I didn't believe in miracles, but I did believe in Cleo. It was all thanks to her.

I'd found her again. I'd had no intention of dying.

The endless compulsion I'd lived with all my life finally tempered. I still needed more. I still needed to fix and improve and create but for now ... I was content. *Happy.*

Her small fingers latched around the lid, unscrewing it, and she took a step back. With a smile of gratitude, I held up the urn and faced my brothers.

"Mo was one of us. He'll *always* be one of us. His motorbike is now the wind. The road is now his home. God speed."

The members murmured their final goodbyes. Other eulogies had already been said at the local watering hole where Mo had wanted his brothers to have one last drink in his honor—he'd even picked up the tab, the crazy bastard.

"Happy trails, brother." I turned downwind and dumped the contents of Mo's earthly remains. The cloud of grey dust took flight, weightless and translucent, spreading quickly with the breeze.

No one spoke as Mo disappeared into the air.

He would become a legend. He would forever be a Pure.

Cleo came closer, wrapping an arm around my waist. "The end of an era."

I smiled; her words couldn't have been more perfect. "The end of war."

With the breeze in my hair and my woman in my arms, I was finally able to let go and just be.

Chapter Thirty-Five

Cleo

I'd always hoped life would pay me back for the pain it'd caused.
Every day with no memory, I'd begged life to be gentle.
Every month with no recollection, I'd pleaded for salvation.
And every year with no epiphany, I'd prayed to be worthy.
My hope had finally paid off. I was whole again. I'd found him again.
And life was now complete. —Cleo, last week

Two things happened a fortnight after Mo's funeral.

Both proved that life moved swiftly and all I could do was hold on, be by Arthur's side, and never let go.

The first was a newspaper article.

I didn't normally read newspapers, but while waiting in the hospital foyer while Arthur had his cast removed, I picked it up out of boredom.

Flicking through the black and white pages, I yawned and glazed over. But then a photo wrenched me to a halt.

There we were.

Arthur and me at the cocktail party at Samson's house.

Beneath the image—taken without my knowledge—was a short but poignant article.

Local motorcycle club president Arthur Killian has recently moved up the ranks from fringes of society to corruption-exposing businessman. This

isn't the first time we've seen him in the media, but it is the first he's been spot-
ted with a woman. Taken at Senator Samson's house, it's been reported that
both Killian and Samson are behind the recent commercial and radio bul-
letins with leaks about the latest spying incident from our government. They
both claim that the world is falling into anarchy with the men and women
in charge unable to rule such a vastly changed economy. They state that the
laws being created aren't to our benefit, and it's up to us, the people who chose
this governing power, to take action and fight for truth and justice.

"Ah, you've seen it then."

My eyes wrenched up, locking onto Arthur. He wore a black
T-shirt and jeans. The cast that'd been scribbled over by Pure Corruption had gone and the shaved patch on his skull was no longer white
against the shaggy length of dark hair—growing back with short bris-
tles, hiding the injury that could've killed him.

"You knew about this?"

He smiled, perching beside me on another chair. "It's not like I'm
hiding them from you, Buttercup. The campaign has been going on
for weeks now." He chuckled. "I can't help it if you don't watch television or read the paper."

My heart raced. After I'd learned his long-term goals with Samson, we hadn't discussed it in great detail. After all, he'd gone to war,
come back injured, and our life turned toward healing and supporting
our Club rather than discussing world revolutions.

But now it was all I could think about.

"What does this mean?"

He ran a hand through his hair. "It means Wallstreet gets out
tomorrow and the moment he does, our life will be very different."

I don't want it to be different.

I *liked* our life. I loved the quiet nights together. I adored the family I'd found in Pure Corruption. I even enjoyed the afternoons I spent
with Molly and Melanie learning the books and diving deeper into the
empire that the Pures ran.

My lips pursed as I rebelled against the thought of our life becoming public property. Of being shoved into the limelight and fighting a battle so big, it would take years to see results.

"Can't you take a step back?" I scrunched up the paper, obscuring our printed faces. "Can't Wallstreet take over now he's free?"

Arthur leaned forward, his green eyes diving into mine. "You know the answer to that, Buttercup. I have to do this. And I need you by my side."

I looked away. The thought of sharing him, of sharing myself with the world scared me to death.

He captured my chin. "Please, Cleo. I can't do this without you."

Despite my fear and hesitation, my heart melted. I had no choice. I wore his jacket. I shared his responsibilities. There was no other way, and I didn't want there to be. "I'll be beside you, Arthur. Every step of the way."

The second thing happened that afternoon.

I received two calls—one I'd been looking forward to and another I'd been dreading.

The first was rather comical and to any other person wouldn't have made sense. "Congratulations, Ms. Price. You've come back from the dead."

I smiled, clutching the phone. "The paperwork is done?"

The past few weeks had been a lot of hoop jumping and proving my identity along with well-executed lies on what'd happened to me the night I disappeared. They didn't need to know about Rubix's death or the raging fire over at Night Crusaders' compound. Justice had been served our way—without involving the police.

"Yes, ma'am. We've reversed the death certificate and reinstated your social security. You'll receive new documentation and will need to apply for a new passport. Your case officer will be in touch once you've confirmed that Sarah Jones is no longer your alias."

The moment the woman hung up, I received another call. The one I'd been dreading.

"Ms. Jones, we'd like to arrange a time for your case worker to come and see you. There are a lot of matters that need clarification, including your sudden arrival back into the United States, your rehabilitation, and memory gain."

Corrine had managed to soothe my case worker after I ran so swiftly from England, but I still had to face the music and answer numerous questions in a debrief. Coming back from the dead wasn't an easy thing. And remembering an entire lifetime from the one I'd lived for the past eight years caused a mass of paperwork.

The familiar flutter of fear that evil would find me once again rose. I couldn't quite silence the terror that my memories would fade or that I'd wake up and forget everything all over again. But every day, I laughed more. Smiled more. I even had my own project in the works that I couldn't wait to share with Arthur. I intended to do something special with the Dagger Rose land I'd inherited. Something that would align my two worlds: Sarah Jones and Cleo Price.

My life had come full circle and once the knots had been tied on the remaining loose ends, I would be free.

"Tell Detective Davidson he's more than welcome to come and see me whenever he likes. I'll look forward to telling him my tale."

With all the illegal activities and murders expunged, of course.

I was now the partner of a public figure.

A biker princess *and* a soon-to-be politician's first lady.

My, how life had changed.

Chapter Thirty-Six

Kill

Mathematics was my forte.
Trading was my calling. Ruling my vocation.
If I couldn't do any of those things...what did that leave me?
Who would I become? —Kill, last night

Wallstreet.

I was so used to seeing him behind bars. So used to the faded cotton of prison uniforms and huddling together to speak in code whenever we had news.

All of that was in the past.

Today was the last day of my current world. Tomorrow, Cleo and I would live an entirely different existence. And I was nervous as well as excited.

My benefactor and mentor stepped out of Florida State. He wore the same pinstripe suit he'd worn the morning the police arrested him at his offices downtown. We were so similar in that respect: He wore his cut and ran with bikers most days, but other days he merged with businessmen and bankers, dressing like them, laughing like them.

Pity he hadn't vetted the women he fucked as well as he did the men he did business with. He'd been sent to jail all thanks to a disgruntled Club bunny.

I waved, catching his eye.

His white teeth flashed in the sun and he followed the same path to freedom I did four years ago. I pushed off from the Mercedes that Grasshopper had paid a fucking fortune for the night we burned Dagger Rose and clasped hands with my friend.

He pulled me into a hug.

"Fuck, Kill. It's good to see you."

My heart raced. I hugged him back.

Breaking away, he raised his head to the sun and inhaled deeply. He looked ten years younger. With an open-necked cream shirt and slicked back white hair, he looked every bit the retired honcho of a Fortune 500 company.

Reaching into the Mercedes' backseat, I pulled out a new jacket. The freshly embroidered cut had no ranking on the pocket—not yet. After all, it was up to him to decide his placement now.

We hadn't discussed in great detail what would happen tonight, but we didn't need to.

Those plans had been set in stone the very first day he tutored me.

My position would be very different soon.

And I'm fine with that.

It was how I wanted it—what I'd requested.

Wallstreet grinned, taking the jacket and sniffing the leather. "Shit, that brings back memories."

"Got a lot to catch up on, and plenty of time to make new ones."

Wallstreet clasped my shoulder. The slight twinge from my previously broken arm made me wince. The shorn piece of hair from my surgery still irritated but the headaches and vision issues were gone. I was on the mend. Thank God.

However, there was one part of me still broken.

I hadn't placed a trade since the battle with Dagger Rose. I hadn't opened my accounts or turned on my computer screens. The codes and algorithms I'd always lived with were still absent and it was fucking lonely inside my head.

"Shall we?" Wallstreet asked, shrugging into the suit and cocking his head at the Merc.

I smiled. The welcome home party we'd planned would kick off the moment I drove him to the Clubhouse. Grasshopper had readied all the supplies required. He still had some getting used to what would happen, but I believed in him.

He was a good guy. A perfect Pure.

Everyone's lives would take some adjusting but the future would only be on the up.

You still haven't told Cleo.

My back tensed. I'd been a pussy not to tell her, but I couldn't. I couldn't give her yet another family and tear it away from her so soon.

"Be my pleasure."

Slipping into the driver's seat, I had the honor of driving the mastermind home.

Pulling up to the Clubhouse, my heart lurched in my chest. This place, with its crumbling brick veneer and rusty barbed wire looked derelict and unwelcoming—exactly how it appeared when I first arrived four years ago. I'd kept the outside charm but renovated the inside.

Just like I did with the brothers.

On the outside, they still looked terrifying but on the inside they were loyal and acclimatized to business rather than battles.

I'd overhauled their thoughts and minds and given them peace instead of war.

I'd done all that at the beck and call of one man who'd saved me.

Regardless of what happened in the future, I would always be proud of that.

Waving at the entrance, I said, "Shall we?"

Wallstreet grinned, tugging his lapels. "Can't wait."

Crunching forward in my boots, I reached for the door handle.

"Wait, Killian." Wallstreet came forward, putting his hand on my shoulder. "You're still okay with this?" His eyes shone. "You've outdone yourself, my boy. I couldn't have asked for a better pupil or friend. You've done everything I ever asked. You've amassed a fortune, kept my Club intact, and begun what I'd tried to do before I was locked up." His voice cracked. "You've been a fucking savior."

Shit, I'd never seen Wallstreet show so much emotion. "Hey, man. It's fine." Patting his arm, I chuckled. "After all, the student is only as good as the teacher."

Wallstreet shook his head, dropping his hand. "Killian, I saw in you something special that not many people have. You would've excelled at anything you put your hand to. Have you ever thought that it might not have been fair of me to ask this of you? To give you a Club—knowing all along that it wasn't yours? Or playing on your obsession for more and making you go after the biggest power in history?" He looked at his feet. "I often had doubts. Wondering if I had any right to drive you so hard."

I cocked my head. He was right. He'd been hard on me, always pushing, never letting me fail. But then again, without him...I wouldn't have been anyone.

Clutching the doorknob, I smiled. "Without you, Cyrus, I would still be locked up or dead. There was no way I would've survived a life of imprisonment and nightmares of Cleo gone—I would never have been free."

Wallstreet ran a hand through his white hair. "That might be the case, but I don't think I ever told you thank you." His gaze glittered. "*Thank you*, Killian, for your hard work and sacrifice. Thank you for being a trusted friend. I'll never take it for granted."

Holy shit.

I grinned. "And thank you for saving my life." Cracking the door, I said, "I think a celebration is in order, don't you? For both of us."

Wallstreet clapped his hands. "I like your—"

"Surprise!"

The celebration hit us the second we stepped foot into Pure Corruption. The women had decorated the space with gay-ass streamers and balloons, while the men had restocked the bar and already guzzled their way to a good buzz.

Wallstreet raised his hands like a returning conqueror, his lined face crinkling in joy. "Fuck, it's good to be back."

Cleo stood beside Molly, her arms crossed but a smile teasing her lips.

"I'll leave you to mingle." I patted Wallstreet's shoulder and darted through the crowd to my woman. The moment I was close enough, I gathered her in a quick hug. "Hello."

She giggled. "Hi yourself."

Nuzzling my nose into her hair, I whispered, "You good?"

She nodded, leaning into my embrace. "I'm great now that you're back." Pulling away, her eyes fell on Wallstreet. Once again the cold dislike she wore when they met at Florida State clouded her face. "So the pioneer has returned."

Turning to face the seething mass of brothers, we didn't speak as we watched the spectacle of back slaps, hugs, and loudly broadcast reminiscing between Wallstreet and the older members of Pure Corruption.

I nodded. "Their leader is back."

"No." Cleo tensed. "Their leader is *you*."

Wrong, Buttercup.

I knew I should've had the balls to tell her before this.

I was only temporary.

I always knew Cleo wouldn't accept Wallstreet's return happily. She'd made no secret that she was wary of him. I understood her need to keep her distance, but at the same time, Wallstreet wasn't Rubix. He wasn't cruel—only ambitious.

And I could deal with ambitious because that curse infected me, too.

Matchsticks appeared, bearing gifts in the form of beer for me and a daiquiri for Cleo. "Good to see the old bloke out of the slammer."

We clinked beers in a toast and downed a few gulps. "He deserves to have a good night."

Cleo stiffened but Matchsticks took another drink. "I think this party will go on all week with the amount of supplies Grasshopper arranged."

I laughed.

Ever since I'd been released from the hospital, I'd let Grasshopper stay in control. To start with, I'd itched to take back leadership—to hold the gavel at Church and oversee every detail. But that wasn't my future and the sooner the members grew accustomed to having Grasshopper lead, the better.

For everyone.

Today was all about celebration. Tomorrow was all about preparation.

We had no time to waste. The past few weeks, our campaign hinting at certain frauds and hidden cover-ups had been leaked to magazines and smaller TV stations. We'd planted the seed of unrest—now it was time to get bigger, louder, and jump into the political stream with the ammunition we'd gathered.

I was looking forward to it but also dreading it at the same time. The moment we put ourselves forward, along with our lofty goals of changing the way the globe was run, we could kiss privacy and indiscretions goodbye.

I'd never wanted to deal with politicians or dive into the seedy world of lawmaking and bills. But sometimes a calling demanded certain sacrifices in order to deliver the ultimate satisfaction.

Look at Cleo.

She'd been forced to live a life she didn't want but in the end she valued everything so much more. I was envious of her contentedness. I wanted that. And the only way I would get it was to become someone I never thought I'd be in order to seek that ever-elusive goal of achieving something far bigger than myself.

Taking another swig, I watched the party atmosphere spread around us. Matchsticks headed toward Roderick and Spokes and Wallstreet prowled the room, nodding at the renovations, occasionally giving me a thumbs-up. I wouldn't admit it but his appreciation and awe at what I'd achieved warmed my fucking heart.

I'd done well.

I was proud.

However, even with the joviality and happiness at having one of us return, there was an aura of loss and sadness. Mo should've been here. He was an original. He deserved to see his Club go full circle.

Every time I thought about Mo and Beetle, a dagger dug into my heart. I missed them. A shitload. Especially Mo because he'd been staunchly on my side once I'd won him over.

He was loyal to the end.

"Arthur?" Cleo popped into my thoughts. Her red hair flamed like living hell with burgundy, gold, and bronze.

She truly was a walking fire.

I forced myself to focus. "Yep?"

Her long legs captured my attention. Encased in tiny jean shorts, the elongated muscles of her thighs and calves made my mouth dry. The grey T-shirt she wore hung off one shoulder revealing a black bra strap. We'd kissed and petted over the past few weeks but we hadn't had sex.

After my head surgery, I was given strict rules on what I couldn't do. Unlike last time, I followed them religiously.

It didn't stop my cock from swelling now, though, or the over-whelming need to be inside her. Yanking her close, I breathed in her ear, "I want you tonight."

Her eyes hooded. "How long did the doctor say to abstain?"

I licked the shell of her ear. "Yesterday. I'm in the clear to fuck you, woman."

She shuddered. "I don't think I've heard anything better."

My cock hardened even more. "You eager to have me inside you?"

"Eager is an understatement." She lowered her voice. "I've been wet for you for weeks."

Fuck me. I groaned under my breath.

Would I ever get used to how beautiful and perfect she was?

Positioning herself in front of me, she whispered, "Why wait until tonight?"

The moment the words registered, I couldn't stop the inevitable. I needed this woman. I needed her now.

"You don't know what you've just done." Grabbing her wrist, I stalked forward.

Her laugh webbed around us as we beelined toward the exit. Moving past Matchsticks, I shoved my beer into his hands followed by Cleo's half-drunk daiquiri. "Keep that. We're leaving."

Matchstick's mouth popped open but he didn't have a chance to say anything as I yanked Cleo across the room.

It wasn't easy navigating the swarms of people or avoiding the intoxicated happiness infecting everyone. Each delay, each mumbled conversation, only made my cock harder. My jaw clenched. Cleo didn't help fucking matters by wriggling forward to sashay in front of me and biting her lip whenever my fingers graced her lower back.

By the time we made it to the corridor, we were both panting hard. I could barely fucking walk with needing her.

"Goddammit, I can't wait much longer." Choosing the room I'd had when I first arrived, I threw her inside and locked the door. The décor was a lot different than the first night I'd spent here. The dirty wrappers, awful stench, and disgusting carpets were gone. It had a fresh coat of paint and blankness of personality that came with being a guest bedroom.

My mind skittered back to the incident that'd occurred in this room. I'd lost my virginity in here. I'd cheated on Cleo all because I was a fucking rehabilitated convict who'd somehow found himself the youngest ever president of the Corrupts.

For a second, I wanted to switch rooms but then Cleo wrenched off her top and stood before me in her shorts and black bra.

"Fuck."

I launched myself at her.

The weight of missing her—of living a life of purgatory believing she was dead—suddenly dissolved. The last dregs of fear that she might disappear again faded and my hands shook as we tumbled to the mattress with our legs and lips locked in an unsolvable puzzle.

She gasped as I captured her nipple in my mouth, dragging her bra down to reveal her delicious flesh. Her skin was soft and supple, my suction fast and greedy. I plumped the heavy weight of her breast, kneading possessively. "Christ, I want you."

"Then take me." She hooked her legs around my hips, gripping my ass and tugging me into her.

I bit her swollen flesh, licking the slight salt from her skin. Her hands skated up my back to capture my head, holding me against her chest. Her breathing stuttered as I sucked her nipple and the words I would never grew tired of spilled from her lips. "I love you, Art. So damn much."

Her fervent declaration slammed into my soul. My eyes stung. My hands fumbled. And my heart cracked open all over again.

Climbing her body, I shoved my hands into her thick hair and held her still. "As you wish, Buttercup."

I love you.

Her face collapsed and fresh adoring tears glassed her eyes.

Her favorite quote from her childhood movie echoed around us, binding us closer.

I cradled her jaw, stroking her lower lip as a single tear escaped her.

My heart lurched. "Don't," I breathed. "It fucking shreds me when you cry."

She reached up and kissed me. "It's too much." Her gorgeous emerald eyes captured mine. "How I feel about you. What you do for me. Finally being together. It's all..."

"More," I murmured, brushing my lips against hers.

I slid my hand reverently along her bare arm. I'd killed for her. I'd cried for her. And now I hoped I deserved her.

Lowering my hands, I fumbled with her shorts and pulled them free.

She squirmed as my fingers trailed between her legs.

"Fuck. You're not wearing underwear."

Her grip tightened around my shoulders. "I hoped something like this would happen." Her cheeks flushed. "It's been a long few weeks."

Her hands slid down my front, blazing a hot trail across my skin. "Get naked, Arthur. You're wearing far too many clothes."

I chuckled, suffering heart palpitations with the need in her voice. Rolling off her a little, I shrugged out of my cut and tugged on my neckline, tearing the T-shirt over my head.

"Much better." Cleo caught the waistband of my jeans and unbuckled them in record speed. Arching my hips, I helped her discard every item of clothing I wore.

Reaching behind her, I unclasped her bra and smothered her. Naked to naked. Skin to skin.

"I'll never get sick of this." I kissed her.

"You never have to."

Our lips met again and the urgency of before came back with every needy demand. Her fingers tightened around my cock, stroking me hard.

I growled, burying my face into her neck, biting her throat. "I have to know that you're prepared for what will happen now. That you're ready to do what needs to be done."

She wriggled beneath me, rubbing her breasts against my chest.

I groaned as her fingers worked harder. "I'm prepared to face anything as long as it's with you."

I stroked her inner thigh, tracing her warm skin toward her pussy.

She went rigid beneath me, vibrating for my touch. Her body was a seductive piece of art with tattoos and scars. I'd never met anyone so complex or unique.

She kissed me again, her teeth catching on my bottom lip and biting gently. She moaned; the sound of her pleasure slid over me like a caress. "Touch me," she demanded. "Please..."

As I cupped her core, she bowed off the bed. My heart clenched as she grabbed my wrist, forcing me to touch her harder.

I thrust my cock shamelessly into her palm. "Goddammit, Buttercup."

Her fingers curled tighter and I pressed two of my own inside her. She gasped. "Yes..."

"Fuck, you make me insane." I couldn't hide the effect she had on me. I would never be able to pretend that I was the one in control. She was my master. My ruler. I was just her prisoner—content to do whatever she wanted me to if it meant I got to spend the rest of my life with her in my arms.

My chest tightened. I was the only one privileged enough to see her this way: hungry, wild, a firecracker just waiting to explode.

Spreading her legs, Cleo guided me with the hold she had on my cock. I groaned as I settled firmly in the V of her thighs and removed my fingers from her pussy. The wetness spread over her naked hip as I clutched her.

Her nipples kissed my chest; sensation rushed through my system. I couldn't stand it any longer.

Nudging against her pussy, the tip of me entered her searing heat. We froze.

My erection throbbed; her core quivered. We paused in the delicious anticipation of joining.

Her nails raked down my back. "Do it. Please...take me."

"As you wish."

I slammed inside her.

She cried out, arching in my rough possession, a feral growl echoing in her chest. Her head threw back in erotic abandon. "Again," she cried. Her face flushed and tight with desire.

Surging upward, I obeyed. I sank my teeth into her shoulder and thrust inside the woman I fucking loved with all my heart.

Cleo hissed, taking my every rock. I couldn't contain the ferocious swell of emotion—the thankfulness, the fear, the happiness, the primal urge to make her mine forever.

I wanted to punish her as well as pleasure.

I wanted her to cry and also laugh.

I wanted to fucking marry her.

We lost sense of time as we thrust and grinded.

Her breath was a velvet lash against my overheated flesh. Her teeth across my pectoral were tiny sinful blades and her pussy was warm and inviting...home.

She clutched at my hair, swept away with lust and far from gentle. Her legs wrapped around me, gluing herself to me forever. She had me under a fucking siege, seducing me with her smell, body, and heart.

Grabbing the pillow behind her head, I drove deeper. I grunted with every stroke, teaching her a lesson in ownership.

"You're mine, Cleo."

Her spine bowed. "Yours. All yours."

Something overflowed inside me with ravenous greed. My skin shone with perspiration as I claimed her elegant body.

"Mine," I said harshly, pushing up and pulling out—driving into her.

I stole her mouth in a lust-drunken kiss, attacking her tongue, stealing her breath.

Our flesh slid against each other. Her body strained against mine, meeting my every thrust. No matter how hard I took her, I couldn't slake my thirst.

"God, Arthur...don't stop."

I couldn't breathe. I couldn't think. I was utterly consumed by her. The moans and begs spilling from her lips caressed my skin. Her body sucked me deep, taking me to the hilt and gathering a catastrophic orgasm.

God, she was a sexual deviant. So responsive. So pure.

Her legs stiffened as her mouth parted.

I drove harder, knowing she was on the cusp.

"Take it." I thrust again. "Take me." I fucked harder. "Give me your pleasure."

She screamed, gripping my shoulders like an anchor as she snipped from gravity, detonating around my cock. Her neck strained, her mouth hung wide and waves upon waves of her release hurtled me toward my own.

Deep inside her, I penetrated her heart not just her body and when I came, I gave her everything I had left.

"Fuck!" I orgasmed in thick ribbons of bliss, shooting deep inside her heat. The blistering pleasure-pain made me desperate for air.

My hands fisted the pillows as I rode out the final waves of the most intense orgasm I'd ever had.

Our heartbeats whirred to the same psychotic beat, relearning one another and reaffirming the vows we made as children that we would always be together.

There was no more amnesia to fight.

No more sadness to ignore.

We were together and we were one.

Nothing could be better than that.

"Arthur?"

My attention changed from pulling on my cut and slipping into my boots. We'd been missing from Wallstreet's welcome back party for over an hour. It was time to be sociable.

Spinning to face Cleo, I scowled at the worried look on her face.

She said, "I know you trust Wallstreet implicitly, but what if—"

Unlocking the door, I held out my hand for her to take. "What if?"

It amused me that so many people thought Wallstreet had an ulterior motive. A hidden agenda that would hurt me and everything we'd worked so hard to build. He'd been nothing but transparent . . . working toward the same goal as me.

Why couldn't Cleo see that?

She wrapped her fingers around mine, and we headed from the sex-laced room and down the corridor toward the raucous of intoxicated people having fun.

"Well . . . I've always maintained that I think he's up to something. That he's always had another agenda."

I smiled. "That's because you're smart. And because he does."

Cleo frowned. "What is he going to do?"

My mind skipped back to Florida State—to that very first lesson where he explained everything in black and white. He'd been brutally honest. Told me what he expected from me. What he would do for me. What would happen if everything went to plan. He'd also bowed to my own conditions without too much fuss.

He'd accepted mine like I'd accepted his. And in return he'd given me something no one else had the power to do.

He gave me my life back—a *better* life.

"He's about to change what our future entails."

"What does that mean?"

Dragging Cleo into the common room, I inhaled the reek of alcohol. "You're about to find out."

And I was right.

The moment we appeared, Wallstreet spotted me. His voice boomed over everyone's. "Ah, there you are!"

Cleo stiffened, refusing to let me untangle my fingers from hers. Laughing under my breath, I said, "Let me go, Buttercup. This has to happen."

Her eyes widened. "*What* has to happen?"

I freed myself, then ran a thumb over her cheek. "What must."

Leaving her wide-eyed and wary, I made my way across the floor and stood beside the man who had done more for me than any other father would do for his son. Rubix had ruined that title but Wallstreet had redeemed it.

His papery, dry hand squeezed my shoulder. "Stand right there, Kill. We have an announcement to make."

This is it.

I grinned. "Sure thing."

Someone passed me a beer and I waited as Grasshopper was summoned to the front and made to stand on the other side of Wallstreet. His eyes met mine. He shook his head once.

I toasted him. Every heartbeat I felt lighter ... as if *this* was my true freedom. The day I'd checked out of jail, I'd left behind lessons for an apprenticeship, but tonight was my graduation.

I wasn't sad.

I was fucking joyous.

Once we were in place, Wallstreet addressed his Club.

"As you all know, I enlisted the help of Kill to lead you guys away from temptation and into the light."

Some men snickered.

Cleo crept closer to the front.

"Killian has done everything I ever asked of him with absolute precision and loyalty. I couldn't have asked for a better acting president and will always be indebted to him."

A few beers were raised; agreement passed around the room.

Signaling for quiet, Wallstreet continued. "We all agree that without Kill the peace and wealth enjoyed by our members wouldn't have been possible. We can also agree that Kill is more than just your acting president; he's been fundamental in saving others outside our brotherhood. He's taken on my quest and excelled at it."

"Here, here!"

"Damn right!"

Brothers laughed and applauded.

"Long live Pure Corruption!"

I held up my hand. "Enough. I have a big enough ego as it is."

Wallstreet chuckled. "You never had an ego." Turning his attention to Grasshopper, he eyed the crowd. "All of that you know. I don't need to tell you what a great man Kill is. However, what you might not know is Hopper is my biological son."

The room suddenly lost its party vibe, screeching to a stop. Men poised with bottles on their lips; women froze.

Despite all our talks in prison, Wallstreet had never mentioned in exact detail how he would get his Club to approve another chain of command. Placing me in his stead hadn't been easy. There'd been scuffles and in-house battles—men had been killed over loyalties to unworthy leaders. But Grasshopper was one of us. He'd been there with every reform and was loved by everyone.

The exact sequence of handing over leadership hadn't been planned because a future could change so fast. So many variables could've gone wrong. I might've been killed trying to tame the Club— he might never have gotten an early pardon.

Life had an uncanny way of changing carefully laid plans.

But it was an unwritten rule: even though Pure Corruption had been mine—it had always been borrowed not permanent. Ultimately it was Wallstreet's conception and would always be his.

I glanced in Cleo's direction. Her jaw was tight, eyes locked on the man who gave me the skills I needed to not only survive but also to extract the perfect revenge.

An ending that'd given me the peace.

Wallstreet continued. "It's true. Back in my youth, I met a woman who turned out to be the love of my fucking life. Unfortunately, I was too stupid to know it at the time and only found out after her death that I had a son." He smiled proudly at Hopper. "Jared has proven himself just as trustworthy and hardworking. He's gone above and beyond and ruled beneath Kill with grace befitting any VP. They truly are brothers, in every sense of the word, and I'm so happy to say that I've been graced with *two* incredible sons."

Shit.

My heart squeezed.

Wallstreet flung an arm over my shoulders. "I don't care that you're not blood, Kill. I don't care that there's no law abiding document saying you belong to me. As far as I'm concerned, I'm your father and Hopper is your brother." Slinging his arm around Grasshopper, he grinned. "You're my family. I couldn't have picked worthier men."

His blue eyes glowed with sudden intensity. "I'll never discount what you did for me or forget your allegiance, Kill. I know I speak for everyone that you'll be one of us for fucking ever."

I was a grown man—a fucking president of a Club. I'd killed and tortured and lied. But hearing such praise from a man who I'd looked up to for so long squeezed my lungs with pride.

Grasshopper laughed, punching his father lightly in the gut. "All right, old timer. Enough scotch for you. You've gone fucking sentimental."

The Club continued to watch, not interrupting our strange, fantastical family moment.

Family.

Shit, I had a new family.

A family who got me—who understood my drive and cherished the gifts I'd been born with.

Cleo glided closer. Her body wasn't as fluid as normal, her feet hesitant and unsure. Her suspicions and concerns about Wallstreet were unfounded but I couldn't deny her instincts had proven to be right.

All along he'd had ulterior motives—motives she might not like—but once she understood why, she would grudgingly admit that it made sense.

Everyone would admit that in order for us to move forward, this was how it had to be.

Wallstreet locked eyes with Cleo. He nodded respectfully. "And while I'm mentioning people, I can't forget you, Ms. Price."

She froze.

"Killian did an incredible job, but you were fundamental in making him become the man he is. So I extend my gratitude."

Cleo pursed her lips. "It was nothing."

Taking a pull on my beverage, I fortified myself with things to come.

Wallstreet was never one to bounce around a topic. He'd been that way since I met him and I doubted he would ever change.

Sure enough, he dismissed Cleo and looked around the room with purpose. "Along with running my MC, Kill was tasked with another mission. As you all know, our goals far exceed turf wars and controlling trading routes. Through Kill's undying fealty, Pure Corruption has extended to chapters not just in the States but all around the world. We have allies in other Clubs, staunch supporters in other presidents, and that's just the beginning. We've made friends with governors, become bedfellows with journalists and people in media power. We're exactly where we need to be to deliver our final strike of justice."

The Club grew serious. Beers were forgotten; excitement laced the air.

My skin prickled as I waited with the rest of the men for Wallstreet's next speech.

"I'm so proud of what you've achieved. So impressed to see a blended mix of old rules and new—not to mention the wealth accumulated while I've been gone. This is the finest fucking Club I've seen and it's all a testament to Kill."

Members toasted in my honor.

Cleo smiled lovingly, blowing me a kiss.

My cock twitched, wanting a rerun of what'd just happened.

"However," Wallstreet said, halting the happy thread buzzing around the room.

The bikers and their women tensed, sensing a change in direction. "I have to do something that pains me today."

Grasshopper dropped his eyes, shadows darkening his face.

Cleo gasped, her gaze accusing.

Wallstreet cleared his throat. "No matter how much I value Kill's efforts and appreciate all he's done for this Club, he can no longer be your president."

The Club sucked in a collected breath. "What?"

"No...that's..."

The words didn't hurt nearly as much as I'd imagined.

This was my family. But I wasn't being cast out—in fact, it was the exact opposite.

"No! We don't want him—"

"We want a vote!"

I held up my hand. "I appreciate your loyalty but there's nothing to discuss."

Besides, even if I *didn't* want this, Wallstreet's word was law. There was no board to contradict him. No voting required. Wallstreet *was* the board with the majority vote.

By stripping my rank, he wasn't making me homeless. He wasn't casting me out with nowhere to go.

He was making my future infinite.

Cleo balled her hands, baring her teeth. "I *knew* you had an ulterior motive! How could you *do* that? Let him create you an empire then shove him out the moment you're freed?"

Other men and women shifted, confusion coloring their faces.

Before me, I saw the truth. I might've taken over this Club against people's wishes. I might've inherited Wallstreet's followers and fought tooth and fucking nail to get them to follow me, but now...the tables had turned.

This was *my* Club. My members. They were loyal to both of us.

Wallstreet shook his head. "Don't jump to conclusions, Ms. Price." Looking at me, a flicker of concern appeared. "We discussed this. We agreed this was the best way. However, if you've changed your mind, Kill..."

I finished my beer. "No. I haven't changed my mind."

I want this.

Wallstreet relaxed, pride once again glowing in his eyes.

I'd been waiting for this day for four years. I feared I'd resent him—that I wouldn't handle being forced into a new career. But surprisingly, I felt...fine. It was right. It was the perfect end to this reign and the perfect beginning to another. "I'm ready for this. Truly."

Grasshopper looked mortified. "Kill, you have to know Pure Corruption is yours. You're our prez."

Wallstreet held up his hand. "Actually, he's not anymore."

The room went deathly silent.

I'd just been stripped of my patch in front of every brother I ruled.

It should've been fucking horrifying. A death sentence.

But it wasn't, because I knew more than them.

It all came back to the "more" obsession. Wallstreet knew me better than I knew myself. He was doing me a fucking favor.

I wasn't losing my family. I would still be welcome. Still loved and permitted to sit in Church and my opinions would still hold power— I'd been promoted rather than demoted.

"So you're taking back the chair?" Matchsticks asked Wallstreet.

Wallstreet grinned. His trimmed black eyebrows were the only pigment left compared to the snowy hair on his head. "Nope. You'll have a new president."

All eyes turned to Grasshopper.

Wallstreet raised his glass. "This is your new prez. My one true heir. My flesh and fucking blood."

Instead of looking proud and humbled, Grasshopper ran a hand through his hair. "I'm so sorry, Killian."

Tossing my empty bottle to the side, I shook my head. "Nothing to be sorry for." Shrugging out of my cut, I passed it over. "Here. No fucking apologies required. I always knew this was a temporary gig."

When he continued to stare at the leather, I threw it at him. "Take it. It's yours."

"But, Art...," Cleo said.

I held up my hand, silencing her. She didn't know the full story yet. Patience was always a virtue in these situations.

Wallstreet nodded as Grasshopper reluctantly slipped off his cut and yanked on the one labeled prez. He'd have to stitch over my name but it was official.

I was no longer a president. Just like that.

Grasshopper swallowed. "The position is yours, Kill. I'm content to remain your VP—"

"No, he can't," Wallstreet interrupted. "Kill can no longer be seen to be associated with this Club."

"Why the hell not?" Cleo snarled. She moved forward, anger and unhappiness painting her face. I loved that she was pissed on my behalf, but this wasn't a betrayal.

This was a favor.

"Because the next part of my life can't mix underworld with glossy pages of newspapers." I smiled. "I can't be president and politician."

How could I let her see that this was the sacrifice I was willing to make to ensure I found happiness? The Club had given me everything I needed: revenge and a home. But I'd made an oath when I was a kid and made Wallstreet promise the same.

I'd made him swear that if I did this for him, then he would do something for me.

I would run his Club. I would be his leader in his stead but when he was free, I wanted out. I'd been born into this lifestyle. But I didn't intend to die in it.

I had too much more to experience to stay in one role forever.

That had been the final seal on our bargain: Wallstreet wanted a stand-in...I wanted a ready-made army. We both had higher goals that required sacrifices, both wanted the same thing.

Cleo's eyes burned into me but I didn't look at her. I would cherish and protect her. I would keep her in my heart always. But it was time for a change. It was time for something *more*.

"You'll still see a lot of Kill," Wallstreet said, smoothing ruffled feathers and concluding his upheaving speech. "He's forever welcome in our homes, our hearts, our Club. He will always be a Pure, but privately not publically. We're family and will always be family, just like Cleo will forever be one of us, too." Wallstreet glanced at Cleo's jacket. She'd slipped it on after we'd sneaked away. "You wear our emblem and oath, Ms. Price. I would never take that allegiance or home away from you. I know your past. I know the loneliness of being stripped of friends and love." He placed his hand on his heart. "You have my ultimate word your ranking within Pure Corruption will not change. Killian will always be respected and listened to but from now on, we will no longer call him prez... with time and luck we'll hopefully be calling him senator and he'll be ruler to thousands."

The gruffness and authority in his tone melted into love and pride. "Kill will give others what he's given us. And that is a fucking hero in my book." Opening his arms, he embraced me like a son and friend.

I hugged him back, feeling the weight of the past eight years fizzing away with every heartbeat. *This* was what I'd been searching for.

I knew the goals of becoming a true senator would be hard—if not impossible. Every aspect of my past would be used against me. The newspapers would have a fucking lifetime of ammunition with my background—but it wouldn't stop me from trying. I didn't need the title to become a leader in politics.

I liked the unknown—the upcoming trials.

One challenge defeated and another new to conquer.

Freedom.

Power.

A blank slate where the past no longer dictated my future and a present where I could be eternally happy.

"You gave me back my will to live, Cyrus."

He kissed my cheek. "You gave me an empire in return."

We broke apart, clasping hands like equals. We were no longer mentor and student.

We were family.

And that was all I ever fucking wanted.

Epilogue

Cleo

One year later...

For a long time, I was a stranger to my life, my past, my family.

But now I was home. I'd found peace. I'd found joy.

Arthur was finally mine—like I always known he would be. We were happy—like I'd always known we could be. And we were safe—like I'd always hoped.

Our scars were still healing, our futures still evolving. But we were together and that was all that mattered. —Cleo, today

Life had a way of tearing someone apart before granting their utmost dreams.

The tribulations we had endured in order to be triumphant made everything so much brighter, intense, and precious.

So damn precious.

Sitting up in bed, I looked over at the man who held my heart.

My heart fisted and leapt like it did every morning. It was so easy to forget his radiant force when sleep carried us off into different worlds. But every time I woke in his arms, I was reminded of his dangerous power. His immense force of will.

No wonder he'd had such success in front of the cameras.

No wonder people flocked to him and listened—*truly* listened—to his ideals and suggestions.

With reverent fingers, I brushed aside the inky strands of hair from his cheek. Twelve months had wiped away lines that'd graced his eyes and washed away the stress from his face.

Being cast from the lifestyle we'd always known turned out to be the best thing that'd ever happened to us.

Not only did we visit Pure Corruption regularly, but I'd also become best friends with Melanie and Molly. Only a few days would go by without me seeing them, and our phones would ring constantly—asking Arthur's opinion, shooting the breeze, and generally being the best family I'd ever had.

So much had changed in a year, but it'd all been positive.

Grasshopper was president; Wallstreet was the oracle, but Arthur... he was the prodigal child reforming the world and bringing about revolution. Somehow he'd become more to them than just a president—he became a true idealist, a savior to everyone who needed speaking for but had no one to trust.

I'm so happy that he's happy.

He'd done the impossible and straddled the line of lawlessness and law-abiding. And because of his background, everyone flocked to him. Criminals believed in him and listened. Middle class were intrigued by him and paid attention. And the men in power who'd treated the globe like their own personal playground were afraid of him.

A perfect combination of power and threats.

Finally, after a war, secrets, double-crossing, and drawn-out vendettas, we were finally enjoying our hard-won peace.

Shifting carefully, I propped my head on my hand and studied the decadent man who graced my heart and soul. He slept on his stomach, his arms wrapped around a pillow. The huge tattoo on his back was the only reminder of the world we'd given up in order to save it as a whole.

At the beginning, he'd been nervous, fumbling with how to speak, trying to pretend he was something he wasn't in front of newscasters and journalists. But one night, I'd reminded him that this was *his* idea. This was his choice and people would react better if they saw the truth.

On paper he'd distanced himself from the outlaw world, but in his heart he was still a biker. And for the public to follow him—he had to be true to his heritage.

The next day, he'd undone his shirt and presented his tattoo to the world. He'd opened up—spoken about his incarceration, his love for his Club, and even skirted the tricky topics of what'd happened to Dagger Rose and Night Crusaders.

Overnight he'd gone from wannabe politician to someone taken seriously. And with that public investment, he finally evolved into the man I always knew he was.

He became Arthur "Kill" Killian—mastermind, genius— spokesperson for the mistreated and disadvantaged.

He sighed heavily, eyelids flickering with dreams. His chiseled biceps and rugged jawline looked so distinguished. The more immersed he became in uncovering international crime and fraud, the more delicious it was.

I was so proud of him.

So proud of all that he'd become.

I was also proud of my own endeavors. Dagger Rose was no longer a rubble wasteland. It'd been transformed into a veterinary homestead for mistreated and injured animals. Corrine had come across from England to help me and when I was away with Arthur, she ran it single-handedly with our staff of three vets.

When I'd approached Arthur with my idea, he'd chuckled and said it couldn't be more perfect. Not only were we saving the world for humans, but I was saving it for animals, too.

Tugging the sheet down, I bit my lip as a few crescent-shaped marks appeared adorning his ass. *My nails from last night.* My tummy clenched, remembering the way he'd filled me. Taking me on my

back, my front, against the wall, on the floor. He'd fucked me tirelessly
and loved me eternally.

The longer we were together, the more insatiable we became. It
could become a real issue. But then again, could being in love ever be
considered a problem?

No, never.

I shifted restlessly, my body stirring with new desire.

I'd always been grateful for my life. I was intelligent—had a healing skill I could use anywhere, and a lifetime of love from my perfect
other. All of those were gifts and big gifts—*wondrous* gifts—especially
Arthur.

I liked to think I was deserving of them, but fate had wanted a
guarantee from me.

So, it'd made me lose everything. It'd stolen my parents, my home,
my soul mate, and washed away my past. I could've floundered. I
could've embraced darkness and anger and never found my way back.

But I didn't.

I stayed true to myself even when I didn't know who that was.

I never stopped believing.

And in return, fate decided I deserved my gifts. I received them all
over again and from that day onward I cherished them deeply.

I would never take anything for granted.

Ever.

"Buttercup, whatever you're thinking about, stop it."

My heart fluttered at his sleepy voice. "You can hear my thoughts?"

His green eyes cracked open, looking as perfect as the glassy ocean
on the horizon. We'd been here for a week and I still couldn't get used
to the view of soaring cliff tops, sparkling beaches, and jewel-encrusted
rain forests.

Arthur had finally honored his promise to take me wherever I
wanted.

Our first vacation together.

A year late . . . but better than never.

Yawning, he propped himself up on an elbow. His long hair curtained one eye, making him look like a ravaging pirate about to claim me. "Your opinions are very loud."

I giggled. "You never complained before."

Our private paradise in the Dominican Republic was barricaded to everyone but us. We'd rented an exclusive treetop villa for three weeks and the space filled with my laughter as he scooped me beneath him and tickled me. "Perhaps I'm too afraid of you to complain."

"Whatever."

His lips touched mine and we slipped into the waltz that never failed to arouse me.

I'd never been so deliriously happy.

The moment Wallstreet had taken away Arthur's position, I'd been hurt, pissed, and downright livid. Not only were the Pures Arthur's success but they were also his friends and surrogate family.

Arthur had been born on the back of a motorbike and inhaled the lifestyle since before he could speak. But in one move, Wallstreet took that away from him.

I expected him to fight. But once again, Arthur and his juggling act of plans surprised me.

He was the one who wanted to step down.

He was the one who wanted *more*.

And to be honest, I thought it was a mistake leaving a world we'd always known, but now I had different conclusions.

Waging daily battles on bent politicians and delivering information to the people gasping for help was Arthur's perfect vocation. He stood up for people who couldn't and fixed messes others didn't understand.

The enormity of what he'd taken on didn't faze him. It only energized him to the point of joy.

It was as if the shadows of guilt and hate were gone. All that was left was the happiness he could never find before.

Arthur pressed me onto my back, capturing my wrists and holding them above my head.

My hand landed on the television remote, heralding the news to boom on the flatscreen and tear apart our interlude.

The international news channel blared.

"Early this week, up and coming political superstar, Arthur Killian, revealed yet another fraudulent fact on the nationwide bank Cross Fund. Through an independent regulatory committee, the house and senate denied emergency funding provision set forth by Cross Bank representatives. New audit reports reveal the company has been running at a deficit for seven years and owe their investors millions of unpaid loans."

Arthur groaned as his own voice filtered from the screen.

"We, as a society, have to stop believing men in power are gods. They're human. They make mistakes and get caught up in deals suffocated with fine print. Most of the world's problems are caused not from illegal activities but from illiteracy when it comes to dealing with long-winded contracts for the exact purpose of blindsiding taxpayers."

"Fuck, I sound like a stuck-up asshole."

Kissing the tip of his nose, I shook my head. "No, you sound divine." I looked over his shoulder, eyeing up the marvelous man in a suit, dripping with sex appeal and breaking all laws of business with his untamed long hair and unbuttoned blazer.

My mouth went instantly dry.

He's mine.

That delicious spectacle on TV was currently between my legs. My hunger for him increased exponentially. "Eight three one . . ."

His lips parted. "What?" Then understanding brightened his face. "You've been studying sequences again."

I giggled. "Well, seeing as you're back to speaking in numbers and codes that fly over my head, I figured I could put in a little effort."

Awe glowed. "You'd do that for me?"

My heart lurched. "I'd do anything for you. You know that."

He brushed aside a strand of hair from my cheek. "Eight three one, huh?" He bowed his head, inhaling me. "Let me see if I can guess. Eight…letters…am I right?"

I nodded. *He's so smart.* It'd taken me days to figure it out when I'd first seen the code, before having to cheat to find the answer.

"Three words?"

I nodded again.

His eyes lit up, glowing rich emerald. "One meaning. I know what it is."

"Smarty pants." I pouted. "So…what is it?"

Arthur kissed me. "It means I love you. Eight letters, three words, one meaning."

I huffed, wriggling away from his kiss. "Fine, Mr. Genius. Way to show me up."

He chuckled. "You're the one who started it." His forehead furrowed. "Hang on, I've got one."

I rolled my eyes. "What, just like that? You can come up with them that fast?"

I'd spent an entire afternoon studying cheesy mathematic sayings online and he could conjure one in a second.

If I didn't love you so much I'd be jealous.

"One four three two…," he said with a flourish.

My face scrunched, trying to work it out. Arthur didn't move, didn't help.

Finally, I gave up. "No idea."

He beamed. "One letter, four letters, three letters, two." He gathered me close, his warmth melting my bones. "I love you, too."

My heart skipped and I hugged him hard. "Always…"

Our reflection bounced from the mirrored ceiling above. The villa had an entire wall of glass, inviting in trees and soft island breeze to whisper around us and keep the muggy island heat at bay. The sound of insects buzzing and birds cooing was the perfect backdrop to this wonderful vacation.

Along with getting away from the press and interviews and research, Arthur had finally jumped back into the world of trading. He'd fought me for a full year whenever I asked if he would trade the FX market again. I knew he feared the concussion had ruined his mathematical abilities. I didn't believe that. *He just proved it.* But there was only so much encouragement I could give before it became a nag.

I hadn't said a word when he'd unzipped his laptop bag and opened the familiar charts and accounts. I didn't want to pry, but so far he'd only placed successful trades, rather than bad.

I hoped it proved to himself that he wasn't broken. That he was fully himself with every gift he'd been graced with.

My lips twitched, thinking about last night. We'd awoken to a torrential downpour. The thunder cracked above as if the very fabric of the universe would shred to smithereens. Instead of staying in bed, Arthur had gathered me in his strong arms and carried me to sit on the cool tiles by the windows with our hands pressed against the glass watching the rain obscure the rest of the world.

I'd never felt so happy or complete as I did in his embrace.

His love for me hurt my heart.

Tackling me, Arthur rubbed his five o'clock shadow over my cheek. "No matter how many times I have you, I'll never stop being awed by how beautiful you are." His lips touched mine, pressing me into the mattress. "After all this time. You're mine."

I didn't have time to respond as his hand dropped between my legs, brushing against my core. He growled when he found how wet I was.

I gasped as he pushed a finger inside me. "I've been yours since I was five." My hips bucked and I stopped thinking.

All I focused on was Arthur. My Libran. My lover.

Arthur climbed on top of me, fisting the heavy weight of his erection and coating his tip in my wetness.

"I've never wanted anyone as much as I want you," he panted in my mouth as we both gasped at the delicious friction. Heat sprung over my skin that had nothing to do with the island warmth.

"I want you, Buttercup."

"You have me."

He shook his head, tracing his tongue over my bottom lip as he sank inside me slowly, effortlessly, coming home where he belonged.

I moaned as he settled his weight over me, holding my head in his hands as he jammed his elbows in the mattress on either side of my ears.

"I want you forever."

"I *am* yours forever."

Again, he shook his head. "*I* know that. *You* know that. But fate... I'm not so sure..."

I frowned, worried at the intensity in his gaze. "What do you mean?"

He rocked, hitting the perfect place inside, spiraling me into a whirlpool of lust. "Fate brought us tougher. It tested us. It took away everything, then gave so much back."

I cupped his face just like he cupped mine. Holding him like that felt as if I held his very soul. "What do you mean?"

He swallowed. "When we die, we'll have to start all over again."

"Arthur, what—"

"It will start all over again because even though we're fated to be together, it's not official. You're still a Price."

My tummy twisted as my thoughts raced. *Was he...*

"I want you as my wife. Not just as my old lady—shit, I don't have a Club anymore so that means nothing. I want you as my *wife*. I want you to wear my name. I want vows to bind us for eternity. I want there to be no doubt that we belong to each other irrevocably."

Tears tickled my eyes as I arched up and kissed him. "Are you asking me to marry you?"

He half chuckled, half gasped; his eyes glittered with emotion. "Do you want me on one knee?" His hips pulsed, making us both groan with pleasure.

I shook my head. "No, I like this method."

He smiled. "You can't run away from me while I'm inside you." Dropping his head, he nuzzled into my neck. "You can't say no."

I clutched his head to me, wrapping my legs around him, reminding myself that no other woman had embraced this man. No other woman had the right to his body, heart, or mind. Not since I captured it that fateful day in our youth.

"I could say no...if I wanted."

He reared back, fear striking the depths of his eyes. "What?"

I laughed quietly. "In my mind, we were married the day you gave me my mood ring. That was the day I bound my soul to yours."

Arthur grabbed my hand with the ring on it—the fake metal was tarnished and the stone waterlogged from all the swimming we'd done in the bay, but I wouldn't take it off. I loved having it there. It was a constant reminder that we'd fought and won.

"I'll ask you this one last time, Buttercup, and watch what you say because if I don't like your answer, I'll deny you an orgasm and leave you miserable."

I wrinkled my nose, rocking my hips. "Now, that wouldn't be fair."

He growled as I dropped my hands and dug my nails into his ass, forcing him to thrust into me. "Goddammit, you keep doing that and I'll come."

I smiled wickedly. "I bet I can make you come before you can make me say yes."

His gaze lit up with challenge. "Is that so?"

I nodded, already thrilling and regretting the gauntlet I'd set.

Arthur suddenly sat up, dragging me with him to straddle his lap. His cock hit the top of me and I flew closer to a release.

"Marry me, Cleo Price. Become Mrs. Killian and let me keep you forever." His face contorted as he thrust hard, burying himself inside me.

I moaned, gripping his strong shoulders. "You'll have to do better than that."

A tortured groan echoed in his chest as he clamped my hips and drove deeper, faster. Every rock tightened my muscles, determining who would win the bet.

Our breathing weaved together as we locked bodies and gave into instinct—the basest need to join and bond and love.

"Please, Cleo...," he growled, his thrusts becoming faster, primal. "Fucking marry me, woman."

My head fell back as his cock stretched me in perfect ways. I rode him as he rode me, living in glitter and stardust as my orgasm sharpened.

Arthur's fingers dug into my thighs, holding me, driving deeper inside me. "Say yes."

I smiled. "You're not trying hard enough." Grabbing his hair, I locked eyes with him.

Green to green.

Soul to soul.

"Come for me, Art. Then I'll marry you."

He gritted his teeth as I tugged on the long strands, rocking in his lap. His body stiffened as I took over the rhythm, setting a relentless intoxicating pace.

His eyes tightened. "Shit, you're...not...going...to..."

I bit his ear, increasing my speed. "Not going to do what?" I licked his jaw. "Win?"

He suddenly flipped me onto my back, pinning me down with his hips. "Say yes. Now. Do it. I'm about to fucking explode." He turned feral, giving me no room to hide and no breath to gasp.

My body turned rigid as every nerve ending shot between my legs. His thickness, his length, the pure undiluted way he loved me all soared me into the stratosphere.

The playfulness disappeared.

Seriousness tinged every thrust.

Everything else disappeared under an avalanche of bliss.

His mouth crashed on mine, drinking my heart and soul. "Say yes, Buttercup. Make me the happiest man alive."

The beg in his voice undid me and in that blissful moment of piercing pleasure, I thanked the universe for making me worthy of this man.

That he was mine forever.

Giving in to him, I let go of everything, sewing my heart to his for eternity.

His tongue entered my mouth, tasting of desperation and desire; I couldn't hold back any longer.

I came.

Oh, God!

Every cell exploded, obliterating loneliness and lost years. "Arthur…"

"Take me," he grunted. "Tell me you'll have me forever."

My release grew stronger. Wave after wave, I relished our connection and the adoration I found in his arms.

I'd found home.

I'd found my perfect other.

Throwing my head back, I threw myself into the final band of my orgasm and said one single word.

Three tiny letters.

The ultimate immortal promise.

"Yes."

About the Author

Pepper Winters is a *New York Times, Wall Street Journal*, and *USA Today* international bestseller. She loves dark romance, star-crossed lovers, as well as the forbidden and taboo. She strives to write stories that make readers crave what they shouldn't and delivers complex plots and unforgettable characters that keep readers talking long after the last page is turned.

On a personal note, she loves to travel, has an addiction to crème brûlée, and is married to an incredible Canadian who puts up with her endless work hours and accompanies her on signings. She's also a firm believer that the impossible can become possible.

Her Dark Romance books include:

Tears of Tess (Monsters in the Dark #1)
Quintessentially Q (Monsters in the Dark #2)
Twisted Together (Monsters in the Dark #3)
Debt Inheritance (Indebted #1)

Her Grey Romance books include:

Destroyed

Upcoming releases are:

First Debt (Indebted Series #2)
Je Suis a Toi (Monsters in the Dark novella)
Forbidden Flaws

To be the first to know of upcoming releases or subscribe to Pepper's newsletter (she promises never to spam or annoy you), visit her website at PepperWinters.com. You can contact her at pepperwinters@gmail.com.

You can also follow her on Pinterest, Facebook and Facebook Group, Twitter, and Goodreads.

Extra note:

I love you line taken from: *twoology.com/36-ways-to-say-I-love -you-in-secret-code/*

Playlist

Paloma Faith, "Picking up the Pieces"
Adele, "Skyfall"
Muse, "Uprising"
Ellie Goulding, "Burn"
Backstreet Boys, "I Want It That Way"
Katy Perry, "Dark Horse"
Creed, "My Sacrifice"
Monsters and Men, "I of the Storm"
The Wallflowers, "One Headlight"
Florence and the Machine, "Cosmic Love"
Snow Patrol, "Signal Fire"
Coldplay, "Yellow"
Ellie Goulding, "I Know You Care"
Ellie Goulding, "Love Me Like You Do"

Find out how their journey of forbidden
pleasures began...

Please see the next page for an excerpt from

Ruin & Rule.

I always believed life would grant rewards to those most worthy. I was fucking naïve. Life doesn't reward—it ruins. It ruins those most deserving and takes everything. It takes everything all while watching any remaining goodness rot to hate.

—*Kill*

Darkness.

That was my world now. Literally and physically.

The back of my skull hurt from being knocked unconscious. My wrists and shoulders ached from lying on my back with my hands tied behind me.

Nothing was broken—at least it didn't feel that way—but everything was bruised. The fuzziness receded wisp by wisp, parting the clouds of sleep, trying to shed light on what'd happened. But there *was* no light. My eyes blinked at the endless darkness from the mask tied around my head. Anxiety twisted my stomach at having such a fundamental gift taken away.

I didn't move, but mentally catalogued my body from the tips of my toes to the last strand of hair on my head. My jaw and tongue ached from the foul rag stuffed in my mouth and my nose permitted a shallow stream of oxygen to enter—just enough to keep me alive.

Fear tried to claw its way through my mind, but I shoved it away. I deliberately suppressed panic in order to assess my predicament rather than lose myself to terror.

Fear never helps, only hinders.

My senses came back, creeping tentatively, as if afraid whoever had stolen me would notice their return.

Sound: the squeak of brakes, the creak of a vehicle settling from motion to stopping.

Touch: the skin on my right forearm stung, throbbing with a mixture of soreness and sharpness. A burn perhaps?

Smell: dank rotting vegetables and the astringent, pungent scent of fear—but it wasn't mine. It was theirs.

It wasn't just me being kidnapped.

My heart flurried, drinking in their terror. It made my breath quicken and legs itch to run. Forcing myself to ignore the outside world, I focused inward. Clutching my inner strength where calmness was a need rather than a luxury.

I refused to lose myself in a fog of tears. Desperation was a curse and I wouldn't succumb, because I had every intention of being prepared for what might happen next.

I hated the sniffles and stifled sobs of others around me. Their bleak sadness tugged at my heartstrings, making me fight with my own preservation, replacing it with concern for theirs.

Get through this, then worry about them.

I didn't think this was a simple opportunistic snatch. Whoever had stolen me planned it. The hunch grew stronger as I searched inside for any liquor remnants or the smell of cigarettes.

Had I been at a party? Nightclub?

Nothing.

I hadn't been stupid or reckless. *I think...*

No hint or clue as to where I'd been or what I'd been doing when they'd come for me.

I wriggled, trying to move away from the stench. My bound wrists protested, stinging as the rope around them gnawed into my flesh like twine-beasts. My ribs bellowed, along with my head. There was no give in my restraints. I stopped trying to move, preserving my energy.

I tried to swallow.

No saliva.

I tried to speak.

No voice.

I tried to remember what happened.

I tried to remember...

Panic.

Nothing.

I can't remember.

"Get up, bitch," a man said. Something jabbed me in the ribs. "Won't tell you again. *Get.*"

I froze as my mind hurtled me from present to past.

I'll miss you so much," she wailed, hugging me tighter.

"I'm not dying, you know." I tried to untangle myself, looking over my shoulder at the FINAL CALL *flashing for my flight. I hated being late for anything. Let alone my one chance at escaping and finding out the truth once and for all.*

"Call me the moment you get there."

"Promise." I drew a cross over my heart—

The memory shattered as my horizontal body suddenly went vertical in one swoop.

Who was that girl? Why did I have no memory of it ever happening?

"I said get up, bitch." The man breathed hard in my ear, sending a waft of reeking breath over me. The blindfold stole my sight, but it left my nose woefully unprotected.

Unfortunately.

My captor shoved me forward. The ground was steady beneath my feet. The sickness plaiting with my confusion faded, leaving me cold.

My legs stumbled in the direction he wanted me to go. I hated shuffling in the darkness, not knowing where I came from or where I was being herded. There were no sounds of comfort or smothered snickers. This wasn't a masquerade.

This was real.

This is real.

My heart thudded harder, fear slipping through my defenses. But full-blown terror remained elusive. Slippery like a silver fish, darting on the outskirts of my mind. It was there but fleeting, keeping me clear-headed and strong.

I was grateful for that. Grateful that I maintained what dignity I had left—remaining strong even in the face of the unknown terrors lurking on the other side of my blindfold.

Moans and whimpers of other women grew in decibels as men ordered them to follow the same path I walked. Either death row or salvation, I had no choice but to inch my way forward, leaving my forgotten past behind.

I willed snippets to come back. I begged the puzzlement of my past to slot into place, so I could make sense of this horrible world I'd awoken in.

But my mind was locked to me. A fortress withholding everything I wished to know.

The pushing stopped. So did I.

Big mistake.

"Move." A cuff to the back of my head sent me wheeling forward. I didn't stop again. My bare feet traversed...wood?

Bare feet?

Where are my shoes?

The missing knowledge twisted my stomach.

Where did I come from?

How did I end up here?

What's my name?

It wasn't the terror of the unknown future that stole my false calmness. It was the fear of losing my very self. They'd stolen everything. My triumphs, my trespasses, my accomplishments and failures.

How could I deal with this new world if I didn't know what skills I had to stay alive? How could I hope to defeat my enemy when my mind revolted and locked me out?

Who am I?

To have who I was deleted ... It was unthinkable.

"Faster, bitch." Something cold wedged against my spine, pushing me onward. With my hands behind my back, I shuffled faster, negotiating the ground as best I could for dips or trips.

"Step down." The man grabbed my bound wrists, giving me something to lean against as my toes navigated the small steps before me.

"Again."

I obeyed.

"Last one."

I managed the small staircase without falling flat on my face.

My face.

What do I look like?

A loud scraping noise sounded before me. I shied back, bumping against a feminine form. The woman behind me cried out—the first verbal sound of another.

"Move." The pressure on my lower back came again, and I obeyed. Inching forward until the stuffy air of old vegetables and must was replaced by ... copper and metallic ... *blood?*

Why ... why is that so familiar?

I gasped as my mind free-fell into another memory.

"I don't think I can do this." I darted away, throwing up in the rubbish bin in the classroom. The unique stench of blood curdled my stomach.

"Don't overthink it. It's not what you're doing to the animal to make it bleed. It's what you're doing to make it live." My professor shook his head, waiting for me to swill out my mouth and return white-faced and queasy to the operation in progress.

My heart splintered like a broken piece of glass, reflecting the compassion and responsibility I felt for such an innocent creature. This little puppy that'd been dumped in a plastic bag to die after being shot with BB gun pellets. He'd survive only if I mastered the skills to stem his internal bleeding and embrace the vocation I was called to do.

Inhaling the scent of blood, I let it invade my nostrils, scald my throat, and impregnate my soul. I drank its coppery essence. I drenched myself in the smell of the creature's life force until it no longer affected me.

Picking up a scalpel, I said, "I'm ready—"

"Holy fuck!" The man guiding me forward suddenly whacked the base of my spine. The hard pain shoved me forward and I tripped.

"Wire—get me fucking reinforcements. He's started a mother-fucking war!"

Wind and body motion swarmed me as men charged from behind. The darkness I lived in suddenly came alive with sound.

Bullets flew, impaling themselves into the metal sides of the vehicle I'd just stepped from. Pings and ricochets echoed in my ear. Curses bellowed; moans of pain threaded like a breeze.

Someone grabbed my arm, swinging me to the side. "Get down!" The inertia of his throw knocked me off balance. With my wrists bound together, I had nothing to grab with, no way to protect myself from falling.

I fell.

My stomach swooped as I tumbled off a small platform and smashed against the ground.

Dirt, damp grass, and moldy leaves replaced the stench of blood, cutting through the cloying sharpness of spilled metallic. My mouth opened, gasping in pain. Blades of grass tickled my lips as my cheek stuck to wet mud.

My shoulder screamed with agony, but I ignored the new injury. My mind clung to the unlocked memory. The fleeting recollection of my profession.

I'm a vet.

The sense of homecoming and security that one little snippet brought was priceless. My soul snarled for more, suddenly ravenous for missing information.

I skipped straight from fumbling uncertainty into starvation for *more.*

Tell me! Show me. Who am I?

I searched inside for more clues. But it was like trying to grab on to an elusive dream, fading faster and faster the harder I chased.

I couldn't remember anything about medicine or how to heal. All I knew was I'd been trained to embrace the scent of blood. I wasn't afraid of it. I didn't faint or suffer sickness at the sight of it pouring from an open wound.

That tiniest knowledge was enough to settle my prickling nerves and focus on the outside world again.

Battle cries. Men screaming. Men growling. The dense thuds of fists on flesh and the horrible deflection of gunshots.

I couldn't understand. Had I fallen through time and entered an alternate dimension?

Another body landed on top of mine.

I cried out, winded from a sharp poke of an elbow to my ribs.

The figure rolled away, crying softly. Feminine.

Why aren't I crying?

I once again searched for fear. It wasn't natural not to be afraid. I'd woken up alone, stolen, and thrown into the middle of a war, yet I wasn't hyperventilating or panicked.

My calmness was like a drug, oozing over me, muting the sharp starkness of my situation. It was bearable if I embraced courage and the knowledge that I was strong.

My hands balled, grateful for the thought. I didn't know who I was, but it didn't matter, because the person who I was in this moment mattered the most.

I had to remain segmented, so I could get through whatever was about to happen. All I had was gut instinct, quiet strength, and rationality. Everything else had been taken.

"Stop fighting, you fucking idiots!"

The loud growl rumbled like an earthquake, hushing the battle in one fell swoop. Whoever had spoken had power.

Immense power. Colossal power.

A shiver darted over my skin.

"What the fuck happened? Have you lost your goddamn lovin' mind?" a man yelled.

A sound of a short scuffle, then the fresh whiff of tilled dirt graced my nose.

"It's done. Throw down your weapons and bend a fucking knee." The same earthquake rumbled. The weight of his command pushed me harder against the damp ground.

"I'm not bending nothing, you asshole. You aren't my Prez!"

"I am. Have been for the past four years."

"You're not. You're his bitch. Don't think his power is yours."

Another fight—muffled fists and kicks. It ended swiftly with a painful groan.

The earthquake voice came again. "Open your eyes and follow the red fucking river. Your chosen—the one you hand-picked to slaughter me and take over the Club—he's dead. Did you ever stop to think Wallstreet made me Prez for a fucking reason?"

Another moan.

"*I'm* the chosen one. I'm the one who knows the family secrets, absorbed the legacy, and earned his way into power. You don't know shit. *Nobody* does. So bend a fucking knee and respect."

Another tremor ran down my back.

Silence for a time, apart from the squelch of boots and heavy breathing. Then a barely muttered curse. "You'll die. One way or another, we won't put up with a Dagger as a Prez. We're the Corrupts, goddammit. Having a traitor rule us is a fucking joke."

"*I'm* the traitor? The man who obeys your leader? Who guides in his stead? *I'm* the traitor when you try and rally my brothers in a war?" A heavy thud of a fist connected with flesh. "No...I'm not. You are."

My mind raced, sucking up noises and forming wild conclusions of what happened before me. Was this World War Three? Was this the apocalypse of the life I couldn't remember? No matter how I pieced it together, I couldn't make sense of anything.

The air was thick with anticipation. I didn't know how many men stood before me. I didn't know how many corpses littered the ground, or how such violence could be permitted in the world I used to know. But I did know the cease-fire was fragile and any moment it would explode.

A single threat slithered through the grass like a snake. "I'll kill you, motherfucker. Mark my words. The true Corrupts are just waiting to take you out."

The gentle foot-thuds of someone large vibrated through the ground. "The Corrupts haven't existed for four fucking years. The moment I took the seat, it's been Pure Corruption all the way. And you're not fucking pure enough for this Club. You're done."

I flinched as the sulfuric boom of a gun ripped through the stagnant air.

A crash as a body fell lifeless to the grass. A soft puff of a soul escaping.

Murder.

Murder was committed right before me.

The inherent need to nurture and heal—the part of me that was as steadfast as the beat of my heart—wept with regret.

Death was something I'd fought against on a daily basis, but now I was weaponless.

I hated that a life had been stolen right before me. That I hadn't been able to stop it.

I'm a witness.

And yet, I'd witnessed nothing.

I'd been privy to a battle but seen nothing. Knew no one. I would never be able to tell who shot whom, or who was right and who was wrong.

My hands shook, even though I managed to stay eerily calm. *Am I in shock?* And if I was, how did I cure myself?

The woman beside me curled into a ball, her knees digging into my side. My first reaction was to repel away from the touch. I didn't know who was friend or foe. But a second reaction came quickly; the urge to share my calmness—to let her know that no matter what happened, she wasn't alone. We faced the same future—no matter how grim.

Voices cascaded over us, whispers mainly, quickly spoken orders. Every sound was heightened. Being robbed of sight made my body seek other ways in which to find clues.

"Get rid of the bodies before daybreak."

"We'll go back and make sure we're still covered."

"Send out the word. It's over. The Prez won—no anarchy today."

Each voice was distinct but my ears twitched only for one: the earthquake rumble that set my skin quivering like quicksand.

He hadn't spoken since he'd condemned someone to death and pulled the trigger. Every second of not hearing him made my heart trip faster. I wasn't afraid. I should be. I should be immobile with fear. But he invoked something in me—something primal. Just like I knew I was female and a vet, I knew his voice meant something. Every inch of me tensed, waiting for him to speak. It was wrong to crave the voice of a killer, but it was the only thing I wanted.

Needed.

I need to know who he is.

Wet mud sucked loudly against boots as they came closer.

The woman whimpered, but I angled my chin toward the sound, wishing my eyes were uncovered.

I wanted to see. I wanted to witness the carnage before me. Because it was carnage. The stench of death confirmed it. It was morbid to want to see such destruction, but without my sight all of this seemed like a terrible nightmare. Nothing was grounded—completely nonsensical and far too strange.

I needed proof that this was real.

I needed concrete evidence that I wasn't mad. That my body was intact, even if my mind was not.

I sucked in a breath as warm fingers touched my cheek, angling my face upward and out of the mud. Strong hands caressed the back of my skull, fumbling with my blindfold.

The anticipation of finally getting my wish to see made me stay still and cooperative in his hold.

I didn't say a word or move. I just waited. And breathed. And listened.

The man's breath was heavy and low, interspersed with a quick catch of pain. His fingers were swift and sure, but unable to hide the small fumble of agony.

He's hurt.

The pressure of the blindfold suddenly released, trading opaque darkness for a new kind of gloom.

Night sky. Moonshine. Stars above.

Anchors of a world I knew, but no recognition of the dark-shrouded industrial estate where blood gleamed silver-black and corpses dotted the field.

I'm alive.

I can see.

The joy at having my eyes freed came and went as blazing as a comet.

Then my life ended as our gazes connected.

Green to green.

I have green eyes.

Down and down I spiraled, deeper and deeper into his clutches.

My life—past, present, and future—lost all purpose the second I stared into his soul.

The fear I'd been missing slammed into my heart.

I quivered. I quaked.

Something howled deep inside with age-old knowledge.

Every part of me arched toward him, then shied away in terror.

Him.

A nightmare come to life.

A nightmare I wanted to *live*.

If life was a tapestry, already threaded and steadfast, then he was the scissors that cut me free. He tore me out, stole me away, changed the whole prophecy of who I was meant to be.

Jaw-length dark hair, tangled and sweaty, framed a square jaw, straight nose, and full lips. His five-o'clock stubble held remnants of war, streaked with dirt and blood. But it was his eyes that shot a quivering arrow into my heart, spreading his emerald anger.

He froze, his body curving toward mine. Blistering hope flickered across his features. His mouth fell open and love so achingly deep glowed in his gaze. "What—" A leg gave out, making him kneel beside me. His hands shook as he cupped my face, his fingers digging painfully into my cheekbones. "It's not—"

My heart raced. *Yes.*

"You know me," I breathed.

The moment my voice webbed around us, storm clouds rolled over the sunshine in his face, blackening the hope and replacing it with pure hatred.

He changed from watching me like I was his angel to glowering as if I were a despicable devil.

I shivered at the change—at the iciness and hardness. He breathed hard, his chest rising and falling. His lips parted, a rumbling command falling from his mouth to my ears. "Stand up. You're mine now."

When I didn't move, his hand landed on my side. His touch was blocked by clothing but I felt it *everywhere*. He stroked my soul, tickled my heart, and caressed every cell with fingers that despised me.

I couldn't suck in a proper breath.

With a vicious push, he rolled me over, and with a sharp blade sliced my bindings. With effortless power, so thrilling and terrifying, he hauled me to my feet.

I didn't sway. I didn't cry. Only pulled the disgusting gag from my mouth and stared in silence.

I stared up, up, up into his bright green eyes, understanding something I shouldn't understand.

This was him.

My nightmare.